Advance praise for *Serenade* by Emily Kiebel

"An absolutely haunting and lyrical read. The captivating use of music and a darkly seductive magic will have readers singing its praises and longing for more."

—Colleen Oakes, author of *Queen of Hearts*

SERENADE

Emily Kiebel

SparkPress, a BookSparks imprint
A division of SparkPoint Studio, LLC

Published by SparkPress, a BookSparks imprint,
A division of SparkPoint Studio, LLC
Tempe, Arizona, USA, 85281
www.sparkpointstudio.com

Printed in the United States of America.

ISBN: 978-1-940716-04-6 (pbk.)
ISBN: 978-1-940716-05-3 (ebk.)

Cover design © Julie Metz, Ltd./metzdesign.com
Formatting by Polgarus Studio

To my sisters, my sirens, my inspirations.
Mia sorella, ti voglio bene.

PART ONE

CHAPTER ONE

Lorelei stepped onto the stage and squinted to block out the glare of the blinding spotlight. After a few seconds, her eyes adjusted until she could vaguely discern the faces of the four silhouettes seated at the table at the far end of the recital hall. It never got any easier. Furrowed brows, pursed lips, and always the scribbling—that infuriating, constant note-taking that made her want to scream, *Could you stop writing for just one second and at least pretend to appreciate what I'm trying to do here?* Every time it was the same. Her heels clicked as she crossed the wooden floor, the sheets of music in her hand becoming damp. Lorelei swallowed hard and forced down the lump in her throat before handing the pages to her accompanist. *You've done this a hundred times. There's nothing to worry about.* She straightened out her skirt with her hands in one last attempt to delay the inevitable. "Lorelei Clark, soprano. I'll be singing 'Gretchen am Spinnrade' by Schubert."

A loud click resonated through the recital hall and the spotlight dimmed. The piano began to play in a frantic circular pattern that conjured up images of the hypnotic spinning wheel for which the song was named. Suddenly she was swallowed up in the piece, the strident German lyrics filling her lips.

My peace is gone, my heart is heavy, I will never find it again.
Where I do not have him, that is the grave, and the whole world is
bitter to me.
My head has gone crazy, my mind torn apart.
My peace is gone, my heart is heavy, I will never find it again.

Her tone was clear, the cadence lilting, the diction crisp. Technique was the easy part. Connecting to the lyrics was another thing entirely. Pretending to be in love was the worst, but trying to convey both love and desperation was especially difficult. She twisted her face into a feigned expression of desire and torment that made her look tortured more than anything else. Try as she might, she could never quite nail it. Finally the music came to a halt. Lorelei took a deep breath and rolled back her shoulders.

"The second piece is 'The Trees on the Mountain' from *Susannah*, by Carlisle Floyd." There was a momentary silence, and Lorelei closed her eyes briefly before her accompanist played the pitch.

The trees on the mountains are cold and bare,
The summer just vanished and left them there,
Like a false-hearted lover, just like my own,
Who made me love him, then left me alone.

She breathed into the aria, her body a vessel for the music. With calculated grace, she approached the last high note carefully, sang it delicately, and let it shimmer with light vibrato: *"Come back... Come back... Come back..."*

Her voice diminished until only echoes reverberated through the hall. The only woman seated at the judges' table nodded her head and made notes on a piece of paper. The dean of vocal music, on the other hand, appeared unaffected. He pushed his glasses up on his nose, looked at her, and said, "Thank you." Even Maria Callas, arguably one of the best sopranos of all time, wouldn't have been able to illicit a more enthusiastic response from him.

Lorelei grabbed her music back from the pianist, smiled tersely, and ducked behind the curtain. She nearly collided with a tenor who was pacing the corridor while rehearsing the "Major-General's Song." A lanky girl from her music history class was doing a strange breathing exercise near the water fountain. Lorelei leaned up against the wall to steady her nerves.

"You survived." Lorelei's roommate, Breanna Matthews, sat on the floor beside the backstage doors with a book laid open in her lap. Dark eyes peeked through a fringe of black bangs.

"I guess so," Lorelei said. "Dr. Nielsen didn't seem too impressed."

"Eh, he's kind of a jerk. I think you sounded great. That Schubert is wicked."

"Thanks." Lorelei took a sip of water. "You next?"

"I'm after Jocelyn," Breanna answered. Lorelei glanced at the girl who was now intermittently contorting her face in a series of stretches and making little high-pitched noises through her nose. Some people had to make such a big production out of everything. "Hey, are you going out with us tonight? We're going to grab some pizza down at Little Antonio's."

"I would, but my dad should be here soon and I have to show him around town. His flight was supposed to get into Bangor at four, so he'll probably be here in an hour or so."

"I see how it is… ditch your friends to go hang out with your dad," Breanna said. Lorelei rolled her eyes. "You know I'm only kidding. You guys have fun on your little road trip. We'll have to plan a girls' night when you get back."

"Sounds good. See you next week."

Lorelei stepped outside and the breeze picked up her hair, whipping it in front of her face. *Stupid wind,* she thought, and snatched her hair band off her wrist before pulling her hair up into a messy ponytail. The trees covered the courtyard in a kaleidoscope of rich crimson and vibrant orange. The fall colors brought back memories of all the times her father took her and her mother up to the mountains to look at the aspen trees changing color. She usually used those trips as an opportunity to nap in the backseat of the car, but her dad dragged her along for their ritual drive over Guanella Pass every year, despite her complaints.

She walked up the steep hill that led to the front steps of her dorm. The stonework of the building made it look older than she suspected it really was, perhaps an attempt to make the campus feel more historic, though it lacked any of the usual wear and tear or ivy-covered brick that always seems to accompany the architecture found at most East Coast colleges. She turned the key in the lock of her bedroom. Inside, wrinkled clothes were tossed carelessly on the twin beds and bits of trash littered the floor. She grabbed a plastic garbage bag from her desk drawer and hastily filled it with the clothes and books that had piled up around the room, then shoved everything else in her closet and shut the door. A half-eaten sandwich and several empty soda cans were chucked into the trash can. If she could at least hide the mess, maybe she'd have a chance at convincing her father that she and Breanna didn't live in total depravity. The floor now visible, Lorelei changed into a pair of comfy jeans, a green T-shirt with an elephant on it that her cousin had given her before she'd left home, and some well-worn tennis shoes. She took her suitcase down from the storage area above the closet and packed just enough clothes for the week.

Lorelei was zipping up the suitcase when there was a knock at the door. "Come in!" she yelled. The door opened and her father's broad face greeted her, his mouth spread into a warm smile.

"Hey Dad!" Lorelei jumped up and embraced him.

"Hi, honey," he kissed the top of her head, "I've missed you, kiddo." He gave her a squeeze and then let go, stepping into the room. "How's it going?"

"Pretty good. I was just packing."

"So, this is the place, huh?"

"Yep," said Lorelei. "What do you think?" She grabbed her makeup bag from the vanity and threw it in her backpack.

"Hmm… Not too shabby," he replied. Lorelei was pretty sure he had spotted the pile of dirty laundry poking out from under the bed. He took a cursory walk around the room and then looked out the window. "Nice view." Behind the dorms was a tiny stream that flowed from one of the many lakes in the small town of Calais down to the estuary. The school had installed an arched steel bridge over it so students could follow the stream through town to the riverside. "You ready to go?"

"Yeah, I think I'm all set," Lorelei looked around the room one last time, making sure she hadn't forgotten anything.

"Is this everything?" he pointed to her suitcase. She nodded and hoisted her backpack over her shoulder. Her father followed her down the hall and out of the dormitory to where the rental car was parked in front of the building, its hazard lights blinking. He tossed the luggage in the trunk and pulled his belt up around his belly.

"Did you know they don't even feed you any real food on those flights anymore? They only give you these teeny packets of trail mix. What good's that?" he said as he turned the key in the ignition. "This town have any decent restaurants?"

"I'm sure we can find something. You must be *starving*." The collection of candy bar and beef jerky wrappers scattered beneath her feet caught her eye and she smiled.

"It's a nice campus," he said as they drove away from the dorm. "Looks like a pretty safe town."

The town square was only a few blocks away from the conservatory. She pointed out all of the important landmarks to her father as they drove. Lorelei loved it here. She loved the way everyone in town seemed to know everyone else. She loved the lighthouses and the fact that she could see Canada from the bank of the St. Croix River. But more than anything, she loved watching the tide rise along the waterfront in the early morning.

On the weekends, Lorelei and her friends would pack their lunches and head to Dochet Island. She always brought along a few textbooks and notebooks, thinking she'd be inspired to study, but inevitably she would end up sitting on the shore for hours, mesmerized by the motion of the cold water tickling her feet. There were reservoirs and lakes back home in Colorado, but the water there wasn't like the water in Calais. The water here was *alive*, an organic and moving thing; she was captivated by it.

They arrived at a restaurant on the edge of town called Harry and Ben's Seafood Shack. Lobster being plentiful in Maine, it was also surprisingly cheap. The place was lined with high-backed wooden booths beneath walls that were covered with nautical maps and whaling-ship replicas. Lorelei and her father found a booth near the window; they both ordered the lobster dinner.

"Your mother and I are thinking of going on an Alaskan cruise in the spring," he remarked.

"Really? Mom wants to go away on a cruise?" she asked.

"Well, I'd like to go, at least. I'm still trying to talk her into it." A plastic bib that was much too small for him was wrapped around his neck.

"Oh yeah? Good luck with *that*," Lorelei sounded less than enthused. She clenched her jaw. "So, how's Mom doing?"

"You know your mom, busy as ever. She just started a new project at work, and she's repainting the guest room." The waiter arrived, placing two plates brimming with bright red lobster on the table. Lorelei's father bent over his plate and inhaled the rising steam before cracking off a claw and pulling out its sweet flesh.

Lorelei crossed her arms over her chest and stared out the window. Her mother was always busy. A *multitasker*, wasn't that what she always called herself?

"What's wrong?" he asked.

"Nothing," she picked up her fork and tapped it nervously on the table.

"Honey," he picked a piece of corn from between his teeth, "you've got to let this thing go. I mean, let bygones be bygones, right? We both know she's not going to wake up one morning and have a change of heart and be okay with all of this, but she does love you, and I really think you two should try to work this out..."

"She's the one who won't take *my* calls, remember? I haven't done anything wrong, but she's not going to talk to me until *I* apologize? Why does she have to be so damn difficult? She should be happy for me, not trying to make me feel guilty! She is *so* ridiculous."

"I don't want to hear you talk that way about your mother again. I know she thinks she knows what's best for you, and no one's going to convince her otherwise, but she does love you, Lori."

"Whatever," she slunk down in the booth, her appetite gone. She thought about her friends who'd likely be out having fun. At the moment, she'd rather be out with them instead of feeling the need to defend her reasons for avoiding her mother.

Her father wiped his butter-soaked fingers on his napkin and laid a road atlas across the table. He flipped open to the page with the map of Maine.

"Okay, so here we are," he pointed up to the top of the map where Maine married Canada on the coast, "and we're going to drive down I-95 to Portland tomorrow, and spend a day there."

"Fine," Lorelei was in no mood to talk, her mind painfully recalling the showdown she'd had with her mother back in August. She didn't *want* to let this ruin her time with her dad, but now that the subject had arisen, it was all that was on her mind.

"From there, we should be able to make it to Boston in just a few hours." His fingers traced the route as he spoke, "I went to Boston when I was just about your age. Neat city. Lots of history. Oh, and Plymouth, too... ," her father trailed off, his mind engaged in the map.

They sat there for a while, her father plotting his route and picking at his food while Lorelei stared out the window. She finally excused herself and went to the ladies' room. When she came back to the table, their plates had already been cleared. Her father was waiting for her beside the booth, holding her food in a white cardboard to-go box.

"Ready, kiddo?" he asked.

"Yep," she replied, "let's go."

They walked out of the restaurant and he put his arm around her shoulders, kissing the top of her head. Their feet crunched the broken clamshells that covered the parking lot. The sun had already set, and Lorelei shivered in the cold, damp air. She looked up and thought she saw a shooting star flash across the sky. As they walked toward the car, her father suddenly stopped and pointed across the street.

"Look over there," he nodded toward neon lights that read *Mabel's Ice Cream Parlor*. Next to the sign was a picture of a cow standing on its hind legs, wearing an apron, and holding an ice cream cone. Sure, it was cheesy, but they did have an unbelievable mint chocolate chip.

"You want ice cream? Now?" Lorelei asked him. "How can you still be hungry?"

"You sound like your mother." A herd of children ran around the porch of the ice cream shop, eagerly licking their cones and giggling, "I may have to follow that diet of hers when I'm home, but I'm on vacation and I want ice cream. Is that okay with you?"

"Fine, but can you unlock the car so I can get my coat?"

He fished the keys out of his pocket and popped open the trunk with the remote. Lorelei reached in and unzipped her suitcase then took out an orange hoodie, which she had unfortunately packed underneath everything else. Her father waited by the side of the road while she wrestled to get it over her head. He called her name, beckoning her to hurry. Lorelei was still shoving her clothes back into the suitcase when the sound of squealing tires cut through the chatter of the children's voices. She looked up in time to see a car speeding around the bend in the road. Its engine revving, the driver reacted, twisting the wheel to the right, but the car continued to screech forward to where her dad was standing in the road. The car skidded over the gravel, sending a huge plume of dust into the night sky and side-swiping him. His body flew through the air, landing in the street, his head hitting the ground with a loud crack. The driver threw the car into reverse, spun around and sped back down the road from where it had come, until it rounded the corner and was no longer in sight. Her father was motionless on the ground. Lorelei screamed and ran out into the road. She knelt beside his body and leaned over him. She put her hand down and she felt something warm and wet on the asphalt. Everything seemed to stand still and grow quiet. The children's screaming had stopped. Lorelei's mind became focused and she took his hand in hers.

A weak sound left his throat. His eyes focused on her face and he gasped. She lifted his head toward her chest and murmured, "You're okay, you're going to be okay." Tears rolled over her cheeks as he struggled to breathe. She looked down at his face. His body shuddered and he mouthed the words, "I love you." Lorelei shook her head. This couldn't be the end. Not here. Not now. Someone would help him. He was going to be okay.

A cold burst of wind whistled through the trees. It grew louder, the whistle turning into a mournful hum. The sound filled Lorelei's ears and ran down her spine, setting her teeth on edge. It called to her, the fervent drone of an empty night, devoid of all light. She choked back her sobs and wiped his brow, the blood streaking from her hands across his forehead. "I love you, Dad." The streetlights clicked on to reveal a blanket of fog that had settled around them. The wind howled its lonesome refrain and Lorelei's voice rose within her. She was singing. There were no words, only the deep, plaintive cry of her heart that poured from within. The song filled the silent street and found harmony with the wind. Her father squinted as if trying to see something far off in the distance. His lips curled up in a contented smile and his eyes softly closed.

Lorelei stopped singing and looked around her. A throng of people encircled them. Men, women, and children who, moments earlier, had been at the ice cream parlor or beside the restaurant, now surrounded Lorelei and her father. Why wasn't anyone helping? "Someone *do* something!" she screamed. No one moved. "Help me!"

The crowd stood transfixed. Their eyes were vacant and they stared at Lorelei with no thought to propriety. No one seemed to notice the man crumpled on the ground beside her. She stood to her feet and ran to the man closest to her and shook him. "Call the paramedics! *Please!*" He blinked hard several times, as though he was waking up but he kept staring at her, unmoving. She grabbed the cell phone that hung on a clip by his pocket. The others had turned in her direction and were still looking at Lorelei alone as she placed the call. All of these people standing here, and not one of them had offered any help. She ran back to her father and cradled him in her arms, collapsing in hysterics. The crowd moved in around them until Lorelei felt suffocated by their presence. She held her father close to her chest until the sirens broke the silence.

CHAPTER TWO

The events to follow were a dreamlike haze. Lorelei could only vaguely remember seeing the car slam into her father, or the moment after when his body was thrown to the ground. She remembered that panicked feeling, her stomach clenched so tightly that she could scarcely pull air into her lungs, her father covered in blood and lying in the road. The paramedics arrived quickly after she had called. They moved her aside and she trembled while she watched them work on him, fear washing over her like a flood. One of the policemen ushered Lorelei into his car, and they followed the ambulance to the hospital, neither speaking to the other on the way there.

The first person Lorelei called from the hospital was Breanna. She didn't have the courage to call her mother right away. How could she explain it, when she couldn't put into words what was happening? If she spoke it aloud, then it meant that the accident was real, and at that point, she wasn't ready to admit that, not even to herself.

Her friends arrived at the hospital and rushed to her side. Chelsea and Breanna wrapped their arms around her, a buffer from the cold waiting room. Chelsea took Lorelei's cell phone and walked away from where she was sitting to call Mrs. Clark. She returned a few minutes later and handed the phone over to Lorelei, who couldn't think of anything to say besides, "Hello."

"Are you okay?" her mother asked, frantically. "Is Dad okay?"

"I don't know," Lorelei replied. Her thoughts, which were racing only moments earlier, had now come to a dead stop, and she had trouble speaking.

"What do you mean? What's going *on*? What are they doing?" Her mother helplessly sought answers, trapped in another state while her husband fought for his life.

"They haven't told me anything." Tears met at the corners of Lorelei's mouth, and she wiped them off her cheeks with the back of her hand. "But it was terrible. I mean, it looked really bad when it happened. There was blood everywhere… and he, I… I don't know. Mom, I don't know what to do. I'm so scared."

Gone were the harsh words and sentiments they had shared over the past several months. She only wished her mother was there to hold her and to tell her everything would be okay. Her mother could keep things together, but Lorelei was falling apart on her own. She felt like she was drowning, imagining herself swept away in the waters of the river that she loved. She could almost feel the frigid fingers of the St. Croix closing over her, slowly pulling her under the dark surface as she was carried away by the great river.

"It's going to be okay, honey," her mother said, her voice suddenly soothing and calm on the line. "Everything's going to be fine. I love you."

"I love you, too, Mom," Lorelei's throat was closing up, "and I miss you. I wish you were here."

"I know, sweetheart. I miss you, too. But you're going to be okay, just try to stay calm. Everything's going to be fine. Now, is there anyone I can talk to? A doctor or a nurse or someone like that?" her mother asked.

"Yeah, I'll try to find somebody," she took the cell phone over to the main desk where a pretty, blonde nurse, probably not much older than Lorelei herself, smiled as Lorelei approached. "Hi," she said, her words shaky. "My mom is on the phone and she wants to know if there's anyone she can talk to about my dad."

"Ms. Clark, right?" the nurse asked.

"Yes," Lorelei answered.

"Just a moment, let me go speak with the attending physician."

The nurse disappeared behind two swinging doors and Lorelei put the phone back to her ear, "They're going to look for the doctor."

"What happened? Your friend said he was in a car accident?" Cassandra Clark was no longer frantic. She sounded calm as she attempted to assess the situation.

"He was just walking across the road, and there was a car, and it hit him and he fell, no, he flew across the street and the car disappeared, but the ambulance came, and the—"

"Lorelei, please, slow down. You're getting yourself worked up. Take a deep breath and start again. Your father was hit by a car when he was crossing the road?"

"Yeah."

"How long was he down before the paramedics arrived?"

"I guess maybe three or four minutes," Lorelei responded, much calmer now.

"Was he conscious? Was he breathing?"

"Yes, for a while, at least," Lorelei began to remember the details a little more clearly. "He looked at me, and I held his hand. I think he was breathing, but after a while, he closed his eyes. Then the ambulance showed up, and they wouldn't let me stay with him."

The nurse returned, followed by a man wearing a white coat that matched his thinning hair. Lorelei reluctantly handed the phone to him, and he walked back through the double doors. She sat on a nearby chair in the waiting area and her friends gathered around her. Breanna took hold of her hand, and they prayed together quietly while Chelsea stayed close with her arm around Lorelei's shoulders.

It was nearly two hours after they arrived when the doctor finally came out to speak with Lorelei. His face told her all she needed to know, even before he said a word. They had tried everything to save her dad. The doctor's words sounded garbled, as if he was speaking underwater. She caught phrases here and there… massive hemorrhaging… internal bleeding… trauma… bleeding in the brain…

Chelsea and Breanna waited with her through the night, never leaving her side even as several policemen interviewed her, each trying to get a clear description of the event. She couldn't remember what the car or the driver looked like. One of the officers suggested that she might remember better in a few days, once the shock had dissipated. He gave Lorelei his card and asked her to call him if she thought of any new details.

It was after eleven when her school advisor, Professor Camden, arrived at the hospital. She wore a neatly tailored gray pencil skirt and white blouse. "Oh my god," she swept her hands dramatically at her sides as she approached Lorelei, "are you all right? Oh, dear, come here." Professor Camden embraced Lorelei tightly. She smelled like strong perfume and cigarettes. Lorelei had to come up for air.

"Thanks for coming. I really appreciate it."

"Well, you certainly don't have to *thank* me. Anything I can do to help; I'll be here for you, understood?"

Lorelei nodded in reply.

"Oh, you poor girl," Camden held Lorelei's shoulders and looked her in the eyes, "I just can't imagine how you're feeling."

Professor Camden helped fill out some hospital forms, and spent a great deal of time talking to Lorelei's mother on the phone, as well as a barrage of doctors, police officers, and hospital staff. At some point, Camden had asked Lorelei if she wanted to be taken back to her dorm, but she simply looked past her teacher with a catatonic stare. Breanna led her to a couch, covered her eyes with a few wet paper towels, and stroked her forehead.

The front of Lorelei's head throbbed and her eyes were swollen and raw. She kept them closed for the moment, tucked in the fetal position on the couch. *When did I fall asleep?* She cautiously opened one eye and squinted. The fluorescent lights amplified her headache. The clock above read 4:15. *Must be morning,* she thought. She turned over. Chelsea was on another sofa, still asleep. Chelsea's boyfriend, Tony, sat beneath her legs, reading a magazine. In the corner of the room, Breanna stood watching the news and sipping a cup of coffee.

"Hey," said Breanna, noticing that Lorelei had turned over on the couch, "can I get you anything? Maybe something to drink?"

"Water." Lorelei sat up only to feel the tightness in her head intensify, and pressed her hands against her pounding temples. She rubbed her fingers over them in circles. She was disoriented and dehydrated, and her head was killing her.

Breanna filled a cup from the water cooler and brought it to her. "Here you go," she sat beside her and put a hand on her back. "You hanging in there?"

"I don't know. I just… I don't know how to feel," Lorelei's eyes started to pool up with tears again. She closed them, and breathed in deeply. She didn't have the strength to cry anymore.

"Let me know if there's anything you need."

Tony glanced up at them from the magazine he was reading. He looked like he hadn't slept for days. His brow furrowed and lips tightened, he tried to be stoic, but she could see the concern in his eyes. He slowly shook his head, knowingly, and then averted his eyes from hers. Lorelei sipped the water and stared blankly at the wall.

"They wanted us to take you home last night, but you fell asleep here and we didn't want to wake you," said Breanna, "You were obviously exhausted. We thought it would be best to let you sleep."

"Thanks," said Lorelei, "and thanks for being here last night."

"I'm your best friend. Of course I'd be here for you." She put her arm around Lorelei's shoulder, "You're going to get through this. I know it's going to take a long time, but someday you'll wake up, and it won't hurt so much. It will get better."

"Why did this have to happen to him? It just doesn't seem fair."

"I don't know."

Lorelei took another sip of water.

"Camden booked a flight to Denver for you for this afternoon."

"What about… ," she couldn't say *my dad.* "Am I just supposed to leave him here? I can't…"

"The hospital's made the arrangements. Don't worry about that. They worked everything out with your mom already. She just wants to get you home."

Lorelei placed the cup on the table next to the couch and stood. Her entire body ached. Tony nudged Chelsea, who was sprawled out across him, and she yawned.

"Chels, you awake?" Breanna asked.

"Mm-hmm," Chelsea responded quietly.

"Let's get going, then," Breanna motioned to the nurse standing at the front desk that they were heading out. The nurse approached, and handed Lorelei a small box.

"Personal effects," she said, and then returned back to her station.

The group stepped outside. The darkness was a welcome relief to the sterile fluorescent lighting that filled the hospital. A thin, crescent moon hung low on the horizon, but there were no stars in the sky. Chelsea tossed a set of keys to Tony and entered the front seat of her old Buick. Breanna opened the back door for Lorelei.

No one spoke on the drive back to campus. The empty streets were bordered by glowing streetlights and Lorelei let her eyes remain unfocused as they passed; everything outside was a colorless blur, a dance between the darkness and the light. Tony pulled the car up to the curb in front of Lorelei's dorm.

Breanna and Chelsea helped Lorelei to her room while Tony waited in the car. She slowly trudged up the stairs to the third floor and walked down the hall. Breanna fumbled with her keys before she finally found the right one and opened the door. Chelsea closed the blinds and Lorelei made her way to the bed. She faced the wall and let herself sink into the mattress, her comforter wrapped securely around her body. Isolated from the world under the thick blankets, Lorelei was fairly certain that she would never leave this bed again.

"We'll be back to get you at eight, okay?" said Chelsea.

Lorelei didn't respond.

"Let's go," Breanna whispered. "Let's just leave her alone."

With that, her friends retreated, shut the door quietly behind them, and left Lorelei alone in her bed. She tried to keep herself from being swallowed up in her fears, to stay afloat amidst the hundreds of questions that swam through her mind. *Why did he stop in the street like that? Couldn't the driver see him? Why didn't I go with him right away instead of complaining about the cold? Why didn't I see this coming? Why couldn't I save him? Why did I sing to him when he was dying right in front of me? It's my fault... It's all my fault...*

Whatever rational thought Lorelei had left told her she wasn't to blame, but she couldn't stop the nagging feelings that she had played a role in her father's death. What could she have done, anyhow? Short of having lightning-fast speed and superhuman strength, she wouldn't have been able to stop the car from hitting him, nor could she bring him back to life, yet she had a sense of indescribable guilt that she was unable to reconcile in her mind. Lorelei buried herself deeper under the blankets, tried to block out her thoughts, and succumbed to a restless sleep.

CHAPTER THREE

The few hours Lorelei had alone to herself were gone. She awoke to Breanna sitting on her bed, gently shaking her into the morning. It took her a moment to remember why she was back in the dorm. A few fleeting seconds of oblivion passed before Lorelei recalled the events of the previous evening. Part of her was convinced that it had been a dream, but Breanna's face reconfirmed the fears that hovered on the outskirts of her consciousness. Memories rushed back to her. Everything had changed. Her father was gone.

"Hey," Breanna said. "Time to wake up. We've got to get going soon."

"Yeah," she replied. "I'll be up in a minute."

Lorelei didn't want to leave the security of her bed and face the day ahead of her, but eventually her body started to move. Chelsea fidgeted on the other side of the room, averting her eyes when Lorelei glanced in her direction.

Lorelei walked to the sink to wash her face and was startled by her reflection in the mirror. Her round face was puffy and red. Her eyes had dark circles underneath them and the whites were bloodshot, which made her irises look like pieces of pale green seaglass. She splashed cool water on her face to remove the traces of tears that marked her cheeks.

"Tony's going to drive you down to Bangor," said Chelsea. "He's flying out today, too, so we figured he could take you and the rental car. I mean, if that's okay with you."

"Sure," said Lorelei. "That was nice of him to offer."

"If you want us to go with you, we totally will, but we just thought…"

"No, it's fine. You don't have to babysit me. I'll be okay. I promise."

Lorelei scooped her hair up and tied it back in a messy bun. She pulled a clean shirt out of her closet and changed into it, then slid on a pair of flip-flops. It was strange to be around Chelsea and Breanna without their normal banter and easy conversation, but she realized it must be awkward for them, too, trying to help her manage without knowing what to say or do. They didn't have any more experience coping with death than she did.

"Here's your flight schedule," said Breanna. She handed a folded-up sheet of paper to Lorelei, "Your mom's going to pick you up from the airport when you get there."

"Thanks."

Lorelei followed them downstairs. Outside the sky was clear and the grass was covered with tiny dewdrops. Tony was standing beside the rental talking on his cell phone. He wore a dark blue polo shirt paired with sharply pressed khakis. As the girls approached him, he hastily ended his conversation and put the phone in his pocket. He gave Lorelei a sympathetic smile, then kissed Chelsea quickly on the cheek.

"Promise you'll text me when you get there," Breanna said to Lorelei.

"Of course I will."

They hugged each other tightly, "Have a safe trip. I'll be praying for you."

"Thanks, Bree. That means a lot."

Lorelei climbed into the front seat of the car, and Tony started the engine. The candy wrappers that had earlier littered the car floor were now conspicuously missing. Lorelei gazed out the window as the girls waved goodbye to her.

"You want to listen to the radio? What do you like?" Tony asked.

"I don't care, whatever you want is fine," she replied.

He scanned the channels and landed on WMED, the local NPR station. Billie Holiday's small-but-intense, bluesy voice came across the radio.

Sunday is gloomy, my hours are slumberless,
Dearest, the shadows I live with are numberless.
Little white flowers will never awaken you,
Not where the black coach of sorrow has taken you.
Angels have no thoughts of ever returning you,
Would they be angry if I thought of joining you?
Gloomy Sunday...

"Shit. I'm sorry. Maybe we should just turn this off." Tony pressed a button on the console, and the music stopped.

"That was awkward," said Lorelei.

"Yeah, no kidding." He shifted his body in the seat and stared straight out at the road ahead. They sat in silence for a few minutes, tense and uncomfortable, before Tony spoke again. "Maybe I shouldn't ask, but, are you going to be okay? I'm worried about you."

"Yeah," Lorelei said, taken aback by his question, "I'm all right. I just feel out of place, I guess." She sighed, and then tried to explain, "You know how it is when you're in a dream? Like you're sort of there, but you're not sure if it's real or not? I feel a little like that. Numb mostly, like I don't know what's going on around me. Besides that, I just feel empty."

"I know, it's not easy. There's a part of you that thinks if you can just concentrate hard enough on waking up, you could bring him back, right?"

"I guess so. I can't stop thinking about that moment, replaying it in my mind and trying to figure out if there was something that I could have changed, something I could have done to stop it."

"It was that way when my mom died," he said. "She had ovarian cancer. She fought it for a long time, but it took her in the end. It was two weeks before I could say it, before I could say 'my mom died.' Sometimes I still wake up and think of calling her before I remember she's not there."

"I didn't know. I'm sorry."

"It's okay. I was really angry about it at first. I tried to channel it into my music for a while, and I wrote a ton of crappy songs that I thought were so epic and original at the time, but they turned out to be really terrible."

"I'm sure they couldn't have been *that* bad."

"Believe me, they were awful," said Tony, "but it was something I needed to do. Somehow you need to let go of the pain, or it'll drive you crazy. Turn it into something good. You have to find something to hope for."

"It sure doesn't feel like it's going to get any easier. I can't see the silver lining in all of this just yet."

"Well, what doesn't kill you makes you stronger, right? You're always going to miss him, but you'll go on with your life, and that's okay. I'm sure that's what he would have wanted. He must have been really proud of you." He reached over and put his hand on hers, squeezing it gently with his long and graceful pianist's fingers.

They made their way along the highway amidst a dazzling display of orange and red, but Lorelei leaned her seat back and rested her eyes. She didn't exactly feel like taking in the scenery. It took them two hours to reach the airport. Tony pulled the car up to the passenger drop-off. He opened the trunk and lifted up her suitcase. Lorelei stepped out of the car, then grabbed her father's luggage and put it on the sidewalk beside her own.

"Will you be okay from here?" Tony asked.

"Yeah," she said. "Thanks for driving me."

"No problem," he leaned over and gave her a nervous hug. "Good luck, Lorelei."

"Thanks again. See you later."

She walked into the terminal, dragging the suitcases behind her. It was a very small airport, so she checked in and moved through security quickly. At the gate, she found a place to sit, away from everyone else. She took a protein bar and her MP3 player out of her purse. While she waited for the plane to begin boarding, Lorelei listened to a playlist her cousin Jennifer had made for her. Eventually they proceeded to board the plane, and she settled into her seat, thankful the seat beside her was empty. She tried to clear her mind, but the flight seemed to take longer than normal. Lorelei wanted so badly to simply fall asleep, but it was useless. She cursed the restless toddler behind her that kept kicking the back of her seat. Without being able to drift off, every minute felt twice as long.

When they had finally landed, she followed the crowd to baggage claim. Her mother was waiting for her at the top of the escalators in the light-flooded Denver airport terminal. Her mother's lean physique, normally so strong and tall, seemed to be slunk in on itself. Tears tingled in Lorelei's eyes as she sidestepped the crowds of people around her and went straight to her mother. Cassandra Clark's arms wrapped around Lorelei firmly; she stroked her daughter's hair and kissed her forehead. They were bound in their mourning, mother and child.

"Oh, sweetheart," her mother said, "I love you so much."

Lorelei sobbed on her mother's shoulder, her body shaking with grief at her homecoming. She felt small and vulnerable like a young child, and the familiar clean scent of her mother made her feel safe again. Lorelei clung even tighter and her mother instinctively began to rock her, back and forth, gently shushing her. Part of Lorelei wished she was a child again, so that her mother could pick her up and carry her when the world became too overwhelming.

"I'm so sorry, Mom," Lorelei cried, her words barely audible. "I can't... I'm sorry..."

"Honey," her mother's long, manicured fingers traced the side of Lorelei's cheek, "it's not your fault. What happened... it happened, and we can't change the past. We're going to get through this. You're here with me now, and we'll be strong together, okay?"

Lorelei took a deep breath and nodded.

"I wish there was something I could do, some way to fix this and bring him back. It's not fair..."

"Of course it's not fair, but bad things happen to good people all the time. We don't get to determine what happens in this life. The only thing we *can* control is how we choose to react. You can't blame yourself for what happened."

Lorelei and her mother went around the corner to baggage claim and waited for her luggage to come circling around on the carousel. They each lifted one of the suitcases, and Lorelei followed her mother through the airport garages toward the car.

"Mom, I'm sorry I haven't been a very good daughter."

"What are you talking about?"

"You know, how I fought with you last summer. I'm really sorry."

Cassandra stopped walking and turned to face her. "We both were a little irrational, and maybe I overreacted, but you're still a good daughter. There's never been a moment in your life that I haven't loved you. You're just strong-willed, like me."

It was true that they could both be stubborn, which made compromising difficult. Her mother could be absolutely infuriating with her frequent edicts of behavior or her declarations of moral superiority. Lorelei was usually able to disarm her mother by placating her and then going and doing whatever she pleased, but their last argument had been particularly brutal. When Lorelei's mother had found out about her choice to move to Calais and study music on a scholarship, she put her foot down.

Cassandra Clark abhorred things that she viewed as being "unproductive," like television, vacations, or sleeping. For her, having a daughter who thought she wanted to be something as inconsequential as a singer was beyond frustrating. Lorelei knew that her mother loved her very much, and in most aspects she had been a good mom, but for as long as Lorelei could remember, she had tried to talk her daughter out of "this singing nonsense." Time and time again, Lorelei was told that her singing was distracting her from her studies, how she would never get into a good school, and therefore would never get a decent job if she didn't put aside this foolishness and focus on more serious endeavors. They had screamed at each other, neither willing to back down from their position.

Even Lorelei's father hadn't been able to persuade Cassandra to let her go, but he ultimately gave Lorelei his blessing, and bought her plane ticket to Maine. Their "little conspiracy" made her mother so mad she lit up like a firecracker. She raged for hours, her face contorted with anger, and then refused to speak to either one of them for weeks. When Lorelei left Colorado, her mother wouldn't even say goodbye.

She looked at her mother through different eyes now.

Cassandra lifted the bags up into the back of the SUV with her toned, muscular arms, then shut the hatch. She looked tired and worn-out as they drove away from the airport into the cold night. Her pale skin glowed with every set of headlights they passed.

Lorelei looked at her mother, "I love you."

"I love you, too, Lorelei. Always have, always will."

Tears welled up in Lorelei's eyes again. During the last few months, she hadn't felt much sadness in her distance from her mother. She had been irritated, certainly, that her mother refused to speak to her as she watched all the other parents help their children settle in at the beginning of the school year, but she did not regret her decision. She could see that their separation had impacted her mother more severely.

The Clark home was in a quiet neighborhood in the suburbs just south of Denver. Despite the darkness, Lorelei noticed that her mother's gardens were dying as they pulled up the driveway. The giant maple tree in the front yard had lost most of its leaves, but the burning bush next to the front door was a vibrant shade of crimson under the faint glow of the porch lights. Lorelei could see Gizmo, their little red-and-white corgi, through the French doors. He had spotted them, too, and jumped up against the glass.

Cassandra pulled the car into the garage, and Lorelei took her bag out of the trunk and carried it upstairs. Gizmo followed on her heels and happily licked the backs of her legs. Her bedroom was pale lavender; it had been the same color since she was in fifth grade, its walls covered with photos. On her dresser was a picture of Lorelei, who couldn't have been more than four years old, sitting on her father's shoulders. Her mother stood beside them with her hand on his forearm, laughing. Next to that was another photo of Lorelei with her dad, the two of them standing on the bank of a river, each holding a fishing rod. She grinned up at the camera, a tiny bluegill hanging from her hand. His face beamed down at her.

Another picture of the two of them hung above her nightstand. It had been taken at Coors Field when she was seven. They each wore a baseball glove, and Lorelei was missing a few teeth. Every summer, she looked forward to going with her father to the baseball games he loved. From an early age, he had taught her how to keep score and record each hit and every run during a game. They'd eat hot dogs and yell at the pitchers, but what she really looked forward to the most was singing with him during the seventh-inning stretch, belting "Take Me Out to the Ball Game" for the whole park to hear. As a teenager, she'd sung "The Star-Spangled Banner" there, her father watching from the seats above home plate, and her mother, not surprisingly, absent.

Lorelei sat down on the edge of the bed and picked up the dog. "Hey, Gizzy," she said, rubbing his soft ears. He seemed to smile up at her gleefully, leaning into the scratches she was providing. "How's my boy? Huh? Missed me?" Gizmo cuddled up against her and licked her hand.

"What a good boy," she patted him on the back, then rested her head on the pillow and pulled Gizmo up beside her. He stretched his stubby little arms toward her, yawned and made a funny noise. Gizmo licked Lorelei's cheek and she rubbed his belly. She turned on her back and stared at the ceiling, which was covered in little pink prisms, each dangling from a string of fishing wire. At the moment they looked dull and lifeless, for there was no light shining through them, but at dawn, they would cast rainbows of light across the entire room.

Lorelei rolled back over onto her side and tucked her legs up beside her chest. Each breath she took was shallow and painful. She reached over to her nightstand and picked up a small wooden music box, then wound it very slowly, as it was quite old and wanted repair. Lorelei opened the lid delicately and watched the small brass drum start to spin as it plucked the tiny silver keys inside and played one of Brahms's waltzes. She remembered all those years when her mother and father would come to her bedside, play her little music box and sing her to sleep. Her father would sing her "The Teddy Bear's Picnic," *If you go out in the woods today, you're sure of a great surprise. If you go out in the woods today, you'd better go in disguise…* acting out the words and singing the verses, making her giggle with delight.

Then Cassandra would take her turn, carefully tucking her into bed, stroking her brown curls, and singing a song or two of her own, always ending with what Lorelei simply knew as her mother's lullaby. She didn't understand what the words meant; they certainly weren't words that she recognized, but the tune was sweet, if not a bit melancholy, and Lorelei always fell asleep by the end of it. If she closed her eyes, she would see herself lying in a boat on quiet water, gently swaying with the breeze, her mom's voice like a harp. As she grew older, the nighttime rituals disappeared, and the song lost its place in her memory.

The music box stopped playing, and the silence of the room rang in her ears. She started to hum the tune of her mother's lullaby, since she couldn't remember the words, and in her mind she was swaying in the boat once more, surrounded by an inky black sea.

CHAPTER FOUR

Lorelei and her mother walked hand in hand into the small, white church. The buzz of women cooking in the parish hall echoed through to the narthex before one of the ushers had a chance to close the door. The Clarks weren't regular church-goers, but when they did make the effort to attend, usually on Christmas or Easter, they went to St. Stephen's. As a child, Lorelei had spent a week every summer here with her cousins; they played with the other children in the courtyard during vacation bible school. One year Lorelei had discovered a secret passageway behind the sacristy that led up to the bell tower, which was not so much a secret as it was simply a staircase whose door had been inadvertently left unlocked.

Lorelei and her mother crossed the entryway of the church to where her Uncle Mike and Aunt Linda stood with their two children, the blond-haired twins, Joshua and Jennifer. Despite being two years younger than Lorelei, her cousins were the closest thing to siblings that Lorelei had. Jennifer had spent most of the week with Lorelei since she had returned home, and her presence had been a great comfort. Together they picked out pictures of her father to display at the funeral, reminisced about their family's annual camping trips, and worked on the tribute that Lorelei would read at the service. Jennifer patiently waited with Lorelei when she didn't feel like talking, and listened to her when she did.

The myriad of family, friends, neighbors, and Andy's co-workers seated in the wooden sanctuary pews grew quiet when the organ began its prelude. The mood in the sanctuary was somber and the reality of the service that was about to take place gripped Lorelei in the chest. *My father's funeral,* she thought, *this is surreal.* She was light-headed and had difficulty containing the loss inside of her body. The pastor approached the family, a middle-aged man wearing a white alb and a gold stole around his shoulders, neatly tied by a rope at his waist.

"Excuse me," he said, "we're ready to begin seating the family now."

Her aunt, uncle, and cousins followed the pastor into the sanctuary, and Lorelei and her mother trailed behind them. They walked down the center aisle and sat in the reserved pew at the front of the church. The congregation stood up as the organist began the introduction to the opening hymn, but Lorelei remained in place, as if there was a massive weight pushing down on her shoulders.

Cassandra leaned over and whispered in Lorelei's ear, "You need to stand up, sweetie. You can do this. I know you can." Her mother's hand wrapped itself firmly around Lorelei's upper arm and pulled her up. Lorelei stood silently as the congregation sang behind her, the words of an old spiritual filling the spacious sanctuary.

Some glad morning when this life is over, I'll fly away.
To a home on God's celestial shores, I'll fly away.
I'll fly away, O Glory, I'll fly away in the morning.

When I die, Hallelujah, bye and bye, I'll fly away.

The service began, the little church packed full of people who loved Andy Clark, filling Lorelei with a quiet, inexplicable joy to see how many people had been touched by his life. She recognized many of the faces of the people around them, people who had helped to write the story of her father's life, as well as her own. Her mother's strength beside her, Jennifer's steady, calming presence, and the love of the multitude of friends around who had come to remember Andy Clark gave her the courage to go forward and speak when it was her turn.

The walk to the pulpit seemed impossibly long. The front of the church was filled with fragrant casa blanca lilies and there was a large floral spray directly in front of the altar. The musky aroma hit her in the face. Through the stained glass, blue light filtered into the sanctuary. Lorelei reached the pulpit and turned around, steadying herself with both hands.

"I want to thank you all for being here. It means so much to our family, though I know my dad would think you are crazy to be here instead of at home watching the playoffs, which is certainly where he would be, probably throwing things at the TV." Many in the congregation chuckled at the reference. "You all knew him, so you already know that he lived life to the fullest, that he had a wonderful, genuine spirit, and that he loved his family above all else. Those are just words, but my father was so much more than that."

"Anybody who spent any time with my father was touched by his kindness, his warm smile, his sincerity. My dad loved to make people laugh. His jokes were usually pretty cheesy, but he never grew tired of telling the same ones over and over again. He couldn't understand why people would choose to be unhappy if they could be having fun instead. And he always gave people the benefit of the doubt. That's why everyone loved spending time with him. He always made me feel better if I was in a bad mood and he always pulled the best out of me.

"This past week has been really tough… for all of us. Losing him was probably the most difficult thing that I've ever experienced, but I wanted to tell you all how much he meant to me, personally. He was caring, funny, generous, and he loved his family immensely. My mother and I were so lucky to have had him in our lives. I've been reminded a lot of all the things he did for us and of the time we spent together as a family, but I wanted to tell you all a story of something he did for me in particular that I won't ever forget.

"When I was eight years old, our third grade class was doing a play, a sort of animal version of *Robin Hood*. I was a bird. I had about three lines, total, but I had worked and worked to memorize those words and truly capture the essence of an outlaw parakeet. My performance was awe-inspiring; or at least I thought it was. One week before the play, I jumped off a swing too high and came down hard on my ankle, breaking it in several places. It had to be reset and I was put in a cast. The pain was terrible, but it wasn't as terrible as knowing that I wasn't going to be in that play.

"The night before the production, my dad came back to the house, carrying a huge bag of multi-colored feathers. He spent the rest of the night hot-gluing hundreds of feathers to my cast. Dad was determined that I was going to be in this play, almost as much as I was. He rented a wheelchair for me, and during the performance, he pushed me around *on his knees,* so he wouldn't be seen. I'm sure it looked a little ridiculous to the audience, but that didn't matter to me. He told me how beautiful I was, praised my acting, and gave me a dozen roses afterwards. He made me feel like the greatest actress in the world."

Lorelei ached as she remembered all the little things her father used to do for her. The way he got up early to brush the snow off her car in the winter. How he used to slip extra money into her wallet when he knew she was going out with her friends. The necklace he bought for her graduation. But she also thought about everything he would be missing—seeing Lorelei at her wedding, being a grandfather to her children, being a part of her future. She reached up and tucked a piece of stray hair behind her ear before she continued.

"My dad told me I could do anything. He used say, 'When you decide to do something, you have to just go for it, and never look back.' I trusted that he would help pick up the pieces if I ever failed at anything, but he would never let me give up at anything without trying my best. He'd just brush me off, help me stand up, and tell me to try again. When I told my parents that I wanted to pursue singing, my father was so supportive of me, and encouraged me through it all. He just wanted me to do something that I loved, and he helped give me that opportunity. Whenever I sing now, I will sing for him." She choked on her final words, "I'll miss you, Dad."

She took a moment to look out at the congregation. Her mother's jaw was clenched and she sat straight and rigid, her lips drawn together into a tight pucker, her back barely touching the pew behind her. Suddenly Lorelei's eyes were drawn to a woman seated alone in the last row. She was strangely familiar, but Lorelei didn't know who she was or when she may have met her. The woman had long, silver hair that was streaked with shining blond highlights, all of which was pulled back loosely at the nape of her neck and let loose to drape around one of her shoulders. Lorelei was transfixed by her. She appeared to be well into her sixties, but had obviously been a statuesque beauty in her youth. A strand of gray pearls lay delicately around her neck and over her dress she wore a black, silk shawl that stood out in sharp contrast to her pale, white skin. Lorelei couldn't take her eyes off of her. There was something so recognizable about her, but what was it? The woman gave Lorelei a half smile of condolence and put her hand on her chest before she stood up and left through the back door of the sanctuary.

Lorelei took her place with her mother again and the service continued. Two of Andy's friends said a few words before the pastor gave a sermon about the promise of the resurrection, and then the congregation celebrated Eucharist together. Lorelei wasn't very religious, but taking the elements made her feel less alone, wrapped in warmth, kneeling beside her family. They returned to their seats, before the pastor proceeded to commend the ashes and offer a benediction. Lorelei brushed away tears and nestled closer to her mother whose firm arm wrapped around her shoulders once more.

The congregation rose to their feet as the organ swelled and filled the space with music, the low notes sending reverberations under Lorelei's feet. Two young acolytes, each wearing red and white robes that dragged on the floor, extinguished the candles and led the procession from the sanctuary. The smell of smoke, which now mingled with the floral fragrance, signaled the end of the service. At that moment, Lorelei was confronted by how much her life had changed at this point. She was awash in memories that flooded her senses; she closed her eyes, and she could see her father there, so close. She didn't want to open her eyes, because the second she did, she knew his face would be gone from her sight. Lorelei wanted to hold on to his smile, aching for his hand to hold hers. Right now, she could picture him so clearly in her mind, she could almost hear his laughter. She was afraid that the memories wouldn't last, that they might start to decay like everything else. Would she wake up one day unable to recall what he looked like?

Lorelei and her mother followed the procession past the congregation and into the parish hall. Lorelei felt smothered; she couldn't breathe, so she pulled away from her mother's grasp and went outside. A cool mist had formed around the small church. Lorelei filled her lungs with air as the thick haze left water droplets clinging to her face. She prayed at that moment that it would rain, that the clouds would burst open with a cold downpour to completely drench her, hiding her tears and soaking her thoroughly. *Yes,* she thought, *rain. That would be good.* The mist floated around her; it caressed Lorelei and surrounded her body. She no longer felt the chill, and the haze became like warm breath upon her neck. The fog was spinning and she was in its midst; it blew her skirt around her knees and her hair in front of her face. Her mind spun with it, as though she was outside of her body, like she was floating. A cold hand grabbed her arm, and she was pulled back from her trance and landed firmly in her body.

"Hey," said Jennifer, "what are you doing out here? It's going to rain."

"I don't care," said Lorelei, "I wish it would."

"Your mom wants you to come back inside."

"No, I just, I can't be in there right now. I need to get some air."

"Aren't you freezing?"

"I'm fine," Lorelei said. "Will you tell her I'll come inside in a minute?"

"Okay," said Jennifer. She gave Lorelei a quick hug and walked back into the church.

Lorelei wanted to bring back the feeling that she'd had before she was interrupted, when she had been lifted away from the world around her, but the moment was lost. She took a big breath and steeled herself to face the hordes of relatives and friends back in the church. Her mother stood inside, politely shaking the hands of the mourners, but her eyes were on Lorelei, cutting through her skin like ice. Lorelei reluctantly opened the door of the church and stepped inside, pulled in by her mother's gaze. She didn't want to face all of these people, each of them offering uneasy words of grievance. Death was like that though, it made people uncomfortable. The church bell began to toll, and each time it sounded, Lorelei's memories of her father drifted further and further away.

Lorelei and her mother had hardly said a word to each other since they left the house that morning. The week had been a long goodbye, and as they drove up the mountains, Lorelei clung to the urn. She wasn't sure if she would be able to let go of this last tactile element when the time came. The car crested the divide and a valley spread itself in front of them. It was something she'd seen a hundred times before, but this time it was more beautiful, even a little like heaven. The sun blazed through pink clouds in straight beams of light and rested atop the weathered tress. Snow had already fallen in the high country once this year and small patches of white hid in shady spots among the towering pines that covered the mountainside. *He would love it here,* she thought.

Cassandra turned the car up a narrow dirt road away from the main highway. Through the thick cover of the forest, dappled light blanketed the road that wound steeply up the hill. After several miles, she pulled into a parking lot and stopped the car. Lorelei climbed out, still holding the urn, and went to meet her mother beside the trailhead. Hand in hand, they walked up the path through the woods, toward a small bridge that crossed over a briskly moving stream.

The water churned against the rocks, the last of the season's snowmelt plunging from the mountaintops. Along the banks of the stream, the aspen blazed yellow and gold, their small, delicate leaves quaking with the slightest breeze. Beyond the bridge, the path diverged sharply to the left and made its way toward a clearing that opened beneath the blue-gray peaks in the horizon. The sweet smell of the trees mixed with the smoke of a campfire somewhere deeper in the forest. Lorelei's eyes were fixed on the stream; the continuous rhythm of water sliding over the boulders was hypnotic.

"Are you ready?" her mother asked.

Lorelei didn't answer. She looked down at the brass urn in her hands, and knew that this… thing… it wasn't her father. But why couldn't she let go?

"Lorelei, is there anything you want to say?"

"No, not really. Mom, do we *have* to do this?"

"Yes. We've already decided this. It's what he wanted, and we, as a family, are going to honor that. Don't make it any more difficult than it has to be."

Cassandra took the urn from Lorelei and faced the downward flowing stream, her back against the breeze. She twisted off the lid, and began to pour the contents into the water. The wind picked up some of the ashes and carried them several feet before they lighted on the current, small swirls of gray visible only for a moment before they were carried beneath the surface. Lorelei looked at her mother who was standing only a few feet away with an empty urn in her hands. A halo of soft light flooded around her mother, and it glinted off the tears on her cheeks. Lorelei wrapped her arm around Cassandra's waist; there was a fragility that Lorelei hadn't seen before, and for the first time she understood that her mother needed comforting, too.

"I love you, Mom," said Lorelei.

Her mother held her close. They stood together on the bridge and watched as the rest of the ashes floated downstream, the water carrying away not only ashes, but also their hopes and expectations. The stream headed from its source to the ocean, and Lorelei thought about the sea, and then of Calais, and the water there beckoned to her. It was time to return, time to leave the safe protection of her mother and go back to Maine. Lorelei crossed the bridge and went to the side of the river. She sat beside it, and let her fingers trail in the ice-cold water, her heart whispering its final farewells.

They stayed in that spot for a while, undisturbed except for the birdsong in the trees, before they left the river. Lorelei followed Cassandra back toward the car. She always had difficulty keeping up with her mother's long, graceful strides. They reached the car and Cassandra placed the empty urn in the backseat. Shifting into a low gear, she drove the car slowly down the steep decline toward the main road. The clouds were passing above quickly, now thick and dark in the western sky.

"When we get back to the house, I think I'm going to book my flight back to Bangor, okay?" Lorelei said.

Her mother scoffed.

"What?" Lorelei asked.

"Is it really necessary? We can just have everything shipped out here. You don't need to go back and get it yourself."

Lorelei shot her mother a cold look. She did not want to have the same argument with her mother that she'd had over the summer, which had left them giving each other the silent treatment for months.

"Did you think I wasn't going to go back to school?"

"I know we haven't had a chance to discuss it yet, but I think it would be best for you to stay home for a while. I thought you could transfer to a state school next semester."

"No, Mom. I'm going back to Calais. They have a really good program, and I have friends up there…"

"You can make new friends. You've only been up there a few months, Lorelei. There are plenty of good schools here."

"Were you even planning on asking me what I thought about this? I don't want to move back home. I *like* it out there, and I want to go back and finish."

"There's no reason you can't go to school here. I'd like you to be closer to home."

"I know you do, but I have to go back… It's something I need to do. It's what Dad would have wanted."

"We'll talk about this later. I'm not discussing it now. Not today." Cassandra's mouth wrinkled tightly and her tone was matter of fact.

"I know you don't want to talk about it now, but you're not going to want to talk about it tomorrow, either, or the next day. You know he'd want me to go back. At least he thought I had something special. He'd want me to use my gift."

"Don't give me that nonsense. This isn't about your father, so stop using him as an excuse. This is about your stubbornness, and I'm not fighting about this anymore. You're staying home."

"Oh, really? You may not realize it, but I'm an adult now, Mom, and I don't have to ask your permission. I'm going back to Calais. I was left an inheritance, and I should be able to decide how to use it."

"Your father worked very hard to make sure you were provided for in case anything ever happened to him. That does not give you the right to spend his money foolishly. You need to start thinking about your future. I'm glad you like to sing, honey, but we both know you're never going to make a living doing it. I just wish you'd—"

"Why do you feel the need to crush my dreams?"

"For crying out loud! I am not trying to crush your dreams. Have you even stopped to consider that I don't want you to leave? That I'm going through a hard time, too? Maybe you could try not being so damn selfish and thinking about what's best for our family. You're all I have left, and I can't stand the thought of you leaving again."

"Haven't you ever just *felt* something, just known that there's something you were meant to do? Something you were meant to be?"

"Yes, actually, I have, but it doesn't matter…"

"It does matter! It absolutely matters! I know this, Mom. And you may not believe it, but I'm actually a pretty good singer, okay? I've been given an opportunity, and I'm not willing to throw it all away just because Dad died. This is all I've ever wanted…"

"Why does it have to be Maine? Is there some reason you're so adamantly opposed to staying in Colorado?"

"Why *not* Maine? It just feels… right. I like it there. I like the school, I like the town, and I've learned a lot. I have Bree and Chelsea and they're really fun…"

"We are not paying twenty grand a year just so you can have 'fun,' Lorelei. You can learn just as much at any school here in state as you can up there. You can even minor in voice, for all I care, but there's no reason you need to continue going to a school that's going to put you hugely into debt with a degree you can't even use!"

"I don't care! I don't care how much it costs! I love it there, and I'm going back. And Professor Camden thinks I have a really good shot at winning the Elmsbrook scholarship next year..."

Her mother screamed, slammed on the brakes, and pulled over to the side of the road.

"No! It is out of the question. I am finished with this conversation, Lorelei Anne. Finished! I do not want to hear another word about it."

Cassandra started driving again, her knuckles white against the steering wheel as she stared at the road. Lorelei's face was flushed with anger and she slouched down in her seat before she reached for her headphones on the floor. Her mother would never understand why she needed to go back to Maine. There was a part of Lorelei that didn't fully understand it either, but she knew that was where she belonged; she knew it as certainly as rivers find the sea.

CHAPTER FIVE

Lorelei came downstairs a little after six in the morning with Gizmo trailing behind her. Her hair was still wet and pulled back tightly in a ponytail. A thin headband held back the frizzy curls she constantly battled. She let the dog outside, and went back into the kitchen, where on a small, yellow piece of paper her mother had left a note:

Lorelei,

Went for a run. Should be back shortly. I need you to unload the dishwasher and feed Gizmo. And eat something, please.

See you soon,
Mom

Cassandra Clark was a strictly regimented individual. Every morning began with an hour-long run, unless it was snowing, in which case, she did a Pilates video. Her workouts were concluded with a protein shake and a glance through the paper before she took a shower and tackled her day. Lorelei checked the clock on the wall. Her mother wouldn't be back for at least half an hour, but her stomach was still uneasy. She didn't know if her anxiety was because she was afraid, or because she felt guilty.

She scooped dog food and poured it into Gizmo's bowl, then went to let him back inside. He jumped up on her and licked her hand before he went to his dish. Lorelei found her mother's planner—the burgundy, leather-bound binder which she kept on the desk in the kitchen. She quickly thumbed through the list of contacts until she found what she was looking for, a small card with the words: Harrison Standard Insurance, Carl Peterson, Agent. She scribbled his name and phone number on a notepad, then tore out the piece of paper, folded it up, and stuck it in the back pocket of her jeans. She went back to the table in the kitchen, and under her mother's note, she wrote:

Mom,

I fed Gizmo, but I didn't get a chance to put away the dishes. Went back to Maine. I love you, and I'll miss you. Please try not to be too mad.

Love,
Lorelei

There was the sound of a car honking from in front of the house. Gizmo ran to the door, barking. Lorelei darted upstairs and grabbed her small suitcase and cloth purse. She swung the purse over her shoulder and across her chest, and bounded down the steps. Gizmo was still growling in the foyer.

"Be a good boy, Giz," she patted him on the head and maneuvered her suitcase out the door.

Her cousin, Jennifer, hopped out of the little orange Kia that sat in the driveway. She ran up the sidewalk and threw her arms around Lorelei's neck.

"I can't believe we're doing this," Jennifer whispered, "it feels so… bad."

Lorelei snickered. Jennifer was such a good girl. She felt the tiniest bit of remorse for dragging her cousin into this, but she knew any trouble Jennifer would find herself in would be minimal, and Lorelei would try to make it up to her, somehow. She opened the back door of the car where Jennifer's twin brother, Joshua was sitting, looking up at her from under a pair of dark sunglasses.

"Here, I'll take it," he said and reached for her suitcase.

Lorelei handed it to him and then shot Jennifer a look. Jennifer shrugged and rolled her eyes. Lorelei shut the door and sighed with exasperation. As much as she loved Jennifer, Joshua had always been the pesky little brother who needed to tag along with them wherever they went, and he always seemed to know exactly when they were planning to do something. Jennifer blamed it on the psychic twin connection. Lorelei just thought he was nosy. Growing up, he had been tolerable, but lately he'd become a mopey, sarcastic nuisance with a penchant for shoplifting.

"Aunt Cassie is going to kill you," said Joshua as Lorelei sat down in the front passenger's seat.

"Shut up," snapped Jennifer, turning around to face him. "I said you could come only if you left us alone."

"So now you're not going to let me talk? You don't have to be so bitchy, Jen."

"Better than being a loser like you."

"At least I'm not a fat, stuck up—"

"Enough! Would you both just stop it?" Lorelei yelled.

The twins ceased their bickering and Jennifer backed out of the driveway. The first rays of sunlight glinted over the rooftops of the houses which were laid out in perfect formation, each a slight variation of beige.

"I printed out your flight information," said Jennifer. "It's there, on the dash."

"Thanks," said Lorelei as she reached for the papers that were stapled together, "how much was it?"

"Four-twenty-five."

"Crap. That's a lot. I'll pay you back as soon as I can."

"It's okay. I know you will. Besides, I used my mom's credit card…"

"You didn't! You are going to be in so much trouble."

"That's what I said," interrupted Joshua. "She's going to be so pissed off."

"We didn't ask for your opinion, moron," said Jennifer, "besides, by then, Lorelei will have her money, and I can just pay Mom back for it. She won't care."

"Yeah, maybe not if it's little-miss-perfect. She'll probably give you a freakin' medal, but if it was me—"

"Well, you know, if you weren't so busy getting in trouble with your idiot, wannabe-punk friends—"

"You don't know what the hell you're talking about—"

They were at it again. All they did lately was argue with each other. Lorelei tried to tune them out as they continued bickering. She pulled a bottle of water out of her purse and drank it, the cool liquid sliding down her throat. They headed east, straight toward the sun. Lorelei tried to relax, which was nearly impossible with the twins still fighting. In her head, she pictured her mother chasing the car, and she was almost certain her mother would be able to catch them, too. The sooner they got to the airport and she made it through the security gates, the less she'd have to fear about her mother trying to stop her.

"So do you think she's ever going to speak to you again?" asked Jennifer.

49

"Yeah, I'm sure she will," said Lorelei, "but it'll be awhile. She definitely knows how to hold a grudge."

"That's too bad. Maybe she won't be as upset as you think. Maybe she'll get over it."

"You obviously haven't seen her *really* mad. I love her, I really do, but when she gets angry, there's nothing you can do to make her compromise. The only way I'm getting back in her good graces anytime soon is complete repentance, which isn't going to happen. And it sucks, too, because she'll be alone now that Dad's gone, but she can't expect me to live at home forever."

"You're doing the right thing. It's not like you're trying to hurt her. You're just doing what's best for you, and you've got to follow your heart."

"I know," Lorelei sighed. The guilt weighed upon her as she tried to reconcile the two truths in her mind. To leave her mother was near abandonment, but to give up on what she had started was a betrayal to a part of her own spirit. Both her mother and her singing had given her life. Music made Lorelei feel alive and complete; when she sang she was fully connected to both her body and to the world around her. Would it be worth sacrificing her own happiness for her mother's? She hoped they would eventually reconcile, but that day may be many weeks, or even months, down the road, and this transgression would not quickly be forgotten.

The airport was bright white in the morning sun, and swarming with cars. Several policemen were outside, directing traffic and blowing their whistles at those cars that were parked for too long. Jennifer pulled up to the side of the building and Lorelei hopped out of the car. By now, Joshua was dozing in the backseat, his mouth agape.

"Good luck," said Jennifer, hugging her cousin. "Call me when you get there, okay?"

"I will. Thanks for everything, Jen. You're the best, you know?"

With that, Jennifer got back into the Kia and pulled away. Lorelei checked in and picked up her boarding pass. On the first floor of the airport, streams of people waited to pass through security. Her stomach was queasy. She eyed the large clock in the terminal, anxious that at any moment her mother might show up and drag her back home. Part of her even wondered if her mother would go so far as to call the police when she found Lorelei's note. *They couldn't actually stop me though, could they?* She thought. *I'm eighteen now. I have as much of a right to get on a plane as anyone else.* Lorelei tried to put the thought out of her mind.

The line of people crept ahead slowly. Just a little more than a week earlier, she had been embracing her mother here, at this very airport. Her mother's love had been so palpable and concrete as she had brought Lorelei into the security of her arms. She wondered for a moment if this was the right decision, if it was really fair to leave her mother alone. But what was fair, really? Was it fair that her father had died so suddenly? Was it fair that Lorelei should have to put her life on hold?

One of the security guards motioned her forward and she showed him her boarding pass and driver's license. He made a quick mark on the boarding pass and gestured for her to go through. Lorelei removed her sneakers and set them, along with her small carry-on luggage and her purse, on the conveyer belt. She walked through the metal detector. It didn't beep. *Safe,* she thought.

The plane glided into a smooth landing outside the Bangor airport. Lorelei was restless. Her legs ached after sitting all day and she desperately needed to stretch. The plane taxied down the runway. Lorelei sifted through her purse, pulled out her cell phone, and turned it on. The screen lit up, and a minute later displayed that she had five new text messages.

Mom: *Where are you? Just joking about Maine, I hope?*

Mom: *L – would like to know when you plan to be home. Going over to Mike and Linda's later.*

Jen: *Your mom is here. I had to tell her. She is freaking out. I'm grounded now.*

Mom: *CANNOT BELIEVE THE STUNT YOU'VE PULLED TODAY. THIS GOES BEYOND BETRAYAL. VERY UPSET!*

Jen: *OMG…Your mom is scary when she's mad*

Lorelei sent a text back to Jen to wish her good luck with her parents. She stuck the phone back into her purse and pulled down her carry-on from the overhead compartment. It was several minutes before Lorelei was off the plane and heading for the entrance of the airport. Bree was already waiting at the curb in her clunky, beat-up Honda. She waved at Lorelei and reached over to unlock the door.

"Hey, sorry it's such a mess," said Breanna. She grabbed some empty water bottles that were scattered across the front seat and tossed them into the back.

"Don't worry about it," said Lorelei, as she climbed in the car. "Thanks for picking me up."

"No problem." Breanna focused her eyes on the road and pulled away from the curb, "How are you doing?"

"It was a rough week, but I'm doing okay. I'm hanging in there, I guess."

"I can't believe you're coming back to school so soon. I mean, I'm really glad you're here, but I'm a little surprised."

"I needed to come back. Staying at home... everything there reminded me of my dad, and it was too much to handle. Every morning I'd wake up, and I see his chair sitting there empty, and I'd remember him reading the paper with a cup of coffee and how he used to say 'morning, kiddo' when I came down the stairs. I can't go anywhere in the house without seeing his face."

"I'm so sorry, Lorelei. I can't imagine what it would be like to have to go through that."

"Thanks. I just really want things to get back to normal, you know?"

"That's understandable," said Breanna.

The skies were cold and gray as they drove north toward Calais. The two girls settled into an easy conversation about the latest school gossip and before long they had arrived back at campus. After Breanna had parked the car, they walked back to the dorm room. Lorelei fumbled for her keys in her purse and opened the door. She remembered the excitement she had felt when she had first entered this room at the beginning of the semester, and the first time she met Breanna, the short, stylish mezzo from Rhode Island, who was Lorelei's first friend at Calais.

The room was as she had left it. Clothes that needed laundering lay in a pile next to the door. Lorelei's body was tired from the flight and the emotional toll of the day; she couldn't help feeling terrible that she'd disobeyed her mother's wishes and acted like an ungrateful and selfish daughter. She flipped open her phone and texted: *"I'm sorry."*

CHAPTER SIX

"Stop pushing so hard!" snapped Professor Camden. "You're straining your voice and these melismas need to be light, crisp. Again, from the top of the page."

Lorelei's eyes focused back to the music on the stand, where hundreds of notes were huddled together. Quick runs led to the top of her range and then circled around and around, dipping and twirling. Just looking at the notes made her head hurt. Singing melismas was a matter of memorization, training your muscles to go through the notes almost as if by instinct. She knew she was overthinking the runs, putting too much emphasis on each note, but then she started to overcorrect herself, and the notes became sloppy, so then she started forcing it. Professor Camden was obviously frustrated.

"What are you doing? No, no, no. Just go back and sing it on an 'ah' again," Professor Camden was one of the more difficult professors, and ordinarily Lorelei loved how challenged she was in Camden's studio, but today she was simply irritated with herself, annoyed that she wasn't improving. In fact, each time they ran through this section, Lorelei was sure she was singing it worse than the time before.

The piano started again and Lorelei gritted her teeth and closed her eyes. *Get it right,* she thought, *just this once.* She took a full breath and started up the first measure, forcing out the melody, her throat tight around the music. The quick scales caught her off guard and she was behind the beat, rushing to catch up, her voice cracking on the top notes. Lorelei stopped singing and slapped her hand on the top of the grand piano, defeated, her shoulders hunched over.

"What's going on Lorelei?" asked Professor Camden.

"I'm sorry," said Lorelei, "I don't know why I just can't get it. And I swear, I really did work on this yesterday, but I can't get it to come out right."

"Let's take a break for today," said Professor Camden. "It doesn't seem like we're making a lot of progress here anyhow, and I don't want you to hurt yourself."

"I don't know why I can't get it. I must be out of it today."

"Lorelei, I don't want you to take this the wrong way, but it seems like you've been somewhere else for the past couple of weeks. You haven't connected to the music since you came back. The effortless quality your voice had earlier this semester didn't come back with you. It's like you're trying too hard. It's too mechanical."

"I don't know why I can't seem to get it. In my head, I know exactly what I'm supposed to do, but it's coming out all wrong."

"Lorelei, I know this has been a difficult month for you. I don't want you to think that I'm trying to get on your case about this, because I really do have a great deal of sympathy for you, but it seems like the joy is gone. I can't hear the passion in your voice, and the freedom that you used to have. I know it's still in you, somewhere. That sort of thing doesn't just disappear, but you haven't reconnected to it. I wonder if a little break wouldn't do you some good, just a little time to find your happiness again."

"No, I'm fine, I promise. I'll practice more."

"I don't think that's the problem. I'm not questioning your commitment to the program. I respect your hard work, but I feel like you're forcing yourself into this in order to forget what's happened to you, and it's coming out in your voice. You're tense, and I think rather than trying to push yourself so hard, it might be best for you to take a little time for yourself, to refocus, to reconnect with what it is that makes you love to sing."

"You want me to quit for the rest of the year?" Lorelei asked.

"Not necessarily. You are a very talented young woman, and your place here in the program would be waiting for you when you're ready to come back."

Lorelei panicked. If her advisor thought she should take some time off, where was she supposed to go? She certainly couldn't go running home with her tail in between her legs. Her mother would be so smug, and Lorelei couldn't stand the thought of it.

"You don't have to decide right now, but think about it, okay?"

"Sure, I'll think about it."

"Have a good weekend."

"Thanks Professor," said Lorelei as she gathered together her books and shoved them in her backpack. "I'll see you later."

The door shut behind her as she left the studio. The wind had been knocked out of her. She couldn't hide the fact that it was more difficult to control her voice now than it had been before. The pressure to prove herself was making her more nervous every time she went to her private voice lessons, and the stress made it that much harder for her to sing the challenging music that she was expected to perform. Lorelei had been going through her days in a haze, but every morning she would wake up, hoping that this would be the day when life returned to normal. In the meantime, she was simply going through the motions, without being fully present in her own body.

She wrapped herself in her black peacoat and pulled a gray knitted hat over her hair and left the music building. Heavy snowflakes clumped up on the branches of the evergreen trees and melted on Lorelei's cheeks. She pulled up the collar of her coat and tried to bury her ears within it, but it was of little use. Her bare fingers were freezing. Lorelei trudged her way through the snow, alone against the biting cold wind. Her feet made fresh tracks through the virgin white powder on the sidewalks that blinded her as she walked to the edge of the forest on the outskirts of campus.

A narrow, snow-covered path led through groves of bare trees and crested at a ridge before finally sloping down to the river. She stood at the riverbank and watched as it bubbled below its icy crust, then reached forward and delicately rested her fingers on the solid ice. It chilled her to the bone, but she could feel the motion of the water still flowing beneath it, like a slumbering giant. Almost every day she came to the water's edge. It was quiet and still, the only place her thoughts were calm. Lorelei recalled watching her father's ashes drift downstream from the mountainside and felt connected to him here. In this place, she felt alive again, like the river beneath its icy facade.

Lorelei rose to her feet and placed her hands in her pockets. She headed back through the forest and toward the student union. Stomping the snow from her boots as she entered the building, Lorelei pulled her keys from her pocket and found her mailbox. She opened it and pulled out a small stack of mail and put it in her now-soaked backpack.

Lorelei turned the corner toward the dining hall, grabbed a bowl of thick, rich broccoli cheese soup and a piece of crusty bread, and found a table near the window. The snow had drained all the color from the landscape, turning it into an empty palette of gray, white, and brown, with students fighting against the snow as they walked between the buildings. From across the room she could see Chelsea and Tony, laughing and eating; Chelsea was practically hanging on Tony, her beautiful blonde hair seemingly untouched by the wet winter weather. They hadn't noticed Lorelei enter, but she didn't make a point of going and sitting with them either. The truth was, she didn't want to sit with them, they were enjoying themselves too much, and Lorelei didn't feel much like talking anyhow.

Her eyes scanned the dining hall. Groups of students sat in their little cliques as they ate lunch. Lorelei envied them. Everyone else seemed so happy, but she felt empty and strange. She turned around and faced the window, and tuned out the voices of the other students. Winter seemed to swallow everything. She looked out, past the trees on the field to where the wall of snow obscured everything beyond it and her mind gravitated there. The white abyss of melancholy she had tried so hard to suppress was gaining a foothold in her chest. She finished her soup and headed back outside, out into the snow. It was cold, but beyond the cold, what she noticed most was the silence. There was nothing and no one, no noise but the sound of her own footsteps as she made her way up the hill toward her dormitory.

The warmth of her bedroom was a welcome relief. Lorelei peeled out of her wet clothes and changed into a pair of flannel pants and an old, worn hoodie. She decided she would call in sick to music history and spend the rest of the afternoon watching tawdry soap operas, eating Pringles, and curled up in her favorite blanket. She flipped on the television, took the mail out of her backpack, and sat on her bed with her legs crossed in front of her.

Most of the mail was junk: credit card offers, ads, and coupons, which she placed in a pile to her left. There were some other bills and notices, which she placed on her right, and behind everything else was a blue envelope, hand addressed to Lorelei in delicate script and postmarked from Massachusetts. Lorelei furrowed her brow and ran her finger through the top of the envelope, carefully ripping it. She pulled out a piece of crisp white paper and unfolded it, revealing a handwritten letter with perfect penmanship.

Dear Lorelei,

My name is Helen Deleaux, your great aunt on your mother's side. I send you my deepest condolences at the passing of your beloved father. He was a good man, and his death is a great loss. To be separated from one's parent is heartbreaking. Your father nurtured you in your childhood, and with his death, a part of your innocence was stripped away too soon. I hope that in time you may feel his loss less intensely as you remember the fond memories you have of your time together.

I saw you briefly at your father's funeral, did you know? I was so pleased to see what a beautiful and self-assured young lady you have become. You remind me so much of your grandmother, my dear sister Lucia, may she rest in peace. She had the same cherubic face and bright eyes, and from what I understand, you share other gifts, as well. I haven't seen you since you were just a little child, and it pains me now to think that I've been absent from your life for so long. It would be my great hope that we might meet sometime soon, to get to know one another.

I heard that you are living in Maine now, studying music. You probably don't realize it, but you come from a long line of musicians and it makes me proud to see you continuing in such a legacy. I am sure you are exceedingly gifted, like the many Deleaux women who have preceded you. Our family has long been touched by Song, so it is no surprise that you have discovered this gift within yourself.

In addition to offering you my sympathy, I also wanted to invite you to visit my home in Chatham whenever you wish. It's a quiet town in Cape Cod, where I live with my niece, Calliope Deleaux, and another distant cousin of ours, Deidre Malone. Our home is on the water, and has been in our family for generations. We have more than enough room for you to come and stay for awhile, if you would like to do so. I think you would find solace here—a time to reflect and renew, perhaps. As for me, I would like nothing more than to see you again.

With love,
Helen Deleaux

Below her name, Helen Deleaux had written her address and a phone number. Lorelei stared at the letter for a minute before she folded it up and held it in her hands. She stared blankly at the wall in front of her. She had never heard her mother mention anything about having an Aunt Helen, but her mother had never really disclosed much about her family. She knew her grandmother Lucia, whom she had never met, had lived in Massachusetts. Lorelei's mother had grown up there, but she very rarely had spoken about her family or childhood, and she always seemed guarded when Lorelei asked questions about her past. It seemed peculiar that she had an aunt and cousins living in New England that, until just moment before, Lorelei had no idea existed.

A bunch of spinsters… or lunatics, Lorelei thought, as she wondered why her mother had kept this information from her. *Or maybe they were never close to begin with.* And yet, the letter indicated that this aunt had known Lorelei as a child, had maybe even spent time with her. Lorelei certainly didn't remember that. But then she suddenly remembered the woman at the funeral, the only guest that Lorelei hadn't recognized, the older woman who had seemed so familiar to her, must have been her great-aunt. The woman had left so quickly, not even paying her respects to the family. How strange that she would have traveled so far and not even made time to speak with her own niece.

The door opened and Breanna walked into the room. She dropped her backpack and began shedding her layers of clothes on the floor.

"It is so cold out there," said Breanna. "I think my hands are gonna fall off."

Lorelei didn't reply. She stayed motionless, her thoughts still on the letter in her hands.

"Hey, Lorelei," said Breanna, "what're you doing?"

"Oh, sorry, I'm not really doing anything," Lorelei answered. "I just came back. Reading the mail. That's all."

"Anything good?"

"Well, my first car bill showed up, and there was a letter from my aunt."

"Sweet. Did she send any money?" Breanna picked up her laptop from the desk and sat down on her bed.

"No," said Lorelei, "no money. She wants me to come visit her."

"Ugh. My parents used to make me visit my Aunt Jane every summer. She collected cats and she made me go with her to sell junk at the flea market. It sucked. She was sort of a freak. Is your aunt cool?"

"I don't know, I can't remember her."

Breanna pulled back her head and wrinkled up her face.

"I didn't even know about her until I read this letter," said Lorelei.

"Then why would she want you to visit?"

"I don't know, but I get the feeling that she and my mother aren't on speaking terms."

"Well, you're not exactly on speaking terms with your mother, either."

"Or maybe they've just fallen out of touch. But it did seem strange that my mother's never even mentioned her, and that this aunt of mine felt it necessary to come to my father's funeral…"

"She did *what*? Can I read the letter?" Breanna snatched it from Lorelei's hands before she had time to respond. She paced the room as she read the contents of the letter.

She finished reading and handed the pages back to Lorelei.

"So, what do you think? Weird, right?" asked Lorelei.

"Yeah, it's a little bizarre that she decided to contact you after all this time," said Breanna, "and you say your mother never told you about her?"

"Not that I can remember. I always knew my mom grew up in Cape Cod, but I figured that all her family must be dead. My grandma Lucia raised her alone and she died not long after I was born. My mom was an only child. You'd have thought if we had other relatives they would have come up in conversation. That's why I think something must have happened to make my mother stop talking to them altogether."

"I love it. A mysterious aunt pops in from out of nowhere; maybe she's your mother's nemesis seeking you out to pull you under her influence and use you against her formidable opponent… It's like a soap opera."

"Very funny."

"So, are you going to go meet her?"

"Do I look crazy to you? I have no idea what she's like, or if she's even telling the truth. It seems a little dangerous."

"I think it's exciting. I mean, you've found a living skeleton in your mother's closet. Who knows what else she's been hiding from you all these years? Maybe you could go visit for Christmas. It's not like you're going to be going home."

Lorelei winced. Her father's death had been difficult enough, and Lorelei couldn't imagine spending the holiday without her mother. Lorelei's emails of apology to her mother had gone unanswered, and she knew if she went home for Christmas break, her mother would make her miserable unless she decided to stay home for good, but the thought of being alone on Christmas made her sick.

"I may not even be here that long."

"What do you mean?"

Lorelei took a deep breath and braced herself. "Camden wants me to take a 'break' for a while. She doesn't think I'm performing well, and she's right, I haven't been. She said I should think about taking some time off from school."

"She actually said that?"

"Yep. And I don't know what to do. But maybe she's right. Maybe I came back to school too soon. But if I leave, I don't know where else to go."

"You can't leave, Lorelei. If you really think you've got a chance at making a career with your voice, you've got to stay."

"It wouldn't be forever, just for a while, until I can get myself together. No matter how much I work or how long I practice, I'm not connecting. I think Camden might be right. I think my heart isn't in it right now."

"But that could change. It takes time to heal from something like what you went through. She can't expect that you'd come back and not be affected by what you experienced."

"It's more than just that," said Lorelei. "I walk around campus and everyone seems so happy and I'm here stuck inside my own head. I don't feel like I belong anymore."

"You're not the only person who has lost somebody. I'm sure lots of kids here have suffered some kind of loss."

"I know that, but right now, for me, it's still too fresh to try to smile and act like everything's okay. There have been days when even getting out of bed seems next to impossible."

"And if this aunt of yours turns out to be legit, would you go stay with her?"

"I don't know. Should I? It all just seems a little too convenient."

"The timing's definitely peculiar, for sure, but you never know, it could be interesting. Maybe she has some great fortune and she's looking for an heir."

"Doubtful. Didn't you read she already has a niece living with her?"

"I wonder how she knew where you go to school, or that you're a singer, or even that your father had passed away. Your mother must have told her at least that much. Maybe they're not as estranged as you think. I think you should go for it. It's probably, what, an eight-hour drive? Just go scope it out, and if she turns out to be nuts, you can always come back."

"Maybe you're right. I guess I could call her."

"Yeah, it couldn't hurt. Where's your phone?"

"Hold on, you think I should call this woman now?"

"Yeah, why not?"

Lorelei didn't feel quite prepared to call Helen Deleaux. What would she say to her? What if this was some sort of hoax? She went to her desk and pulled her cellphone out from a drawer and took it back to her bed. She sat down and dialed the number listed at the bottom of the note. The phone began to ring. Lorelei's stomach lurched with anxiety.

"Hello?" a female voice answered.

"Yes, is Helen there?" Lorelei asked.

"She is," the voice replied, "and who may I tell her is calling?"

"Lorelei Clark."

"Thank you," the phone went silent for a moment. Lorelei looked up at Breanna, panic in her eyes.

"Hello?" another woman had picked up the line.

"Hi, is this Helen Deleaux?"

"This is she."

"My name's Lorelei, and I think I received a letter from you today."

"Yes, that would be correct. I'm so glad to hear your voice. I didn't know if you would call me or not."

"Well, I just wanted to call and introduce myself. I wanted to say hello."

"My dear, you don't have to be so formal with me. I'm sure my letter took you quite by surprise."

"Yes, I... well, I didn't know I had any relatives in New England, actually."

The voice on the other line chuckled, "You most certainly do! And I'm very glad we've found each other. You're in Maine, I understand?"

"Yes, way up north, just across from Canada."

"Oh, I know the Maine seaboard quite well. You're on the St. Croix River, I believe. It must be unbearably cold up there right now, not that it's much warmer down here."

"Yes, it's really cold right now."

Breanna kicked Lorelei's leg and she motioned for her to get to the point.

"Well, the reason I'm calling," said Lorelei, "is that I thought maybe I would take you up on your invitation to come visit—"

"Wonderful!" Helen interrupted her, "I think you'll really enjoy it. The house is very spacious and the view is beautiful. I may not be a very exciting companion, after all, I'm just an old woman, but I think you might like to spend some time with your cousin, Deidre. She's only a few years older than you are."

"Sure, it would be nice to meet you all."

"When were you planning on arriving?"

"Um, I was thinking, maybe next week sometime?"

"So soon! That's splendid! I could fix up a room for you… maybe the loft…"

"You don't mind? I don't want to intrude."

"You wouldn't be intruding; after all, I was the one who invited you. I wouldn't have written you if I hadn't meant it."

"I'd have to talk to my advisor first, but then I can let you know what day I would be able to leave."

"I'm so looking forward to seeing you again, my dear."

"Thanks, I mean, I'm really excited to meet you, too."

"Until then," said Helen, "take care."

Lorelei hung up the phone and looked up at Breanna.

"So?" Breanna asked.

"I think I'm going to Chatham next week."

CHAPTER SEVEN

Lorelei spoke with her professors and her advisor about leaving Calais for a while. Most of them were very understanding and accommodating, with the exception of her music history teacher who told her she would have to repeat the course. Breanna made her swear that if there was anything strange about the situation, she would come back right away. The better part of the following weekend was spent packing up her clothes and helping Tony and a few of his friends load everything into her new car.

After Lorelei had received the life insurance money, the Jeep was the only major purchase that she made. She put most of the money in a savings account, with the intention of using it to pay for her tuition and books while she was studying in Calais, but she decided to spend a little to buy herself a car. The Jeep was used, and it needed a new paint job, but it was in good shape and the four-wheel drive made her feel safer on the snow-packed roads. It gave her the freedom to drive the backcountry roads when she needed to clear her mind.

Monday morning came and Lorelei stepped outside. The air was still, but very cold. She could see her breath and even the little hairs in her nose had turned to ice, but the sun had come out and the skies were mostly clear for the first time in weeks. The Jeep roared to life and Lorelei sat inside the car for several minutes while it warmed up before she left the parking lot. The campus looked like a postcard with snow frosting the pine trees and icicles hanging from the buildings. Lorelei imagined that she was quite possibly the only person in town who was up so early.

For just a moment Lorelei stopped to question what exactly she was doing. She had often been told she was impulsive, and she usually made decisions quickly, but her decisions had always been backed with some sort of rational explanation. But this, this wasn't just impulsivity, this was bordering on stupidity. She had no evidence that Helen Deleaux was even a relative of hers, but there was something in the letter that had intrigued her. Helen had written that Lorelei came from a family of musicians. Her mother certainly had shown no inclination of musical ability, but Lorelei wondered if it was true that her talent could have been inherited. *Maybe*, she thought, *they can help me find my voice again*. As her anxiety started to calm, she turned and started down the highway.

Just outside of Bangor, she stopped for a cup of coffee and grabbed a few pastries for the road. Lorelei sipped from the cup. The coffee tasted good, warm and bitter. Brown, sludge-covered snow was layered on the shoulders of the highway. The length of the interstate was bordered with tall, snow-encrusted pine trees, dotted along the way with some bare deciduous trees that stood out like skeletons. She watched the mile markers tick down the mileage toward New Hampshire and ate a chocolate chip muffin. At the border between the states, the jumbled town of Portsmouth was perched on an icy harbor; bits of land that jetted out into the water were connected by a spiderweb of bridges that stood over sleeping fishing boats. Lorelei stopped to fill up with gas and washed the windshield of the Jeep.

The snow on the roadside seemed to lessen south of Boston. Beyond Plymouth, the highway curved east and wrapped itself around the arm of Cape Cod. Lorelei drove past the small towns, each with their own proper English moniker, and she started to sweat. She wiped her brow on her sleeve. Her jaw clenched tighter and her fingers dug into the steering wheel. Lorelei rolled her neck in a wide circle to try to loosen her shoulders, which had begun to ascend toward her ears. She took a deep breath and looked at the map. Exiting the highway, she drove south, toward Chatham, and found Old Queen Anne Road that led to Main Street. The town itself was small, but the shops along the road seemed nice and the old-fashioned colonial homes that Lorelei spotted were immaculately kept. The afternoon sun reflected glimmers of light from the powder upon rooftops like a snow globe that had just settled.

Lorelei took a sharp right turn onto New Nigamo Street. To either side were evenly spaced old homes with gracious lawns and classic architecture. On the other side of these houses, she could make out the coastline. She checked the address of each and kept going. There were fewer homes as she headed down the street, until there were none at all. As the road bent to the left and changed its name, Lorelei spied a house beyond an old iron gate. The fence itself has brick pillars and ornamental iron rods, and bore a sign that read *4 Nehwas Road, Deleaux Cottage.*

The house could hardly be described as a cottage. A tall Victorian mansion that sat on an inlet just on the edge of the cape, the house looked as though it had been pieced together. Little additions and porches jutted out from the taller central foundation. Lorelei drove the Jeep through the gate and pulled up in front of the gray house. It towered over her, swallowing her car in its shadow. Strands of seashells hung from the top of the porch that wrapped itself around the first floor. Lorelei shrunk as she sat parked in the long front driveway.

What was I thinking? What am I doing here? Lorelei's face was flushed and her body tingled with a combination of excitement and terror as her heart beat a frantic pattern in her chest. She opened the door of the car, pocketed her keys, and began to ascend the steps. The house was surreal, like something from her dreams. She had been there before. The tower on the side of the house seemed so familiar, with its spiral steps winding toward the roof like a lighthouse. *No, no, this was a terrible idea. There's no way I'm going up there. I'm such an IDIOT...*

The wind started howling and a large clump of snow slid from the roof of the house and landed directly beside her. She gasped, and dug her fingernails deep into her palms. Her mind flashed with the scenarios of a dozen different horror movies, with each stupid heroine putting herself directly in harm's way, unwittingly becoming the target of some psychotic murderer. *That's it,* she thought, *I can't stay here. What the hell was I thinking?* Lorelei grabbed hold of the banister and turned around, carefully avoiding the slush that was piled next to her feet. The stairs creaked beneath her as she began her way back down toward the Jeep.

"Lorelei?" a voice called out from behind her. She turned her head around to see a woman standing at the top of the steps. Her hair was pulled up in a high bun and she was covered in a rich brown pashmina. Wisps of hair framed her face and fluttered in the wind. Lorelei met the woman's pale green eyes with her own; comfort and warmth replaced the fear that had been holding her back.

"Yes, uh, hi," Lorelei stuttered.

"I didn't think you would actually come, but I'm glad you did," said the woman. "Come here and let me see you."

Lorelei faced the woman and took two steps back up the stairs toward her.

"You're a real beauty," she said. "I still can't believe how much you've grown."

She reached a thin hand out and brushed Lorelei's cheek. Her hand was soft and warm. It reminded her of her mother.

"I'm sorry, but I don't remember you."

"Of course you wouldn't. When you lived here you were just a tiny little thing, barely walking. You were the sweetest child though, always happy, playing, singing. My own dear little niece."

"I lived here?" Lorelei asked.

"For a few years, yes. You were born in this house. Just up there, actually." She pointed up toward a gable on the second story beside the spiral tower.

Lorelei was shocked and confused by Helen's claim. Her mother had never told her that she was born in Massachusetts or that she had lived anywhere but Colorado. Shouldn't every child know where they were born, at the very least?

"Let's not stand out here in the cold," said Helen. "Come inside and I'll make you a hot cup of tea."

Before she had time to answer, Helen had opened the crimson door and crossed the threshold. Lorelei followed, entering the house behind her. Helen took Lorelei's coat, shook the snow from it, and hung it up on a peg next to the door. The foyer was cavernous with hammered tin ceilings and a massive wooden staircase. At the bottom of the banister the wooden figurehead of a woman perched toward Lorelei; its round breasts and slender figure the epitome of feminine beauty, but its face was weathered and the features had been worn away. They entered the kitchen through a brick archway and Helen led Lorelei to a large oak table and pulled out a chair.

"Here you go," she said. "Make yourself at home. I'll just get the kettle started."

"This is a beautiful house," said Lorelei. "How long have you lived here?"

"The Deleauxes have owned this property and this home, in one form or another, for hundreds of years," Helen filled a teakettle with water and sat it on the gas stove. "Our history here goes back a long, long way."

"I had no idea we even had family out here."

"Well, we're it, really. And I'm sorry we haven't done a better job of staying in touch." Helen went to the pantry and pulled out two thick mugs. She hummed as she placed a tea bag in each and brought them over to the table, moving with such grace that it seemed almost as though she were floating across the room. In one swift move, she took the chair beside Lorelei and sat.

"We can go get your things in a few minutes, but I'll let you warm up first. I have your room all ready for you. I hope you like it."

"Thank you. It's really nice of you to let me stay here."

"You can stay as long as you'd like. We certainly aren't short on space."

Lorelei smiled. The kitchen was cozy and smelled of fresh bread. Copper pots hung from the ceiling above the stove and a mosaic of pale blue and green tiles covered the backsplash behind the countertops.

"Did you get to see much of the town when you were driving?" Helen asked.

"I saw a little bit. Just the main street."

"We'll have to show you around town. Maybe Dee can take you to see the marina tomorrow."

"Dee?"

"Deidre's one of our cousins. She lives here with me and my niece Calliope. They should be home in a few hours and we'll all have dinner together."

The kettle began to whistle and Helen stood. Within seconds, hot water was being poured into Lorelei's mug. The aroma of sweet cinnamon wafted up and the steam warmed Lorelei's face as she blew on the cup. It was perfect—hot, spicy, and fragrant.

"Are you hungry? Can I get you anything?" asked Helen.

"No, I'm fine. Thank you."

Lorelei sipped her tea, and Helen relaxed back in her chair and crossed her legs.

"How was the drive?"

"Pretty long, but the roads were okay. It wasn't too icy or anything."

"Good." Helen spied Lorelei's empty cup, "Any more tea?"

"No thanks, I've had enough."

Helen stood, picked up the mugs, and rinsed them in the sink.

"Let me show you to your room, and you can settle in for a bit."

Lorelei followed Helen back out through the foyer and up the main staircase. The landing overlooked another room, with plush yellow chairs, a leather sofa, and a bookcase that had been built into one of the walls. A great gray stone fireplace between two large picture windows held a small fire that was sputtering, but still holding onto life before becoming embers. The windows themselves were shrouded by long, blue silk curtains, but beyond them, Lorelei caught just a glimpse of what must be the sea.

Helen led Lorelei past the landing and down a long hallway, at the end of which was a narrow door. She opened the door and a steep staircase led to an upper floor. There was very little light in the staircase and Lorelei felt a sense of claustrophobia overtake her.

"This used to be the servant's quarters," said Helen, "a very long time ago. We renovated it several years ago."

At the top of the steps, Lorelei was overtaken by light. A big, round window cast rays of sunlight across the hardwood flooring in the room. The side walls were sloped up and met at a point at the top of the ceiling. A white daybed sat under the window, covered by a green paisley quilt and lots of pillows, and next to the bed was a cream colored chair with a small ottoman and a lamp.

"Wow, this is so nice," said Lorelei. "It's really pretty up here."

"I'm glad you like it. Let me show you everything. Here is a closet for all your clothes," said Helen opening the door to a walk-in closet. Lorelei's luggage had already been placed inside the closet, "Good, it looks like Aeson already brought up your things."

Lorelei was taken aback to see her luggage already neatly lined against the closet wall. "Who's... Aeson?"

"Aeson Hunter works for our company, but he does some odds and ends around the house for us sometimes, too."

"What company?"

"The Deleaux family has controlling assets in a company called Aquaitor," she paused. "It's a maritime salvage company. Other companies hire us to clean up shipwrecks and spills, retrieve sunken goods, tug out grounded ships, that sort of thing. I still do a consult every now and then, but I've retired for the most part. Calliope's been the one really running the company for the last five years. She has very good business sense."

Lorelei spun around to face another door on the other side of the room.

"What's over there?"

"Let me show you." Helen opened the door and a burst of cold air swept through the room. She disappeared beyond the door and Lorelei followed.

The door led to a balcony that hung on to the side of the house, jutting out just above the roofline. They walked several paces and rounded the corner. Lorelei clung to the handrail as she stepped carefully through the fresh snow. The height was dizzying, but Lorelei could see the cliffs beneath them and the water slapping the rocks where it met land. It was breathtaking. The coastline stretched out, full of twists, turns, and inlets that cut into the side of the earth. A little bit of sunlight hit the water and had turned it into a sparkling cloth of deep blue, moving and constantly changing.

"This is amazing," said Lorelei. Her eyes could hardly absorb the view. From the height of the balcony was a panorama of ocean that went on forever. At the horizon, she could nearly make out the curve of the earth. The wind stung her cheeks, and she rubbed her arms to warm them, but she had no immediate desire to go back inside.

"This is one of my favorite places, too. There's something special about this place."

"It's beautiful. You can see everything from here."

"I'm glad you like it."

They stood together for a few minutes looking over the ocean. Lorelei's hands were like ice curled around the metal guardrail that enclosed the balcony. Her eyes panned the sea; rows of stately houses beyond the cliffs clung to another shoreline farther up the coast. The land the home sat on was a peninsula sticking into the ocean. Within the jetty was an enclave where the water circled up against the rocks around it. Lorelei could see a path that trailed from the house down to the top of the cliffs and steps that descended from the path to the pooling water below.

Helen turned and headed back for the door. The warmth of the house was a comfort. Lorelei blew on her hands to warm them as they entered.

"Over here's the bathroom, if you want to freshen up a bit," said Helen. "Take your time, and come down whenever you want. I'm going to start fixing dinner."

Helen left her alone in the room. Lorelei went to the closet, took a small bag of toiletries and cosmetics out of the suitcase, and headed for the bathroom. She ran the water in the sink until it became warm and then scrubbed her face. Lorelei let her hair down from its ponytail and ran a brush through it. Her hair was frizzy, but she did her best to pull it back and secured it again with a rubber band. She went back to the bed and rested her head on the quilted pillowcase. Hanging from the ceiling above her were several silver paper stars dangling from fishing wire, each spinning slightly, back and forth. Lorelei closed her eyes and allowed herself to simply breathe.

CHAPTER EIGHT

Lorelei made her way downstairs; she could hear pans clanking in the kitchen as she crossed the foyer and headed toward the sound.

"I don't know *where* the mandoline is, Helen. Can't I just chop them up on the cutting board?"

"Yes, fine. Just go take the onions over there. I need to use this counter to clean the chicken."

Lorelei stepped into the kitchen where there were two women facing away from her toward the wall. One obviously was her Aunt Helen, the other had long, blonde hair that fell straight down her back. She turned around, her hands full of onions and a cutting board, and spotted Lorelei standing across the kitchen.

"Oh, hi there," said the young woman, smiling. Lorelei immediately noticed the woman's perfect teeth. She flashed Lorelei a smile and sat everything down on the island in the middle of the room.

Helen turned around to face Lorelei. "Did you get a little rest?" she asked.

"Yes," replied Lorelei, "I think I fell asleep for a while."

"Lorelei, I'd like you to meet Deidre. Dee, Lorelei."

Deidre grinned again, her gorgeous smile spread wide under glossy burgundy lips and her green eyes danced in the light when she blinked. Lorelei was mesmerized by Deidre's face. It was as though she had been plucked from the cover of a magazine. Everything about her was stunning, even her flawless skin, which was silky and bronzed. *She must make men melt,* thought Lorelei.

"It is *so* nice to meet you. Another Deleaux girl!" Deidre winked.

"Clark," replied Lorelei.

"Huh?"

"My name's Lorelei *Clark.*"

"Yeah, well we're all Deleaux girls here," said Deidre, "and you're so pretty! Look at that face, and you have the Deleaux eyes for sure. The sailors are definitely going to go for you."

"Dee, *please,*" said Helen, placing a hand on her shoulder. Deidre rolled her eyes.

"Hey you wanna help me with the onions?" Deidre asked Lorelei.

"Dee, you can slice the onions yourself," said Helen, "Lorelei's our guest tonight."

"Is there anything I can do to help?" asked Lorelei.

"No, you just relax. You've had a long day."

Lorelei took a seat on a bar stool at the island. She watched Helen and Deidre as they cooked. Helen moved quickly from one task to the next as Deidre slowly peeled her onions.

"So you're from Colorado, huh?" asked Deidre.

"Yeah, lived there my whole life," Lorelei corrected herself, "well, *most* of my life. But I've been going to school in Maine this year."

"Helen told me. So you're singing, right?"

"Uh-huh."

78

"Good for you. You'll have to sing for me sometime. We can go karaoke together!"

Lorelei heard Helen sigh deeply.

Deidre leaned in closer to Lorelei and whispered, "She doesn't like me singing karaoke for some reason. But whatever. We'll go anyway." Deidre smiled coyly at Lorelei and continued her task.

"Don't think I can't hear you," said Helen. "It's not that I mind you going out once in a while, but one would think, that at your age, you could find something better to do with your time."

"It's not like there's anything else to do in this town. So I like going out with my friends. How am I supposed to meet anyone if I stay cooped up in this house?"

"Have you lived here very long?" asked Lorelei.

"Going on three years now, actually. I moved out from LA when I was twenty-two. I didn't have a job, so Helen and Calliope hired me to work for them."

"Is your family still out in Los Angeles?"

"No," Deidre replied, "my mother passed away when I was a baby. My father remarried and I grew up in Ohio. I didn't move to LA until I was twenty. I had this dream that I was going to be famous, but things didn't turn out exactly as I had planned, ya know? Los Angeles was great, but I couldn't afford to eat and I was living on my friends' couches, so I moved out here."

"Are you an actress?"

"No, I'm a singer, too. I was in a band for a while, and we had a demo tape. Actually almost signed to a label, but it didn't work out."

"That's too bad. Do you think you'll try again?"

"Eh, probably not. I'm pretty sure that chapter in my life is over. And it's okay, really. I don't mind living out here too much;

it can just be a little boring sometimes. It's better in the summer, though."

Deidre took the board full of chopped onions and dumped them into a big pot that was sitting on the stove. "Anyway, Helen wanted me to take you around town tomorrow. You interested?"

"Sure," said Lorelei.

Helen was now standing beside Deidre and dusted the counter with flour. She emptied a bowl full of dough and began to roll it out until it had reached the thickness she desired. A rusty-looking biscuit cutter turned out perfect circles of dough that were laid to rest on a metal tray. Helen and Deidre worked side by side, and the smell of savory chicken soup filled the kitchen. The teakettle whistled and Helen poured mugs full of the same sweet cinnamon tea that Lorelei had enjoyed when she first arrived. Outside the window, the light was fading, the sun making its retreat from the sky.

Lorelei heard the front door open. It creaked on its hinges and was closed just as quickly as it had opened. Several seconds later, she heard the clicking of high heels on the wood floor approaching the kitchen. Another woman was approaching them from the front of the house. She was tall and wore a black pencil skirt that stopped just above her knees with a well-fitted, cream-colored silk blouse, and had jet-black hair with a streak of white toward the front that framed her pale face and hung in front of her shoulders. Her intense and striking face was tempered by her cool, green eyes.

She stopped at the entrance of the kitchen and eyed Lorelei intently, as if she were sizing her up, before entering. After hanging her black leather purse on the back of one of the kitchen chairs, she approached Lorelei.

"Hello, I'm Calliope," she said, extending her hand toward Lorelei.

"Hi, I'm Lorelei Clark," Lorelei stood up and took Calliope's powerful hand.

"Pleasure meeting you," Calliope walked over to the sink and filled a glass with water. "How's your mother?"

"Fine, I think. She's in Colorado. I haven't talked to her lately."

"Well, when you do, tell her I send my regards."

Calliope reminded Lorelei of her mother very much. Her build was the same, lean and muscular, and she had the same commanding presence when she stepped into the room.

"How did everything go today?" asked Helen.

"Fine," said Calliope. "We bought new scuba gear for the dive team today. Aeson insisted the old gear needed to be replaced. And we put a bid in at Port Newark for a job that would start next week."

"That's good news."

"We sent some of the guys to pull out that car that skidded off the bridge on Bells Neck Road last Thursday, remember?"

"The accident in the reservoir? Of course I remember," replied Helen.

"There's a memorial service down in Harwich the day after tomorrow, if you want to go," said Calliope.

"Maybe," Helen stirred the pot on the stove.

"So when did you get here?" Calliope turned her attention back to Lorelei.

"A few hours ago."

"All settled?"

"Not exactly. I ended up falling asleep for a little while."

Calliope smiled at her. "Well, there will be plenty of time to unpack tomorrow."

"I think Deidre's going to show me around town tomorrow."

"Make sure she takes you to the candy shop," said Helen. "They have wonderful truffles and excellent fudge."

Lorelei watched as they continued to cook. Helen had covered the pot of soup and was slicing apples to make a pie. Deidre stepped out of the room to take a phone call and Calliope set the table before leaving to change her clothes.

"So what do you think? Are you glad you came?" asked Helen, as she placed the pie carefully in the oven. She wiped her hands on a towel that was hanging over her shoulder.

"Yeah, I guess so," said Lorelei. "You know, to be honest, I really didn't know what I was doing driving all the way down here, but now that I'm here, it sort of makes sense in some weird way. And I can't believe this house. It's gorgeous."

"Thank you," Helen smiled at her. "I hope you make yourself at home. You can help yourself to anything while you're here."

"Thanks."

"I think Deidre is really excited you're here. It will be good for her to have another young person in the house."

"She seems really nice."

"Dee has a good heart. I'm sure the two of you will get along well." She lifted the lid and stirred the soup, grabbed some salt from the cellar next to the stovetop and threw it in the steaming pot.

"Can I ask you something?"

"Of course."

"It's really strange that my mom never mentioned you, or that we lived in Chatham at all. I was just... is there... some reason she wouldn't have wanted me to know about you?"

"It's complicated, Lorelei. She and I had very different ideas about how to raise children, and I think at some point, I may have overstepped my bounds. Your mother always wanted what was best for you, and she decided that she wanted to raise you in Colorado. Who was I to try and stop her?"

"She's impossible."

"I can't blame her, really. Your mom and dad wanted a different life for you than the life they had here."

"So why would my parents lie to me?"

"Well, did you ever ask them? I'm sure your mom figured you wouldn't be interested in a bunch of old maids living up in Cape Cod. We still write to each other, sometimes. She sent me a few of your school pictures. They're over here somewhere…" Helen pulled out an envelope from one of the drawers near the stove. She rifled through a collection of wallet-sized photos, "Look, here you are… sixth grade."

"Ugh, braces."

"And here's your senior picture," Helen said, handing over the photograph.

The photograph of Lorelei showed her leaning up against the side of a bridge crossing a stream. Her hair curled around her face in perfect ringlets and freckles dotted her nose. She remembered picking out that outfit, a cute purple top with a long orange scarf that hung from her neck and her favorite pair of skinny jeans.

"I love this picture of you," said Helen. "You look so happy."

Lorelei tried to remember that feeling—happiness. A warm breeze playing through her hair. Laughing. It had been a long time since she had laughed.

Deidre walked back into the kitchen, her silky blonde hair swaying on her back as she sashayed toward Helen.

"I'm going to meet Tyler after dinner, so are we going to eat soon?"

"The bartender?"

"No, that's Taylor. Tyler is the guy I met last weekend at the grocery store. I think he might be like a teacher or something."

"Oh, I see," replied Helen.

"We're just going to watch movies over at his place."

"Well, dinner's almost ready. Can you get out the butter? Lorelei, you can sit wherever you'd like."

Lorelei went and took a seat at the table. The table was covered with a light brown tablecloth, and had a basket of bread and a pitcher of water in the center of it. Each place setting had a soup bowl and small plate. The china itself was lovely and delicate, with a scalloped edge that contained a blue and brown pattern, while in the very center of the bowl was the emblem of a small red flag with a white star in it, beneath which was a scroll bearing the words "White Star Lines." Deidre sat down in the chair to Lorelei's right. Helen brought a white tureen of soup to the table and began to ladle it into their bowls. Thick chunks of chicken and vegetables spilled into the dishes and hot steam rose in front of her face. It smelled like home.

Calliope had returned to the kitchen wearing a sweater and jeans and joined them. Sitting at the table, Lorelei noticed how beautiful the three women were, so uniquely different, but still so individually stunning. But it was their eyes that tied them all together; their eyes were opalescent and full of light, a cool green that Lorelei had only ever seen before in her own eyes. Helen reached out and took Lorelei's hand in her own. Their hands clasped together, the women bowed their heads and Helen led them in a sung prayer, *"We thank Thee for the gifts that Thou hast given from Thy bounty. Bless us today and teach us to love one another more perfectly. Amen."* Their voices were full and rich, moving together in harmony.

As their prayer was concluded, Helen squeezed her hand and Lorelei looked up to see Deidre give her a smile. What Helen had told her about their musical gifts had been true. Lorelei hadn't imagined that they would have such pure and perfect voices, and when they sang together as one, it had become something sublime.

They continued through the meal pleasantly, enjoying the flavorful soup and homemade bread. Lorelei took in the conversation and started to feel at ease with these relatives of hers. For a day that had started with such apprehension, it had ended with a sense of peace. Helen's presence was particularly calming; when she spoke Lorelei was relaxed and sedate—the exact opposite of what she had expected.

After supper, Helen and Deidre made quick work to clean up the kitchen, refusing Lorelei's offers to help, and Calliope brewed a pot of coffee. Deidre left the house after the dishes had been scrubbed, dried, and put away in the cupboards. As she headed out, Lorelei decided to retreat to her room after thanking Helen and Calliope again for their hospitality. Night had already settled upon the house and Lorelei found her room, dark and a little cold. She turned on the small lamp by the bedside, changed into her pajamas and then found her phone and called Breanna.

"So you're okay?" Breanna sounded relieved.

"Yeah, I'm fine. You should see this place, though. It's, well, it's hard to describe, but it's amazing. The house is really old, but it's interesting. I'm staying on the third floor and there's an unbelievable view of the ocean from up here."

"And they're not too... weird?"

"No, they're all right, actually. Helen's been really sweet, and I'm going to go check out the town tomorrow."

"How long do you think you're going to stay?"

"I don't know. Maybe a week or two. Maybe more. I'm just going to see how it goes."

"Well, call me tomorrow night, all right? I'm glad everything's okay."

"Thanks. I miss you guys. Tell Chelsea I said hi."

"Sure. Bye, Lorelei."

She hung up the phone and finished getting ready for bed. Moonlight streamed in the round window and painted itself across the room. The stars that hung above the bed caught bits of the moonlight too, and cast their shadows on the wall. Lorelei crawled into bed and pulled the quilt up beneath her chin. As she waited for sleep, she knew that finding these Deleaux women had been more than a leap of faith; she felt a surprising and unexpected connection to this place, and to the sea that surrounded her.

CHAPTER NINE

The sun gently woke Lorelei, its familiar warmth spreading across her cheeks in lines cut by the wooden blinds on the window. She rolled over, sat up on the edge of the bed, and rubbed the sleep from her eyes. The room was filled with light, but Lorelei knew that the sunlight this time of year was deceptive; it simply created an illusion of summer, while the wind and the surf would certainly remind her of the impending winter as soon as she went outside. She crawled out of bed, wiggled her toes into her slippers, and headed downstairs.

From the kitchen, Lorelei could hear Deidre talking on the phone in the next room. There was a box of bran flakes sitting on the counter. Lorelei wrinkled her nose at the sight of them. She looked in the pantry to try to find a more suitable option, and only found three more boxes of bran flakes. She made a mental note that she would need to buy some cereal when she went to town today, grabbed a banana and a glass of milk, and walked out the door from the kitchen that led to the back porch.

The wind stung her cheeks slightly when she went outside, but she liked the feel of it. It was invigorating. She took a deep breath to fill her lungs with the cool salt air. At least the sky was clear, and she could see forever. The beach stretched out for miles on either side of the old house, and the ocean seemed calm, like it was sleeping, with long and easy breaths. The back of the property that faced the sea was gently sloping, and had few trees. Beside the house were several terraced gardens, empty for winter. The path she had seen yesterday from the porch above started here at the back deck and was made of river rock. It was still mostly covered with blown snow, but a single set of footprints led from the house to the edge of the property, where a set of wooden steps met the water. Down below, she could make out a figure standing in the cove, not very far from the shore.

Lorelei walked to the edge of the deck and peered down to the beach below. She recognized the silver hair of her aunt. Helen was wearing a long, white, cotton dress and was standing in the frigid water, up to her thighs. The skirt of the dress swirled about her on the surface of the sea, following the waves, back and forth. Her hands skimmed the water, palms touching it lightly, caressing the ocean itself. And Lorelei could hear her, over the steady noise of the waves.

I'm just a poor wayfaring stranger
trav'ling through this world of woe.
There's no sickness, toil nor danger
In that bright world to which I go.
I'm going there to meet my father
I'm going there no more to roam;
I'm just a'going over Jordan
I'm just a'going over home.

Helen's voice was so plaintive and eerily ethereal. Her song rose up, smooth and slow, and was carried on the breeze, line by line, gentle and sorrowful, as Helen wept to the ocean. Lorelei was captivated by it, but she still wondered why her aunt was standing in water that must be nearly freezing.

"She does that sometimes," Lorelei turned, startled to see Calliope standing behind her on the deck.

"But it's so cold outside," Lorelei said, "the water must be freezing."

"She doesn't seem to mind," replied Calliope. "I think she enjoys the solitude."

"And she's... singing," Lorelei remarked.

"Yes," said Calliope, "that's her way. Everyone has their own way of singing their sorrows. This is Helen's. She's lived here so long, the sea is like an old friend to her. Singing out there clears her mind."

Lorelei stood, watching her aunt below and listening to her wailing her song of sorrow, and she was overcome with a great sympathy for her. Helen's grief wrapped around her like a cloak, as heavy as the sadness she bore for her own recent loss. Lorelei's anguish for her father rose up in her, but there was a part of her that was less alone. She suddenly knew she wasn't the only person in the world with a burden on her heart. There was a strange feeling inside her that wished that she, too, could cry out to the sea and have it take away her pain, her fear, and her emptiness. As Lorelei continued to listen, Helen's song faded into silence, and she turned around and started walking back to shore.

"Come on, let's go back inside," Calliope led Lorelei back into the house.

Back in the kitchen, Deidre was chopping fruit and putting it in a blender. "You guys want a smoothie?" she asked.

"No thanks," Calliope replied, "I'm heading out now. Did you get last month's invoices put together?"

"Yep," said Deidre, "they're labeled and on your desk."

Calliope picked up a Blackberry from the table and looked at it, "And the conference call's still on for this morning?"

"Uh-huh, 9:30."

"Thanks. You two have fun today. I'll see you later tonight."

Calliope grabbed her purse and pulled on her coat. She turned to walk out of the kitchen, but as she did so, she nearly bumped into a young man who was heading toward her.

"Sorry, Ms. Deleaux. Are you okay?"

"Yes, I'm fine. I didn't see you there," Calliope replied.

"I just came by to bring Helen a message, but I'll be back at the office in a few minutes."

"You know, you could have just called."

"Yeah, I know, but I was already out, so I thought I'd just drop by."

"All right. Do you think you'll have a chance to go over the payroll today? I think some of the guys have been padding their overtime."

"Sure, absolutely."

"Great. I'll see you soon," she said before turning to leave.

He walked in and hopped up on the counter, sitting beside Deidre as she started the blender.

"Aeson, *please*," said Deidre, shoving him in the leg.

"What, no good morning kiss?"

"Would you stop? Seriously."

As Deidre turned around and made her way toward the sink, Aeson jumped down and pulled her into his arms. She elbowed him in the ribs. Hard.

"What the hell was that for?" he bent over, holding his side.

"You just don't know when to quit. You drive me crazy!" Deidre was staring him down now.

"Sorry! I was only kidding," he rubbed his side and grimaced. Aeson turned his attention toward Lorelei, who was sitting on the bar stool at the island in the middle of the kitchen. "And who do we have over here?"

"Oh, this is Lorelei. She just came down yesterday. Cassandra's daughter. Lorelei, this is Aeson Hunter, total juvenile. You'll have to learn to put up with him, though, because he is *always around.*"

"Hey," he smiled at her. "Welcome to Chatham."

Aeson wore a plain white T-shirt over blue jeans. He had dark golden hair that hung in front of his deep blue eyes and stubble that covered his chin. Lorelei guessed that he was a few years older than she was, but he looked somewhat more weathered. His calloused hands picked up an apple from beside him and he began tossing it playfully and catching it in his hands.

"Nice to meet you," Lorelei blushed.

"Aeson, what are you doing here?" Helen spoke as she entered the kitchen from the back door. Her dress was wet and clung to her legs, but she offered no explanation.

"Just brought a message for you," he said. He placed a piece of folded-up white paper in her hand.

"Thank you," she unfolded the paper and glanced it over. "Looks like we've got an early appointment tomorrow, Deidre."

Deidre poured her smoothie into a plastic cup. "How early?"

"Pretty early, 5:30, I'd say."

"Are you *kidding* me? That *sucks.*"

"You know the routine. You don't have to like it, but you need to be there."

"Hey, I'm going to leave now," said Aeson, "but it was a pleasure meeting you, Lorelei. See you 'round." Aeson grabbed

Deidre's cup, patted her on the butt and then ran out of the kitchen.

"You... JERK!" Deidre yelled after him. "Can't you *do* something about him?"

"Oh, Deidre," said Helen, "Don't be so sensitive."

Helen left them and headed for the stairs. Deidre was still fuming, but she tried to regain her composure and asked Lorelei, "So what do you want to do today?"

"I don't care."

"Well, nothing's open yet anyhow, so I'm going to get ready. You wanna meet me back down here in an hour or so?"

"Sure, sounds good."

Lorelei put her bowl in the sink and went upstairs to shower and get dressed. She found a pair of jeans and paired it with a zip-up fleece and pushed her hair back into a headband. She looked in the mirror and put on some blush and just a little pink lipgloss. Satisfied, Lorelei ran down both flights of stairs and found Deidre waiting for her at the bottom. She wore a short, flared skirt over gray leggings, a little plum houndstooth-patterned jacket, a pair of black, strappy, platform stilettos, and enormous silver sunglasses. Beside her, Lorelei was extremely underdressed.

"All set?" asked Deidre.

"I guess so," said Lorelei.

Outside, the clouds had retreated to the eastern sky, letting the sun warm the Earth below. The snow was melting from the rooftop and had begun to trickle down the gutter beside the porch steps. Lorelei's Jeep was still parked in the driveway at the bottom of the stairs, and in front of it was a black Volkswagen Jetta. Deidre unlocked the doors and Lorelei got in the passenger's side. She headed up the road, found Main Street, and made a right.

"So, I thought I'd show you the lighthouse first," said Deidre. She parked the car on the side of the road, next to a white building that resembled a modest house with a bright red roof that was peeking out under the layer of snow. Beside it stood a white lighthouse tower. "It's still operated by the Coast Guard, so most people don't get to go in, but I know a guy that works here."

As they got out of the car, the door of the house opened and a man walked down the sidewalk toward them. He was muscular and clean cut, and was wearing khaki cargo pants and a black shirt.

"Deidre Malone!" he yelled at her. "Girl, you are a sight for sore eyes, and you are looking *particularly* beautiful today."

"You like?" she asked as she twirled around for him.

"Sure do. Get over here."

She leaned over the short fence that surrounded the property and planted a quick kiss on his lips. He opened the gate to let them in. Petty Officer Jeremy Douglas, of the US Coast Guard, shook Lorelei's hand.

"Lorelei wanted to know if you could take us up in the tower," said Deidre.

"I'm not supposed to take civilians up there, not unless it's been approved."

"You'd do it for me though, wouldn't you?" she looked at him intently; her eyes were impossible to resist. He started to sweat a little and he looked back over his shoulder nervously.

"Well, all right," Jeremy replied, "just this once. You're going to get me in trouble one of these days."

He wrapped his arm around Deidre's shoulders and they headed toward the lighthouse tower with Lorelei trailing behind them. Jeremy unlocked the door at the bottom of the tower and led the way. Lorelei followed up the giant spiral staircase that circled around to a platform housing the light inside. The lens twirled in its enclosure of huge windows that overlooked the beach and the great expanse of ocean that lay beyond it.

"Beautiful, isn't it?" asked Deidre.

"Yeah, this is incredible," said Lorelei. She put her face up near one of the panes of glass, trying to take in the view.

"Been around since the early nineteenth century," said Jeremy, "although it's had some renovations along the way. Before they put the lighthouse here, there were lots of shipwrecks in this area. Pretty treacherous waters, actually. There were land pirates that would climb up on these dunes out here with their lanterns and lure the ships up to the coast. When the boats would wash up, they'd plunder them and take what they could. People around here called them 'mooncussers' because apparently they would cuss at the moon if it was too bright, because the sailors wouldn't see their lanterns. So, the village built a lighthouse here, so the ships would be guided safely."

"Interesting," said Lorelei, more impressed by the view than by the history lesson.

"You know, Helen told me that one of our ancestors was the keeper here back in the 1800s," said Deidre. "She kind of inherited the job after her husband died. Not many women were lighthouse keepers back then. Weird to think someone in our family used to actually live here, isn't it?"

Lorelei walked around the platform of the lighthouse slowly. The beach here was a lot different than the cliffs by the Deleaux house, much more open and less rocky. She could imagine swimmers enjoying the water and sun with their families in the summer, but for now, the beach was empty; dead grasses stuck up through the snow and swayed in the wind, while the ocean itself was covered with a thin fog.

After they had finished up in the lighthouse, Deidre continued her tour of the town. They had lunch at a restaurant tucked away behind some shops on Main Street, where Deidre was quite friendly with one of the waiters. They drove past the marina and Deidre pointed out several of the boats that Aquaitor kept docked there. The stores along Main Street were charming, full of antiques, expensive jewelry, home decor, and various novelties, and many of the shops were advertising end-of-season sales. Deidre and Lorelei browsed, humming to the music that was playing in the stores. Afterwards, they went to a grocery store not far from town to do a little shopping for Helen before they headed back to the house.

"I had fun today," Lorelei said as she heaved a bag of potatoes into the trunk of the car. "Thanks for taking me out and showing me the town."

As they brought the sacks of groceries in through the front door of the house, Lorelei heard a voice coming from the living room, singing. She dropped her groceries in the foyer and went around the corner to listen. Helen was looking out the windows as she sang, and Lorelei knew every word.

Sofðu unga astin min
uti regnið grætur.
Mamma geymir gullin þin
gamlan legg og voluskrin.
Við skulum ekki vaka um dimmar nætur.

The song was slow, and haunting. Helen turned around and saw Lorelei watching her from the doorway. "I *know* that song," said Lorelei. "That's my mother's song. She used to sing it to me every night when I was a child."

"And I used to sing it to her," said Helen. "It's a lullaby."

"I thought I had forgotten the words, but I remember them now."

"That's good. Maybe someday you can pass it on to your daughter. Lullabies are a little bit like an inheritance that way. We collect them from our mothers and pass them on to future generations and that little piece of us stays alive with our children."

"It's beautiful. I love how you sing it."

The evening was filled with more of the same domestic pleasantries that had occupied their night before. A pot roast filled the house with delicious fragrant aromas and the women joined together to dine, starting their meal again with their sung prayer. After supper, Lorelei found a book in the study and retreated up to her room early to read and take a bath. She spent time on the phone with her cousin, Jennifer, but did not mention to her that she was no longer in Calais.

Lying in bed, her thoughts drifted back to that morning, when she had seen Helen wading in the ocean, singing. It was such a peculiar thing, and while Lorelei's day had been filled with so many other diversions, she hadn't thought about it much since then. Why had she been out in the water, crying to the sea? There was no other way to describe it, but it had seemed as though she was mourning, and her voice had carried farther up to the house than it should have naturally. It bothered Lorelei, because it seemed so unusual for a woman as seemingly lucid as Helen to walk into the ocean in the middle of the winter, fully dressed, and sing; but deep inside, seeing Helen in the water was the most natural thing in the world.

CHAPTER TEN

A surge of electric pain ran down Lorelei's spine and she bolted upright from her sleep. Her stomach was uneasy and her hair was wet with sweat as she awoke from a night terror. In her dreams, she could see the man drown, his cries unanswered as he struggled in the waves. His arms flailed about him as he tried to breathe, but every time he went for air, he sucked in more water, stinging his lungs. Lorelei went to the bathroom and splashed cool water on her face, trying to ignore the images from her dream that were still playing through her mind.

She pushed her feet into her warm, furry slippers and walked down the long, narrow staircase that led from the third floor bedroom down to the floor beneath it. She tried to turn the handle of the door at the bottom of the stairs, but it wouldn't budge. Lorelei pushed against the door. It was stuck fast. The handle seemed to be locked from the other side, and in the dark staircase, she was having a hard time trying to determine if or where there might be a keyhole. She banged on the door, but there was no answer. After a minute, she tried banging again, but still nothing and no one came to her aid. *This kind of thing happens in old houses*, she told herself, *the lock must be jammed.*

Lorelei walked back up the flight of stairs and toward a door that led out to the balcony. *Maybe there's a fire escape out that way,* she thought. She grabbed a hoodie and pulled it on before heading outside. Most of the snow had melted from the porch, but small patches of ice remained, so Lorelei held tight to the handrail as she walked along the side of the house. There was no stairwell, only a railing where the porch ended from which she could see the edge of the roof. If she jumped, she might be able to slide from that to the second story porch below. *No*, she thought, *that's too dangerous*, but still she walked over to it, just to see how difficult it might be.

From the corner of the porch she could see the cove and the cliffs covered with thick, quickly moving fog. It was still mostly dark; the sun hadn't risen yet, but deep orange streams of light had started to reach out from the horizon over the sea. The fog began to swirl together intensely. It gushed in from the ocean and rounded itself about the edges of the inlet, like clouds. As she watched, the fog separated itself into three distinct spinning columns of mist, with green light emanating from within them. The light and the mist began to solidify, and Lorelei could see each column taking a human shape. *It must be a dream*, she thought, remembering the images of the drowning man.

In the cove, the water glowed electrically, a blue-green pool lit up from under the surface. The figures were almost translucent, like vapor. Turbulent waves lapped up against the sides of the cliffs as the figures became clearer. The ocean reached up with liquid fingers around them, until each column of water and mist had become opaque in the form of a woman. The water calmed and flattened out beneath them, and little by little, the forms drew closer and closer to the beach.

The women floated above the water effortlessly, and by the time they had reached land, Lorelei recognized them, even from a distance, illuminated by the sun that was rising behind them. Helen, with long silver hair that hung in front of her shoulders. Deidre, perfect and beautiful. Calliope, dark and mysterious. They were obviously naked, but the mist continued to circle around and cover them, rising from the water like pieces of silk. *What the hell is going on?* Lorelei panicked, goose bumps covered her body and the hair on her arms stood up. Maybe she was seeing things, she wasn't sure. The women walked up onto the beach and behind a large boulder. She hoisted herself up to look over the edge. They had disappeared.

Lorelei ran inside, grabbed her car keys, and flew down the stairs. *I've got to get out of here. Now. I should have known all of this was too good to be true. What is happening?* She reached the door. It was still locked. She pounded both of her fists on the wood. Were they keeping her captive?

"Let me out!" Lorelei yelled. She tried to use her shoulder to heave herself against the door, but it was useless. The door was locked. She sat down on the steps and put her head in between her knees, as she tried not to hyperventilate. There was only one way out. *Outside,* she thought, *just go.*

She ran back up the stairs and jumped out onto the porch once more, then darted around the side of the house. *If I can just get over this ledge,* she thought, *I can climb to the roof and slide down.* She braced herself against the railing and began to crawl up, one foot balanced on the porch beneath her and the other on the icy metal rail. The roof was still slick with snow, but Lorelei reached for one of the gutters and held onto it as she pulled herself over the balcony. She landed on the roof on her stomach, and as she slid down, the wetness of the snow crept under her shirt. Finally, Lorelei's feet hit the edge of the roof.

There was nothing else below her, but if she could make her way across the roof just a little bit farther, she could drop rather easily onto the second-story porch. She couldn't see anything behind her or below, and she said a frantic prayer that she wouldn't fall. As she let go of the gutter, adrenaline coursed through her veins and she began to move. Inch by inch, Lorelei edged herself to the left, keeping herself low and close to the roof. A pile of snow slid down from above and hit her in the face, nearly making her lose her balance.

After several minutes, she could see that the porch was beneath her. Very slowly, Lorelei turned until she was on her side, then she reached down for the side of the roof. She brushed away the snow to make a place for her hands to grasp, then bent over, took hold of the gutter on the edge of the roof, and swung herself onto the porch. She landed hard; one of her feet took the impact and twisted. Lorelei tried to rise up, but her right ankle was wrenched in pain and wobbly. She hobbled to the turret with the spiral staircase, and as she held on to the railing, she hopped down the stairs, trying to ignore the pain.

At the bottom of the stairs, she let go of the rail and took a step toward the car, but she found that her ankle wouldn't support her weight and it buckled beneath her. It was still quite dark; the crescent moon hung above her head, but the sky had started changing to blue as daylight began its approach. Lorelei dropped to her hands and tried to crawl toward the car, through the mud and snow, dragging her right leg behind her. *Just a little farther,* she thought. *I can do this.* She bit her lip to try to keep herself from screaming.

A dark figure emerged in front of her and spoke her name.

SERENADE

"Get away from me! Get away from me!" Lorelei recoiled at the sound, and attempted to turn from it.

"Lorelei, stop!" Helen's voice resonated. She stood directly in front of Lorelei, flanked on either side by Deidre and Calliope. She was trapped, with no way to outrun all three of them. She pulled herself upright, and stood up to them, face to face. They were all fully clothed now and made a semicircle around her.

"What the hell *are* you? Are you all witches or something?" Lorelei screamed.

"Well, we've been called worse," replied Helen. "Where are you going?"

"Away from here. Away from this house," said Lorelei.

"Why?" asked Deidre, her voice sweet and childlike.

"I have to get away from *you!*" She made an attempt to dodge them, but her ankle gave way, and she stumbled.

"You're hurt," said Calliope. "Let me see—" she moved closer to Lorelei.

"No! Leave me alone. Don't touch me!"

"What's wrong?" asked Helen. "Why are you so upset? You need to come inside and sit down. You've hurt yourself."

"No. I have to leave. Right now."

"You're in no condition to be going anywhere," said Calliope. "You're soaking wet and you're injured. Now, would you please tell us why what has made you so upset?"

"Down there... what *was* that?" she motioned to the cliffs at the water's edge.

The three women looked at each other, silent for a moment. Helen walked toward her. Lorelei flinched, but was fixed to the spot where she stood.

"I take it you saw us in the sea," said Helen calmly.

"You were walking on the water!" Lorelei yelled emphatically, "Whatever you were doing down there was not natural, it's not even human."

"I can explain it to you, if you'll let me."

"Explain what, exactly? Explain how I got to be locked in my room, or maybe what you and Deidre and Calliope were doing floating around on top of the ocean?"

Lorelei made another move toward the car and her foot twisted again. Helen reached out and grabbed her arm.

"No! I said not to touch me!"

"Lorelei, calm down. I'm not going to hurt you. Nobody is going to hurt you."

"I don't understand what's happening. This isn't real, is it?"

"Come inside, Lorelei. I'll tell you everything you want to know."

Deidre and Calliope each took an arm. She tried to shake free from their grasp, but they held tight. Knowing she wouldn't be able to outrun them in her condition, Lorelei surrendered. There was no way to escape from this situation. Reluctantly, she allowed Deidre to help her inside the house. They made their way up the stairs to the front door and entered. While Calliope hurried to her room to find a robe to wrap around Lorelei, Helen led her into the main sitting room and helped her into one of the large, plush chairs. Deidre brought in a bandage and gently wrapped Lorelei's ankle. After Deidre had attended to the sprain, Helen motioned for the others to leave her alone with Lorelei.

"You told me you'd explain," Lorelei said. "What's going on? What are you?"

"We hadn't planned to tell you yet," said Helen.

"Tell me what?"

"What we are. What we *all* are," Helen crossed the room and knelt in front of her. Helen's green eyes, with their little flecks of amber and purple, were like an opiate, calming and reassuring. "Our family is... unique, Lorelei. We have a gift, an inheritance really, that has been passed down from one generation to the next. What you saw today is part of that gift. We can do things other people can't."

"Like magic or something?"

"No, not magic. Magic is something you do, but this is something we are." Helen stood and walked toward the window, "We've been around a very long time, as far back as written history can record. Some have called us enchantresses or nymphs, while others have confused us with mermaids, but what we've been most commonly called is *sirens*."

"I don't understand. You're *what?*"

"Sirens. Do you remember reading about them in Greek mythology? Beautiful, powerful women who sing and lull sailors to their deaths. That's our purpose. It's what we are."

"No way. That's ridiculous. That's the most insane thing I've ever heard."

"So how else would you explain what you just saw?"

"I don't know! But that can't be possible. Those are just myths. They aren't true."

"Many myths do have some basis in truth, Lorelei, but that's not to say that what you know as myth hasn't been distorted from reality. The stories they've told about us, killing men for pleasure or spite, well, those simply aren't true. Those sailors who have seen us and survived tend to fabricate things a little."

"I'm really trying to understand this, believe me, but it just doesn't make any sense."

"I can't force you to believe, Lorelei, but it true, and I have no reason to lie to you about this. You've seen it with your own eyes." Helen put her hand on Lorelei's shoulder. She could feel Lorelei still shaking under her touch. "Listen, you have no reason to be afraid."

"I'm not afraid," she lied. "It just doesn't seem like any of this could be possible," Lorelei wondered why Helen had sought her. She felt a strange suspicion as she remembered them singing around the table, voices entwined like rope, voices so similar to her own. And she knew how the sea called to her since her first day in Calais, as though it were alive. She paused, and then asked, "So you're it? Just the three of you?"

"No, we aren't the only ones. You need to know… this gift of ours, it runs deep in our veins, even though we didn't choose it. Generations of sirens have lived under this roof, been a part of this land, and there's a reason you were called here, too." Lorelei was numb. Her face drained very pale as she listened to her Aunt Helen's words. "You are here with us, because you are one of us."

Lorelei couldn't move. She could barely breathe the words, "No. Impossible."

"I can only imagine that it would be very difficult for you to believe me," said Helen. "None of us believed when we were first told, either. It seems illogical, I'm sure, to an intelligent young woman like yourself to believe in such… fairy tales, but know this: you have the gift, and it is your birthright. You are a siren, and have been such since the day you were born. You just haven't heard the Song until recently."

Lorelei took a moment to try to understand what Helen was telling her. If she had really been set apart as a siren from birth, why was she only finding out about it now? Her mind spun as she tried to make sense of it.

"No… How could I, how could I be?" Her voice choked in her throat.

"You are a true Deleaux. I've known since the day you were born. I can see it in your eyes. You are a siren, Lorelei. A living, breathing myth."

She sat in absolute shock and silence, and had to remind herself to inhale.

"It will take you a while to get used to the idea. I had hoped to prepare you a little better for this, to ease you into it. But that's the truth. You've been brought here to take your place among us."

"How does it… work, exactly? I mean, what do I *do*?" Lorelei asked, her brow furrowed as she tried to wrap her mind around everything she'd been told.

"You already have the gift. You just need to learn to hone it, that is, to tune your voice, but more importantly, you will have to learn to listen. We never act on our own; everything we sing has a purpose, but we can't sing without first learning to listen."

Lorelei's face contorted. Helen's explanation was leaving her more confused.

"So, just what is it that I'm supposed to be listening for?"

"Do you remember when your father died?"

"Yes," she answered quickly. Painful memories surged through Lorelei's body. Her heart sped as she remembered the moment of his death. She could see his body lying in the road again, unmoving and broken.

"And what did you do?"

"I panicked. Everything happened so suddenly. The car slammed into him, and I could barely move, and then…"

"Yes? What happened next?"

"I walked over toward him, and I, oh my god, I *sang* to him."

For a moment Lorelei could picture her father in the street, just outside the ice cream shop, bleeding to death. She was above him, involuntarily singing as he clung to life. But it was his eyes she remembered most—his eyes had fixed to hers and there was no pain in them. She remembered how peaceful he was despite the chaos around him as the paramedics tried to keep him alive.

"You heard it, Lorelei. You didn't sing of your own volition; rather, the Song found you and sang itself through you. And it wasn't just any song either, it was a song of passage, albeit a rudimentary one, certainly. That was the moment the gift was kindled within you."

"So is that why I'm here? Because I sang to my father when he died?"

"Yes, partly."

"And is that the reason *why* he died?"

"Of course not," replied Helen. "Your father's death was an accident. He did not die so that fate could force your hand into becoming a siren before you were ready, but this *is* what you were meant to do, and when an opportunity came for you to use your gift, it happened."

"Then did I, did I kill him? Is that what happened?" Lorelei's voice croaked and a lump rose in her throat, "Would he have lived if I hadn't sung to him?"

"Oh, my dear, of course not," Helen embraced Lorelei and held her to her chest. "That isn't what we do, not at all." Helen took Lorelei's head in both of her hands, and looked her in the eyes, "Listen to me, Lori, you are not responsible for his death. What you did for your father was the greatest gift you could have given him."

"I don't understand. I don't know what I did."

"The song of passage is a song that guides the dying into death. It makes the transition easier. Painless. Because you sang, his death was an easy one. He didn't feel any pain, or fear. He was at peace when he died, and he didn't struggle with it. It came to him as naturally as breathing. When you sang to him, you took away his suffering."

Lorelei choked back tears, "I just wish I could have stopped it."

"Sometimes things happen when they happen, and sometimes there's no making sense of it. Bad things are inevitably going to happen. We can do our best to make good in the world, to make people's lives better, to make their suffering easier, but we can't stop that which was destined to happen. We can't control death; we can only do our best to make it less frightening."

"How? I didn't even know what I was doing when I sang to him. It just... *happened.*"

"Like I said, there's a part of the gift that's innate. It will push its way into you, without your approval, until you learn to listen for it, and control it."

"And you're really sure that I am one of these, um, sirens?"

"Without a doubt," Helen smiled at her.

"How will I know when I hear it, whatever this thing is that I'm supposed to hear?"

"It's all around you, all the time, everywhere you go. There are times when it is stronger than others, but it's always present. You just need to learn what it sounds like. Do you want me to show you now?"

Lorelei quivered. Her chest was tight, her stomach was in knots, but she needed to know. She needed to hear it with her own ears, to know what it was that made them this way.

"Yes."

CHAPTER ELEVEN

Helen stood abruptly and hastened toward the door. She flung it open and called up the staircase.

"Deidre! Calliope! I need you at the waterfront, now!"

Helen turned back to face Lorelei, her eyes sparkling.

"Come with me. It's time for you to see what you were born to do."

Helen swept back toward her, her light-blue, cotton dress flowing behind her like waves and her silver hair secured in a high bun. She looked regal, elegant in her simplicity.

"Let's see if you can stand."

Lorelei stood up and tested her weight against her bandaged ankle. It still hurt, but she could walk again. "I think I'm okay." Helen helped her into the foyer.

Deidre opened her bedroom door and called down from the balcony. "Right *now*, Helen? I'm on the phone…"

"Yes, right now," said Helen, with cool composure. "You can call him back later."

Calliope was already standing beside the front door as Lorelei and Helen approached. She wore a stark-white, sleeveless dress that hugged her body and stopped just above the knee. A thick, black patent leather belt was at her waist. Her hair was so beautiful and shiny that it appeared to be almost iridescent as it cascaded over the front of her left shoulder. She smiled, knowingly.

Deidre emerged from her room, rolling her eyes. She wore a loose, pin-striped blouse over tight-fitting, black jeans and red, high-heeled boots. She crossed her arms in defiance, "You couldn't have let me just finish *one* phone call?"

"Drop the attitude, Dee," said Calliope.

"Fine, let's go," said Deidre, visibly irritated.

They walked along the terraced gardens, still girded with snow, until they reached the edge of the cove, to the same inlet where Lorelei had seen Helen standing waist deep in the water and singing just a few days earlier. Calliope held her arm as they walked down the stairs that led from the gardens to the water's edge. The coast was dotted with rough and jagged boulders. The surf hit the rocks, creating white foam that rocked back and forth between the sea and the shore. At the bottom of the steps, Helen, Calliope, and Deidre took off their shoes and stepped into the ankle-deep water. Lorelei took off her robe and laid it on the beach.

She stopped, unsure what to do next. Was this a twisted joke? It couldn't be *real*, could it? Certainly her aunt and cousins were not some sort of mythical creatures. Maybe she had misunderstood. The three women, so ethereal, stood in the bay but the water made it easier to believe that they were something else, something altogether inhuman, as though they were a part of the ocean itself.

Helen held out her hand, and Lorelei reached for it. She trembled when her feet hit the water. It was so cold, icy on her skin, and her body wanted to retreat, but she moved, inch by inch, closer to where they stood. They walked farther out into the cove, water moving up Lorelei's shins, sending shivers up her spine. Her teeth chattered as the water reached her thighs, and her steps slowed once her legs were fully immersed. The waves bobbed up and down against her torso; her body was freezing—it hurt to breathe. Lorelei gasped as they went deeper and deeper into the bay, farther and farther from shore.

The women formed a circle around Lorelei. Helen stood directly behind her, Calliope and Deidre stood to her sides, facing her.

"I need you to lie back in the water," Helen said.

"I can't," said Lorelei, "it's too c-c-cold."

"It's not too cold," said Calliope. "Just do as she says."

Lorelei spread her arms out to her side and leaned back into the water, as she had been instructed. Her body was heavy. She lifted her legs, until she was floating on the surface. Helen cradled Lorelei's head in her hands, and Calliope and Deidre moved in closer, holding on to Lorelei's sides. She closed her eyes while the waves lifted her body up and down. The cold sting of the water began to disappear. She could hardly feel anything around her save for her own heart beating, her body floating, drifting, weightless. Helen stared down at her. Lorelei could see her mouthing the word, "*Listen.*"

She closed her eyes again, allowing herself to be rocked by the ocean, vaguely aware of the women still holding her, unsure of what it was that she was supposed to be listening for, exactly. All she could hear was the sound of water passing by her ears, sloshing and gurgling. Nothing else. Swoosh. Crash. Shush. *This is ridiculous,* she thought. *How do I know what I'm supposed to be listening for? How much longer do I have to stay here?*

The water rose over her body with the pressure of the women pushing her down below the surface. She struggled, but they held her under, her face covered with water, the taste of salt in her mouth. The water continued to fill her ears with a blurry kind of noise. And then, underneath that, was a faint hum. Not even a hum, really, just a distant tone, almost imperceptible, like the sound of silence, the ringing one's ears make when there is no other noise to distract them. But this noise, this noise was *real*, not just the absence of other sounds. Lorelei turned her attention to it and the humming seemed to come nearer to her, closer to her body.

Warmth spread over her feet and worked its way up her body as the tone approached. It swirled around her head, it was no longer just one note, but several, dancing in the waves. Her face broke through the surface of the water and the notes made their way through her; Lorelei's mouth opened and a strong, clear sound emerged, more crystalline and pure than any she had ever sung. Just a single note—crisp, unadorned, and powerful. It began to spin a little, as the noise made its way into her ears, up through her body, and out into the air around her. She was connected to the water beneath her, a channel for the music, the Song, that was surging through her.

The three women pulled Lorelei upright. She spun around to face Helen.

"It's true, isn't it?" she asked.

"Every word," replied Helen. "And now you've heard it for yourself."

"That was unbelievable. The sound moved up through me and then it just poured out of me."

"Pretty neat, huh?" asked Deidre.

"Yeah," said Lorelei. "That was unbelievable."

"This is only the beginning of your journey," said Calliope. Her radiant face glowed as she embraced Lorelei, "Welcome."

Helen stood beside Lorelei and turned her to face the horizon which was glowing with morning light. The ocean was broad and magnificent; deep blue, sparkling water stretched out in front of her until it met the sky. Lorelei belonged to the sea.

"There is power in the water," said Helen, "a power that we can hear and feel and even touch. It runs over the waves, and deep below the surface. The voice of Idis has called each of us by name and brought us together. And now it has called you to take your place among us, Lorelei."

Lorelei understood more clearly what Helen had tried to explain to her. The tones she had heard when they held her under the waves must have been what Helen called the Song.

"Let's get you back to the house," said Calliope. "We'll get some warm clothes on you."

They helped Lorelei out of the water and back onto the beach. She picked up the robe and slipped it on. As she followed them up the stairs, she realized that her ankle, which had been so painful before, was now only slightly sore. In fact, she could hardly tell that it had been injured at all, if it weren't for the bandage still wrapped around it. Lorelei could hear the waves crashing behind her as she ascended the staircase, as if they weren't ready for her to leave.

The house was warm when they entered. Deidre took her upstairs to the third-floor bedroom. Lorelei went into the bathroom, and slipped out of her wet clothes and dumped them in the tub before changing into a pair of warm flannel pajama bottoms and a sweatshirt. She dried her hair with a towel and then combed it back. Deidre was sitting on the bed when Lorelei came out of the bathroom.

"I'm sorry we scared you this morning," said Deidre.

"I think maybe I overreacted," said Lorelei.

112

"No, you didn't. We kind of expected it. Everybody freaks out when they find out for the first time. I did."

"Really? How did you find out?"

"Well, you remember how I told you I moved out here a few years ago?"

"Uh-huh."

"I came out because I needed a job, and they told me I could work for them. So, I did, and everything seemed to be working out pretty well. It was like a month after I'd been here, they took me down to the beach and then they just… *transformed* in front of me. I swear, I thought I was hallucinating or having a heart attack or something."

"What did you do?"

"I tried to scream, but I couldn't—I was literally paralyzed with fear. At some point, I pulled myself together and tried to run away, but Calliope caught me. Don't let her fool you… she may not look it, but she is *fast*. Then Helen sang to me until I was so calm, you would have thought they drugged me. They brought me into the house and explained it to me, but it took me a really long time to accept it."

"What made you believe?"

"Helen's persistence. She kept trying, every day. She finally made me see what was there all along… and then it just came together for me."

"And then you were a siren, just like that?"

"It isn't like they're going to send you out tomorrow or anything. It takes a long time to really learn how to do it. You'll know when you're ready." Deidre took her hand. "Listen, I just wanted to tell you, I'm really happy you're here. I think we're going to be good friends, the two of us."

"Yeah? That would be nice."

They went back downstairs together and found Helen and Calliope drinking tea at the table. Helen pulled out a chair for Lorelei and went to fill two more mugs with hot water.

"Are you better now?" asked Calliope.

"Yes, much better. Thanks," Lorelei replied.

Helen sat down beside her and handed her the warm mug. She took a sip.

"Can I ask you something?" Lorelei turned toward Helen.

"Of course. I'm sure you have many questions."

"How did you know about me singing to my father?"

"Well, in many cases, the first time a siren sings, it's an accident. You don't really know what you're doing, rather, it's something that happens *to* you. And, when a siren sings her first Song, the others in her family with the gift can feel it. We knew the day it happened. We could hear it. For you, it was only a matter of time."

"And you have to be close to the sea for it to work, right?"

"The song is stronger in the water, it's easier to hear. Most of time, we do our work while we're in the ocean or beside it, although there are some exceptions."

"So what if I'd never come out here? What if I'd stayed in Colorado?"

"A siren cannot resist the call of the sea forever. It will find her, one way or another. When you were a baby, I used to take you down to the beach to play. You would have spent all day down there if I had let you. I remember one day watching you sit on the beach, with just your little toes splashing in the water, giggling. The mist passed around you and cradled you. It was like you and the water were playing together, and she's been calling you back ever since."

"And my mother? She's a Deleaux, right? Is she a siren, too?"

"No, your mother is not a siren," said Calliope. "She wasn't born with the gift."

Lorelei was relieved, in a way, that her mother was not one of them, that she could have this secret.

"She doesn't even know I'm here," said Lorelei. "She still thinks I'm living in Calais, and she was already really mad about my being there. I don't want her to find out that I'm here, not yet."

"Fair enough," said Helen. "I won't let her know you're here."

"So, what were you doing when I saw you this morning?"

"There was a man down in Falmouth," said Calliope. "He was drunk and fell off a pier during the night. We went to make it easier for him."

"I saw it," said Lorelei, "in my dreams. He was struggling and sinking."

"That's not surprising," said Calliope, "in fact, you should begin to feel these things intuitively."

"But couldn't you have saved him?" she asked. "If you knew he was going to drown, why didn't you rescue him?"

"We aren't in the business of rescuing people," Calliope replied. "If someone's fate is already sealed, we can't interfere with that."

"Well, how do you *know*? How did you know that he was supposed to die? Maybe you were supposed to save him."

"We know before it happens. You'll understand eventually," said Calliope.

"But isn't it hard to watch people die? Isn't there a part of you that wants to help?"

"We *are* helping," said Deidre. "If we weren't there, that guy would've died anyway, but he would've been cold and alone, full of pain and fear. I mean, isn't that worse?"

"I guess so, but it seems so morbid."

"It's not all that bad really," said Deidre. "I mean, yeah, it sucks the first couple of times, but then... you get used to it. Singing someone into death is never easy, but just by being there, you're making a difference to that person. Once they hear us, it's like all the fear is gone. They get swallowed up in all of their happiest memories, then they can let go. And we always go together, which makes it better."

"Tomorrow I'll begin teaching you to sing," said Helen.

"I already know how to sing," said Lorelei. "I've been singing for years."

"Yes and no," said Helen. "You may have mastered the mechanics of using your voice, but I'm going to teach you how to connect yourself to what you heard today. There are a number of different songs that we sing, and you need to learn to use them all. It will be several months before you're ready to go out to sea with us."

Months? Lorelei's thoughts suddenly jumped back to school. Was she making a commitment to stay here in Chatham? Did they expect her to live with them indefinitely?

"I can't stay here that long," said Lorelei. "I had only planned to be here for a few weeks, maybe until the end of the semester, but I wasn't planning on moving here permanently."

"I understand that's a decision you're going to have to make," said Helen, "but as long as you're here, we might as well teach you a thing or two."

Lorelei nodded in agreement.

"There's one more thing," said Helen, "I almost forgot."

She got up and left the room. Lorelei could hear Helen's footsteps on the stairs. When she returned, she handed Lorelei a small, blue box. Inside was a silver necklace from which hung a large, purple gemstone that reflected the light, and little specks of blue sparkled within it.

"It was my sister's," said Helen. "It belonged to your grandmother, Lucia. She was a remarkable woman, a very powerful siren in her own right. She would have wanted you to have it. I've been saving it for this day."

"Thank you. It's beautiful." Lorelei put it around her neck. As she clasped the necklace, she almost thought she could hear the Song again.

Helen's eyes watered, "You look so much like her. The resemblance is amazing."

"Really? I don't think I've ever seen a picture of her."

"Come with me. I'll show you what she looked like."

Lorelei stood up and followed Helen from the kitchen. She led her into another room next to the parlor that had a baby grand piano and a harp. In the corner was a large photograph of a woman standing on the shore holding the hand of a young child.

"That's your grandmother," said Helen.

The woman did look very much like Lorelei. She had the same round face and button nose, and her brown hair framed her face in spirals. Her complexion was fair, with just a few freckles on her nose, and she had the same light green eyes. But there was such energy in her face, and her smile illuminated the photograph. In the photograph, Lucia held the hand of a little, smiling child. Lorelei recognized the girl immediately as her own mother.

"She's stunning," said Lorelei.

"Just like you," replied Helen.

"No, I'm not beautiful like that. She's gorgeous. I'm just sort of... plain."

"You're the exact image of Lucia, in every way. She would be so proud of you. You are going to be amazing, just like her. I can tell."

Helen leaned over and kissed Lorelei's forehead and then left the room. Lorelei stood and looked at the portrait for several minutes, her own eyes reflecting back at her from her grandmother's face. It was hard to believe how much her world had changed in less than a day. Yesterday, she was just an ordinary young woman, but now she was a siren, charged with sending sailors to their deaths. Lorelei put her hand on the necklace that hung on her chest and prayed for strength.

CHAPTER TWELVE

"You can't think about anything but what you're singing," said Helen as she placed another book on Lorelei's stomach. "Believe me, because there will be plenty of distractions. You have to stay focused, but it gets easier with practice."

Lorelei lay on the floor facing up, a stack of books on top of her belly. She concentrated on the rhythmic sounds of her breathing, in and out. This wasn't unlike other techniques she had learned in her voice lessons, but Helen insisted that she work on her breathing to clear her mind. In through her nose, out through pursed lips, the air came and went in a circular pattern.

"What you are going to learn now is how to calm a frantic mind," said Helen, "but if you're going to do that, your own mind has to be at peace. When someone starts to drown, the first thing they do is panic. Your job is to settle them down, make them stop struggling. Once you can do that, the rest is easy."

Helen sat beside the harp and played long, arpeggiated chords. Her graceful fingers plucked the strings in succession and the music filled the small studio. "Listen for the overtones. Do you hear them?"

"Yes," said Lorelei as she closed her eyes. She could hear the sounds that seemed to resonate above the notes that were being played. Helen began to hum in harmony with the chord, gradually increasing in volume as she played faster. She broke into full singing, a minor tune with no words. It sounded like a plainsong chant, as there was no discernible rhythm, but with a much wider range of notes. Eventually, she stopped playing the harp and stood up, adding words to the melody.

Fog and shadows meet in vain
'Gainst the silver drops to strain;
Whilst the silent waves abound,
Courting depths with empty sound;
From the mirrored waters part,
Still the mind and calm the heart.

The same notes that Lorelei had heard beneath the water in the cove were woven in and around Helen's voice. The tone was clear and piercing, like a bell. Warmth spread down Lorelei's body. Her pulse slowed and she melted into the floor beneath her.

"Sing with me," said Helen.

Lorelei pulled air through her lips and the song was on her tongue. She hummed along with Helen until the words were familiar and then she began to sing. Their voices complemented each other, and once Lorelei had become confident with the melody, Helen began to add rich harmonies. She kept her eyes closed and listened to the sound of their voices combining together. Helen stopped singing completely and Lorelei continued to sing the words through once on her own, fully immersed in the ripples of song that spun in her head.

Lorelei opened her eyes and removed the stack of books from her stomach. Helen had a forced smile on her face. She reached out her hand and helped Lorelei to her feet.

"So, that was okay, right?" asked Lorelei.

"It's coming along. Why don't we take a break and have some lunch. Sound good?"

"Sure," said Lorelei, confused. Helen had been less than enthusiastic in her assessment of Lorelei's singing. She shrugged it off; this was just her first try, she would certainly improve with practice.

Calliope was paying bills at the kitchen table when Lorelei and Helen entered. She peered over her wire rim glasses toward them, sending a piercing glance in Lorelei's direction.

"How are things going?" Calliope asked, her eyebrows arched in expectation.

"Fine," said Helen. "We're just taking a break. What would you ladies like for lunch?

"Nothing for me," said Calliope as she scooped up the pile of unpaid bills from the table. "I was just finishing some work."

"You don't want to stay and eat with us?" asked Helen.

"I'm sorry, I can't today. Wish I could, but I've got a million things going on at work." The edges of Calliope's blood-red lips lifted up in a smile. Lorelei stared at Calliope's eyes and they softened from glistening ice to moving water. Her smile disappeared and she squinted intently at Lorelei. "You remind me of your father, you know? You look like him."

"Really?" Lorelei asked. "Most people say I look more like my mom."

"Well, you look a little like her," said Calliope, "but more like your dad, I think. It's there, in your smile."

"Thanks," said Lorelei.

Calliope's softness was gone as quickly as it had appeared. She tucked the bills away into her planner and threw her coat over her arm. "I'll be home late. Don't wait for me for dinner."

Lorelei picked at the sandwich that Helen made for her. Every thought she had was on her newfound identity. Remembering Helen's reaction to her singing earlier, she wondered if she had been disappointed, but Lorelei was determined that she could perfect whatever she learned. The sun had made a triumphant return and was spread across the kitchen table. Lorelei's necklace reflected back thousands of little specks of light that danced on the wall beside the window. She pushed her food aside, unable to eat more than a few bites.

Helen cleared the table and instructed Lorelei to put on a jacket. Lorelei went to the coat closet obediently and found her winter coat and then returned to the kitchen. Without saying a word, she followed Helen out of the house and down the path toward the shore. She could hear the surf and focused on the rhythmic sounds as they drew ever closer. Helen approached the water reverently with short, measured steps. Lorelei stayed behind a few paces, unsure what her aunt would do next.

"A siren is at once a part of the sea, and the master of it," said Helen, still facing the horizon. "The ocean holds that element that gives the siren her abilities, but she, in turn holds within her the ability to bend the sea to her will."

Helen bent down and touched her palm to the water. She made little counterclockwise circles and the waves began to calm, now only gently bobbing. Helen's hand stopped, and she spread out her fingers and pushed the heel of her hand deeper into the water, fingers now pointing up toward the sky. The water in the cove went completely still—a solid mirror of light. The sand and silt that had been churning beneath the surface now began to settle toward the bottom of the ocean floor and the water cleared.

She stood upright again, tall and strong as a woman half her age. Helen turned her face upwards and stretched her hands out toward her sides, her palms facing up. She stood like that for several seconds, like a priest before an altar, before she brought her hands together, touching as though she were in prayer. Helen bent down and dipped her fingers into the sea. She began to rise again, slowly, bringing her hands up separately. A column of water followed Helen's hands out of the water and up toward her face. Lorelei gasped and took a step forward, mesmerized.

"Give me your hand," said Helen.

Lorelei reached out and Helen took hold of her hand. She pulled Lorelei close and guided her hand toward the column of water so that both she and Helen had one hand on it. The water was solid beneath her palm, like wet marble. She wiggled her fingers and it moved beneath the pressure, but remained firm. Helen took her own hand off of it so that Lorelei held the column by herself. Lorelei had both palms on it now and could feel the power of the water surging up though her arms; she braced herself to keep the column fixed in place. The pedestal of water became wider and taller, and lifted Lorelei's hands up as it grew. The energy from the water was battling with her for control; her mind became flooded with indiscernible noise. The water pushed toward her. Lorelei dug in her feet and planted her hands firmly against it, pushing the weight of her body toward the column that now seemed unrelenting and massive.

She gritted her teeth and she tried to keep her balance. Her mind wouldn't stop spinning long enough for Lorelei to call out to Helen for help. Fatigued, she mustered her strength and bent back her arms, only to thrust them straight out toward the mass of water. The column dissipated and formed itself into one large wave. The wave gathered force and headed out toward the small bit of space between the cove and the ocean. It was large in size, at least twice as tall as Lorelei from the surface of the glass cove. With a loud crash, the wave ricocheted and bounced back before the cove settled once again.

Lorelei bent over, her muscles shaking. Helen knelt beside her and wrapped an arm around Lorelei's shoulders.

"Are you okay?" asked Helen.

"I think so," said Lorelei. "Just give me a minute."

"Why did you do that? Why did you let go?"

"I panicked. It thought it was going to swallow me. I... I didn't know what to do, but I had to get rid of it."

"You lost control."

"Whatever that was... it was too strong, I couldn't stop it..."

"No," said Helen, "you didn't lose control of the water, you lost control of yourself. If you can't keep your mind and your emotions under your own control, how can you harness the sea?"

"It was taking over me. I couldn't hold onto it."

"You could have handled it, Lorelei. Remember what I told you earlier? Your mind must be at peace. You need to be able to tune out the busyness of your thoughts or they will control you. If you act erratically, you're going to end up hurting someone."

Lorelei's frustration with herself boiled to the surface.

"Yeah, well I guess I'm having a hard time controlling my emotions since I just learned yesterday that I'm a *siren*," she snapped. "I guess you could say my mind isn't really at *peace* with that yet."

"Lorelei, you have a choice to make. You can either choose to dwell on being afraid of these gifts, or you can choose to stand up and keep practicing. But if you're going to linger on your disbelief, you'll never realize your potential. What's it going to be?"

"I want to do this, but…"

"What? Are you scared?"

"Yes, of course I am! I'm scared of what I don't know. I'm scared of what I am, of what I'm supposed to do. I don't understand any of this. So, I'm magical. Don't you think that requires a bit of a mental adjustment?"

"We don't use the word 'magic,' Lorelei. This isn't magic, this is who we are. It's our purpose. I'm not teaching you spells or charms, or any of that nonsense. Magic is something people look to in desperation because they cannot make sense of their lives on their own. It's a false hope. Look at it this way: you wouldn't have these gifts if you weren't going to be able to use them."

"But what if I fail? What's my purpose then?"

"You aren't going to fail. The Fates wouldn't allow it. You can do this, but you need to trust me, your sisters,… and yourself." Helen stood up and pulled Lorelei to her feet. "Now, you're going to try again. Go on."

Lorelei reached her arm out over the water and pressed her palm flat against the surface of it. She moved her hand in a circular pattern, and then very slowly and deliberately, she lifted it up. The water followed behind her hand like translucent silk. It cascaded over her fingers and little streams of cool liquid slid from her wrists down to her elbows. Lorelei focused only on taking long, deep breaths and moving her hands in small, calculated patterns. It was beautiful, really, like a waterfall half frozen before winter.

"Now," said Helen, "I want you to push it away from you *gently*. Push it to the opposite side of the cove, but before it hits the rocks, summon it back to you."

"How am I supposed to do that?" Lorelei asked.

"Just pull it back to you. You'll use your hands and call it back."

"Okay, here goes."

Lorelei pulled her hands apart and the water grew wider. She coiled her arms back toward her chest and then pushed it away deliberately. The water obeyed and turned itself into a gentle rolling wave that headed slowly for the other side of the cove. As it drew closer to the rocks, Lorelei steadied herself. Her arms held forward, she did her best to try to stop the wave which was bearing down on the distant shore. *Stop*, she thought, *get back here.* The wave continued on its forward trajectory, immune to any sort of commands Lorelei was trying to send toward it. It hit the side of the boulders and the water sprayed upwards in white foam.

She gritted her teeth. *Am I incapable of doing even the simplest things?* Lorelei twisted her mouth into a tight pucker and balled her hands into fists. With anger and an audible scream, she punched downward. The water parted in front of her; full walls of shimmering aqua rose on either side and were sent furiously toward the sea. The ocean floor was exposed for a brief moment before the surge pushed back toward her and splashed Lorelei and Helen, soaking them both.

"Lorelei!" chided Helen. "What was that for? You need to calm down!"

"I'm just so frustrated! I suck at this!"

"You're just learning. No one gets it right away," said Helen as she wrung out her hair. "But we can't have any more outbursts like that, you understand? There's no reason to overreact."

"I'm sorry. I don't know what got into me. I promise it won't happen again."

"It's okay. Now, let's give it another try."

"Haven't I done enough damage for one day?"

"Come now, that isn't the kind of attitude we need. Just once more. This time, don't try to stop the wave, just try to turn it. The wave is energy. All you need to do is to try and change its path, all right?"

Lorelei nodded reluctantly and started the process once more. This time, as the wave neared the shore, she pushed her hands left, sending her energy in that direction and then pulled them in toward herself, willing the water back to its origin. As if on cue, the wave actually turned around and began to head toward her. She smiled a little and held her hands as if to catch it. The water came up and splashed around her feet and then retreated back to the cove, which was as still as glass once again.

"Well done!" shouted Helen.

Lorelei beamed. The power to control the water was something she had not even imagined was possible before now. The wind, the waves, and the tides were a part of her, an extension of her body. Peace settled over her. Helen placed her hands on Lorelei's shoulders and brought her face up against Lorelei's.

"You see what you can do?" she asked. "This is just the beginning."

A little wave leapt up and hit Lorelei in the shins.

"She's happy to have you back," Helen said, and chuckled under her breath.

"Thank you," said Lorelei, "for bringing me back here."

"I didn't bring you back. Idis called here and you followed that call on your own. Even after your father's death, you came back to the ocean because you're connected to it. All I can do is to try and guide you."

"Idis? What's Idis?"

"It's sort of the power of the sea, the power in all things. It's what gives you the ability to call to the waves. The sound you heard, here, under the water, that was Idis, too. She moves through us to do her work, to comfort the dying and to stand watch in the sea."

It seemed to Lorelei that this *Idis* must be some sort of a deity that Helen revered. She wasn't entirely convinced, but she also figured that there was no reason to argue, so she nodded her understanding and let Helen continue with her theological discourse.

"Idis was the spirit that moved over the water in the beginning of time, and from the moment of your birth until your last breath, she's known your joys and sorrows, your hopes and dreams. And as a siren, your job is important because you work on her behalf. For some, you'll be the final blessing that Idis gives them before they leave this life."

Lorelei and Helen stayed and worked for several more hours in the cold water of the cove. She ran through more patterns with the waves, drew up columns of water of different sizes, and had even been able to pull up an orb of spinning water and hold it aloft before tossing it like a beach ball. Each new task seemed easier than the one before it, but Lorelei tried to remain calm, and not let herself celebrate her success too much. When the light began to fade, they left the cove and walked back toward the house. She hated leaving it; she had only begun to realize what she could do.

Helen walked beside her. She looked so elegant even with her hair wet and flattened against her forehead. The day spent near the water had revived her and her face was glowing; it looked almost youthful in the fading light. Or perhaps it was glowing for another reason, Lorelei wondered. *Is she proud of me?*

As though she could hear Lorelei's thoughts, Helen looked at her. "You were magnificent out there, once you let go of your fear.

I couldn't be more satisfied with what you did today. You're going to be amazing."

CHAPTER THIRTEEN

"You up yet?" Deidre knocked on the door.

Lorelei sat up in bed and yawned. She swung her legs over the side of the bed and stretched. "Yeah, I'm just getting up now."

"Can I come in?"

"Sure," said Lorelei. She stood up and grabbed her robe from the closet door.

Deidre opened the door, already dressed and perfectly coiffed. Her hair was in a ponytail pinned on the top of her head by a barrette, with her bangs pulled up into a sleek, full poof. She walked toward Lorelei on impossibly high heels. Lorelei ran her hand through her hair and rubbed her eyes.

"So, I was wondering if you wanted to drive up with me to Boston," said Deidre. "I have to courier some documents up there, and I could use some company. It'll be fun!"

"Right *now?*" Lorelei asked.

"Well, we'd need to get going soon. You don't have to go, I just figured you might want to tag along."

"I'd probably need to check with Helen first. I'm not sure if she wanted to work with me today or not."

"Oh, she's not even going to be here. Calliope needed her to come along on a consult down in Newport. They left about an hour ago."

"Sure, then. I'll go with you. Can you give me a few minutes to get changed?"

"Absolutely. Meet me downstairs when you're ready, okay?"

Deidre's heels clicked on the hardwood floor on her way out of the room. Lorelei quickly ran a brush through her tangled hair and pushed it back into a headband. She layered a camisole with a long-sleeved T-shirt and wiggled her feet into a pair of well-worn, canvas shoes. A skinny scarf wrapped around her neck, Lorelei scampered down to the foyer. The smell of coffee drew her to the kitchen where Deidre was steaming milk.

"Latte?" she asked.

"Sure," said Lorelei. She didn't generally drink coffee, but she was still groggy and figured the caffeine would wake her up a bit. Deidre filled two travel mugs with espresso and topped them off with sugar-free, vanilla syrup and hot, frothy soy milk. She handed one to Lorelei and grabbed her purse before they headed out toward Deidre's car.

"Ever been to Boston before?" asked Deidre. She started the car and then began to shuffle through her MP3 player.

"I drove through it coming down here, but that's it."

"Boston's great. There's a lot to do. After we drop off this stuff," said Deidre, tossing two manila envelopes into the backseat, "we could go shopping. You want to come with me?"

"Yeah, I haven't been to the mall since, well, since last summer."

"We're not going to the *mall*. I'm taking you to Newbury Street. You'll love it."

"That'll be fun. I could use some new jeans actually..."

"C'mon, you've got to get something more fun than just *jeans*. That's all you ever wear. We should get you something really cute. You know, something more girly."

Lorelei sighed and rolled her eyes. Deidre decided on a playlist of show tunes, and as they drove the stretch of highway that led north toward Boston, they belted out hits by Gershwin, Rodgers and Hammerstein, and Andrew Lloyd Webber. Deidre's voice was full and dynamic; she could emulate almost any of the singers with a zesty, carefree style and a dramatic, piercing quality to her sound. This was all Deidre Malone, vivacious, free, and confident. Lorelei could picture her onstage lighting up a room as she filled it with her intense voice. Cole Porter's "Night and Day" began to play on the radio. Deidre reached over and turned down the volume.

"Helen said you were great yesterday, with the water and everything."

"She did?" Lorelei asked.

"Uh-huh. She said it took a while, but you really seem to have a strong ability."

"I guess so. It was overwhelming, but sort of incredible, too. After I figured it out, everything felt so natural, like I've just opened my eyes and seen something that was there all along."

"Has she started teaching you how to sing yet?"

"Yes, but… I don't get the feeling that she thought much of my singing."

"That's the thing—it's not *your* singing. You can't think about it that way. You almost have to imagine yourself as an instrument. The harder you try to get it right, the worse it will be. You've just got to let yourself go and not worry about it."

"Easier said than done. I've spent so much of my life training and perfecting my technique, it's hard to let go of that."

"Just don't push yourself too much. One day it'll just click for you, and you shouldn't worry—Helen doesn't expect it to happen all at once. You've got to relax and let the Song do the work for you."

They entered the city and Deidre navigated around a labyrinth of streets, dodging pedestrians and negotiating the traffic pattern. The city's streets seemed to be like an unorganized maze, each neighborhood with its own design. The architecture was similarly disheveled; modern buildings stood juxtaposed against colonial churches and historic storefronts. Sidewalks full of people lined the streets in front of several tall skyscrapers in the center of the city. Deidre parked the car in a garage and then led the way toward one of the buildings that stood next to the harbor.

Lorelei followed Deidre into the building. Deidre winked at the security guard who was seated at the desk in the entry way and he quickly waved them along their way. They went to the elevators and ascended to the twenty-second floor. The elevator door opened revealing a large panel of glass that bore an emblem for Marshall UK Maritime Investments. A stocky, brunette receptionist stood up from her desk and opened the door for them.

"Miss Malone," said the receptionist, peering over her red glasses, "it's good to see you. Had a safe trip?"

"Yes, thanks," Deidre replied. "Colleen, this is my cousin Lorelei. Lorelei, Colleen Jordan."

"Nice to meet you," said Lorelei. She reached out her hand to shake Colleen's.

"I'm just going to run these down to Michener's office. Is he available?" Deidre asked. Colleen nodded affirmatively. "I'll be back in just a minute, Lorelei," she said and then started down the hallway.

"So, you guys have any plans for the rest of the day?" Colleen asked.

"I think Deidre wants to go shopping, then we'll probably go back home."

Colleen started laughing.

"What's so funny?" asked Lorelei.

"Oh, nothing," said Colleen, "but Deidre's a fun girl. You know, a really *fun* girl. When she comes up to the city, she's gonna have a good time."

Lorelei stared back at her.

"I'm just saying, don't expect to be going back to the Cape tonight, unless you plan on carrying her there," Colleen walked to the other side of her desk and opened the drawer. She pulled out a key and began to write a note on a scrap of paper. "Here, take this. It's just a spare key and my address. Don't lose it."

"Okay, thanks," said Lorelei. She tucked the key and her note into her jeans pocket.

Deidre returned moments later. "Ready to go?" she asked Lorelei.

"Yep," Lorelei replied. "It was nice meeting you," she told Colleen as they left.

Outside the building, Deidre hailed a cab. Lorelei jumped in the backseat.

"Newbury Street," said Deidre, "Vonnie Biermann's."

The taxi rolled away from the curb. The cabbie maneuvered through traffic, only honking occasionally, as they made their way out of the financial district. Along the way, Deidre pointed out the highlights of the city as they headed toward the quieter, brownstone-lined streets of the Back Bay neighborhood. The cab pulled up beside a quartet of boutique shops, each with perfectly dressed window displays. Deidre paid the driver and gracefully stepped out of the car.

The scene was very different here than on the other side of town. Young urbanites sauntered casually past the shops with their organic, fair-trade coffees in hand. Lorelei walked up toward one of the shop windows and peered inside. She couldn't imagine herself wearing any of the clothes on display. Mannequins were dressed in tiny, trendy skirts, angular blouses with plunging necklines, and ridiculous high heels that seemed so impractical Lorelei couldn't understand why anyone would actually wear them in public. Deidre beckoned and Lorelei followed her into the shop next door.

"Welcome to Vonnie Biermann's," said a young, blonde girl in the entrance. "My name's Stephanie. Let me know if there's anything I can show you."

"Ummm… could you tell me if Margie's in today?" asked Deidre.

Stephanie, looking dejected, nodded and went to find her coworker.

"No offense to her, but some of these girls they have working here don't have a clue what they're doing," Deidre whispered to Lorelei. She broke away and started touching several shirts that were hanging on the racks.

"Deeeeee!" an olive-skinned woman came trotting quickly toward them with her arms outstretched. "How the hell are you?"

"Oh my god! You look so amazing!" Deidre hugged the woman and then stood back to look at her. "What are you wearing? It is gorgeous!"

"Oh this? This is *only* the new Ricard Pirzetti from the spring collection. It's not available yet, but you know me, I talked Vonnie into letting me wear it. Just in the store."

The Pirzetti ensemble consisted of a short, one-sleeved orange dress that hung over her frame like an oversized T-shirt, and a thick leather belt. The dress had been paired with gray leggings and furry boots. Lorelei thought she looked like a train wreck, but then again, she had never really followed the fashion trends.

"So… ," said Deidre, smiling mischievously, "I have a bit of a challenge for you."

"Okay," the woman said, "I love a challenge."

"This is my cousin, Lorelei."

"Oh, my goodness," the woman said, "isn't she a pretty little thing? But she is just hidden behind these terrible clothes."

"I know, right?" said Deidre.

"I'm standing right here!" said Lorelei. "I don't think my clothes are *that* bad."

"Honey, they are. They really are. My name's Margie, and I am going to take care of you. We are going to make you look like you just stepped out of a magazine."

"We're going out tonight, so if you could find something, you know, chic and stunning," said Deidre, "something really sexy."

"Wait a minute," said Lorelei, "I didn't realize that this was going to be a 'make-over-your-ugly-cousin' day. I'm perfectly comfortable in my own clothes, actually."

"You may be comfortable, but you're going out with Deidre Malone tonight, and for that you need to look *hot.* You don't really want to be compared to her looking the way you do now, do you?"

Lorelei caught a glance of herself in the mirror. She had never really disliked her casual appearance until this moment. Wrinkled, faded jeans and a long-sleeved, worn-out T-shirt next to Deidre's perfectly polished, immaculate ensemble did make her look, well, grungy by comparison. But, on the other hand, she didn't want to look like some sort of bizarre fashion experiment like Margie. What was the worst that could happen?

"Fine," Lorelei relented.

"Let's look at you," said Margie. She walked around Lorelei and looked her up and down. "Long limbs, curvy hips, defined waist, beautiful neck, I'd say a size six?"

Margie took Lorelei by the hand and led her around the store. As she went, she grabbed pieces of clothing, threw them over her arm, and continued. Silk, satin, suede, leather, linen, and sheer fabric in a rich variety of colors and patterns piled ever higher on Margie's petite arm. "Here we go," said Margie, ushering Lorelei into a dressing room. She handed her a deep purple dress. Lorelei slipped out of her clothes and pulled the dress over her head. It was short and sleeveless with an empire waist and a sequined trim at the bottom.

Deidre gasped as Lorelei emerged from the dressing room. "That is so cute! You look so hot! I love it."

Lorelei turned around to face the mirror. Still wearing her socks, she did think the dress looked good. It was flattering. Even from the back, she looked stylish. She looked like she could almost pass for being in her early twenties.

"Your legs look amazing in that dress. Seriously amazing," said Deidre.

"It's okay, but I think we can do better," said Margie.

Lorelei tried on outfit after outfit, each one carefully inspected by Margie and Deidre. She stood captive as they added accessories and fussed over the details each time Lorelei came out wearing a different dress. They were each beautiful in different ways. Some were very feminine and flirty, with accents of ruffles and soft hemlines, while others were sophisticated and sharp, and made her look provocative. Hours after they had started, Lorelei was tired of being made to model a never-ending stream of dresses. She was tired, hungry, and annoyed with being made into a human doll.

"Are we done yet?" Lorelei asked, as she slipped on yet another design, this one a black, linen, wrap-around dress that looked like a peacoat.

"You aren't having fun?" Deidre asked.

"It's not that I'm not having fun, I'm just tired. You guys want to choose one for me and we can go?"

"Hold on a moment," said Margie. "Will you try on just *one* more? There's one in the back you just have to try before we call it quits." Lorelei took a deep breath and blew it out in a forceful sigh. She nodded. Margie swept away to a back room and came back out, holding an opaque dress bag. She hung the bag on a hook and carefully unzipped it. "Okay, this you are going to *love*," said Margie. "It's a Jacques Cavier."

She held up a tiny, slinky piece of silk fabric. It started at the top almost ivory and then faded in an ombré to a bright fuschia at the bottom. With disdain, Lorelei took the dress and returned to the dressing room yet again. She kicked the black dress to the floor and pulled the pink one over her head. It was light and breezy, and the silk slid over her like water. She zipped it up on the side and walked out to her waiting audience.

Deidre's mouth dropped when she saw Lorelei in the dress. "Stunning," she whispered. Margie also nodded her approval. Lorelei faced her reflection in the mirror. What she saw staring back at her didn't even seem real. The dress hugged her curves in all the right places; spaghetti straps and a V-neck that was alluring, but left just enough to the imagination. It emphasized her shapely shoulders and neck, and the skirt was perfectly flared and moved with her as she turned. Lorelei was entranced by her own natural beauty. She looked like a woman.

A simple silver necklace and sparkling earrings were added. Margie brought over a pair of strappy heels that made her legs look long and toned. Deidre pulled a makeup kit out of her purse. A little blush, soft pink lipgloss, some eyeliner, mascara, and a little shimmery eye shadow were expertly applied on Lorelei's face. Meanwhile, Margie was grabbing pieces of Lorelei's hair, twisting it into spirals on the crown of her head and securing them with bobby pins so that little tendrils of curls framed her face. Once they were done, Deidre and Margie stood back to admire their masterpiece. They looked at each other and smiled.

"Perfect," said Deidre, "we'll take it. And these over here, too," she motioned toward a stack of apparel that was spread over the back of a chair. Lorelei looked at her to protest, but before she could, Deidre held up a black credit card and said, "My treat. Don't worry about it."

"You want it shipped, Dee?" asked Margie.

"Sure," said Deidre.

Moments later, Lorelei and Deidre left Vonnie Biermann's. Back in daylight, Lorelei had stepped out from Deidre's shadow. She could have sworn that all eyes were on her.

CHAPTER 14

"Table for two, please," said Deidre.

The maître d', a bald, heavy-set man in a pinstripe suit, was facing away, eyes focused on a computer screen. "I'm sorry, madam, but we are all seated for the evening. We won't be able to accommodate any more guests tonight."

"Certainly there must be *something* you can do," she said, her voice like honey. He turned and looked up at her. Deidre leaned in, her eyes fixed on his. The corner of her lip raised in a playful smirk. "Maybe someone's canceled?" she asked.

His hands fumbled with the reservation list. He stared at her intently and then coughed a little, "Well, um, yes, let me see…" He shuffled the papers anxiously. "We might have an opening, just a moment."

The maître d' left his station and scurried to the dining room where he beckoned two of the wait staff toward him. He spoke to them with large gestures, and they hurried away, only to return minutes later carrying a table and two chairs. The table was set between the bar and a large wooden fireplace. A busboy quickly laid out linens and china before the maître d' returned, holding menus. "Ladies," he said, "right this way."

"Thank you," said Deidre as she brushed his cheek with the back of her hand, and whispered, "sweet man."

Vincento's was an old, North End establishment. It was a place to see and be seen. The swanky bar was dimly lit with uniformed bartenders that stood behind it shaking drinks. Deidre ordered a martini for herself and an iced tea for Lorelei.

"I can't get over how hot you look in that dress," said Deidre.

"Thanks," said Lorelei, "it's really nice. This place is so fancy, it almost makes me uncomfortable."

"Well, you fit in perfectly. You look like you belong here."

They opened the menus. Lorelei's eyes gazed over the choices. Descriptions of delicious Italian food jumped from the page and Lorelei was nearly ready to choose until she saw the price.

"Thirty-five dollars for lasagna?" said Lorelei, aghast. "They can't be serious."

"Get whatever you want," said Deidre. "Seriously. You don't have to pay for it."

"Deidre, you've spent too much on me already. I feel bad having you buy my dinner, too…"

"Let me worry about that. You just enjoy yourself. You're beautiful, young, and single. I want you to have fun tonight, okay? Let me worry about the money."

The waiter returned and took their order. Lorelei conservatively asked for the eggplant parmesan, as it was only twenty-four dollars. Deidre, on the other hand, ordered lobster and several different types of hors d'oeuvres and another cocktail. While they were waiting for their food, Deidre stood up and walked toward the bar. She casually approached one of the gentlemen seated at the bar and started to talk to him.

He was a good-looking man, much older than Deidre, but distinguished, and obviously wealthy. From a distance, Lorelei watched how Deidre interacted with him. She smiled, leaned in toward him, and her eyes glittered as she spoke with him. She touched his shoulder lightly and he stood up, never taking his eyes off her face. She leaned toward his face and whispered in his ear. He laughed and she looked down, coyly. Her hand found his and she led him away from the bar and back toward their table.

"Could you hand me my purse?" Deidre asked.

Lorelei picked the purse up and gave it to her. Deidre searched through it until she found her camera. She handed the camera to the man beside her. "Take our picture?" He agreed. Lorelei stood up next to Deidre, arms around each other's waist, and smiled. "Lorelei, this is—"

"Malcolm," he interrupted.

"Yes," said Deidre, "Malcolm is just in town from Chicago."

"Nice to meet you," said Lorelei.

"If you aren't meeting anyone else," said Deidre, "we'd love for you to join us."

"How could I refuse?"

The waiters made room for another seat and Malcolm sat between them. He was very handsome, with salt-and-pepper hair, blue eyes, and broad shoulders. Deidre and Malcolm exchanged small talk. She smiled at him and he blushed. Her delicate hand was on the table, and Malcolm went to cover it with his own, a gold band on his ring finger. Dinner arrived and Lorelei enjoyed the sumptuous meal that had been prepared for them. Malcolm was still captivated by Deidre, but he managed to politely include Lorelei in the conversation occasionally. After they had finished eating, the waiter brought the check to the table. Without hesitation, Malcolm reached for it.

"Thank you for a lovely meal," he said as he pulled out his wallet. "I have truly enjoyed the pleasure of your company."

"You are too sweet," said Deidre, "but you don't have to pay for us. Here, let me see the check."

"Absolutely not. It's the very least I can do for two such beautiful women."

Deidre leaned over toward him, holding his face up with her hand. "Thank you. That is the sweetest thing anyone has ever done for me. You're so generous."

They stood up to leave and Malcolm put his arm around Deidre's waist as they left the restaurant. Outside, they stood and faced each other; Malcolm's hands tenderly held Deidre's hips and her arms rested on his shoulders. Lorelei stood apart, uncomfortable with their public display of affection. Malcolm bent over Deidre and kissed her on the cheek. She turned her lips up toward his ear and whispered. He pulled back, clasped her hands briefly, and then walked away.

At the curb, Deidre hailed a cab. She and Lorelei entered.

"Where to?" asked the driver.

"The Jade Room," said Deidre. The cab lurched forward. Lorelei watched the lights of the street twinkle past the car as they made their way through the city.

"I hope you were paying attention back there," said Deidre.

"Paying attention to what?"

"To what I was doing with Malcolm."

"What you were doing? Making a move on a married man? That was pretty obvious. It was kind of awkward, actually."

"Oh my god, are you blind? That whole thing was for you."

"What was for me?"

Deidre turned and faced Lorelei. "What happened back there is one of the... um, *perks*... of us being what we are. We can tap into

143

a man's desire, make him yearn for us, make him beg for us, even. They can't resist it. And Malcolm back there, he was innocent enough. He didn't want to cheat on his wife, and I wouldn't have let him either, but he couldn't help himself."

"So, seduction is one of our… *gifts*?"

"Helen tells us we should only use our powers for good, but every now and then, you have to make an exception. And I really wanted lobster."

"How do you do it?"

"It's easy, really. First, you have to figure out who you're going to pursue. In my experience, it's easiest to start with a man who's alone. Then, just walk up to him, confidently, and catch him with your eyes. Hold his eyes with yours. Make him think he's the only man in the room. Smile, but not too big a smile, you know, there still needs to be a little mystery. Talk to him a little just to warm him up, ask him his name, where he's from, it doesn't matter. Then you touch him. Stroke his face, hold his hand, whatever. After that, he's yours. That's when you sing to him."

"Is that what you were doing when you were whispering to him?"

"Uh-huh. You just lean in, real close, and sing. Just something sultry, or romantic, he just needs to hear your voice. He'll be bound to you then, until you release him, and he'll do anything you want. He'll follow you around like a puppy dog."

"That hardly seems fair."

"Oh, what's fair anyway? Women have been seducing men for thousands of years. What's a little harmless fun? No one's gonna get hurt. It's just a game."

A line of young men and women were lined up the sidewalk in front of the Jade Room when they arrived. Deidre grabbed

Lorelei's hand and pulled her to the front of the crowd. An imposing bouncer stood between them and the door.

"Hey Jake," said Deidre, "how's it going?"

"Fine. Who's this?" he gestured at Lorelei.

"Just a friend of mine."

"She got an ID?" he asked.

"Oh, c'mon, you don't trust me?" She stepped forward and brushed up against his arm. "We just want to have a little fun. I'll keep an eye on her."

The bouncer stepped aside and let them into the club. The place was dark and intoxicating. Deep plum and chocolate walls and large Buddha statues lined the room, and red lanterns hung from the ceilings. Hypnotic music pulsed through the room where dancing couples moved in the darkness amidst a visually dazzling light display. Others were seated in plush leather loveseats along the walls sipping on exotic drinks. The DJ stood above the crowd, watching the dancers from his perch. Deidre led Lorelei to a quiet corner of the room, away from the crowd.

"Look at all of them," said Deidre. "There's a lot of hot guys here tonight. Anybody out there you like? I want you to pick one."

Lorelei's eyes scanned the room. A group of men was huddled near the bar, laughing and drinking beers with their shirts hanging out of their pants. Frat boys. *No thanks,* she thought. Several other men had approached a bachelorette party that was seated at a table. They had greasy hair and shirts that were partly unbuttoned, revealing gold chains and curly chest hair poking out from the top. The party of women looked less than impressed. Lorelei wished they would get a clue.

There was another man, standing alone, not far from the dance floor. *He looks nice,* she thought. *Normal.* He had a drink in his hand and was bobbing his head to the music as he watched the dancers. She couldn't see his features too closely, but he was alone. Lorelei pointed in his direction.

"Good choice," said Deidre. "Do you remember what you have to do?"

"Uh… I go make eye contact with him, smile, talk a little, touch him, then sing to him? Is that it?"

"Well, those are the basics. You look gorgeous. Get out there. Be brave."

Lorelei stood up straight, and made her way across the room, trying to strut the way she had seen Deidre do before. The closer she got to him, the more nervous she became. Her stomach clenched and she was light-headed. *Keep breathing.* She approached him, trying not to blink. *Look at me.* His head turned toward her. Dark brown eyes caught her glance. *That's it, keep looking at me.* She smiled at him. As soon as she did, she realized her smile was forced, and she closed her mouth, so that her lips were just slightly turned up.

"Hi," she said nervously.

"Hey there."

"Having fun?"

"Yeah, I suppose. Just relaxing."

"Wow. Cool. I mean, um, yeah, that's, uh, cool." She nearly looked away, but forced herself to keep her eyes on his.

"What's your name?" he asked.

"Lorelei. What's yours?"

"Garrett."

"Cool. That's a cool name."

"Yeah, thanks."

He thinks I'm weird. He thinks I'm a total freak. 'That's a cool name?' What am I doing? Okay, calm down. I just need to reach out and… She tried to touch his arm at the same time he lifted his glass to his mouth, and instead ended up with her hand on his stomach. *Oh crap,* she thought, and then pulled her hand back abruptly, losing her balance in the process. As she started to fall, she grabbed at his shirt. He caught her arm, keeping her from landing on the ground, but in the process he spilled his drink on himself.

"I'm so sorry!" she yelled. "I can't believe I just did that!" She ran over to the bar and picked up a handful of napkins. "Here. I'm so, so sorry."

"It's okay," he said as he dabbed the front of his shirt.

"No, it's not. I ruined your shirt."

"Hey, it's just a shirt. Don't worry about it."

"I am *so* embarrassed. I'm really, really sorry." Lorelei's eyes began to water.

"Stop apologizing, okay? I don't care. Let me get you a drink and we can go sit down, all right?"

Lorelei nodded and Garrett went to the bar. He returned with two glasses of wine. Lorelei considered for a moment telling him that she was too young to drink, but she decided not to risk any further humiliation. Garrett took her hand and led her to a small table away from the dance floor. He pulled out a chair for her.

"Here, have some wine," he said.

She took a big sip of wine. It was crisp and acidic. *Now's the time,* thought Lorelei. *It's now or never. I've got to sing to him. What am I supposed to sing? Something romantic, something about love. Oh, come on, Lorelei, you have to think of something. Okay, a romantic song... c'mon, you just have to think of one song.* She leaned in close and started to sing.

Why do birds suddenly appear every time you are near?
Just like me, they long to be close to you...

"The Carpenters, huh?" Garrett looked at her wide-eyed, and then started to laugh. "You're a weird girl, Lorelei," he said, "but I like you."

"You think I'm weird?"

"Maybe weird isn't the right word. But you are a little quirky. You want to dance?" he asked.

"I don't know, I think I've done enough damage for one night."

"It'll be fun. I promise." He smiled and took hold of her arm.

Lorelei chugged the rest of her wine and then followed Garrett to the dance floor. He pulled her close to him; his hands were firm around her waist. She swayed with him and rolled her hips back and forth with the music, moving fluidly with the rhythm. He reached behind her and dipped her backward. Her back arched and Lorelei tried to convince herself that he wouldn't drop her. Garrett snapped her body up toward him and he traced the contour of her face with his fingers. Lorelei enjoyed the closeness and she was transfixed by his smile that glowed under the black light.

He turned her around so that her back was pressed up against his back. Across the room, Deidre was dancing on top of a table. The frat boys had gathered around to watch and were encouraging her. She dropped down, slapped the table, and rolled back up. Her hips spun in a circle and she was lifting her shirt up to reveal her midriff. One of the young men reached up and pulled her into his arms. She laughed until he swung her over his shoulder. She began to struggle to get down, but the other frat boys were cheering him on, lifting up their beers in a salute of their machismo.

"I gotta go," Lorelei told Garrett. She ran toward the group of men. The guy who was holding Deidre couldn't have been much older than twenty. He had stubble on his chin and wore a Red Sox shirt. "Hey! Hey, put her down!" Lorelei yelled.

He laughed. "You want a ride next? I bet you would. Or are you just another tease like this one?"

Lorelei took a deep breath and calmed her racing thoughts. She focused on his eyes and pulled them into her own. She could feel him staring back at her, and suddenly, she knew that she had found it—the power over him.

Lorelei smiled, just a little, and said, "You will let her go now. Now."

He obeyed, willingly. Deidre was back on her feet again and straightened out her skirt. Lorelei stepped forward and touched his arm. His jaw dropped.

"We're going to go now, and you're going to leave us alone, understand?"

"Don't go," he replied. "Stay with me."

"No," said Lorelei, "I think we've had enough fun for now. We're leaving."

She grabbed Deidre's forearm and headed for the exit. Deidre stumbled and caught her balance on Lorelei's shoulder.

"Where are we going?" Deidre reeked of alcohol. "Why do we have to leave?"

"We're going," said Lorelei. "Come on."

Lorelei lifted Deidre's arm around her shoulders and helped her back to her feet. They cut through the crowds and into the cold night air outside.

"Lorelei, wait!" a voice called from behind her. She spun around to see Garrett. "You're leaving so soon?"

"Sorry, I meant to say goodbye, but my friend… she needs to go home. She's had too much to drink," said Lorelei.

"I'm fine… ," Deidre countered. Lorelei shushed her.

"I'm sorry," she said, "I had a great time tonight. Thank you."

"Can I take you home?" he asked.

"No, we'll be fine. I'm going to go get a cab."

"Let me." Garrett walked to the curb to hail a cab.

"Lor... you gotta release him," Deidre stuttered. "Or he's going to follow us."

"What?" Lorelei asked.

"Did you sing to him?"

"Yeah, but it didn't even work."

"It obviously did. You've got to release him."

"How?"

"Touch him again... and then you've got to tell him goodbye forever."

Lorelei helped Deidre into the cab and then stood back up and faced Garrett.

"I really wish I could stay," she said.

"Then stay. Don't leave."

"I've got to go. I'm sorry." Lorelei put her hand on his shoulder and stood on her toes so that she could whisper in his ear, "I'm not going to see you again. So thanks for a nice evening... and goodbye." She gave him a quick peck on the cheek and entered the cab. Without another look, Garrett turned and walked away in the other direction.

CHAPTER FIFTEEN

It took Lorelei a few moments to get her bearings when she woke up to the sound of a ringing cell phone. She wasn't sure where she was at first, waking up on a sofa in a strange apartment, but then she vaguely remembered taking an intoxicated Deidre to Colleen's apartment the night before. On the floor, her cousin was asleep on a heap of pillows and blankets. The phone stopped ringing for a minute before it started up again. Lorelei lifted herself from the couch, stepped over Deidre, and found the phone inside a purse beside the door. The caller ID displayed the Deleaux home number.

Lorelei flipped the phone open. "Hello?" she whispered.

"Where are you?" the voice on the other end was shrill.

"In Boston... somewhere," she said.

"Seriously? You know we have a summoning today, did you forget?"

"Huh? A what?"

"Who is this?" the caller was clearly agitated.

"This is Lorelei. Who's *this*?"

"Sorry, Lorelei. It's Calliope. Is Deidre there?"

"Yes, hold on." Lorelei bent down next to the pile of blankets on the floor and gently shook Deidre. "Hey, you have a call." Deidre mumbled something and rolled over. "It's Calliope. She sounds mad."

"Fine," said Deidre. She sat up, rubbed her temples, and squinted at Lorelei, "I'll talk to her." Lorelei handed over the phone and sat back down on the sofa.

"Hello?" she asked. There was a long pause before Deidre said, "I forgot. Sorry… Chill out. We'll leave now, okay? Well, what time is it? Oh, crap. Yeah, we're coming. Bye."

"What did she want?" Lorelei asked.

"We have to go. They need us back home."

They quickly straightened up the blankets before they left the apartment. They walked briskly in the cold morning air to the parking garage where they had left the car.

"You okay to drive?" asked Deidre. "My head is killing me."

"Yeah, sure. I can drive." Deidre tossed her the keys and sat in the passenger seat. Lorelei found her way to the highway. "Why are we in such a hurry?"

"You'll see," said Deidre.

Deidre leaned her seat back, put on her sunglasses, and promptly feel asleep. She hadn't explained to Lorelei what the urgency was in their returning, but Lorelei could sense that it had something to do with the sirens. Her eyes on the road, Lorelei was compelled to drive faster. Whatever it was, she was needed. She was being called back to the house, and to the water. An unseen force pushed her down the highway; her shoulders ached under the pressure. A little more than an hour on the road, they were back in Chatham. Calliope was waiting for them on the front porch. Lorelei and Deidre exited the car and headed toward her.

"Helen's waiting for us at the cove. We need to hurry," said Calliope. "Lorelei, you can wait inside."

"I want to go," said Lorelei. "Whatever it is, I want to see."

"This isn't the time. We're already running late and you aren't needed today."

An uncontrollable panic welled up inside Lorelei. Lightheaded, her thoughts raced through her mind. The waves were crashing beyond the house, beckoning her. Adrenaline coursed through her veins, making her heart pound inside her chest. She was going to pass out if she didn't go down to the cove. "I have to go," she said. "I can't explain it, but I have to be there."

"I'm not going to argue this with you right now. Go wait inside," said Calliope.

Lorelei was breathing fast and nearly at the point of hyperventilating. Her body was physically reacting in a way that she couldn't control. She grabbed Deidre's arm to steady herself.

"C'mon Calliope, she can't fight the summoning any more than you or I can," said Deidre. "You can't make her stay here. It wouldn't be fair."

"Fine," Calliope relented, "just try not to get in the way."

Calliope led the way into the house; her long, black hair cascaded over her strong shoulders. Lorelei still had on the dress she had worn the night before while Deidre somehow managed to look radiant despite her bloodshot eyes and messy hair. Deidre found a white, silk robe for Lorelei and told her to change into it as she did the same. Lorelei quickly obeyed, her thoughts racing too frantically for her to question otherwise. After they had changed, Lorelei, Deidre, and Calliope proceeded to make their way to the cove. Lorelei's mind became still as she approached the water and her heart returned to a normal rhythm. She carefully walked down the steps toward the cove and kicked off her shoes in the sand.

Helen stood at the edge of the water, facing out toward the horizon.

"Stand here," said Deidre. She and Calliope left Lorelei for a moment and approached Helen.

The three women stood silently next to one another, their feet being lapped softly by the waves. Helen's arms lifted to the sky as Deidre and Calliope started to hum a low note, a sound that was rich and soulful. There was no breeze, not even the slightest movement of air, but there was electricity that was tangible to Lorelei and made the hair on her arms stand on end. She was almost afraid to breathe for fear of disturbing the stillness. Helen sang one loud note and started scooping her hands above her head in circles. Immediately, a rush of gray clouds converged above them. The light of the sun was blocked out and the clouds covered the cove completely.

Amazed, Lorelei stood transfixed. The water itself had begun to move in an unusual pattern, bobbing steadily up and down along the shore. Lorelei noticed the walls of the cove were now draped in spirals of fog that were climbing upwards from the water. The fog reached the top of the walls and then began to fill the cove in a thick, gray haze. Helen, Calliope, and Deidre, removed their robes, dropped them on the ground and walked bare skinned into the water. When the water hit the curve of their hips, they stopped. Together, they began to sing, their voices intertwining. The song was ethereal, like a dream. Their voices wove, like shimmering threads, binding the women together in song.

A mist approached from the sea, snaking across the water, a faintly glowing green vapor. The mist was alive, twisting and turning as it flew over the surface of the water. It cut through the fog and dipped into the water before it rose back out and approached the women. The mist split into three distinct tendrils, still bound together, but each piece moving independently. It began to widen and glow more brightly as it came closer to them. Without warning, it leapt from the water and rushed up the front of their bodies completely encompassing them, before pulling them violently under. Lorelei stifled a scream. The surface of the water was still like glass and the mist continued to hover above it; the women had vanished.

Lorelei's heart pounded in her chest. A lump rose in her throat, but she was so scared she couldn't make a sound. Everything was silent. The fog had stopped moving and even the clouds overhead were completely frozen. Lorelei walked timidly toward the shoreline, her feet unsteady beneath her.

A whisper came over the water. Helen's voice rang in her ears, "Do not be afraid, Lorelei." She let out a low whimper.

The water began to stir around where the women had been standing. The mist formed a circle amidst a growing whirlpool. Slowly, Lorelei saw the tops of three heads emerge slowly. Their stares were penetrating; light shone through their seaglass eyes and was so blinding Lorelei could barely stand to look directly at them. Their heads rose above the surface. The women glided up out of the water so effortlessly it appeared as though they were being lifted from beneath the waves. Their hair blew wildly, billowing behind them and around their faces.

Lorelei saw Deidre—a vision of sublime beauty. She was surreal in her transformation, unlike anything Lorelei could have imagined. Her skin was opalescent and shimmered in the light of the mist like a pearl. Blonde hair streamed out behind her and curled around her shoulders. Her hands brushed the surface of the water gently and the mist snaked around her body, gracefully covering her breasts and wrapping around her hips. Likewise, Helen and Calliope were breathtaking in their new form.

Calliope's dark hair stood in bold contrast to her pearl skin. Next to Deidre, her features were much sharper, and her fierce beauty made her an imposing presence. Helen, regal and statuesque, stood tall and serene over the water. The lines that had been carved into her face had all but vanished, and her eyes, so bright with a fire that lit them from behind, radiated a force that pulled Lorelei ever closer to her. Lorelei tried to run, but it was impossible. Their eyes drew her toward them against her will.

"Come here, child," Helen turned and beckoned for Lorelei.

As if there were arms about her waist pulling her into the sea, she found herself amongst them, surrounded by these powerful creatures. Deidre's berry-stained lips parted in a half smile; she helped Lorelei disrobe, and then took her hand and led her deeper into the cove. The water was warm on her skin, so different from the last time she had been here with the three of them. The fog became thick again and their features were less pronounced. Lorelei trembled.

"Don't be scared," said Helen. "It will be done quickly."

They began to sing once again, a lyrical song that bounced off the walls of the cove. Lorelei gazed out toward the sea and saw the mist careening toward her. It jumped out of the water as it approached, circling and writhing like a serpent. The other women stepped back and Lorelei faced the mist alone. The mist darted toward her and suddenly leapt up at her face; it was excruciatingly cold, like ice on her skin. She found herself plunged into the water. Beneath the surface, the glowing mist coiled tightly around her body. It constricted her limbs and forced the air from her lungs and bound itself around her chest. Lorelei struggled against the bondage, but it pulled her deeper under the water. It was as though her muscles were being torn from her bones. Every movement she made only heightened the pain. Unable to scream or breathe, she arched her back and tried to free herself, but the more she thrashed, the tighter it gripped her.

At the point of nearly losing consciousness, Lorelei stopped struggling. Her thoughts went to her mother and the words that had gone unsaid between them since her father's death. She pained to see her mother once again, but it was too late. *This was all a mistake,* she thought. Her eyes closed and her body clenched in a spasm, choking water into her lungs. The cold liquid filled her with a tingly sensation, but she came to her senses once again and the pain subsided. She expelled the water and took another large breath of liquid. As she did so, she heard a loud, wailing sound in the water. It got closer, increasing in intensity to the point that it hurt her ears. She recognized it immediately as the Song, but it was so strong this time that it was unmistakable. The mist loosened its hold on her and began to push her up toward the surface of the water. Lorelei's face met the air and she found the eyes of the other women staring down at her.

"Are you okay?" Helen asked.

"I don't know," Lorelei shivered. Her body was tender, like it had been bruised all over. She looked down to see how much damage there was and she saw that her skin had changed. It was as flawless as silk. Like the others, Lorelei's skin had taken on an opalescent hue with flashes of pinks and blues that passed under the creamy surface. Electricity surged under her skin, tingling. Her fingertips felt charged with power. She clearly could hear the Song, a melody above her head. The green mist was wrapped around her body, but it was also holding her up waist deep in the water. Lorelei's soft face was framed by perfect brown spirals of hair and her seaglass eyes glowed as brightly as the others.

"I think you're going to be all right," said Calliope. "Just a little stunned, but you'll get over it."

"The first time is always the worst," said Deidre. "It's not so bad once you've done it five or six times. Just don't fight so much next time and it'll be easier."

"You couldn't have told me that before that thing grabbed me?"

"If we had told you, you might not have gone through with it," said Calliope. "But, it's all over now, and we have to get going."

Helen slid up next to Lorelei and took hold of her upper arm. "Don't forget to breathe," she said. Without notice, Lorelei was pulled back under the water. Her arm was yanked forcefully until they were speeding out of the cove, past reefs and sandbars, and into the ocean. The Song and the rushing sound of water both played in her ears. Beside her, Helen was nothing more than a blur of green mist. She had to force herself to breathe in the water. It was such an unnatural feeling, but she tried to keep her breathing steady. She gazed into the vast expanse of darkness that surrounded them. The ocean floor dropped out of sight and they were traveling through a strange world of light and shadow. Fear tugged on Lorelei's heart, but she tried to put her trust in Helen.

Their pace slowed. Lorelei could see the light of the sun streaming down on them; the way it stretched out its rays through the water, the sun looked like a light at the end of a long tunnel. Helen loosened her grip on Lorelei's arm as their shoulders rose up out of the sea and they moved more deliberately. Lorelei sputtered a little when she reached the surface, coughing out the liquid that had been in her lungs and replacing it with oxygen. Helen pointed out toward a small fishing boat and said, "That's the place. This is where we've been called to lead a soul from this life into death."

Lorelei squinted and saw the boat bobbing in the water. Dark clouds crept in from the horizon and the wind began to pick up. As if gliding, the women approached the nondescript gray boat, a small craft with an enclosed cabin in front and a back end full of lobster traps. At the stern, a weathered lobsterman with a full, red beard threw bait into the traps. A lit cigarette hung from his lips and he cursed when his hand caught on a piece of wire sticking out of a trap. Finished baiting, he went to the side of the boat and hoisted the anchor before calling out, "Spencer, let's go! Let 'er rip."

A teenage boy emerged from the cabin, his shaggy brown hair covering his eyes. He zipped his brown jacket and sauntered across the deck toward the lobsterman who was finishing his cigarette. The man tossed the butt overboard and took his place shipside. Spencer opened a hatch and pulled out a long stick with a hook at the end. As the ship moved ever closer to the women, the lobstermen began to pull in their catch. Lorelei was cloaked with a sense of dread, knowing that fate had already been sealed for one or both of these men.

They worked in tandem; the boy leaned over the side of the boat with the stick to snag the buoys as they passed by. Each buoy was attached to a rope that extended below the water that he would grab and feed through a motorized pulley. As the rope was pulled up, the lobster traps would surface and the man would haul them up and toss them onto the deck. Without a word, the traps were emptied, baited, and tossed back again. Each lobster was weighed and measured; the claws of the acceptable specimens were secured with rubber bands and they were placed in a crate. Too consumed with their work, the lobstermen hadn't noticed the four women that were approaching from behind.

Lorelei waited nervously, her stomach in knots. Spencer baited the final trap and then lifted it above his head. As soon as he threw the trap, there was a loud splash as Spencer was yanked overboard. His leg had gotten caught up in the ropes of one of the traps that had just been pushed back into the water. He cried for help as he hoisted himself up and gripped the edge of the boat while it continued to glide forward, his body stretched out between the boat and his foot that remained tethered to the buoy.

The lobsterman rushed to cut the engine and then ran to his son's aid. "Hang on, Spencer." He grabbed the boy's arm and tried to lift him out of the water. The trap had caught onto a floating mass of seaweed and was proving to be too challenging for him to lift. He reached over the side to try to untangle Spencer's leg, but the boy was losing his grip on the edge of the boat. His father grabbed his forearm and he tugged Spencer toward him, but he wasn't able to get enough leverage to pull him onboard. They were at an impasse; the man could not let go of Spencer's arms or he would be pulled under, but there was nothing he could do to free him either.

"It's time," Helen told the others. "Deidre, do you want to do the honors?"

"I suppose I can," Deidre replied. "And you'll both handle the other one?"

"Yes, we'll take care of him," said Calliope, her voice icy.

"All right, ladies, good luck." Helen turned to Lorelei and said, "Stay here. It won't take long, but this will be a good opportunity for you to watch and learn. I know this won't be easy for you, but you have to see it to understand."

Lorelei nodded in agreement. Helen gestured and the others followed, moving gracefully through the water toward the boat. The mist glowed more brightly than before with threads of light piercing the darkness. They circled around the boat where the man was still struggling to pull his son from the tangled ropes. The fog billowed as Helen and Calliope pulled the water up into a spinning column beneath them. Their bodies rose up with the column in unison until they were at the same level as the vessel. Without a sound, they jumped delicately onto the deck. Lorelei clenched her teeth and shivered as the women surrounded the two lobstermen.

A large wave hit the side of the boat. The man's feet slid as the vessel jerked. Spencer's head hit the side of the hull and his father panicked. Spencer had lost consciousness and his body floated listlessly, his foot still bound to the buoy. Calliope touched the lobsterman on the shoulder. He turned his head. She was resplendent, a masterpiece of feminine beauty, with hollow eyes that penetrated into his. His own son was bobbing helplessly in the water, but he couldn't turn away from Calliope. She opened her mouth and began to sing a melody with words that Lorelei didn't understand. His jaw dropped and he let go of Spencer's arms. Helen came to Calliope's side and together they captivated him. Step by step, they moved away from the edge of the ship and he followed them as if in a trance.

In the water below, Deidre looked like an angel. She was suspended out of the water and her blonde hair poured down her back like silk. Her face, ethereal in its perfection, gazed down at the boy in loving tenderness. She cradled his head in her hands and brought him out of the water to breathe. His eyes squinted open and he stared at her for a moment before realizing his present situation. He looked around and, seeing that he was very nearly pulled under by the trap, began to thrash about wildly. Spencer grabbed Deidre's shoulders to try to pull his body upright again. Her face remained unmoved as she pushed his hair out of his eyes with one of her hands. She began to sing and Lorelei recognized the song as the one Helen had taught her.

Fog and shadows meet in vain
'Gainst the silver drops to strain;
Whilst the silent waves abound,

Courting depths with empty sound;
From the mirrored waters part,
Still the mind and calm the heart.

Spencer ceased all movement and rested in Deidre's arms. To Lorelei, he looked like a baby being put to sleep by the sound of his mother's lullaby. The waves rocked him like a cradle and he rested his eyes, weary of the struggle. Deidre pulled him close against her chest and hummed softly in his ear until his body was completely relaxed, in an apparent slumber. She lowered him gently into the water and his head slipped under the surface of the sea. Spencer opened his eyes again, but made no effort to stay afloat. With his last breath, a series of tiny bubbles made their way up from his mouth. His arms were stretched out beside him and moved like loose fabric as the waves pushed him back and forth.

The last time Lorelei had seen a dead body, she had been the one doing the singing. She was shocked to see the pallid corpse as he was dragged farther and farther down into the watery abyss. His eyes were vacant, the life in him gone. Helen and Calliope retreated back into the water. The lobsterman stood alone on his boat, a solitary silhouette against the darkened sky. When the siren's spell had finally broken its hold on him, he ran for his son. He reached out for the buoy with the hooked stick and pulled it toward the ship, then lashed the rope to the boat's railing. With the rope secured, he found a knife and cut the rope away from the boy's leg. He yanked Spencer's body up toward him and it flopped in his arms, lifeless.

"No! Breathe! C'mon, Spencer, breathe!" he screamed. A lump rose in Lorelei's throat. The man laid Spencer's body on the deck and tried to resuscitate him, but it was useless. He was already gone. The lobsterman began to sob, and tears welled in Lorelei's eyes. The man knelt beside his son and embraced him, his body jerking in desperation and grief. Pulling the boy's body into his arms, he screamed at the top of his lungs, rage and anger exploding from his chest.

How could they do that to this man? Why would these sirens take the life of this man's young son and leave him to suffer alone? Despite their beauty and the amazing things they could do, to Lorelei they seemed to be little more than monsters. And yet, she knew she was one of them. The thought disgusted her, but what had she expected? She had known that there would be a death today, and yet she had insisted to come with them. If this were indeed her calling, she couldn't be a part of it. Not this. Lorelei started to hyperventilate. She was dizzy and nauseous. He mind flashed to the moment of her father's death before she passed out and fell into the cold, cruel sea.

CHAPTER SIXTEEN

Lorelei gripped the covers of her bed. Even lying down, the room was spinning around her. Her chest was so tight that it hurt to breathe. Every time she let her eyes close, if even for a second, the image of the boy's drowning came reeling back. It was always the same, she saw him passing from life to death, his face pale white and his lips tipped with blue. She couldn't shake the memory of his father, hunched over his son's body, crying in grief to the empty sea. Lorelei wondered how the man would be able to face the boy's mother, and how she too would be devastated at such a loss. Her heart ached for them remembering the pain of her own father's death, knowing he was gone forever. How much worse it must be to lose one's child.

After the summoning, the sirens had brought Lorelei back to the cove. She had been in shock, and couldn't bring herself to look at them directly. Helen had let her walk back to the house alone and Lorelei had retreated to her room, where she spent the last four days alone in silence. The women brought food and drink to her door, but when they tried to talk to her, Lorelei refused to respond. She wanted to leave this place, but where would she go? If she left, it wouldn't change who—*or what*—she was. And that thought made her sick to her stomach.

She didn't understand how the others could go on so easily, as if nothing had happened. They had been responsible for a death, and they were completely unfazed by it. Had they become numb to suffering? Could they not see the needless pain that they were inflicting on people? Lorelei didn't worry so much for the dead as she felt sorry for those that were left behind—the ones that had loved and lost. And these women must have attended the deaths of hundreds, if not thousands, of people. Lorelei couldn't do that. She wasn't that person and she didn't want this responsibility.

There was a knock at her door. "Lorelei," said Deidre, "you have to come out of there eventually. Won't you at least talk to me?"

Lorelei rolled over and faced the wall. She said nothing.

Lorelei woke up the next morning and slid out of bed. She opened the door and found toast and tea waiting for her. The tea was tepid, but she drank it anyway. Her hair was a mess, greasy and matted to her head. She saw herself in the mirror and decided to take a shower. Lorelei lathered her hair and scrubbed her face while the hot water streamed down on her. She sucked the steam deep into her lungs. If only it were so easy to clean her mind of the things she had seen, the things she had done. She just wanted to be back in Calais, worrying only about classes and test scores, friendships and the occasional party. When she stepped back into the room, Lorelei noticed her cell phone ringing on the nightstand. She rushed over and answered it.

"Hello?" she said.

"It's Breanna," was the reply.

"Bree, how are you?" Lorelei asked.

"Good. Things are good, but we all miss you."

"I miss you guys, too."

"Hey, I just wanted to see if you could get together today. I'm down at my grandmother's for Thanksgiving, and she doesn't live very far from Chatham."

"It's Thanksgiving already?"

"Well, not until tomorrow."

"Sure—yeah, I'd love to see you," said Lorelei. "Where are you?"

"In Hyannis. We come here every year."

Lorelei agreed to meeting Bree in Hyannis for lunch at 12:30. She needed to get out of the house and talk to someone. The more she stayed in this room, the more she thought about the boy's face slipping under the water, and she knew she needed to get her mind off of it. She found a garment bag of the clothes Deidre had bought for her hanging on a hook on the back of the door and took out an emerald-colored silk blouse and a pair of black trousers. Lorelei straightened her hair and applied a little blush and lipgloss.

The stairs creaked as Lorelei descended. She rounded the corner stealthily and peered over the banister. There was no one in the living room or kitchen. They must be at work, or else they were... she didn't want to think about it. Lorelei ran down the grand staircase and flew out the front door. She hopped in her Jeep, which was parked by the side of the house. As she drove away, she was relieved; she could breathe again.

In Hyannis, Bree greeted Lorelei outside the Thai Gardens restaurant with a quick hug. They entered and were soon seated. The smell of coconut curry filled the air. Lorelei was starving.

"It is so good to see you," said Bree. "You look so beautiful, but... ," she paused.

"But what?" asked Lorelei.

"You seem sad, that's all. Are you okay?"

"I don't know. This week has been rough."

"Really? How come?"

Lorelei sat quietly for a moment. No matter how desperately she wished she could tell Breanna everything that had happened to her since she had come to Chatham, she couldn't imagine trying to explain it when she didn't completely understand it herself. She wanted so badly to confide in her friend, to tell her how strange it had been to not only find out that she was a siren, but also to confess how difficult it had been to deal with the implications of that reality.

"The holidays are hard," Lorelei lied. "I miss my parents."

"I understand. That must be difficult for you," said Breanna. "You know, if you want to come over to my grandma's tomorrow for dinner, you're more than welcome."

"Thanks. I'll think about it." Lorelei wondered if she could just pretend like none of this had happened, to go on with her life as if nothing had changed.

"So, are you going to come back to school in January, or what?"

"Maybe. I'm not sure yet."

"C'mon, you've got to come back. The competition for the Elmsbrook scholarship is in February and I know how badly you wanted that. Just think, you'd get to study abroad for a semester and work with Paola Perlegetti in Rome. You have a real gift, you know. You shouldn't blow it."

If only Bree knew the truth about her gift. The thing Lorelei used to be most proud of, her voice, was more like a curse to her now. Lorelei had loved singing not so long ago, but it was too dangerous for her to consider continuing on with her voice studies. What if the Song made its appearance again unexpectedly and someone else died because of her? And being this close to the water, she couldn't escape that possibility, and she wasn't willing to risk it.

Their food arrived, steaming hot with exotic, pungent aromas permeating the air, making Lorelei's mouth water. The pad thai, her favorite, was delicious, an expert blend of flavors—sweet, spicy, nutty, and savory. After living on bread and tea for the last five days, Lorelei plowed through the food. Breanna filled Lorelei in with the campus gossip as they ate. One of the music theory professors had been fired, there were new qualifications announced to pass the proficiencies that almost all the students thought were biased toward next year's entering freshmen, and Chelsea and Tony had been on the verge of a breakup for the last several weeks.

Despite all the pleasantries, Lorelei couldn't shake the feeling that she didn't belong in that world anymore. After what she had seen, everything she had learned with the Deleauxes had taught her that the world was not as simple as she used to believe. There were deeper forces that pulled lives in unexpected directions. She didn't belong to that life now. Fate had taken her away from Calais, away from Bree and her other friends, and onto a different path. She realized that this wasn't that path she would have chosen for herself, but it was the one that had been chosen for her, and, like it or not, the calling was unavoidable.

"So, have you liked staying down here?" asked Breanna. "Are they nice to you?"

"They're nice enough, I guess. The house is really pretty, right on the water, and they've been very generous to me, I just… I can't decide if I should stay."

"You weren't planning on staying that long, were you? I thought you wanted to go to clear your head for a while, but the more you talk about it, it seems like you're never coming back to Maine."

"I don't know what to do. They're family and I feel—connected, somehow, but I'm not sure if that's where I belong. My Aunt Helen wants me to stay, I know. She's been teaching me things, things about our family and our past, and I've learned a lot about myself—things that maybe I didn't want to know. These women are a part of my life now. I'm connected to them, whether I want to be or not. Does that even make sense?"

"So this is all some big ancestry thing? I guess it's nice to know where you come from, but Lorelei, don't you think your future's more important? They'll always be there for you to visit, and maybe you can spend more time with them after you graduate."

"It's not that simple. You don't understand."

"Then explain it to me," Bree leaned in, her arms resting on the table.

If it were only that easy, Lorelei thought, *I would tell you right now. But I'm not like you. I'm not normal. And you'd never understand.*

"I'm... I'm bound to them now. Part of me wants to leave; I would leave right now if I could, but I can't." Lorelei leaned back and took a sip of water. Her frustration at being unable to tell Bree the truth welled up inside. "There are things I need to know, and it isn't going to be easy, but I have to figure out who I am and where I belong, and I think the only way I can do that is by being a part of that family."

"Have you told your mother yet?"

"No, I haven't talked to her since I left Colorado. She probably still thinks I'm in Maine."

"You should tell her."

"I know. And I will tell her—when the time's right."

Their meal commenced and the two split the check. Lorelei hugged Breanna on her way out to the car and promised to call her if she needed a place to go for Thanksgiving. She watched Bree leave and wondered if they would see each other again. The world was a heavier place to Lorelei, and she secretly envied her friend's ignorance. Her life had changed, and there was no going back. There would be secrets that she would be forced to keep from even her best friends, but Lorelei knew that even though she hated it, the call of the water was too strong to ignore. Sadness filled her heart knowing that she couldn't go back; things would never be the same. Her naive, carefree former life was a thing of the past.

Lorelei had resigned herself to returning to the Deleaux home. There was still so much she didn't understand about everything, and she needed answers. She thought to ask Helen, but Helen had always been so vague in her explanations that Lorelei was generally more confused by the answers she gave. It seemed to Lorelei that Helen had always protected her from the truth, as though she couldn't handle it. And as for Deidre, Lorelei really liked her, but she knew that Deidre wouldn't say anything that Helen wouldn't allow. That left only one option—Calliope. Lorelei didn't know why, but she knew Calliope would tell her the truth. She was so no-nonsense about everything and seemed to be outside the realm of Helen's control.

Leaving Hyannis, Lorelei headed east along the cape. She concentrated on the road, knowing the time for answers would come. Her car zipped through the barren landscape with brown and gray grasses that bedecked the roadside. Lorelei passed along the quiet main street of Chatham, most of its stores closed for the winter, and she was strangely empowered as she drove alongside the coastline. The house appeared in her view, stately and imposing. Lorelei pulled up in the front and climbed out of the car. She walked up the front stairs with certainty, remembering the first time when she had timidly ascended them. Inside, she could hear voices in the kitchen, pots clinking and the smell of cinnamon and nutmeg.

Helen spotted her standing in the doorway. "Lorelei," she said, "it's so good that you've come downstairs. Are you quite all right?"

"I'd really like to talk to Calliope," Lorelei said firmly.

"That's fine, I suppose," said Helen, giving Calliope a sideward warning glance.

Calliope turned in her seat and faced Lorelei. She stood, so tall compared to the others, dressed in chic linen trousers paired with a V-neck sweater. Her black hair was swept back into a ponytail at the base of her neck. She had high, prominent cheekbones and perfectly arched eyebrows, with lips the color of deep red roses. The only feature that was remotely soft about her were her eyes— the pale, green color of the sea during a storm.

"Did you want to go somewhere else to talk?" asked Calliope.

Lorelei nodded. Calliope brushed past her and led through the foyer and into the sitting room with the yellow chairs. She motioned for Lorelei to sit on the sofa and then she herself took a seat in the chair facing it. Calliope crossed her legs at the ankles and folded her hands in her lap. "What is it you wanted to discuss?" she started.

"I have some things I want to ask about, you know, the siren thing, and I want to know that you'll be honest with me," Lorelei felt intimidated. "I don't need to be protected from it anymore. If I ask you these questions, can I trust that you'll be truthful with me?"

There was silence and then Calliope answered coolly, "Yes, I'll tell you anything you want to know."

Lorelei composed herself, dried her sweaty palms on her lap and then asked, "Why me? Is there a reason why I'm a siren?"

"It tends to run in families. Not everyone in a family will be born with the gift, but there have been sirens in our family for generations. It's sort of luck of the draw. Sometimes, like in your case, we can tell which girls have the gift from a very early age, but sometimes it doesn't show itself until later."

"And if I choose not to be a siren, what then?"

"Unfortunately, that's not a choice you get to make. Do you remember how you felt the day you and Deidre came back from Boston? Like you were going to be sick?"

"Yes," said Lorelei, "it was terrible."

"You have a duty to the sea, and if you fail to perform that duty when she asks it of you, you will physically suffer. The more you ignore the call, the worse it will get, until it drives you mad."

"But how can you do it? How can you watch as people die and keep going back? Don't you feel at least a little guilty?"

"We never let it become personal. When you're out there, you can't think about them as individuals. You have a job to do, you just do it and keep moving forward. You don't have a choice. When I'm out there, I'm methodical. I don't think, I just act. And I remember that we are part of a larger plan."

"What plan is that? What plan just lets you stand by and watch people die?"

"Lorelei, don't be naive. Everyone dies eventually. Some people die of old age, some of disease, and some die out there, in the water. That's reality. Like it or not, we're a part of that. Fate has already chosen them and we respect the Fates."

"So are there others out there? Other sirens beside just us?"

"We are only one of many groups, called assemblies, around the world. Each assembly is usually comprised of about three to five women, ranging in age. New sirens are bought into the fold as the matriarch ages. Once in a great while, we'll converge with the other groups when there is a catastrophe too large for us to handle on our own. When a multitude of assemblies unite, we call it a congregation. It's very rare, but it does happen from time to time—shipwrecks, hurricanes, that sort of thing. You'll undoubtedly run into several of these groups in your lifetime."

"How many assemblies are out there?"

"I can't say exactly how many there are in the world. There are many assemblies that I've never encountered. Some have tried to keep records, but it's an inexact practice, at best. We're most familiar with those here in our territory. There's an assembly to the north of us, the Merchansons, who live not far from Montreal. The Waterfords live in Norfolk and there's an assembly in Savannah and another in New Orleans."

Lorelei considered the thought that they weren't alone in this. She had never really thought of it before, but it was understandable that their family certainly couldn't handle all of the drownings in the world by themselves. There were probably other young women like her struggling with these same issues.

"Calliope, when we're, you know, transformed, can everyone see us?"

"Yes, we're visible. That's why we use the cove—it offers a certain level of protection from being seen by outsiders."

"Then if you can be seen, what happens when there are survivors? Like, the other day, that man saw you. Will he remember that?"

"Most of the time, I think people are so stressed by those situations that they don't clearly remember what happened anyway. If they do have memories of us, they usually pass them off as hallucinations. Some have mistaken us for angels. And if anyone is brave enough to talk about what they saw, no one would believe them. But they will dream about us for the rest of their lives. We leave a mark on them that will never fade."

"When we change, does it always... hurt so much?"

"You get used to it. I can't say it's ever pleasant, but it's not so bad after a while. In time, you might even come to crave the change. As sirens we have freedom and power that we don't have on land and it's indescribable. When we're on the water, we control it, make it bend to our will. The feeling of being so strong—unstoppable even—is very addicting. You'll learn to tolerate the change because of what you become."

Lorelei remembered the water surging past her when Helen had pulled her into the sea. She could see them all in her mind, radiant and mystical, with dominion over the ocean and even over the weather above them. It was alluring.

"I know this is a lot to try to understand," said Calliope, "but someday soon it will feel like second nature. You have all the power already, you just need to stop doubting yourself and be more confident. That's ours out there," she said, motioning to the window and the water beyond, "all of it; and it is your destiny, as it has been for generations of your family before you, to control it."

Lorelei reached up and grasped at the necklace that hung around her neck and thought of her grandmother's photo. This was her inheritance. She couldn't turn her back on it any more than she could change her height, or the shape of her face. *It they can do it,* she thought, *maybe I can, too. I'm a Deleaux.*

Calliope glanced at her watch, "Anything else?"

"No," said Lorelei, her brow furrowed, "I'm starting to understand."

"Good, I'm glad we had this talk." With that, Calliope stood up and briskly left the room.

Lorelei turned her eyes to the ocean. It was so infinite that it intimidated her, but she also yearned to be a part of it. Quietly, she said a prayer for the boy who had died and for his family, and promised herself that she would try to continue on this journey. In the silence of the room, she could hear the faint strains of the Song calling to her from depths of the sea.

CHAPTER SEVENTEEN

Oatmeal ferociously bubbled up over the pot's brim, and Lorelei quickly grabbed the pot and moved it off the burner. She turned down the heat, gave the mixture a quick stir and sat it back down on the stove top. Thanksgiving had passed uneventfully, a quiet meal at the Deleaux home, simple and rustic. Lorelei had resigned to stay in Chatham, and thankfully, no one spoke of her nervous breakdown the week before. In fact, Helen was even more gracious and accommodating, as if she were afraid that Lorelei might somehow break if she asked her to lift a finger.

Lorelei gulped down a glass of orange juice and hurriedly ate a bowlful of warm oatmeal. Helen, Calliope, and Deidre were all working today—a busy day for them following the holiday weekend. Calliope had asked Lorelei the night before if she would be willing to help them with a project. A small fishing boat was beached on Monomoy Island and needed to be brought back to the mainland. Lorelei agreed to go with one of their workers and help him if he needed anything. She was excited to get out of the house and to be useful.

At nine o'clock, the doorbell rang. Lorelei grabbed her coat and scarf, opened the door, and found a familiar young man waiting. His blue eyes peeked out from under a mop of unruly dark-blond hair.

"New girl," he said, a playful smirk spread across his lips.

"Uh, yeah," she replied.

"Aeson," he said, reaching his hand out to greet her, "we met a few weeks ago, remember?"

"Sure, I remember." She took hold of his hand and shook it matter-of-factly.

"Ready to go?" he asked.

"Yeah," she followed him out to his truck, which was still idling in the driveway.

He opened the door and gave her a boost up into the passenger's seat. The truck smelled like gasoline and was full of various tools, scattered paperwork that had been hastily thrown about the cab, and a wetsuit that hung from the back window. The engine roared beneath her and the truck began to roll.

"How've you been?" Aeson asked.

"Fine," she replied.

"Just 'fine'? C'mon, you can do better than that," he said.

Lorelei wasn't sure how to reply. She looked over at Aeson, who was staring straight ahead at the road. He was young, couldn't be more than a few years older than she was, but unlike her, he seemed so sure of himself, almost smug. What was she supposed to say to him? Tell him things weren't fine, that she was still lost and scared despite having decided not to run away from her fate? Admit she was confused and terrified of the task before her? No, it was better to lie.

"I'm just fine," she answered.

He laughed. "So they're not driving you crazy yet?"

"Not yet," Lorelei smiled.

"Give it time," Aeson pulled the truck into the marina. He jumped out and grabbed a duffel bag from the flatbed of the truck. A local fisherman approached and waved at them. Lorelei lowered herself to the ground and walked along the pier. The water was shallow and clear, with small waves bouncing against the sides of the dock. Several small rowboats were completely submerged under the surface of the water, either fallen into disrepair or simply had been tipped over by the wind and sunk. Aeson motioned for Lorelei to follow him toward a sturdy, but practical-looking white vessel.

"C'mon up," he said and reached his hand out to pull her onboard. "This is *The Hera*, one of our working ships. She's not a tug, but she'll do in a pinch."

He went to the wheel and steered out into the sea. Lorelei watched the sandy dunes and small gray cottages that covered the landscape as the boat pulled away from shore. Aeson revved the ship faster as they cleared the protected waters of the marina and the wind stung Lorelei's cheeks. She wrapped her arms around herself.

"You cold?" he asked. "There's a few coats under there."

Lorelei lifted the lid to a large metal trunk and found two heavy, bright-orange, canvas jackets. Both of them were much too large for her, but it was better than being cold. It hung down to her knees and the sleeves were far too long for her arms, like a child wearing their parents' clothes. She sighed, zipped up the jacket, and walked to where Aeson was steering the boat.

"Oh my god," he laughed. "You look like a giant pumpkin."

"It's not like there were very many options," Lorelei quipped, suddenly feeling completely self-aware. "Is it that bad?"

"No, it's fine. You don't have to be too concerned on my account. You want to steer?" He asked. Lorelei nodded. "Here, take the wheel. Just keep heading straight this way." Aeson headed to the back of the ship and began to unravel several thick ropes. Lorelei focused on the smooth motion of the ship cutting through the water, her hair blowing wildly behind her.

Aeson returned and put his arms around hers. He leaned in and a rush crept up her spine. "Let's slow her down," he said and pulled back on the throttle. The ship moved slowly toward an island not far in the distance. An old lighthouse sat on top of the uninhabited island while seabirds noisily circled above the coast. He scanned the shore with his binoculars and then pointed to the stranded vessel on the beach to their left. Lorelei turned the wheel and the boat changed course.

"Okay, so here's what we're going to do. We're going to take her in, but not too far, then drop the anchor. I'll try to hook it up and I'll need you out here to lift the anchor and pull the boat. Don't give it too much gas—just slow and steady, okay?"

Lorelei nodded her understanding and Aeson slowed the boat to a crawl until it stopped just outside of the sandbar. He showed her how to operate the anchor and gave her a few more instructions before he attached the ropes to the side of the ship. He handed her a walkie-talkie, pulled on a wetsuit, and then dove into the water. Strong, muscular arms pulled his body through the water until it was shallow enough for him to stand. Aeson approached the beached vessel and then hefted himself aboard. He disappeared up into the ship and Lorelei turned her attention back to the sea.

Gentle waves bobbed the ship back and forth, and Lorelei held tightly to the railing as she walked to the stern. Just visible on the horizon, the cape was veiled behind a thin mist and glinting water.

Cool air filled her lungs and the wind continued to blow past her face. Despite the sting of the wind, she felt lost in the rocking waves and freshness of the salt air. She sat down on the bench and closed her eyes while the boat swayed rhythmically beneath her. Several minutes passed before Lorelei opened her eyes again. The sky was darker, light cirrus clouds giving way to pillars of smoke. The mist was growing steadily thicker; within minutes she couldn't see the shoreline of the cape anymore. And beneath the ship, the water had become a deep, gray abyss, no longer the sparking blue-green that it had been in the sunlight.

She looked around the boat anxiously, and picked up the walkie-talkie. "Aeson?" she said. There was no response. "The weather's starting to get bad out here. How much longer do you think you'll be?" She turned up the volume on the walkie-talkie, but only heard static. "Aeson, are you there?" Still nothing.

From the distance, a droning metallic hum started to sound. Lorelei focused on the deep, jarring tone that resonated from the ocean itself. The clouds rolled over the boat and blotted out the light. Lorelei peered into the water and saw a green glow coming up from the depths. The light was pulsating and the sound started to beat with it, throbbing in Lorelei's head, beckoning her. *Not now*, she thought, *I'm not ready*. She tried the walkie-talkie again, but it was dead.

Lorelei's stomach seized and she thought for a moment that she might get sick. She remembered what Calliope had told her about how sirens couldn't avoid the call of the Song. The dark water looked as smooth and solid as glass, while on the surface, whispers of mist moved in circles and the green light simmered beneath. She felt like she was being tugged toward the sea; light-headed and nauseous, Lorelei clung to the side of the boat. *But I'm alone,* she thought. Helen had never prepared her for the possibility that she might be called without the others, but if she were to believe everything she had been taught, there was a reason and purpose the Song was calling her now.

She gritted her teeth and clenched the railing tightly. Lightning cracked, illuminating the sky and torrents of rain began to fall. The droning sound hurt her ears. It wanted her. Rainwater rolled down her face and drenched her hair. Fear had grabbed hold, but Lorelei told herself that this wasn't the moment to panic—she needed to rise above and do what needed to be done. *Do not be afraid*, she told herself. She unzipped the coat and tossed it to the deck, shivering as the rain soaked through her clothes. Lorelei hoisted herself up on the side of the boat and stood looking down at the water. Helen's words echoed through her mind, *You aren't going to fail. The Fates wouldn't allow it.*

Lorelei let go of the railing and jumped in, feet first. She was quickly submerged in the freezing water, her body tightened and trembled. She bobbed to the surface and gasped for air. Every breath was painful and Lorelei struggled to stay afloat. When she'd been in the water with the others, it had been cold, but not intolerable. This time the water felt like ice; it was excruciating. She waited for the change to happen, but there was nothing. Nothing but water and the cold.

Something slid up against her leg. She couldn't see through the water to tell what it was, but whatever had just touched her was big. Lorelei panicked and she swam to the side of the boat. How was she going to pull herself up? There weren't any steps or rope, and she couldn't reach up to the railing. Another bolt of lightning shot through the sky and the sound of thunder boomed overhead. Lorelei was unexpectedly jerked under the water by her ankle. The water covered her head and the green glow surrounded her. She struggled against it, kicking and fighting to get above—to air.

Lorelei surfaced briefly and grabbed a lungful of air before being pulled down again by unseen hands. Her thoughts were racing. She tried to reach down and find whatever it was that had been bound around her leg, but she couldn't feel anything. Lorelei's arms flailed in her desperation. Again, she was able to just barely get above the water and take a breath before she was swept under. She faced upwards and saw the boat as she was pulled deeper. Her arms locked against her sides. Amidst it all, she could still hear the deep, droning sound…

She began to lose consciousness when she felt something else grab her around the waist. A pair of arms had taken hold of her and was pulling her toward the surface. The two opposing forces yanked at her body. She hung motionless like a rag doll, and then, with all the energy she had left, and on the verge of passing out, Lorelei gave one last, strong kick, and broke free from whatever had been holding her leg. The pair of arms around her waist continued to pull her upwards and when her face broke through the surface, she swallowed in a huge gasp of air and felt her mind return to her. Someone had saved her.

Helpless, Lorelei felt her body being heaved onto the deck of the boat. She was then carried down a flight of steps under the deck and laid on a cot. The face above her—it was Aeson's face. He looked frightened, but he worked quickly and began to strip off Lorelei's wet clothes. She was embarrassed, but too weak to try to stop him. He wrapped her in a blanket and then wiped the water off her face with a towel and tried to wring out her hair while she lay shivering. He rubbed his hands over her arms on top of the blanket. Lorelei blinked up at him.

"Are you okay?" he asked. She nodded feebly. "Your lips are still blue." He placed his hands on her face. Lorelei closed her eyes and relished the warmth. He had taken off the top of his wetsuit and pulled her up against his bare chest and rubbed her back. She melted into him and let him hold her close.

"What the hell did you think you were doing?" She bit her lip and shrugged her shoulders. He lowered her back down onto the cot. "You could have died out there. Really. You're lucky to be alive right now."

Still shivering, she mouthed the words, *I know.*

"Did you honestly think you could have withstood it? You're not nearly experienced enough to be out in water like that."

She closed her eyes and nodded her head, ashamed. The rain was still pounding the deck of the boat above them. Slowly, sensation started to return to her limbs. Aeson brewed a pot of coffee and returned with a mug for her. He helped her sit up and drink it. It was black and bitter, but it was hot and warmed her up as it slid down her throat. Aeson found a large sweatshirt and helped her into it. It came down to her knees. He sat beside her until she stopped shaking.

"So would you mind explaining to me what the hell you were thinking jumping into the water like that?"

"I thought I saw something. I wanted to see what it was." Lorelei couldn't begin to explain to him what had actually prompted her to leap into the frigid sea.

"So you jumped into the Atlantic Ocean in the middle of winter? Without proper gear or even a life jacket? Were you *trying* to kill yourself?"

"Sorry."

"I'm not asking for an apology," he said, "but what you did was crazy."

"Fine. Maybe I am crazy."

"I'm not trying to be a jerk, but I've never known anybody to do something so stupid."

"You wouldn't understand."

He looked at her and put his hand around the back of her neck. "Try me."

There was something in his eyes that made her want to tell him the truth. She looked down at her hands and said, "I don't know. I just felt called to go out there."

"Dammit," he said under his breath. Aeson stood up. "Has Helen told you there are powers in the ocean beyond Idis?"

She looked at him with interest. "How do you know about Idis?"

"Because I'm a messenger," he answered plainly.

"A messenger of *what*?" she asked.

"Just a messenger."

"I'm confused..."

"Look, Lorelei. I know what you are. You don't have to pretend with me."

"Know what, exactly?"

"That you're a siren. Helen told me before you moved down here."

Lorelei was shocked. She couldn't understand why Helen would have told Aeson that they were sirens.

"So you know what we are—what we do?"

He smirked, "Yeah, you could even say I help, in a way."

"What do you mean, you help?"

"Every group of sirens has a messenger. The messenger is responsible for the overall protection of their assembly and to defend them against outside forces. They also give the sirens instructions in regards to the calling. And for the Deleauxes, I'm their messenger."

"What kind of instructions?" she asked.

"We have premonitions," he said, "a limited sight to see when and where shipwrecks and deaths at sea are going to happen, how many people will die, all of that. I tell them what to expect so they know when to be ready and what to do."

"But what happened to me today? I heard the Song..."

"What are you talking about? Nothing happened today. I just saw you jump off the boat like a damn idiot. If it had been the calling, I would have seen it."

"How can you say nothing happened? I heard something and I saw the mist. It was making me sick and it just kept getting louder. That's the reason why I jumped. You didn't see any of it?"

Aeson stood up and towered over her, "Lorelei, tell me what you saw."

"After you left, I was just standing on the boat and watching the water. Everything seemed normal, but the sky started to change. It got darker and there was this sound—like scraping metal almost, it got louder and hurt my head. And the sea was glowing green. I know I've only seen it happen once before, but I thought it must be Idis. That noise, I couldn't stop myself—it wanted me out there."

Aeson paused to think. "Listen, Lorelei, not everything in the sea is good. Like I said, Idis isn't the only thing out there. The sea holds things that would try to destroy you—dark things. And that was something else. At least it couldn't have been Idis."

"It seemed so much like last time. I mean, I was scared because I was alone, but I was also scared about what would happen if I didn't go."

"I honestly can't say what it was. It could have been any number of things."

"So how am I supposed to know the difference?" she asked.

"If there's going to be a calling, I'll see it ahead of time. You'll know because I'll have told you to watch for it. And you're not to go out alone—not yet. You aren't ready, and I can't afford to lose any of my sirens. Now, you take it easy and I'm going to get us home."

"Okay," said Lorelei. She put her head back down on the pillow and Aeson wrapped her in another blanket. He left her to go back up to the deck, she heard the motor start, and they headed back to the mainland.

CHAPTER EIGHTEEN

"You feeling better?" asked Deidre, placing a mug and small teapot on Lorelei's bedside table.

"I feel fine. Actually, I feel great. Can I come downstairs yet?" Lorelei pleaded.

"Nope. The doctor says you need to rest a little longer. You don't just get hypothermia one day and pretend it didn't happen. Sorry."

Lorelei sat up in bed and poured herself a cup of tea. The truth was, she still felt weak, but she was tired of the round-the-clock care given her since the incident at Monomoy Island. She had told the doctor that she had slipped and fallen overboard, not wanting him to think that she had jumped in intentionally. Once back at the Deleaux's, Lorelei had told the others what had happened and Helen spent the last two days trying to determine what it was that Lorelei experienced.

"Are there any updates?" Lorelei asked.

"Helen was on the phone with Veronique Merchansons this morning. None of the sirens in Montreal have seen anything out of the ordinary lately. And nothing unusual in Virginia or the Southern coast, either. But Veronique does have a theory."

"Go on…"

"She thinks it might have been a banshee."

"A *banshee*?"

"It's only a theory, but she remembered a story her grandmother had told her once that sounded similar to what happened to you."

"Back up just a second. What exactly is a banshee?"

Deidre sat down on the bed beside Lorelei, "They're basically rogue sirens."

"Huh?"

"Every once in a while, a siren turns away from her family. She either gets pissed off and leaves, or simply decides to go it on her own. Most of them are just crazy old women who live solitary lives and don't do much harm, but every once in a while, one of them gets angry enough that they try to tempt fate. Banshees live outside the realm of Idis, but they still have their powers. It doesn't happen very often, but they've been known to terrorize entire towns, and they can get violently mean. The thing about the banshees—well, they aren't doing the work of the Fates anymore, but because they're separated from the Song, they literally go mad. An aggressive banshee usually believes she's doing the work of the Fates when she's busy killing people, but that's just because she's become so disconnected from reality."

"What would make a siren choose to leave her family?"

"Usually because they've had some sort of disagreement with the matriarch of their assembly. The eldest member of each family has the final say on all decisions, and some sirens have a difficult time living under the authority of another. We all know that someday we'll each have a turn to be in charge, and our whole life is spent learning and leading up to that day, so that when we finally are the head of the household, we'll make wise decisions and be able to teach the new sisters that join us. Personally, I think it sounds awful. Too much pressure."

"And a simple disagreement would be enough to make a siren turn her back on her whole life?" Lorelei asked.

"You'd be surprised. Some of us can be pretty hotheaded."

"And Veronique thinks one of these banshees is on the loose?"

"Maybe, but there's a problem with her theory," said Deidre. "There are no known banshees in this part of the world. Our area hasn't had any sirens leave the fold in over twenty years, and that one died eight years ago. If it really is a banshee, we have no idea who she is or why she's here. Or how she found you yesterday."

"So what are we going to do about it?"

"There's not really much we can do, at this point. Helen's waiting to hear back from the messengers—see if they saw anything. Until then, we just hold tight."

"That's so frustrating. What if she goes after someone else? I mean, it's a possibility that she could attack someone from town, right?"

"Sure, it's possible, but we don't even know if that's what happened to you. It could have been something entirely different. We just don't know yet."

"I could have sworn it was the Song, Deidre. The way it made me feel, the way it was pulling me toward the water. It was strong. I tried to resist, but it just got worse. I'm so stupid."

"You're not stupid, you're just young. And you still have a lot to learn. Whatever was coming after you yesterday had to have been evil, and evil things have a tendency to imitate the good. I probably would have done the same thing if I'd been there."

"The sound itself was different, though. It was deeper, almost menacing," said Lorelei. "It cut right through me. I only thought it was getting worse because I was being disobedient. That's why I jumped in the water."

"Well, at least you're safe now. And as soon as you're well, we're all going to devote more time to your training. We think it's time for you start doing the work soon."

"Really?" Lorelei asked, taken aback.

"We figure the more you know about your role as a siren, the less likely these little mishaps will be in the future."

"Obviously I'm not ready, not after what I did. I could never…"

"Will you stop it already?"

"Stop what?"

"Feeling sorry for yourself. I've never known anyone who insists on beating themselves up over trivial little things the way you do. No one is mad at you. This is not a reflection of your potential. It's over now. Time to move on." Irritated, Deidre stood up and walked toward the bedroom door, "And I will personally see to it that you will be ready. We all believe in you, and it's about time you showed a little confidence in yourself."

Deidre turned to leave and Lorelei quickly blurted, "Is Aeson still here?"

"No," said Deidre, "I think he's at the office. He didn't stick around long after he brought you home. Why?"

"Nothing really. I just wanted to say thanks."

"I'll let him know the next time I see him."

In her heart, Lorelei knew that Deidre was right. All of her fears and anxieties had only grown stronger because she felt so inept, but perhaps the day would come when all of this would be second nature to her. She promised herself that when her training started again she would give herself to it fully, unafraid of making mistakes.

The following day, Helen summoned Lorelei to meet her in the library. "You look much better today," she said as Lorelei approached.

"Thanks," Lorelei replied. "I take it the doctor told you I can get up now?"

"Yes, I'm happy to say he gave you a clean bill of health. Now that you're well, I'd like to start working with you again every day. I think it might help you understand yourself better if you know our history." Helen reached above her head and took a thick book bound in burgundy leather from the shelf. "Here we go," she said, opening the yellow-tinged volume. "These are the records of all the souls we have sent into the sea." Ornate lettering was scrawled across the pages listing dates, times, locations, and casualties. "It's important for us to keep a record, just to make sure nothing is missed. But this is also a written history of all the sirens who have served here. The earliest records we have in our possession date back to the 1600s, but we know that there were sirens here even before the British settled."

"Really? How do you know that?" asked Lorelei, her fingers brushing the old manuscript.

"The Wampanoag people have a legend about a creature of the sea. It was a woman who rose up from the ocean, could control the weather, and seduced men with her Song. She eventually lured their great hero, Maushop, away from land and keeps him bound underwater in a cave. Sound familiar? It is our understanding that this legend was the native people's attempt to try to understand the sirens that they had encountered. Certainly there must have been women who lived among the indigenous people that acted in this capacity, though if they organized themselves into collective groups like we do today—that we don't know."

"And where are our ancestors from?" Lorelei asked.

"The earliest records in America date back to around 1634. The two families of sirens in England, the Marburys and the Barretts, convened and sent two women, one from each household, to the New World. Anne and Mary settled in New England, along with their husbands," Helen flipped to the first page and pointed to the top. "They lived for several years in the Massachusetts Bay Colony before they, along with several others, were exiled to what is now Rhode Island in 1638, for being, shall we say, a bit too headstrong for their time. Our lineage can be traced back directly to Anne and Mary, and while their daughters and granddaughters scattered to various places throughout New England, we know that they remained associated through letters and diary entries. In the early 1780s, five of them came together and settled right here in Chatham. It wasn't until 1860 that they built this house and began to live as a group. That was when they took the name Deleaux, to bind themselves together as a sisterhood."

"And everything is in here? Every life they took?"

"Yes, we record it so we remember the lost. We must never forget that each soul that perished was a human being—a mother or father, son or daughter. These records are our tribute to the deceased." Helen took another volume off the shelf and thumbed through it until she found the page she was seeking. "Here, April 10th, 1963. It reads, 'Tragedy befell the USS Thresher, American naval submarine, 220 miles due east, the wreck was attended by Viviane, Serena, Lysithia, and Lucia Deleaux. The disaster took the lives of all on board, as the submarine quickly flooded before submerging to the ocean floor. This marks the first calling of Lucia Deleaux, daughter of Serena.' This was your grandmother's first time as a siren." Below that were listed the names of the 129 individuals who perished in the wreck. Lorelei gently ran her fingers over the names.

"Your grandmother was remarkable. She was always so calm under pressure and a gifted leader. When she transformed, her presence was ethereal, so graceful and enchanting—every last nuance, from the way she used her eyes to the way she sang was the perfect embodiment of a siren. Lucia guided me in my first calls, always patient and encouraging as I was learning. All I wanted was to live up to her example. I wish you could have known her."

"What happened to her?" Lorelei asked.

Helen closed her eyes and dropped her head. "My sister had too many burdens. There was a great deal of responsibility put upon her at an early age, and while she handled it for many years, there came a point when she couldn't shoulder the weight of it anymore. My sister, your grandmother, took her own life."

Lorelei head spun and she gasped, "I never knew."

"I think it's one of the reasons your mother never brought you out here after her death or told you about us. I don't think she could handle the memories associated with this place."

"When did she die?"

"Oh, you were just a toddler. It was not long after you had moved away, actually. Your mother came back for the funeral, but that was the last time I saw her." A single tear rolled down Helen's cheek. "I still miss my sister, but the first day you came out here, when you were standing on our porch, it was like seeing Lucia again. And it's not just the resemblance, but your mannerisms, your voice, it's as though she's here. I'm so happy you've come back to us."

Lorelei hugged Helen, "I'm glad, too."

"When I heard what happened to you out there, how we could have lost you, I couldn't believe what a fool I'd been. I should never have let you go out on the water by yourself."

"You couldn't have known," said Lorelei, "and I wasn't alone— I was with Aeson. Besides, he knows what we are and he told me he's supposed to protect us."

"That's true, but he's never had to protect us before. Aeson's only been our messenger for a little over a year, and nothing like this has ever happened to him yet. He wasn't expecting it."

"What *are* the messengers, exactly?" Lorelei asked.

"Essentially, the messengers give us our assignments. We don't have the ability to know when the Song will be calling us, or what we'll experience when we are called, but the messengers have the gift of foresight. They can sense it a few days before it ever happens. Aeson tells us exactly what is supposed to happen so we know how to focus our efforts. The fact that he didn't see you drown is proof in and of itself that you weren't intended to die. But something out there did wish you harm, Lorelei. Whether or not it meant to kill you, I don't know, but it wasn't good."

"It's something evil then? A banshee?"

"I can't say for sure if that's what it was or not, but you must understand, there are malevolent things in the water, Lorelei. As certainly as there is light, there is darkness. So Idis is the light, and the darkness is called Deimus. Each has its own Song and calling. Ordinarily they keep each other in balance; darkness itself is merely the absence of light, but there are times when the darkness can take on a life of its own, when it infringes on the light and overcomes it. A young siren could easily succumb to this kind of entity, unable to recognize it or defend herself. That's why I should never have let you go out there without one of us. You'll always be the most powerful, and yet also the most vulnerable, when you're on the water."

"Why didn't you tell me? If I had known there was something dangerous out there, I would have tried harder to resist it."

"I didn't think it was something you needed to worry about yet. The journey toward becoming a siren takes patience. You need time for your mind to wrap itself around each aspect of yourself before it truly understands, and frankly, you were already having a difficult time accepting it, so I didn't want to scare you any further. I regret now that I didn't tell you about this sooner. You had a right to know."

"So where do we go from here?"

"We're going to devote much more time to your training. I didn't want to overwhelm you at first, but I think this is the time we begin to focus more intently on your skills, starting with this." Helen hoisted a large book from the shelf and placed it in Lorelei's hands. "This is the Compendium, the collection of all of our songs. Every day you will study and work to memorize these." Lorelei opened the heavy tome and leafed through the pages. Much of it was in foreign languages; some of the music was scripted in square notation like Gregorian chants, while others looked more modern.

"The songs have different functions," said Helen. "Some are for producing a calming effect, some are meant to paralyze, there are several that enable you to cause slumber, and even some meant to seduce. You may not end up using them all, but it is important to build your repertoire. Think of these as the framework through which you allow the Song to sing through you." Lorelei turned the pages. There were pieces in the Compendium written for solo voice, with soaring glissandos, technical runs, and difficult high notes, not unlike the music she'd been accustomed to singing at the conservatory. Others were simpler, plaintive folk tunes, and she even found a few pieces that were meant to be sung in three- or four-part harmony.

"We will work on these every morning in the studio. I expect that you will put all of your energy into the study and memorization of these songs. The afternoons will be spent in functional application, putting theory into practice."

"And how do we do that, exactly?"

"You'll go into town and practice what you've learned until you're comfortable."

"You don't mean I'm actually going to try these out on people, do you?"

"Lorelei, our songs and skills will still have effect, even without the change. We cannot fully transform unless we are called, but we still have the power of influence over people. How will you know if you've mastered these skills unless you can demonstrate it on someone?"

The thought of it made Lorelei squeamish. She remembered her less-than-perfect attempt at seduction the night she was in Boston with Deidre and she wasn't inclined to relive that moment. Her face pinched up in disapproval.

"It's like being a hypnotist," said Helen. "You have to know what you're capable of before you perform on a bigger stage, and if you do it right, they won't remember a thing."

Lorelei placed the Compendium on the end table, and leafed through it, overwhelmed by the breadth of it all. "Where do you want me to start?"

"Here," Helen turned the well-worn pages until she found a page with a simple script and shape-note dictation. "This one is fairly straightforward, and useful in many applications." She lifted her chin, silver hair cascading over her shoulders, and closed her eyes. Her voice was brazen and forceful as the music poured from her.

Ancient magic resonated through Helen and filled the room, reverberating from the walls. Lorelei was shocked by the intensity of it, but more than anything, she ached to be able to harness that kind of power herself. "You have to feel it, deep within you, under your feet. You must be completely grounded in it. Here, stand up." Helen pushed Lorelei's shoulders back and widened her stance. She put her opened palm on Lorelei stomach, "Feel it here, and grab hold of the sound," Helen put two fingers right between Lorelei's eyes, "and sing here."

Lorelei held the Compendium in her hands and breathed deeply, then began to sing. The song was raw and unpolished; there was nothing distinctly beautiful about this type of singing, but it was as though the ground had moved under Lorelei's feet. It took a great deal of energy, but the music came out freely. She could feel it rising up in her; life and death comingled in her veins. This went against everything she'd ever been taught about singing—she let go of the rules to which she'd clung for so long. It was liberating. Unconcerned about proper form and technicality, she reveled in the Song that had finally found its place within her. Lorelei let the feeling overtake her body, and as she was consumed by the Song, she emerged a siren.

PART TWO

Come lovely and soothing Death,
Undulate round the world, serenely arriving, arriving,
In the day, in the night, to all, to each,
Sooner or later delicate Death.

When it is so—when thou hast taken them, I joyously sing the dead,
Lost in the loving, floating ocean of thee,
Laved in the flood of thy bliss, O Death.

    Walt Whitman, from "When Lilacs Last in the Dooryard Bloom'd"

CHAPTER NINETEEN

Tiny purple crocuses peeked their heads out from beneath the thin layer of snow and ice that still covered the ground outside the Deleaux home. In the drawing room, Lorelei Clark sat with her mind immersed in a song from the fourteenth century, a French *chant du memoire,* or song of remembrance. She planned to go into town later in the day and try it out on an unsuspecting bystander. The purpose of the song was to allow the listener to drift back to their fondest memories, to escape the current time and place, and to be completely immersed in a moment in time when they were at their happiest.

This was the fourth *chant du memoire* that Lorelei had committed to memory. The first time she had tried such a song on someone had been a disaster. She had sung the clerk at a jewelry store into such a wonderful memory that Lorelei couldn't get her to snap out of it. Calliope had to come to the shop and guide the poor woman back into reality. When the storekeeper came to her senses, she cried at being returned to her mundane existence. The other two times she had sung a *chant du memoire*, both had worked out well, and she felt confident that this new piece would also be successful. Each day the songs seemed to come easier. She found that the more she focused on the feelings the songs were meant to evoke, the tune and lyrics simply fell into place.

She glanced at the clock. If she left now and allowed herself thirty minutes to practice the song on someone in town, she could be back to the house in time for lunch. Certainly some lonely soul would be wandering the beach by the lighthouse. Lorelei placed a bookmark in the Compendium, pocketed her car keys, and walked toward the foyer to get her coat. As she opened the front door, the sunlight momentarily blinded her and it was a few moments before she saw Aeson's truck parked at the end of the driveway.

"Hey kiddo," he called out, "where you going?"

"To town," she replied. Ever since the incident in the fall, Aeson watched Lorelei like a hawk. He was always popping up unexpectedly, or nosily inquiring about her plans. She knew he blamed himself for what had happened that day, but it didn't make his near-constant intrusions any less annoying.

"Come inside for a minute, okay?" he said, walking past her and into the house.

"But I was just leaving..."

"It'll only be a minute. I'll meet you in the kitchen."

Lorelei rolled her eyes, but followed him inside nonetheless. He pulled a box of crackers from the cupboard. She plunked herself onto one of the bar stools.

"Want a cracker?" he held the box out toward her.

"No, thanks. Not hungry."

"Suit yourself," he said, between mouthfuls. Setting the box down, he brushed his hands off on his jeans and approached Lorelei. "There's not really a good way to ease into this, but you've got your first calling tomorrow."

Lorelei's stomach dropped. She had spent months preparing for this, but hearing the words from Aeson sent her head spinning, as though it was disconnected from her body. The confidence she had felt this morning had all but vanished.

"Tomorrow morning, southeast of Long Island, the crew of the K-Land *Australia* will be heading toward Port Newark. There will be fifteen fatalities. Of those, six of them will die on impact, but the remaining will suffer injuries or freezing conditions in the water and will meet their end with the help of the sirens. And you will be responsible for taking lives."

"By... myself?"

"You won't be alone. The others will be there, but obviously, they'll be busy as well. You'll sing to two separate men, and they'll pass on from this world. Helen and the others already know, but I wanted to tell you in person."

"I'm not ready... I mean, I've been working really hard, but I don't think I'm ready to actually sing yet—not on a real call where people are going to die—not yet."

"Believe me, if I had any say in the matter, you wouldn't be going tomorrow, but ready or not, now is the time. You wouldn't be called if you couldn't handle the job."

Lorelei realized what he said was true. Aeson touched her gently on the shoulder, his eyes scanning hers for a reaction. "Listen, it won't be that bad. Really. You just need to go, and everything will fall into place. Once you're there, you'll be a natural."

Lorelei smiled at him and nodded. He pulled her in close and wrapped his arms around her, and she responded, her hands reaching up his back and her cheek resting on his shoulder. She was surprised at how comforting his presence was at that moment; the warmth of another human being stopped her head from spinning and grounded her within her body once again.

"When am I going to stop being afraid?" she asked.

He let go of her and said with a smirk, "Maybe a little fear isn't so bad, if it keeps you from doing something reckless like you did out at Monomoy…"

"Yeah, I know. I don't think I ever really apologized to you for what happened that day. Or thanked you properly for jumping in after me."

"It was my own fault for leaving you by yourself. Just be smart tomorrow, and do whatever Helen tells you to do, no questions asked, okay?"

Lorelei nodded her understanding before Aeson tousled her hair and left her alone in the kitchen. She took off her coat, threw it on one of the kitchen chairs, and ran into the music room. The Compendium lay on the piano. She paged through the great book, fingers running over the music, and shockingly, Lorelei found that she knew, or was at least familiar with, more songs than not. Even more surprising was her realization that she had committed almost half of them to memory; she certainly had the tools, and even some experience in their use. The next hour was spent with her head buried in the Compendium, mouthing the words and humming the melodies that had been passed down from generation to generation in her family, so preoccupied that she didn't notice Helen had entered the room until she felt a hand on her shoulder. Helen sat beside her on the piano bench, took the book from Lorelei, and closed it on her lap.

The side of Helen's mouth rose in a half smile; her features, weathered with age, were still soft and beautiful.

"Tomorrow," Lorelei whispered.

"I know," said Helen. "And you're ready. You're already prepared. This isn't a test you can study for, so let's put this down, for now. Come and help me in the kitchen, okay?"

Lorelei spent the afternoon making pies with Helen, recipes she recognized from her childhood. The act of baking—folding pie dough, rolling it out into perfect circles, simmering tender blueberries, forming criss-cross lattices over the tops of cinnamon-flecked apples—it's simple domesticity, took Lorelei's mind off of the coming events. Helen's hands worked with ease and efficiency, the same hands that had likely taught Lorelei's own mother how to make these very pies.

The day passed quickly and as the sun began its descent, Lorelei sipped a mug of chamomile tea and stared out her bedroom window at the ocean beyond the cliffs. It seemed so peaceful, but she knew that somewhere on that water a group of sailors were spending the last night of their lives under the stars. She felt a sting of pity and even a sense of helplessness in knowing that she would be there, but it didn't scare her like it had before. Lorelei felt tempted to pray for them, but they were already too far gone, beyond even God's hands now.

The silhouettes of four women stood in a straight row on the beach, their naked bodies reflecting the morning sun's soft, pink light. No words were exchanged between them as they walked into the gentle waves on the edge of the cove; the only sound was of the surf splashing on the sand and the occasional cry of a seagull. The women sank farther into the water until they were chest deep in it. While they sang, the eldest among them stretched her hands up and huge spirals of fog poured in from the sea, glowing and coiling around their figures.

Lorelei felt a pull from within the cove and below her. She forced herself to relax and let it take her. Water rushed over her head as she was pressed down, until she was supine, floating just above the ocean floor. The icy-cold water of the sea stabbed her and her skin stretched, like it was being pulled away from her flesh, but Lorelei didn't resist it, she only closed her eyes and gritted her teeth until the pain subsided. Once she had gained control of her body, she took a deep breath and the water filled her lungs, but it didn't sting. The ocean swirled as her brilliant green eyes rose out of the water, piercing through the gray mist that still enveloped her. As she waited for the others, Lorelei placed her hands on the sea and lifted them up to form an orb of water that hovered and spun beneath her palms, a trick she had finally mastered after weeks of practice. Finally the others appeared and she drew close to them, their pearl-like skin matching her own.

Helen nodded at them and without saying a word, they plunged back into the cold. Lorelei angled her hands toward her feet and pushed the water away until she gained momentum. Together, they sped through the opening at the entrance of the cove. Around the shoals and sandbars they darted, focused on finding the target they pursued. Lorelei kept Helen in her sights and tried to mimic her movements, adjusting her hips and legs to change her direction as they flew amidst the water. Dappled sunlight shimmered through the blue sea creating a beautiful world of light and shadow.

Eventually they reached the place where they had been summoned and Helen slowed her pace. The others followed suit; they surfaced together, faces toward the sky until they had stopped completely and were perched in the ocean, the water holding them at their hips. There was no shoreline to be seen, only miles and miles of water, the sunlight glinting like jewels. Calliope pointed to the open sea, but as Lorelei squinted, she could just make out a speck of a vessel in the distance. "We'll wait," said Helen. The women stayed where they were as the ship slowly approached them, growing steadily the closer it came. The mist, hazy and glowing green, still circled around them.

The ship was massive, a large blue behemoth that glided through the ocean with ease. Lorelei could see containers the size of trucks stacked on the deck, row after row, looming many stories over the water. The gigantic cargo ship was as long as three football fields, the name of the vessel emblazoned in white letters on its side: K-Land *Australia.* In the middle of the ship stood a tall white tower at the top of which was a small space enclosed by windows. Orange lifeboats hung from the sides of the tower.

Helen motioned them forward and they headed toward the vessel. She stopped. "Now," she whispered, "be ready." Everything was quiet. There was anticipation amongst the four of them and Lorelei clenched her fists anxiously. The ship continued to solemnly slip through the water; its magnitude seemed impervious to disaster.

A popping noise resonated from within vessel, like loud gunfire inside the hull. A moment later, a fireball erupted from one of the containers beside the tower. A rush of searing heat blazed against Lorelei's face. Aboard the vessel, three men climbed up on deck toward the fire. The tallest one pointed toward the stern and yelled at the other two. Another explosion sent all of them flying onto their backs. They rose to their feet and scrambled in the other direction. The fire swallowed up the containers around it, shooting sparks into the air like fireworks. Beside the fire, three stacks of containers started to tip forward, leaning into the tower and causing it to buckle. The ship belched smoke and row upon row of containers caught fire in succession. A huge explosion ripped a giant crack through the stern of the ship. The sound of the metal ripping apart roared through Lorelei's ears. On the deck, two sailors were trying to untie one of the lifeboats when a brown container broke loose from its stack and rolled down, crushing them. Lorelei winced.

Another row of containers tumbled overboard and the crack in the hull grew wider. The ship's bow tipped upwards just slightly, and a sailor tumbled off the side of the deck where the containers had just fallen. "Deidre, go," said Helen. Deidre slipped away to where the man was holding onto the edge of one of the containers in the water. She bent over him, brushed the hair out of his eyes, and began to sing. He looked up at her like he had never been happier in his entire life.

By now, the hull was almost completely split in half and the front end of the vessel rocked forward violently. The ship's tower leaned back and fell into the hole that was now separating the front of the ship from her stern. The glass from the windows in the observation deck shattered and there were screams as several men fell through the windows into the water below. Helen nodded at Calliope and she departed. Lorelei shivered when she heard the Song, pulsing from below her and moving up her body. *I can do this,* she thought. *Be strong.*

Two of the sailors had successfully lowered the second lifeboat, and were lucky enough to abandon the flaming wreckage, paddling away from the ship as fast as they were able. The vessel creaked again and the last row of containers on the deck careened over the edge. A man slid off the ship after them, his legs flailing about as he fell into the icy water.

"Lorelei, I want you to go to that one," said Helen. "He's dying and he needs you. You can do this, right?"

Lorelei nodded. Her heart pounded in her chest and she turned to face the fiery monstrosity. She moved through the water with ease, nearing the smoking vessel and the man whose life would soon be gone. The man floated in his life vest, but as Lorelei approached, she could tell that he was badly burned. Half of his face was melted—the flesh stripped away to reveal the muscle and bone beneath the skin. One of his arms was missing from the elbow down, and his blood blossomed like crimson flowers in the water around him. He was screaming in pain as she reached him. Her eyes welled at the sight of this man—broken, bleeding, and alone. More than anything, she just wanted to stop his pain.

The mist rose up and held him at her eye level. She put her arm on his shoulder. "Hush," she whispered, her lips against his ear, "I'm with you." He stopped screaming long enough to look at her and she began to sing to him. Her voice floated above the chaos and inferno that was blasting above them. Tears fell from her eyes as his pain left his body. He looked comforted—happy even. At this moment everything made sense. The siren sang her song for love—to end suffering for the hurting, dying soul. Lorelei changed her tune and sang of a land of rest, where men neither toiled nor suffered. Her voice cradled him gently. He smiled, closed his eyes, and took his last breath. Lorelei choked back a sob, knowing that he was gone. In a strange way, she was filled with peace.

A container bobbed beside the vessel. A voice cried out from behind the floating container. The Song called to her, pulled her toward the voice. When she found him, he was clinging to an empty keg that was floating next to the ship. His shirt was burned in places and in tatters around his torso. He looked up at her and gasped. Lorelei realized she must look both beautiful and terrifying. She didn't want him to sense any fear in her face, so she tried to force a small, reassuring smile. It didn't seem to work. The color had drained from his face and his teeth were chattering. The young man tried to swim away, still grasping the keg, but he didn't get far. Lorelei could tell his muscles were clenching from the cold because his movements were wild and unproductive. She moved around the keg until she was floating in front of him, face to face.

Lorelei brushed his cheek with the back of her hand. "Quiet," she told him, her eyes piercing into his. "Do not be afraid." Still he struggled. She took a breath and pulled him toward her, the mist lifting his body up above the water. His hair was dark and wet, he had a prominent scar on one cheek, and though his face was framed by a strong jaw, there was softness in his chocolate-brown eyes. He was young, probably just a few years older than she was. Lorelei was suddenly aware of her own nakedness; she blushed and used her hands to pull a curtain of water in front of her chest to cover herself. She struggled to think of what to sing, but decided to put him in a euphoric state by singing an old English ballad called "The Isles of Bliss." It was short and sweet, sung to create a mood of ecstasy and joy, but when she had finished, the terror remained in his eyes. She tried again, this time with the *chant du memoire* that had worked so well on that clerk in town. Still nothing. He screamed for help and tried to push away from her. *Another song,* she thought, *a song for the drowning.*

Hear the soft slumber of night,
Her melody taking to flight,
All that was hers, will be hers again,
Mortal we all, mere shadows of men.
Slip far beneath, under the deep,
Night cradles all in their last sleep.

The man looked confused, but he didn't seem any less afraid. Nothing was working. *This man could live,* the thought fluttered through her mind. He had stopped struggling and was using all his energy to shiver. His lips were blue, but he held on to life. She looked into his eyes. He was pleading with her, desperate to stay alive. "Please," he said, "help me."

Lorelei knew she didn't have any options. She thought she had come to terms with her role in all of this. Her job was simple, really, but now that she was faced with the reality of the situation, she was having second thoughts. He was going to die soon, of that much she was sure, and his death would not be an easy one if she couldn't find a way to connect with the Song. This was his fate, but Lorelei had lost all resolve to help him perish. She couldn't look at his eyes—those eyes that begged her for mercy, for some small act of compassion—without feeling guilty. And yet, that was the problem, she didn't believe he *should* die. It seemed like such a waste. He likely had a family, someone who loved him waiting for him at home. Even if he didn't, he was young and strong and wanted to live. A vision of her father came to mind, blood pooling around his body, the life fading from his eyes. Lorelei remembered the desperation she'd had when he died, the feeling that there was nothing she could do. She couldn't save her father, but she had to save this man. At that moment, Lorelei didn't care about anything but him, not about destiny or duty, just about this man, this *life*, whose fate she held in her hands. At that moment, Lorelei knew it was her fate to change his.

A shrill noise pierced her ears. She was about to go against her duty, and Idis was trying to pull her back. The sound grew in intensity and pulsated in her head and down her spine, so loud that it seemed like it could split her in half. Lorelei fought back against the noise; she grimaced, and her body trembled, vibrating as though the sound were moving through her until at last, it broke. Like a sonic boom, the water shot away from her, creating a giant tide moving away in all directions. Lorelei's skin glowed with a soft, white light, and the waves circled around her until the ocean was calm once again and the noise had stopped ringing in her ears.

Lorelei reached out for the sailor. She grabbed his forearm and pulled him toward her. His skin was as cold as ice. She remembered that feeling all too well. He looked down where her hand met his arm. "What are you doing?" he choked.

"I'm not going to let you die." His body was shaking so hard she had trouble holding on to him. "Put your arm around my shoulders."

"I'm not letting go." His other arm still clung to the keg.

"Do it. Now." Without another word, he did as she said and wrapped his free arm around Lorelei's shoulders. Lorelei took his right arm with her left hand. She turned away from the ship and swam from the flames.

The two men who had made it onto the lifeboat were several hundred feet away, but getting this man to them was her best chance for keeping him alive. He was so heavy that she had difficulty keeping him above water. It would be so much easier if she could swim below the surface, but he wouldn't survive under there. Lorelei moved as fast as she could, dragging him being her. As long as she could still feel his breath on her neck, she knew he was still alive.

Her muscles burned and she gasped for air, but she managed to keep moving ahead. The space between them and the lifeboat was becoming shorter as she fought to get away from the burning ship. She strained against the weight of him; her free arm sliced through the water and her legs kicked powerfully, using every ounce of energy she had left to pull him the final distance. Lorelei thought she heard a whisper in her ear, "Thank you."

The orange lifeboat bobbed on the water in front of them. Upon reaching it, Lorelei took the man's arm from around her neck and placed his hands on a rope that hung from the edge of the boat. "A little help," he called out, his voice small and shaking. Lorelei ducked to the side, out of their sight.

The two men aboard the raft spotted him hanging onto the rope and immediately rushed to assist him. The bigger of the two reached over him and yanked him up by his belt, and together they were able to pull him to safety. They laid him down and took several blankets out of the emergency supply kit. While the smaller man worked to get him warm, the other turned his attention back to a CB radio. They had issued a distress call and he was talking to the captain of another ship in the vicinity. A flare illuminated the sky.

"My god Tyler, you must be the luckiest man alive," said the larger man.

"It wasn't luck," Tyler replied.

Lorelei looked back at the vessel. By now, only a small part of the ship was still above water, the rest of it was already submerged. She dove under the water, her movements easy and graceful. Within moments she was back at the site of the wreck where the other sirens were looking at her. The mist about them arced with electricity. Helen's expression was sullen, perhaps even a bit angry. Lorelei held her hands up over her face and covered her eyes, the sudden realization of her actions now apparent.

"What were you doing, just now?" Helen asked.

Lorelei was at a loss for words. She furrowed her brow and looked down in shame.

Calliope's nostrils flared and she yelled loudly through gritted teeth. "You stupid girl!" Her hand extended up behind her, ready to strike, but Deidre grabbed her arm before she could let it fly.

"No," said Deidre. "This isn't the time for that. Many people have lost their lives today and we must honor that. We need to go home now."

"I'll take care of this right now. I'll do it myself." Calliope's shoulders heaved with each angry breath. She turned toward the small lifeboat, but Helen reached out to stop her.

"It's too late," said Helen, "There's no way to do anything about it now without more casualties."

"I wasn't thinking—" Lorelei began.

"Yes, that much is clear," Helen said firmly. "You weren't thinking. You were acting on a foolish desire to be a hero, and in the process, you've broken the most important rule we have. You do not interfere with fate. There will be repercussions, Lorelei. I really thought you would have known better."

Lorelei felt like a fool, humiliated by Helen's disappointment. Even though she knew she had a made a mistake, in her heart, she was glad she had saved him. This man, Tyler, would get another chance at life because she had felt pity. Why should she be ashamed for doing what she knew to be right? The four women submerged into the water as the last remnant of the K-Land *Australia* slipped under the sea. They moved like ghosts through the abyss, and Lorelei Clark followed behind them, fearing what awaited her on land.

CHAPTER TWENTY

The three days since the shipwreck were miserable for Lorelei. She had sought refuge in her room, afraid of what the others would say to her. During the day, the house was quiet, but in the evenings, she could hear their voices through the vents, hushed whispers where she was certain her name was mentioned several times. Once night fell and she was sure they were asleep, she would sneak out of her bedroom to gather food, and so had been living on potato chips, apples, and beef jerky since her self-imposed exile began. She had started composing letters to Helen on several occasions to try to explain her actions, but had abandoned each effort. There was no way to justify her behavior; and as good as her intentions were, she had failed at the task she had been assigned and had acted irresponsibly. Guilt and shame—those nagging little words appeared in her thoughts from time to time, but more so because she expected that she *should* be feeling remorse, not that she actually was. In fact, Lorelei still felt that her actions were, in a sense, noble. Her fear of confronting the Deleauxes became more about her inability to apologize for what she had done than facing their anger.

Lorelei had thought about running away, but there was no place for her to go. She could go home perhaps, but what would she tell her mother? Certainly by now her mother must have discovered that she hadn't been at school for quite some time, and she had a suspicion that her mother might have an inclination as to where she had been living the last few months. She knew Helen communicated with her mother periodically, and as she hadn't received any phone calls expressing concern over whether or not she were alive, it was most likely that her mother had bitterly resigned herself to the knowledge that Lorelei had left school without so much as consulting her. An enraged Cassandra Clark was far more frightening than living in silence among the sirens.

It was on this evening, the third night after her failed summoning, that Aeson's truck pulled up in the driveway. From her bedroom window she saw him jump out, brush his hands on his jeans, and saunter up to the house. She wanted to talk to him, to ask him if maybe there was a possibility that what he had foreseen had been wrong. If only it were, this schism with the others would come to an end. Unfortunately, the most she could do was listen to more half-muttered conversations making their way up through the ducts to her bedroom. It was infuriating to know she was being talked about without being able to hear the exact details of the conversation. When she couldn't take it anymore, Lorelei wrapped herself in a duvet and paced along the balcony, watching the ocean from her tower.

The sun was setting and the wind picked up, biting at her cheeks. Dark clouds were forming to the west and the smell of rain was already in the air. Lorelei went back inside and lay down on her bed. She was going to go crazy if she had to spend another day in here. There was a sharp knock on her door. "Yes?" she asked, tentatively.

"It's Deidre. Can I come in?"

"Sure," Lorelei said. The door squeaked as it opened and Deidre stood motionless in the doorframe. There was an uncomfortable silence. Lorelei rolled to her side and sat up on the edge of the bed, blankets draped around her shoulders. "Did you need something?"

"They asked me to come get you. Would you come downstairs?" Deidre wasn't her usual, happy self. She was wearing plain black pants and a cream sweater, hardly any makeup, and her hair was a bit frizzy. Her eyes darted around the room, but she wouldn't look at Lorelei directly.

Lorelei's stomach tensed. "Yes, fine. I'll be down in a minute."

"Okay, I'll tell them you're coming," said Deidre. She turned around and left.

Lorelei took a deep breath. Of course she would have to face them eventually. Now was as good a time as any, she supposed. She pulled her hair back into a tight bun and put on some blush and lip gloss. Steadying herself, Lorelei put on a fake smile and made her way down to the living room where the others were waiting for her. Helen's was not the warm, gentle presence that she had known. The whites of her eyes were tinged pink and her lips had gathered into a worried pucker. She sat in the plush highback chair beside the fireplace and Deidre stood behind her. As Lorelei entered, Calliope approached her from where she had been standing by the windows.

"Glad you could join us," Calliope's words were icy. "Come and sit." She motioned to the large chair beside the sofa. Lorelei was compelled to do as she was told. Calliope picked up the remote control from the coffee table and turned on the television. The evening news lit up the screen and all eyes in the room were focused on the reporter, a pretty young woman with perfect, shiny black hair.

"Tonight's story," said the reporter, "is a story of hope and survival amidst improbable odds. As the container ship, the K-Land *Australia*, was making her transatlantic voyage back from Rotterdam, undeclared explosive cargo ignited, literally tearing the ship apart within minutes. The crew of American sailors suffered great losses. Fourteen members of the crew perished in the sea." She stopped speaking and the pictures of the sailors who had died scrolled across the screen, with their names and ranks underneath their photos. Lorelei recognized the fourth man on the screen as the first man that she had comforted in death. Ronald J Cooper. Lorelei felt a twinge in her throat as a tear fell down her face.

"Only three of the bodies have been recovered," the reporter continued. "Some will be lost to the sea forever, but they will never be forgotten in the hearts and minds of those they left behind. And yet, despite the news of this devastating disaster, there is another story of the three men who lived. With us today are the survivors of the tragedy at sea, Mitch Jordan, Barry Evans, and Tyler Ceyeks. Gentlemen, welcome."

The camera panned to three men who were sitting at the news desk beside her. Lorelei fixed on the face of the youngest. She had dreamt of that face every night since she had returned. Her dreams had been images of his face, slipping under the water, his eyes cold and dead. She would awake from the dream panicked and covered in sweat, and would tell herself that it wasn't real. He had lived. And to prove it, here he was on network television. He was very handsome, especially now; for someone who had come so close to death, he looked particularly healthy.

"So tell us, what were you thinking when the explosion happened? How did you react so quickly?"

"Well, Barry and I were in one of the little rooms below deck looking over the manifest and load plan when we heard a huge bang," said the smaller man who was half bald and wearing glasses. "We rushed up to deck and there was a tower of smoke coming from some of the containers. Then the bridge fell. It was blocking the way through to the rest of the crew. We were able to get to one of the lifeboats. There weren't any other men on that side of the ship, so when she started to break apart, we lowered the raft into the water. We called out to see if anyone else could get to our life boat, but we didn't hear any answers, so we started rowing away from the ship. We didn't know what was going to blow next."

"That must have been terrifying," the reporter feigned surprise. "What happened next?"

The other man, a rough looking fellow with a patchy beard, answered in a thick Boston accent, "We didn't know if some of the other guys had made it onto another life boat or not, but when we were a safe distance away, we started to radio for help. I finally caught the captain of a little local operation on the radio, when Mitch here sees a hand on the side of our life boat and hears ol' Tyler calling up for help. So we heave him in, and he's cold as ice. And we have no idea how in the name of God Almighty he managed to swim from that wreck all the way out to where we was. It was a real miracle."

"Tyler, do you remember anything from that day? How did you manage to make it so far and in such rough conditions?"

The camera zoomed in on Tyler's face. He looked straight into the lens and answered, "I didn't swim out there by myself. There was a mermaid. She saved me."

The other two men chuckled halfheartedly. "That's what he keeps saying," said the bearded man, "but we didn't see any mermaid. I think the cold water left him a little touched in the head."

"So there you have it," said the reporter, "a miracle on the sea, with a little help from... a mermaid. Keep your eyes open. You never know when you might see one. Back to you, Charles."

"What a fool," said Calliope. A bolt of lightning lit up the sky from the window behind her and raindrops began to fall. She turned off the television, sat down, and faced Lorelei, "Do you have any idea what you did? Do you realize the damage you've done?"

"No, I don't. I helped someone. I don't understand what's wrong with that." Lorelei replied.

"That's the problem—you don't have any respect for what we do. We have been given a sacred responsibility. Our job is not to *question* the call, but to be obedient and to act as the sirens that we are. We're not here to save lives. Our *only* job is to move people from life into death."

"But have any of you actually ever challenged it? If you could save a life, why wouldn't you? I know some people are going to die no matter what, but what I can't get my head around is how you could look at a person and not have one ounce of sympathy for them, not a single moment where you think to yourself, *what am I doing?* It doesn't have to be like this."

"Believe me Lorelei, I've had those moments," said Helen meekly. "It's what makes it so difficult. Do you think we haven't shed tears for the dead?"

"I still don't understand why it was so wrong," said Lorelei.

"You've violated the most important rule that we have," said Calliope. "You don't interfere with fate. That is not your place. What the Fates have willed, you must act upon. If you can't abide by that, then you are not fit to be a siren."

SERENADE

"That's not fair," Deidre interjected. "She made a mistake. We've all made mistakes. You aren't going to shun her for one mistake, are you?"

"Of course not," Calliope replied, "not if she makes it right."

"And how am I supposed to do that?" Lorelei asked.

A crash of thunder shook the house and Calliope picked up an old leather book. Lorelei recognized it as the book that Helen had shown her the day she explained their family's history. Calliope opened the book to the last page of writing and handed it to Lorelei. "Look there," she said, "Only fourteen names. There should be fifteen. You must fix this little discrepancy."

Lorelei jerked her head back as if she had smelled something foul. "Are you asking me to kill him?"

"I'm not asking you. I'm telling you you're going to make this right. That man's name will be on this list. He should not be alive. Least of all, he shouldn't be telling the world he was rescued by a *mermaid*, of all things."

Lorelei shook her head and closed the book. She stood up. "I don't care. What's done is done. I'm not going to *kill* someone just because you think I should."

"You can't run from fate, Lorelei," said Helen. "Neither can he. I hate to say it, because I know how hard this will be for you, but Calliope's right. That man's mortal life was supposed to have ended out at sea, and you're the one who should have helped to extinguish it. Terrible things have happened to those who tempt the Fates."

"Really? Like what?" asked Lorelei, indignant.

"Your grandmother," said Helen. "She broke the rules once."

Lorelei was stunned. After all she'd heard about Helen's sister, how perfect she was—the very model of a siren. She couldn't imagine the woman Helen so admired would disobey the call of the Song.

"The consequences were severe for her, and led her to take her own life." Helen looked down, and for the first time in three days, Lorelei was confronted with true remorse. It was clear now why Helen was so disappointed in her. She had been responsible for Lorelei's teaching, and here she was, following in the footsteps of her lost sister.

"I'm sorry, Helen. I didn't know." Lorelei lowered her gaze.

"I've said before that you and she are very much alike. In many ways, that's a wonderful thing, but she was too impulsive and she acted recklessly. I would hate to see you make the same mistake and end up like she did."

"I would never do that," said Lorelei, "I promise."

"It isn't just about you," said Aeson. He ran his hand through his blond hair and approached her. "This could impact people you don't even know. The fate of everyone on Earth is woven together; you pull on one loose thread and everything else can unravel. This could have consequences that even I can't foresee."

"I don't really understand how saving this one person could make that much of a difference."

"You're not seeing the big picture," hissed Calliope. "If you change one person's fate, it will affect the fates of many more; it throws our world off balance, even so far as to create natural disasters—earthquakes, floods, famines—until the balance is restored. Do you want to be responsible for that?"

She felt tiny, small, and insignificant. *What if they're right?*

"I can't do it. I tried, I really did, but it didn't work. He just wouldn't die. I couldn't help it."

"You have to remember, it's not about what *you* do," said Helen, gently, "you're merely the vessel for the Song. You have to let go of yourself, and the Song will manifest itself in you. All you have to do is get him to water, and let it do the rest."

"I won't do it. Singing to someone who is dying is totally different than leading someone who's perfectly fine to their death. That's wrong."

"Fine," snarled Calliope. "If you won't do it, I will. In fact, that's what I've wanted to do since this happened, but Helen thought we ought to give you the chance to correct your mistake on your own since you were the one who ought to have taken him. It's a pity, because I'm sure you would have made it easier on him. I have no problem killing him on land. There are many ways to kill a man."

"What? No!" Lorelei was aghast. She turned to Helen, "She can *do* that?"

"It's certainly not what I'd prefer," said Helen, "but given the choice, if you're not willing to do it, I will allow Calliope to go in your place."

"I agree," said Aeson. "None of us wants to be in this situation, but it needs to be done. You have to make a decision. If you're not up for the job, we'll have to make other arrangements."

Lorelei's head was spinning, like she had been smacked in the face. Her heart raced inside her chest; anger and helplessness clouded her vision.

"That's no decision!" she yelled. "That's an ultimatum! It's not fair!"

"Well, *my dear*," said Calliope, flourishing her hand, "you put yourself in this situation. If you had done what you were supposed to do, we wouldn't be having this discussion, would we?"

Lorelei began to hyperventilate. She felt herself slipping, her body numb. Deidre hurried to her side and put her arm around

Lorelei's waist. "Come on," she whispered, "let's go. Let's get out of here."

Lorelei was breathing erratically as Deidre guided her out of the room. From behind her, she heard Helen say, "That was too harsh. You didn't need to put it so indelicately."

Calliope's voice struck back, "I'm not about to coddle her. She thinks she can take whatever she wants, just like her mother. Let's only hope what was said had the desired effect—and if so, the end will justify the means."

The front door swung open and Deidre ushered Lorelei outside. Though they were somewhat sheltered by the porch, the rain blew toward them. Lorelei closed her eyes and tried to keep from crying but she could still hear Calliope's voice in her head. *If you won't do it, I will.* Tears welled up in her eyes and rolled down her cheek.

"It's going to be okay," Deidre said. Lorelei's breath came in uncontrollable shudders. She wiped her eyes on the back of her hand and sat up a bit. She desperately wanted Deidre to tell her there was some other option, some way for her to get around this and let Tyler live, but the silence was only punctuated by thunder and howling wind. Deidre's beautiful eyes looked pained, but she didn't offer any consolation. "What are you going to do?"

"I don't know," said Lorelei. She sighed deeply. "What should I do?"

Deidre paused for a long time before she answered. "I think you should go."

"Really?" Lorelei asked. The dark tempestuous storm swirled around the house and roared in her ears.

"I do. I know this isn't what you want to hear from me, but I think it's better than the alternative. I think you would be more… *kind.* If you really had compassion for him, you'd do it yourself.

The lives of hundreds of people could be in jeopardy until the balance is restored, and Calliope knows that."

Lorelei pictured herself singing to Tyler in the water, his eyes locking with hers, pleading. She had risked everything to save him, and it all backfired. He was going to die anyhow and there was nothing she could do about it. "You don't think she'd really do it, do you?"

"Calliope? Oh yeah, she'll do it. She takes this all very seriously. They've been fighting you know—Helen and Calliope. She doesn't think Helen's fit to be matriarch anymore. If you don't go, Calliope will see it as a sign of weakness in both you and Helen. She'll go just to prove her point, and as angry as she is right now, it's just a job for her—it won't be pretty."

Lorelei's hair was moist with rain and her eyes were red and swollen. She sat up and looked at Deidre. "I can't do it, Dee. Not any of this. I don't have it in me to watch people die. I thought I was ready, but I'm not. It's too hard."

"I wish I could say it would get easier, but it never really does. This isn't the life I would have chosen for myself, either; it chose me. And it chose you, too. And like it or not, this is your responsibility. This man is your responsibility."

"I know, but I wish there was another way," Lorelei's voice was shaky.

"Me too, sweetie," Deidre gave Lorelei a squeeze around her shoulders. "Let's go inside, okay?"

Lorelei wiped the hair from her face and nodded. Helen and Aeson approached them. Helen's face was creased with worry. "Where's Calliope?" Deidre asked.

"She left to go pack," said Aeson. "She doesn't think you're going to go."

Helen grasped both of Lorelei's hands in her own, "It shouldn't have to be like this, but I'm asking you to do this for me. It would be the most merciful thing you could do for him. Go and set things right. *Please.*" Seeing Helen beg, a woman ordinarily so dignified and noble, Lorelei realized that her inaction was tearing the family apart. "The power that you have is a gift. It can, and should, be used for good. Remember the other man that you helped? Or even your own father? When it was their time to die, you gave them peace. I know you're capable. This isn't a game, it is your duty."

"I can't—" Lorelei started.

"Yes, you can," said Helen firmly. "You're a Deleaux. This is what you were born to do. He should have died peacefully, with your help, and you took that from him. If Calliope finds him, he won't have that. I need you to really think about the choice you're making, because this is the only chance you're going to have to prove that you can handle this responsibility and fulfill your own destiny."

Lorelei felt lost. She wanted so badly for them to just listen to her, to understand that she had already made the right choice, at least what her heart had told her was the right choice, but everyone else felt just as strongly that Lorelei had made the wrong decision in saving Tyler. All the things Helen had taught her about the Song, the call, and Idis—*if fate really wanted him dead, he'd be dead, right?* And yet, the sadness in Helen's eyes reminded Lorelei of what she had said about her grandmother. If the consequences Lucia had suffered by going against fate were bad enough to make her take her own life, perhaps the consequences of Lorelei's own actions would be more far-reaching than she imagined. Rain pelted the windows, furiously beating against the glass; nature itself was avowing its disapproval.

"I'll go," she whispered at first, trying to convince herself. "I'll go." The front door burst open with a gust of wind that sent rain pouring in. Deidre pushed the door shut with force. Lorelei opened the closet door and took out her coat.

"I don't want you driving in this weather," said Helen. "You can leave in the morning."

"If I don't go now, I'll lose my nerve." Lorelei pulled her keys out of her pocket. "Where do I find him?"

"Port Elizabeth," said Aeson, "New Jersey. Go to the union hall and they should be able to help you find him. You can borrow the GPS out in my truck."

"You're going, are you?" Calliope had suddenly appeared on the grand staircase behind them, her right hand gracefully poised on the banister. She looked down at Lorelei, raven hair cascading over her shoulders.

"Yes," replied Lorelei curtly, "but I'm not going for *you*. I'm going to let him have an honorable death. You aren't going to touch a single hair on his head."

"You're doing the right thing," she said solemnly. "I'm sorry it's come to this and I know you probably think I'm a monster, but someone needed to take care of this. It was your actions that were going to force my hand to do something I didn't want to do either. It's not only in your best interest, but it's for the sake of all of us."

"Do you want me to come with you?" Deidre asked.

"No," Lorelei answered. "You're right. I have to do this alone."

"Be careful," said Helen. She kissed Lorelei's forehead.

"I will be." Lorelei hugged Deidre tightly and pulled the hood up over her head. She followed Aeson outside into the storm. He led her to his truck and handed her the GPS. They ran to her car and he opened the door for her. Through the rain, he said something she couldn't hear.

"What?" she yelled.

"I don't want anything to happen to you," he said. "Call me if you need anything." Lorelei got in the car. Aeson shut the door and put his palm up on the window. The rain dripped down his brow and fell over his blue eyes as he mouthed *goodbye*. Lorelei started the car and drove away in the dark, leaving him standing alone in the rain.

CHAPTER TWENTY-ONE

Music played loudly in the car, an effort on Lorelei's part to avoid thinking about what lay at the end of her journey. The rain had let up after she had driven through Rhode Island, and the night enveloped her like a dark blanket. The moon appeared from behind the clouds and reflected off the wet hood of her car. She stopped for gas in a small Connecticut town and bought something to drink in the gas station before continuing. Passing New York City, the lights of the great metropolis illuminated the sky to her left, a beacon in the darkness of the early morning.

The interstate cut through Newark and ran south beside the airport. It was five in the morning and the horizon was beginning to glow ever so slightly with a pale halo of light. Having driven through the night, Lorelei's eyes ached with fatigue, so she pulled off the highway and followed the signs to a hotel that was adjacent to a prison. She wrinkled her nose at the combined smells of fish and hops from the brewery across the highway. This certainly wasn't the best part of town, but then, she knew there were probably worse places. She parked in the hotel parking lot and hurried into the lobby. A bustling group of flight attendants brushed past her on their way out the door, each immaculately dressed and coiffed.

Lorelei approached the young man standing at the desk. "Hi, I know it's early for check-in, but you don't have any rooms available now, do you? I'll pay extra." She dug in her pocket and pulled out her debit card.

"Let me check," he replied. He turned his attention to his computer. "Well, we do have a non-smoking queen available for $145." Lorelei agreed to the rate and he proceeded with the transaction and handed her a room key. She took the elevator to the fourth floor and found the room; it was small, but clean, and the bed was comfortable. She removed her shoes, shut the curtains to block out the light and sank into bed where she fell asleep as morning broke.

When she finally awoke, it took her a few minutes to remember where she was and why she was there. She rolled over and looked at the alarm clock on the bedside table. It was 2:15 in the afternoon. Rubbing the sleep from her eyes, she climbed out of bed and looked at herself in the bathroom mirror. Her hair was a mess and she hadn't even done so much as pack a brush. She had on the same outfit she had been wearing the day before—a long-sleeved T-shirt and a pair of skinny jeans. Lorelei washed her face and pulled her hair back into a messy ponytail. *That'll have to do,* she thought.

Back down in the lobby, Lorelei approached the clerk at the desk. "Excuse me," she said. "You wouldn't happen to know where the union hall is?"

"What union are you talking about?" the woman asked.

"Um, for the port?" Lorelei realized Aeson hadn't given her very specific details.

"Longshoremen?"

"No, for the sailors I think?"

"Hold on," the clerk went in the back room and came back with an address on a piece of paper. "Here you go. Just take this road here down to the wharf and you'll stay on that until you see the sign for the port, then take a right there and follow it down until you get to this address. It should be on the left, before you get to the port."

Lorelei thanked her, took the address, and went out to her car. The sunlight diffused through patched clouds and haze. A jet soared overhead. Lorelei's stomach growled. She hadn't eaten anything all day. Just down the road she found a fast-food place where she ordered a burger and soda. It was delicious—greasy and satisfying. She took out the GPS, plugged the address the hotel clerk had given her into it, and followed the robotic directions leading her toward the port.

It didn't take long before she found her destination. The union hall was an old brick building in an industrial part of town. It sat next to an abandoned warehouse full of broken windows. Most of the vehicles driving by were trucks hauling their loads either to or from the docks. Lorelei could see the massive cranes on the waterfront loading the huge ships. She suddenly remembered the last time she had seen one of those enormous vessels, right before it had exploded, killing many of its crew, save for a lucky few, one of whom she knew shouldn't have been quite so lucky.

The old building reeked of mold. There were several men standing and looking at postings on bulletin boards, lists of vessel itineraries, and available jobs. A large painting of an older, bald man hung on the wall. There were three desks behind a half wall, and two women sat behind them, talking to each other. Lorelei approached nervously. "Excuse me," she said.

One of the women, a blonde with a huge bouffant hairdo, fire engine-red lipstick and a billowy leopard-print blouse, stood up from her desk and walked toward Lorelei, visibly irritated at having been interrupted. "Yes?" she barked.

"Um, sorry, I'm looking for Tyler Ceyeks. C-E-Y-E-K-S. Do you know where I can find him?"

"He's not here," she turned around and walked back to her desk.

"Do you have his address or know where he's staying? I believe he's a member of this union."

"Do I *look* like I'm directory assistance? We don't make a habit of giving the personal details of our members to girls who walk in off the streets." She paused. "You with the press?"

"No," said Lorelei, "no, I'm not."

"Eh, it doesn't matter. He doesn't want to be bothered."

"Well, thanks a lot for your *help*," Lorelei scoffed.

She started to make her way back outside when she was stopped by a gray-haired man with patchy stubble covering his chin. "I overheard you asking about Tyler," he said. "You know him?"

"Yeah, sort of," Lorelei bit her lip.

"Well, as long as you're a friend, he's going to be at O'Sullivan's later tonight. He'll be playing pool with some of us."

"Thanks," she said.

"Maybe I'll see you there?" he winked at her.

"Sure, maybe," Lorelei smiled back politely, but he was old enough to be her father and the way he looked at her made her skin crawl.

She left the union hall and went back to the car. By now it was 3:30. In a few hours she would have to go to some pool hall to find her intended victim. It was like a game of cat and mouse, except the prey didn't know he was being hunted. Lorelei recoiled at the thought, but she started to run scenarios through in her head. How she would lead him away, where she would take him, how he would finally meet his end. *This isn't murder,* she told herself. *This is my responsibility.* But she didn't believe it.

On the way back to the hotel, she passed a run-down strip mall. She stopped and went into the drugstore to pick up some makeup, a brush, and a bottle of hairspray. Beside the drugstore was a clothing store, aptly named *Flash.* It looked like a stripper's closet, the windows full of sequined spandex tops and miniskirts. Hesitantly, she went inside and searched until she found a purple dress that wasn't terribly revealing. Paired with some black leggings and ankle boots and cinched with a gold belt, it almost looked cute. It wasn't her style, but it was better than the clothes she had slept in the night before. She paid for the dress and accessories, and returned to the hotel.

Back in her room, Lorelei started getting ready. After she had showered, she looked at herself in the mirror. Wet hair cascading over creamy white shoulders, a perfect figure, and eyes the color of the sea in the morning—a creature so beautiful that men would willingly follow her to their death, like a drug. *Or a toxin,* she thought. A siren didn't need makeup or sexy clothes; she could wield power with her eyes and her voice alone. The mystique of her kind was staring back at her, bare naked in the mirror. Maybe Deidre needed to dress up when she went on the prowl, but Lorelei decided she would go as she was. She dried herself off and put on her own clothes, then ran the brush through her hair and let it dry in gentle ringlets that softly framed her face. She waited in the room until the sun began to set, then left the hotel to find Tyler.

O'Sullivan's bar was just down the road from the docks. It was tucked away between an old warehouse and a pawn shop. Two of the letters on the sign had been burned out, so it just read

O'Sulliva in glaring orange neon. Three burly men leaned against the brick wall just outside the door puffing on cigarettes. Lorelei drove a few blocks past the establishment and found a parking spot on the street. She sat in the safety of her car and took several deep breaths to steady her trembling body. Waves of nausea seized her stomach and she rested her head on the steering wheel. Lorelei had been nervous like this before her first call, but then she knew the others would be there with her. This time she was completely alone.

Lorelei took her phone out of her pocket and scrolled down to Aeson's number. She wanted to call and ask him if things had changed, if maybe she didn't have to go through with this after all, but she stopped short of dialing. *No,* she thought, *he'll think I'm an idiot. Come on, pull yourself together and take care of this. There's no other choice.* She sat up, put her phone back in her pocket, took the keys out of the ignition, and stepped out of the car. Along the crumbling sidewalk, Lorelei walked toward O'Sullivan's. The men standing beside the door stared at her like she was a strange animal, but they let her pass without saying a word. She opened the heavy wooden door and entered the bar. The thick smoke inside stung her lungs and she started to cough a little. Several weather-worn men sat at the bar, and a few overly tanned middle-aged women stood by them, drinking glasses of whiskey. Lorelei stood fixed to the spot, unable to determine her next course of action.

Behind the bar, a wiry-looking fellow was drying glasses. He nodded in her direction. "Getcha a drink?" he asked.

"Um, no thanks," she replied. "I'm looking for somebody."

"Suit yourself," he said, and went back to his work.

At the back of the bar was a darkly lit room that smelled strongly of beer. Inside the room were two pool tables, a few dart boards, and several tables holding half-empty pitchers of beer. The man Lorelei had run into earlier at the union hall was lining up his shot. He placed the pool cue on the table, leaned forward, and closed one eye, then pulled back on the cue once, twice, and finally snapped it forward sending the small white ball clacking into the others. Lorelei stepped into the shadows to watch.

Across the room, a younger man wearing cargo pants and a fitted black V-neck shirt was perched on a bar stool. He stood up and took his place at the pool table. His thick, muscular arms grasped the cue and he bent over the table to take his shot. A scar stretched across his left cheek and his black hair swooped over his forehead. He hit one of the balls in the pocket and walked to the other side of the table with long strides, cool and in control. Lorelei, on the other hand, wanted to run. Her palms were sweating and she pushed herself against the wall as tightly as she could so she wouldn't be seen. And yet, she couldn't take her eyes off of him. He threw back a drink and then set himself up for another shot.

"Hey, girlie!" the gray-haired man had spotted her. "You made it."

Lorelei's eyes opened wide. *Oh crap,* she thought. *What the hell am I supposed to do now?* She was frozen with panic.

"Tyler, this your girlfriend? She was looking for you earlier today," he said.

Tyler spun around and looked at Lorelei quizzically. He furrowed his eyes and shook his head. "No, I don't know her." She breathed a sigh of relief, grateful that he didn't recognize her.

The gray-haired man turned to face her. "I thought you said you knew him."

"Well," Lorelei tried to find the words, "I only know him from TV. He was on the news yesterday. I was fascinated by the story and I wanted to meet him."

EMILY KIEBEL

The man seemed satisfied with her answer. "And what's your name?" he asked.

She paused before answering, "Lorelei."

"Pretty name," he said. "I'm Hank. We're just about to start a new game. You wanna play?"

She shook her head bashfully.

"Come on, just play one game with us. Okay with you, Tyler?"

"Doesn't bother me," he said.

"No, it's fine. Really," said Lorelei, "I don't know how to play anyway."

"Good time for you to learn, then," said Hank. "Tyler, show her how to break."

Tyler took the triangle from the wall and arranged the balls neatly in the middle of the table. "Come here," he said. Lorelei joined him at the end of the table. Tyler handed her a cue. "Hold it like this," he wrapped her fingers around the cue. "Okay, now put your left hand here." He placed her hand on the table. Tyler arranged her fingers so the cue slid over her thumb easily. The skin of his hands was surprisingly soft. He took her hips in his hands and angled them slightly, and then he reached around her side and put his hand on top of hers. Lorelei had rarely been this close to a man before and his scent was intoxicating. Tyler's arms wrapped around her delicate frame, trapping her between his body and the pool table, but she felt a rush of adrenaline being so close to him. His head was just above her shoulder and she could feel his warm breath on her neck. He pushed her down with his chest so that her upper body was over the table.

"Easy now," he said. He held her right hand and pulled the cue back and then sent it suddenly forward. The ball jumped and hit the others with a loud crack. "That's it. You're a natural."

For a moment Lorelei forgot the reason why she was there and smiled at him. He released his hold on her and she began to crave the warmth of his skin against hers again. She caught herself staring into his dark eyes and remembered the last time she had gazed into them. It was so different seeing him now—not helpless or afraid like he had been the day of their first encounter. She found it a little ironic that he could look at her brazenly and without the slightest trace of apprehension because for him, Lorelei Clark was the most dangerous thing in the city.

Five more men entered the room and hung their coats on pegs that were mounted to the wall by the door. They greeted Hank and Tyler with handshakes and ordered some pitchers of beer.

"You gonna play?" Hank asked Tyler.

"I'll sit this one out," said Tyler. "You guys go ahead." He poured a glass of beer and offered it to Lorelei.

"No thanks," she said, "I'm not old enough to drink yet."

"You from around here?" Tyler asked, putting his pool cue up on the wall.

"No," she replied. "I'm living in Massachusetts right now. Cape Cod."

"I thought maybe I'd seen you before. You look familiar, but I'm having a hard time placing it." He took a sip of his beer, "Bit of a drive, coming all the way out to New Jersey just to see me."

"It's really not that far."

"True, but it's still strange that anybody would go that great a length just to find a stranger they saw give an interview on TV. Is that really why you're here?"

"I was intrigued by you," she said. "Your story was so unbelievable, I had to meet you in person."

He laughed, "I'm not that intriguing—just a regular guy who managed to survive an accident more or less unscathed. I didn't even do anything heroic. The only reason people are even interested is because of how I was saved."

"You mean the part about the mermaid?"

"I don't expect you to believe it. Nobody else seems to," he sat his drink down on the table beside him. "I can't really blame you if you don't, but these guys—I've known them for years, and they think I've lost it. Even Hank thinks so, and he's my uncle. He knows I'm not the type to make things up, not like this, but he still thinks I'm crazy."

"I don't think you're crazy," said Lorelei. "I'm sure there's a perfectly good explanation."

"Yeah, I know, it was a figment of my imagination, my mind coping with a near-death experience. I've heard it from everyone. I may not be the smartest person alive, but I know what I saw. I didn't imagine it. There was something, or *someone*, in the ocean that dragged me to that lifeboat."

Lorelei blushed. She put her hand on his arm, feeling the firmness of his muscles below his skin. "I believe you."

"Then you'd be the first person who does, Lorelei," the way he said her name made her weak. He looked directly into her eyes. She was losing her resolve to do the job she was sent to do, and the longer she listened to him talk, the less she could picture ending his life.

Lorelei put a hand on his shoulder and stood on her toes to put her mouth up against his ear. She started to hum a little, the tune of an old love song. He put his hand on her waist and swayed with her. Very softly, she began to sing as they danced in the dimly lit corner.

O my love's like a red, red rose that's newly sprung in June;
My love's like the melody that's sweetly played in tune.

238

As fair art thou, my bonnie lad, so deep in love am I:
And I will love thee still, my dear, 'til all the seas go dry.
'Til all the seas go dry, my dear, and rocks melt with the sun:
I will love thee still, my dear, while the sands of life shall run.
So fare thee well, my only love, and fare thee well, a while,
And I will come again, my love, tho' it were ten thousand miles.

They stopped dancing and Tyler backed up enough so that he was once again looking at her face. "You're beautiful," he said.

Lorelei blushed again and turned her eyes away from his. Tyler was captivated by her powers, a victim of the siren's charms. It was time to act—if he was under her spell she couldn't hesitate any longer.

"Let's get out of here," she said, "I need to get some air."

He grabbed his jacket and followed her out of bar, walking past the bartender and the other patrons.

"Where do you want to go?" he asked, once they had stepped outside.

"Let's just walk, okay?"

"This isn't really the type of neighborhood where you can just go for a walk…"

"I'll be all right," she put her hand on his chest and looked up at him, "I have you to protect me."

CHAPTER TWENTY-TWO

Tyler wrapped his coat around Lorelei's shoulders and they walked in the moonlight. Vehicles rumbled on an overpass creating the only sound that disturbed an otherwise quiet evening. A streetlight flickered above an old man who was crouched on the ground, his body wrapped in a sleeping bag. Tyler took his wallet out of his back pocket and handed the man a few dollars. He pulled Lorelei close to his side and put his arm around her waist.

"Stay close to me," he said, "this is a pretty bad part of town."

"Doesn't seem like there's really a good part of town anywhere around here," she said, cautiously looking down the alley they were passing.

"It's not all bad," said Tyler. "There are a lot of hard-working people here, too."

"Did you grow up around here?"

"I'm from Philadelphia, actually, but we moved to New Jersey after my dad died when I was a teenager. Mom wanted to be closer to her family. She wasn't working and we didn't have a lot of money, so we lived with my grandparents for a while."

"I'm sorry," she said. "That must have been hard on you."

Tyler didn't respond and she didn't want to push the issue. They continued down the street, walking alongside empty parking lots with high fences lined with barbed wire. At the end of one of the sidewalks Tyler jumped across a particularly large, dirty puddle. He turned back to Lorelei, lifted her by the waist, and helped her over it. Tyler's dark eyes searched her face; they were framed by thick eyebrows and each of his pupils held a tiny reflection of the moon. His hands slid down her sides until they rested on her hips.

"God, you're gorgeous," he said. His stare was so intense, it made her uncomfortable. This was the power of her allure. Deidre had told her about the power she could wield over men—the ability to make them do whatever she wanted, and yet, the way he looked at her made her feel naked. Ironically enough, the first time they had encountered each other, she had been.

"Thanks," she said. *Just keep him walking. It wasn't like this when he wasn't looking at me.* "So, do you live around here?" She turned and continued ahead and he hurried to catch up.

"I spend so much time at sea I just stay at Hank's when I'm in town. He's a few miles north of here. I could take you to see the place if you'd like."

Lorelei stopped and faced him. "I'm not that kind of girl, Mr. Ceyeks."

"No, that's not what I meant. I didn't mean to imply..."

"It's okay. I just don't want you to think that I came out to meet you for some sort of hookup. I think you're nice and everything, but I just want to talk, okay?"

"Oh god, I'm sorry if I offended you. It's only that, well, you *are* beautiful, but there's something about you, I can't put my finger on it—you seem so familiar to me. But you're right. I crossed the line, I'm sorry. I promise I'll be a gentleman."

"Thank you," Lorelei let him hold her hand and they continued on. "How did you get into working on the ships?"

"I got a job at the port and I worked there for a year after high school, but I knew that's not what I wanted to do for the rest of my life. The pay was good, but it was pretty grueling work. Hank had some connections and I ended up going to the Merchant Marine Academy. I graduated two years ago and started sailing with the K-Land fleet. The freedom was great at first—traveling the world and getting to see so many different places—but most of the time you're just on the water and it's not easy being away from civilization for so long. It's isolating."

"I can imagine it would be," said Lorelei. "But you probably make friends with the other guys on the ship, right?"

"Yeah, sure you do. But as you know, a whole lot of my friends didn't make it back on our last voyage." He paused and looked up at the sky, "You know, Lorelei, I actually feel guilty about it. A lot of those guys had families, even children at home, but I survived and they didn't. Look at me. What do I have? Nothing really. There's no reason I should have survived instead of them."

Lorelei was speechless. Ever since she had rescued him, and risked everything in doing so, she had comforted herself by thinking that he must have a reason to live. But he didn't. He said as much himself. There was no reason for him to have survived above any of the other men on his ship.

"Just because you don't have a family doesn't mean you're any less important."

"Survivor's guilt, I guess," he replied. "I'm sure I should be grateful, but all I can think about is the unfairness of it all."

"Everybody meets their end eventually, some sooner than others." *It was their fate,* she thought. *It wasn't your fault. They would have died anyhow.* "I'm sure they're in a better place now."

"That's what everyone tells me, but I guess I have a hard time believing it. I mean, nobody really has a clue what happens after you die, and who's to say they're in a better place? Maybe they are, and maybe they aren't. And I get it; people say it to make themselves feel better. To try to convince themselves that if somebody dies, it was meant to be—some great divine plan. But you know what? I think that's bullshit. Bad things happen to good people and there's nothing you can do about that, but you can't go around trying to placate people by telling them that it was their time to go or that it was all for the best."

Lorelei remembered when her father died, people had said the same, and it had seemed so cruel to her, too. Why would death necessarily be better than life? At least she always had the feeling that there was an afterlife, which had given her comfort, but the timing still seemed wrong. Her father wasn't old, he wasn't sick. He was happy. But still fate had called his number and his life was taken from him. Now that she was a siren, she understood it a little better, but it didn't mean that she had to like it.

"You're right," she said, "it's not fair. But I still want to believe that death isn't the end. I'd like to hope that there's more to life than just these physical bodies."

"For all we know, that might be true, but there's no way to prove it," he paused. "Listen, I'm sorry if I'm going off on a bit of a tirade here. The last few days have been terrible. I've still got memorial services to attend and grieving widows to pay my respects to, and all along people keep telling me how lucky I am. I guess I just don't feel like seeing your friends drown or get blown apart is anyone's idea of luck."

"I'm really sorry about what happened," said Lorelei.

"Thanks. You must think I'm ridiculous—I meet a beautiful woman and here I am complaining about all of this. I'll stop wallowing in self-pity now."

"I don't mind. And I don't think you're ridiculous. You're bound to have a lot of emotions after going through something like you did. It would have traumatized anyone."

"You're a sweet girl, you know?" Tyler shook his head. "Maybe everybody else is right. Maybe I'm going crazy. Sometimes I feel like I'm losing my mind."

Lorelei desperately wanted to tell him that he wasn't crazy, that he hadn't imagined what had happened to him out at sea that day. But it wouldn't make a difference. Why waste time trying to explain the mystery of fate and humanity's role in it to a man who would be dead within minutes anyhow? Even though she knew her part in it, she didn't know with any certainty what actually did happen to people after their death, but in her heart, she knew that any force in the universe that had enough foresight to create the sirens must certainly have a greater plan for the human soul than just a brief and temporal existence on the Earth. Why else would these creatures exist to guide souls out of life if death was only a great abyss?

"So, what is it that you do, Lorelei?" he asked.

That was the question of the hour. "I'm taking a break from school right now. I moved in with some relatives last semester."

"Are you working, then?"

"No," she felt embarrassed, afraid he would think she was one of those idle types that allowed others to take care of them. "I'm continuing with some private studies."

"And what are you studying?"

"Music, actually. I'm a singer. My aunt is giving me lessons. She's very talented."

"I bet you have a nice voice," he said. He must not remember when she sang to him back in the bar only a short while ago. "You planning on singing professionally?"

"I don't really know yet, but it doesn't matter. Even if I don't end up making a living at it, I'm always going to be a singer. It's in my blood."

"It's good you have a passion for something like that."

"What about you? Do you have a passion?"

"I thought so," he said. "I really liked sailing, but I don't think I can go back to that life now, not that I'll need to anymore. Mitch and Barry and me, we got ourselves some lawyers and they seem confident we'll reach a pretty big settlement with the company. Those idiots should have known better than to stow explosives next to the engine room."

How easy it was for one person's actions to impact the lives of others so completely. The tragedy that resulted in the loss of so many lives was a result of simple human error, one little mistake with dire consequences. *Did fate act on that person intending to cause that accident?* Lorelei wondered. *I wonder if they had any idea at all...*

"You about ready to head back?" he asked. "Aren't you getting cold?"

"No, I'm okay. Can we walk down to the water?" Lorelei pointed ahead to where the road dipped and turned to the right. At the end of the road was a narrow wooden dock that jutted out over the water, barely visible in the dark. A few cars were parked along the sides of the road, but there was no sign of people either on the street or down the alleyways. The night was cool and damp, and Lorelei's legs were like cement; she forged ahead, one tedious step at time, forcing her body toward the water's edge. Tyler, however, seemed oblivious that the path he was taking was leading to his own end. He blew on his hands to warm them and shoved them in his pockets. Lorelei grabbed his arm with both of her hands. She needed to hold on to him, to cling to something firm and warm to keep herself from shaking. She was overwhelmed with guilt; using him as selfish comfort against her fear was cruel, but it was the only way she could keep moving forward.

A small set of stairs led from the street up to the pier. Lorelei held onto the handrail and pulled herself up with Tyler right behind her. She took his hand and together they walked to the end of the dock. The sound of their footsteps on the wooden boards was drowned out by the rhythmic waves hitting the support beams below the pier. Nothing about this place was reminiscent of the ocean by Chatham—that great, tumultuous, and beautiful body of water that moved like it was breathing. The water here was oily, covered by a film of dirt and grime that floated on its surface. Light from the massive port only a few hundred feet away reflected on the sludgy water around them. Even in the dark, Lorelei could see land on the other side of the channel with its hazy light rising up from the city.

"Nice night, isn't it?" Tyler asked.

"Uh-huh," she turned and faced him. He was so close to her that she had to tilt her head up to look into his eyes. Amidst the harshness of the looming metal cranes and the warehouses of the industrial city, he was out of place. Tyler's eyes were dark and soulful, sparkling under the black sky. He wasn't classically handsome, but he was strong and intense, and his eyes held her gaze with his own. Lorelei was pulled in, unable to look away, nearly forgetting why she was there.

"What really brought you here, Lorelei?" he asked.

"I… I don't know," she said. "Fate, maybe."

"Must be," he said. "I'm glad you found me. I've never seen a woman as captivating as you are."

From the corner of her eye, Lorelei noticed a pale green light emanating from a bright orb that was bobbing just beneath the surface of the water. Her chest was tight and her heart was racing; it felt like someone had a vise grip around her throat. It was here. The time had come and there was no escaping it. The orb floated up, higher and higher, until it broke free from the sea. The light dissipated and spread itself from one side of the channel to the other. A low drone pulsed through the air, calling her, beckoning as it had so many times before.

It has to be done. There's no other way. Lorelei let go of Tyler's hand and approached the end of the dock. Every passing second felt like an eternity. She wanted to prolong the inevitable, but the Song called, and it was her duty as death's handmaid to answer. Lorelei's delicate hands were suspended over the water. The liquid began to swirl beneath her palms to form a whirlpool. While the water circled and glowed with a faint green light, thick tendrils of fog wove above it, snake-like. The mist rose upwards, filling the air until the land on the other side of the channel had become completely obscured by the fog. Lorelei lifted her hands slowly, and a column of water obediently followed, barely touching her palms. The column of water retreated as she willed it so. Now she only needed to lure Tyler to the edge, knowing he would follow without hesitation. Perhaps she could even make him jump off the dock, allow the water to envelop him and pull him under, filling his lungs and choking out the air. Her eyes burned. *Don't cry. Whatever you do, do not cry.*

She turned around to see Tyler watching her. He wasn't scared, or even concerned about what was happening. In fact, Lorelei was sure he hadn't noticed because he was so focused on her. She wiped away a tear and pressed her lips together, trying to fight back her emotions.

"Are you okay?" his eyes searched hers, a look of genuine worry on his face.

"It's nothing," she said. He brushed the hair out of her face and pulled her into his strong arms. She rested her head on his chest, calmed by the rise and fall of his breath. *Don't let him suffer much,* she thought, unsure if fate or Idis could hear her silent prayer, but in her heart, she wanted to tell him to run.

The Song changed from a deep drone to a more insistent hum, buzzing in Lorelei's ear like a mosquito. It flitted around her incessantly, growing steadily louder. The Song was ready for him. Lorelei lifted her head off his chest and took a step back. Tyler relaxed his grip as she pulled away from him and his hands moved from her back to lightly grasping her upper arms, leaving a small gap between their bodies. The Song was rising up Lorelei's body, from beneath her feet up to her chest, forcing itself through her. She closed her eyes, took a slow breath, and parted her mouth…

Tyler's lips suddenly found hers. Lorelei's eyes shot open. This was certainly not part of the plan. Tyler reached behind her head and pulled her toward him. She allowed it—if nothing else, she could afford him one last moment of happiness before the end. His lips caressed hers, each movement deliberate and unrestrained. Lorelei gasped and a chill ran down her spine. She had thought she was in control, but the passion that had been kindled in him was more powerful than she expected. Instinctively, but without meaning to, she found herself reciprocating his kisses, melting into the safety of his embrace. Tyler's lips traced her cheek and Lorelei tilted her head sideways, exposing her neck to his eager kisses. She closed her eyes, her breath coming in shudders.

Lorelei didn't object when Tyler turned his attention back to her lips. All the thoughts of what she was supposed to be doing vanished as she was swept up in the rush of the powerful sensations that were overcoming her. Tyler pulled Lorelei tightly against his body, unaware of the wave of water that was steadily gaining height at the end of the dock. Lorelei had never felt this way before. She'd only had a few boyfriends when she was in high school and all of them had been inconsequential. Never had she been so consumed by this type of desire before. Tyler wasn't like those boys she'd gone out with in the past; he was strong, passionate, and in control. Lorelei, on the other hand, had officially lost control, allowing her physical reaction to overwhelm her normally rational mind.

As she was busily succumbing to Tyler's touch, the dock was surrounded by a semicircular wall of water that began to cascade upwards, like a waterfall in reverse. Lorelei was oblivious to it until the wall broke, splashing them both and breaking her concentration. She was suddenly pulled back into place. She broke free from Tyler's arms and turned to see the tower of water hovering above them. Helen's words came back to her, *All you have to do is get him to water, and let the Song take over.* Apparently the Song wasn't going to wait for Lorelei to decide when the time was right. The sea would claim Tyler as its own with or without her help. She turned and looked back at Tyler, who was standing slack-jawed facing the massive wave. There was something about him that she couldn't let die, it was unconscionable. A dagger of remorse tore through her heart. *They'll never forgive me,* she thought.

Lorelei couldn't even hear the Song anymore; the voice of Idis that had been so loud before she had been sidetracked by Tyler had all but disappeared. There was a whoosh of water and the wave arched up over them and then came crashing down, dowsing Lorelei and Tyler. She lost her footing and clung to him. It started to rise up again, even higher this time.

"Run!" she yelled. Lorelei grabbed his hand and took off running toward land. They dodged to avoid the waves of water that continued to pummel the dock, thwarting their escape. The mist that had swirled about them now tried to grab hold of Lorelei's legs, very nearly tripping her. Unconcerned for her own safety, despite the waves that were trying to toss her into the harbor, her only thought was for Tyler. She had to get him back on land—the farther from the sea, the better. They reached the steps and jumped down just as another massive wave crashed behind them. As they ran, Lorelei turned back just for a moment to see a black figure sink into the water.

CHAPTER TWENTY-THREE

The air on the waterfront was thick with mist, so much so it seemed they were surrounded by steam as they ran from the pier. Lorelei was already out of breath by the time they turned the corner, the heavy fog filling her lungs, suffocating her. The more distance they put between themselves and the water, the more breathable the air became, and the surreal green glow faded away to the flicker of streetlamps again. Tyler sprinted up the hills with ease, but Lorelei strained to keep up with him, pushing her body to the limit until she felt she couldn't go any farther. When they reached the main road, she had to stop and catch her breath. All the times she'd seen her mother leave the house to go running in the mornings, Lorelei absolutely hated it. She had sworn that the only time she would run was if something were chasing her, but she never thought she'd actually have to make good on that promise. If she had known something like this could happen, she might have considered joining her mother on those morning jogs once in a while.

EMILY KIEBEL

"What the *hell* was that?" Tyler shouted. He spun around, his body obviously piqued in a fight-or-flight response, as though ready to fight an unseen adversary.

"I have no idea," she said, between breaths.

"Are you okay?" he asked. Lorelei was bent over, her head between her knees. He put his hand on her back. "Do you need to sit?"

"I'll be fine, just… just as soon as I… catch my breath."

Lorelei forced herself to breath in slowly and deeply until her heart slowed enough that she no longer felt like her lungs were about to explode. She stood up and looked down the road, almost expecting that the wave would have followed them. *Damn.* Twice she had defied fate and now she had seen with her own eyes that fate would not be ignored. She wasn't thinking when she'd started to run; it had only been a reflex to the chaos of the situation. But why couldn't she go through with it and let Tyler be swept up in the wave? Why didn't she let him go?

"I've never seen anything like that," Tyler said, "and I've spent years on the ocean. It must have been some sort of tidal wave or microburst, but where did it come from?"

If you only knew, thought Lorelei. It was amazing what lengths people would go to rationalize the irrational. Still, she figured Tyler must have had some suspicion; after all, he had seen the unexplainable face to face before and had been honest about it then.

Lorelei's wet clothes clung to her body.

"You're shivering," said Tyler. "You need to get somewhere warm. Let's go back to the bar. It's just around the corner."

"No," she said. He couldn't stay here beside the water, unprotected. And they'd be too easy to find so close to the scene of her failed attempt to relinquish him to the ocean. If she had any

252

hope of keeping Tyler safe, she needed to get him away from the waterfront. "I don't want to go back in there—I'm soaked. I want to go back to the hotel. Come with me?"

Tyler's eyes widened. He nodded in agreement and followed her to her car. She unlocked the doors and he opened the passenger door.

"You're cold and wet. Let me drive."

Lorelei handed him the keys.

"The hotel's by the airport," she told him. "It's next to a prison." He started driving and she turned on the heat. The vents blasted out cold air and she turned it off again. Her arms were covered in goose bumps, tiny hairs sticking up straight from the skin.

"That was crazy," he said, "I mean, the way the water just rushed up like that. I thought we were going to get pushed off the dock. We were pretty lucky."

"Yeah," said Lorelei, staring out the car window. "Lucky."

She couldn't understand what had happened. One minute, the Song was there, calling to her while she controlled the water; the next, the power of the Song had taken on a force of its own. Lorelei understood that a siren could direct the water, that she could will it to rise on command, but she could also restrain it. After the first few fateful attempts at the cove in Chatham, Lorelei had become quite adept at managing the water in that way; it was bizarre that it should act without being directed. Perhaps her emotions at the time, the passion she'd felt when she was kissing Tyler had contributed to the huge wave. After all, Helen had taught her right from the beginning that to control the sea, she must control her emotions, and she had let her emotions control her instead.

There was another possibility, though. Lorelei thought back to the vague figure she had seen submerging into the water as they were making their escape. It might have just been a shadow; between the darkness, the water, and the mist, Lorelei wasn't sure it was anything more than an illusion, but perhaps someone, or *something*, else had been there with them. Something that had shown its power to Lorelei once before. A *banshee*. She thought back to the day she had nearly drowned at Monomoy Island. Technically, whether or not she had actually been attacked by a banshee that day had been mere speculation, but this seemed a little too coincidental for it not to be the same force—something that didn't care whether or not Lorelei got hurt in the process. When she'd gone into the sea with the other sirens, she'd been protected by their presence, but she seemed to attract trouble when she was alone.

"How long are you staying in town?" he asked.

"I'm leaving tomorrow," she said. Lorelei had to leave, that much she knew, but where she would go, or what would be done with Tyler—those were things she couldn't answer.

"Too bad, I'd love to show you around town," he said.

"That's okay. I think I've seen enough already."

"Well, if you don't want to stay in Newark, we could always go to Manhattan…"

"We'll see," Lorelei would think about that later.

The hotel was quiet when they arrived—only the desk clerk and a janitor were in the lobby. They took the elevator up to the fourth floor and Lorelei pulled the hotel key from her back pocket. The room was clean and the bed was made. She closed the door and latched the deadbolt behind her.

"I'm going to take a shower, okay?" she motioned to her hair that was wet and sticking to the sides of her face. It dawned on her that she didn't have a change of dry clothes, except for the dress that she had bought earlier in the day. *It'll have to do,* she thought. She snatched the bag with the clothes from the dresser and darted into the bathroom. "I'll be out in a few minutes."

Lorelei felt like she was covered in the grime and sludge that she'd seen floating in the water at the pier. She turned on the tap in the bathtub and waited for it to get hot while she undressed. She stepped in and scrubbed herself clean, picturing the filth running down the drain. Her skin was fresh and soft again. Pure. She dried off and wrapped her hair in the towel. Her jeans and shirt were wet and dirty, piled on the floor. Reaching into the bag of clothes, she took out the purple dress and pulled it over her head and then put on the black leggings. *No belt or boots,* she thought, *at least I'll look less like a prostitute.*

Lorelei hung up the towel and brushed out her hair. She scrunched it up with her fingers into wet curls and tousled her head a bit letting them break free. These clothes felt foreign to her, like wearing someone else's skin. *If only my mother could see me now,* she smirked at her reflection before opening the door to the bedroom. Tyler was sitting on the edge of the bed, watching television, his shirt tossed over the back of one of the chairs. His chest was perfectly rippled and bronzed, just the right amount of muscle beneath taut skin.

"You sure clean up nicely," he said, eyeing her up and down. "You're stunning."

"It's the only other clothing I have," Lorelei blushed and covered her chest with her hands, suddenly self-conscious.

"You don't have to hide from me, you know." He stood up and took a step toward her. His shoulders were broad, and on one of his biceps was a tattoo—some sort of crest with a lion holding a branch in one of its paws and a crown on its head. Lorelei thought him a bit like a lion; the way he stalked her, bold and calculating, dark hair hanging in front of his face like a mane. And she was the prey.

He clicked off the television and stood facing her squarely. Lorelei bit her lower lip. She looked at his eyes, trying to decipher his motivation, but his actions were perfectly clear—he wanted her. On the other hand, Lorelei was in unfamiliar territory and her stomach was in knots. Alone with him, she was completely vulnerable, both attracted to him and afraid of what that attraction entailed. Thick fingers cupped her face. With his thumbs he rubbed her neck, just beneath her ears, and very intently, he bent down and kissed her.

Lorelei's head was floating, dizzy and light, as the rush of being swept up—being pursued and then captured—flooded her body. Even the smell of him, sweat and beer and just a hint of cigarettes, felt dangerous. *This is too reckless,* she thought, *I have to stop this.* While her mind fought against her body, Lorelei arched her back where Tyler's hand was holding her. She leaned into it, amazed how steadfast he was, like being carried away in a storm. She clutched his arms and held onto him. Tyler wasn't gentle with her; there was power behind his lips—heat and pressure. One of his hands went behind her head, fingers moving through her hair and holding her close to him while his other hand descended down her spine, along the side of her hip, toward the hem of her dress... He started pulling the side of Lorelei's dress up her leg. *No. No. I can't...*

"Stop, please stop," Lorelei pleaded between gulps of air, "I don't want to, I can't. Come on, let go."

Tyler kissed her cheek and whispered in her ear, "I need you." His hand crept under her skirt, rough fingers caressing her thigh. Lorelei gasped. She put her hands on his chest and pushed away, but he was stronger than she was. The more she pushed him, the tighter he held onto her.

"Tyler, quit it," she said adamantly. "This isn't right. You don't actually want to do this!"

"You're unbelievable," he stared into her eyes. "I've never met anyone I've wanted more. And I do want you." His desire was unmistakable, and it was her fault. She had seduced him; more than that, she had forced him into wanting her and now she was pushing him away. She hadn't thought it would come to this. He was supposed to be gone by now, out of her hair, a victim to fate. If she couldn't gain the upper hand and control the situation, they'd both be in trouble.

"I'm serious, you have to stop," she pleaded. "Let me go. Now."

"You don't really mean that," he said.

"Yes, I do. I told you, I'm not that kind of girl."

"Not *what* kind of girl? The kind of girl that picks up a stranger at a bar, takes him back to her hotel, puts on a dress like *that,* and then tells him she doesn't want to do anything? No, I don't think so. I know you want me, too."

This is a disaster. He's not going to stop unless I release him from the power of the Song, but if I do he'll leave and he's not safe out there. Fate will find him, or Calliope will figure out I didn't let him drown and she'll come looking for him. I can't let him go, but he isn't going to stop…

"Just slow down, okay?" she needed time to think. That seemed to appease him somewhat. He loosened his grip on her and moved his hand back to her hip.

"You're killing me here," he said. Tyler took a deep breath and let it out through pursed lips, "But I'll slow down, if that's what you want."

"Thank you," Lorelei was relieved.

He started to kiss her again, more gently; she could tell he was struggling to restrain himself. His arms were nearly trembling as he held onto her. He was taking measured breaths, slow and deliberate. His chest tight against hers, Lorelei could feel the muscles strained, barely controlling his need for her. His lips brushed her cheek and she flushed, blood rushing to her face. Her temperature was steadily rising as well. She shuddered a little when he kissed her ear, his soft lips parted and his tongue lightly touched the delicate skin there. Lorelei's head tilted back and she closed her eyes.

Sleep. The thought hit Lorelei. *I could sing him to sleep.* Tyler's lips were on the side of her neck. He was slowly, steadily moving down her neck until he was kissing the small indentation between her shoulder and clavicle. He touched the small of her back with one hand while the other slowly crept up her stomach. Lorelei leaned forward and began to softly sing a song she had learned only the week before, the words by Kipling were a lullaby that Helen said her grandmother had set to the melody of an old German folk tune.

Oh! hush thee, my baby, the night is behind us,
And black are the waters that sparkled so green.
The moon, o'er the combers, looks downward to find us,
At rest in the hollows that rustle between.

Tyler stopped what he was doing and yawned. His left hand moved and grasped Lorelei's upper arm. He pulled her in close and stood, his head against hers, breathing in the smell of her hair. Lorelei continued to sing.

Where billow meets billow, there soft by the pillow;
Ah, weary wee flipperling, curl at thy ease!
The storm shall not wake thee, no shark shall overtake thee,
Asleep in the arms of the slow-swinging seas.

His eyes watered as he fought to keep them open. Holding onto Lorelei, he moved nearer to the bed. Another yawn and they both sat on the edge of the bed. He crumpled forward and Lorelei put an arm around his shoulders before she finished the song. She lowered his body onto the bed before she kneeled beside him and unlaced his shoes, gently removing each one and putting them aside. Tyler was solid and heavy, so it took a good amount of force for Lorelei to roll him onto his side and place his head on the pillow. She lifted his legs onto the bed and positioned him so he was lying straight on one side of it, facing the edge. He was out cold, his mouth gaped open and he breathed deeply, sound asleep, lulled by the sound of her song.

It took her a minute to catch her breath. Who was this man she'd brought back to her room? He didn't seem like such a threat asleep on the bed, but he was so much stronger than she was, he had nearly overpowered her. Lorelei shook her head. *What a mess,* she thought. *What am I going to do with him?* She took a blanket from the closet and covered him with it. His hair hung on his forehead and his dark eyelashes twitched slightly. *Okay, so he's hot. And he likes me. So what? If I don't pull myself together, we're both going to get hurt.*

She grabbed her wet clothes from the bathroom floor and washed them in the sink with a bar of soap, then hung them to dry in the shower. When she returned to the room, Tyler was still sleeping in the same spot, snoring lightly. Lorelei wondered how long he would stay asleep. He'd probably sleep through the night, at the very least, but she had no idea what she would do with him in the morning. They couldn't stay in this town. They would have to leave this place, but she couldn't imagine where they would go or what she would have to say to convince Tyler to go with her. If he was still under her power, he would probably go with her just because she asked him. She wondered if it was fair to take him away from this place under false pretenses and the illusion of love, and if he was still under her seductive spell, how many more times would he try to force himself on her? Lorelei told herself it wasn't his fault, that he couldn't help himself, but she was still offended by how he'd treated her. She'd felt it too—the intense desire to be near him, aching for his touch—but she knew she didn't love him. She barely even knew him.

For a while Lorelei stayed awake and watched television from a chair in the corner of the room. She would occasionally glance over to make sure that he was still sleeping. Besides an intermittent grunt, he was perfectly peaceful. She needed to get some rest, but the floor of the room consisted of a slightly stained industrial carpet that was probably teeming with germs. She couldn't sleep on the floor. The only other option was to sleep in the bed with Tyler. Lorelei crept under the comforter and rested her head on the pillow. The blankets separated their bodies, leaving Lorelei feeling like she had a bit of protection from him.

Lorelei turned off the lights and lay awake facing the ceiling. She desperately wanted someone to tell her what to do, where to go, how to handle this. Of course, even when she had been told what to do, she'd failed at that, too. Strangely enough, the person Lorelei really found herself wanting was her mother, the last person she would have expected. Her mother was so decisive, she would have taken care of this whole situation with ease, but Lorelei was lost and alone. Even worse, she was responsible not only for herself, but also for keeping another person out of harm's way, at least until she could figure out how to keep him safe. *I'll figure it out in the morning.* She closed her eyes.

CHAPTER TWENTY-FOUR

The warmth of the sun cascaded over Lorelei's face. She stretched a bit, then buried her head deeper into the pillow and yawned. Lorelei smiled a little, still half dreaming. In her dreams, she was back in Calais at the beach on Dochet Island, wading in the water in bare feet, the sand between her toes and sunlight on her shoulders. It was an eternity ago, when things were simpler and life was straightforward, before she had found out about the Song that was alive in that very water. Maybe it had been calling to her even then, ever so faintly, without her knowing, without her bothering to listen for it. She could picture herself lying on the beach, peaceful and breathing quietly, young and naive.

Something jostled the bed and Lorelei squinted an eye open. Everything was blurry. By her side was the figure of a man. He was facing her, lying sideways with his head propped up on his hand. And he was staring at her. Lorelei rubbed her eyes and opened them. *Where am I? Who is this person?* The memories of the night before came flooding back.

"Hey there, beautiful. Did you sleep okay?" he smiled at her.

"Uh, yeah, sure did," she sat up in the bed and looked around. "What time is it?"

"Quarter after eight," he replied.

She pulled the covers up to her chest. "Have you been awake very long?"

"Not too long," he said. "You look really peaceful when you're asleep, you know."

Lorelei pulled her fingers through her hair, imagining the rat's nest that was undoubtedly piled on top of her head. She pulled her lips back into a forced smile. *How long had he been watching me?* she wondered.

"There's breakfast in the lobby. I can go grab something if you're hungry. Maybe some cereal and yogurt?"

"Thanks," she said. "That would be great."

"Okay, I'll be right back." He got out of bed and left the room.

Lorelei went into the bathroom. Her jeans and T-shirt were hanging from the shower rod and were dry. She changed into them, brushed her teeth, and tried to pull the knots out of her hair. The events of the previous evening played through her head. Everything that could go wrong had gone wrong. A man who was supposed to be dead now had ended up sleeping in her bed. Twice now she had failed to do her duty as a siren. What perplexed her the most was the fact that as much of an apparent failure she was at heeding the call, the Song had still chosen her for this task. She had all the skills, all the power of her birthright, but none of the ability to blindly act without questioning. Shouldn't it have known—whatever *it* was—that she was going to fail? After all, if it was fate that governed everything, shouldn't fate have picked a more adequate individual to act on its behalf?

Lorelei washed the sleep out of her eyes and returned back to the room. She took her phone out of her purse and flipped it open.

Three missed calls, one each from Deidre, Calliope, and Aeson. *Great. I'm sure they already know.* She sighed and read the text message sent from Deidre, "Hey—what's going on? Call me back, okay?" Lorelei rolled her eyes. There was nothing she could say to any of them to make it right. Helen would be disappointed in her, and Calliope would find Aeson and finish what Lorelei couldn't bring herself to do. That was it, plain and simple. They needed to leave this town, get on the road and put as much distance between themselves and the ocean as possible. She had no idea where they would go or what they would do when they arrived, but she needed to get him away from here, and as far away from the sirens as she could.

There was a knock at the door. Lorelei peeked out the peephole. Tyler stood there waiting, his eyes darting from side to side. She opened the door.

"Here, I grabbed a bunch of different things," Tyler spread the food out on a dresser next to the television. Lorelei picked up a strawberry yogurt and sat on the edge of the bed. He paced the room and stopped to look out the window, "I want to apologize."

Lorelei put down her yogurt and asked, "Apologize for what?"

He turned to face her, "For how I acted last night. That's not who I am, I mean, I'm not usually so… forward. I don't know what came over me."

"It's okay," she said, knowing that most of the blame for his behavior was hers.

"No, it isn't. I was raised better than that. I should have treated you with more respect and not been so presumptuous. It won't happen again."

"Apology accepted," Lorelei felt a blush creep up her cheeks. The night before everything had been so reckless, she had been scared of what she had created with her power of seduction, but he wasn't as intimidating now. The emotions that had taken over her at the dock were still there, but more subdued. She was in control of herself again.

"Cinnamon roll?" Tyler handed Lorelei the roll and sat beside her as they ate. "Can I get you anything else?"

"No, I'm fine," Lorelei brushed the crumbs off her pants. "We should probably get going soon."

"Yeah, I'm sure you need to get home," he said.

This was the time to tell him, the time to convince him leave this town for his own good. "Not necessarily," she said, "I don't have to be back any time soon. I'm actually thinking of doing a little traveling, you know, just to get out of town for a couple of days."

"You have some place in mind?"

"No place in particular. I just want to go and see where I end up. And I think you should come with me."

Tyler tilted his head, looking confused, "We hardly know each other..."

"I know. It's a weird request, but it could be fun. Don't you ever do anything spontaneous? I think it'd be exciting, just getting out on the road to see where it leads."

"I don't know..."

"C'mon, I'm sure you could get away for at least a few days. Last night you told me yourself that you're not even working right now. I could stand to take a little vacation, and I'd love to have some company. It'll only be a couple of days." She looked at him pleadingly, "Please?"

Lorelei could see Tyler processing it. If she had to, she could put him under her spell and she knew he would be bound to follow her, but she wasn't inclined to unleash that lustful monster in him again unless it was truly necessary.

"Well, I guess it would be okay for a few days. I don't have a lot of extra cash right now, so I can't go anywhere too expensive," he said.

"Don't worry about it," said Lorelei, "I can cover the expenses. And I don't plan on going anywhere fancy."

"No, I don't want you paying for me," he paused. "I do have an idea though. Maybe not as spontaneous as you might like, but my family has a little cabin up in the mountains in North Carolina. My dad used to take me fishing there when I was a kid. It isn't much, but it would be nice there this time of year. If you're okay with roughing it, we could go there."

"Is it close to the ocean?" she asked.

"No, it's all the way on the other side of the state."

"Sounds perfect. Are you sure we can use it?"

"Yeah, I have a key to the place. Hank's the only one who really uses it anymore, and I'm sure he wouldn't mind. If we drove, we could get there in about a day."

"Sounds perfect. I mean, I think we should do it, if you really want to," Lorelei was thrilled. The other sirens wouldn't have any idea they were going there, and the distance from the ocean made it safe. The fact that Tyler had made the decision with a completely sound mind and no supernatural coercion was the icing on the cake.

"It's all right with me. We can go for a few days. I'll call Hank and let him know we're heading down there…"

"Do you really have to tell him?" she asked. They needed a clean trail. If Lorelei had been able to find Tyler through Hank, she was sure the others could do the same.

"Why does it matter?" he asked. "It would be rude to leave town without telling him."

"You can tell him you're leaving, but we don't necessarily have to tell him where we're going, do we?"

"I guess not... ," Tyler's face pinched together. "I get the feeling you're not telling me something, that there's something more to this little trip you just decided we're going on that you're not telling me about."

"Oh, that's ridiculous," Lorelei's palms were sweating. "You're a grown man, I just think you should be able to go wherever you want to go, so I don't understand why you would need your uncle's permission."

"It's not like that, Lorelei. I don't need his permission, but ever since the accident, he worries about me, and I don't want to cause him any more stress. I'll just tell him I'm leaving town. I won't say where we're going, okay?" Lorelei nodded. "I'm going to go jump in the shower now, then we can swing by the house so I can grab some clothes before we leave."

She watched the way the muscles in his chest contracted as he lifted his shirt over his head and threw it on the bed, noticing the perfect taper in his body from his shoulders to his waist. Any other girl would envy her, but Lorelei was filled with trepidation even as she battled the feelings she had for him. She couldn't allow her emotions to get in the way anymore. He went into the bathroom and she heard the water running.

Lorelei's phone rang and she glanced at the screen. It was her mother. *Really?* She thought, *Of all the times, she calls me now? What could she possibly want?* The truth was, she wanted to hear her mother's voice, but she didn't actually want to talk to her, so she let the phone ring through to voicemail. What would she say to her mother if she were to talk to her? How could she explain what had happened to her over the last six months or what she was doing now? Maybe she'd call her later, let her mother know she was okay.

Maybe. The phone chimed that there was a new message, and Lorelei hesitantly opened it and dialed to listen to her messages. Hearing her mother's voice, her chest tightened.

"Lorelei, this is your mother. I need you to listen to me. I know we haven't spoken for some time, but this has gone far enough. You're in more trouble than you realize and you need to come home now. Whatever it is you're doing, you need to stop it and get on the next flight back to Denver. I need you to call me when you get this message. I do love you, and we need to talk, okay? Bye." As always, Cassandra was direct in her message. *You have no idea, Mother,* she thought. She didn't need any more texts from Deidre or voicemails from her mother. Lorelei turned off her phone and stuffed it in her purse.

"You ready to go?" Tyler asked.

"That was fast," said Lorelei, spinning around to see Tyler emerging from the bathroom. His hair was still wet and tousled atop his head.

"After you live on a ship with fifteen other guys for a few months, you get used to getting ready quickly." He grabbed his shirt from the bed and pulled it over his head. "Shall we?" He opened the door and motioned for her to go first.

They walked together through the hotel lobby out to the parking lot. It was a warm and sunny spring day, the sky dotted with big, tumbling cumulus clouds.

"Here, you'd better drive," she said, tossing him her keys. Tyler opened the car door for her, and she jumped in and threw her things in the back seat. He changed the radio station to classic rock and they left the industrial confines of the city driving north until they reached a neighborhood Tyler called "the Ironbound." Block after block of small wooden homes, brick churches, and an occasional convenience store lined the grid of streets. Tyler turned down an alley and pulled up behind a gray home with blue shutters that was surrounded by a small lawn and chain-link fence.

"You can come in if you want," Tyler said, "I'm just gonna grab a few things and leave a note for Hank."

"Is he here?" Lorelei asked.

"His car isn't here, so I'm guessing he's probably at work."

Tyler got out of the car and headed up toward the house. Trying to keep up with his quick steps, Lorelei scurried up the pathway behind him. He unlocked the door and it creaked as he pulled it open. The house was sparsely appointed and smelled a bit musty. The well-worn green carpeting and mismatched fixtures in the house obviously hadn't been updated since the late seventies. An old, upholstered recliner was parked in front of an old-fashioned television set. A few pictures hung on the walls—a family portrait of a couple and their two small children, a wedding picture of a much younger Hank and his bride, and on the staircase was a formal picture of Tyler in uniform. Over the mantle was a painting of a coastline with city lights above it. The dark blues made the bright yellow lights jump out of the picture; the color of the water reminded Lorelei of the sea under a full moon.

Tyler lunged up the stairs two at a time and motioned for Lorelei to follow him. She bit her lip nervously, the tiny hairs on the back of her neck standing on end. This was his domain, no longer the neutral territory of the hotel, and something about that unnerved her. Maybe it was the way he paced so casually and with such confidence while she felt small and vulnerable when she was alone with him. She reasoned that she needed to get over it, and fast. They'd be spending even more time alone when they reached their destination and if she didn't feel comfortable being alone with him now, how would she manage when they were on the run together? She took a deep breath and rounded the corner at the top of the steps.

The door to Tyler's bedroom was open, and Lorelei cautiously entered after him. On the opposing wall was a large bay window with a wide window seat looking out at the street below. The room was flooded with bright sunlight that spread over the bed and onto the walls. On nearly every vertical surface were brilliant oil paintings, hung modestly without frames. They depicted all sorts of things, from street scenes in a bustling city where the people's faces were obscured, to countryside landscapes, to more intimate portraits of individuals. Lorelei let her eyes take in the art that filled the room.

"Did you do all of these?" she asked.

"Yeah, I painted them. A bit of a hobby for me, I guess."

"Tyler, this is more than just a hobby. These paintings are really beautiful," her fingers reached up to touch the portrait of a woman. She traced her shape of her neck that curved so delicately toward her shoulders.

"It keeps my mind occupied. Those over there," he pointed to the wall above his bed, "they're some of the cities where I've traveled. There's Rotterdam up there, and over there, those are the beaches of Gioia Tauro in Italy."

A colorful picture of people with large brimmed hats sitting on small boats filled with fruits and vegetables caught Lorelei's attention. "Who are they?" she asked.

"Oh, that's the floating market in Bangkok. It's amazing. The people sell anything you can imagine and the line of boats goes on as far as you can see."

"You're very talented. Have you really been to all these places?"

"I'm lucky I've been able to see so much of the world. Some people never even get out of their little towns, but there's so much beauty in the world, it would be a shame not to experience it."

"They are really incredible. All the colors, all the variety of places and people are amazing." She looked up at him, "You didn't tell me you liked painting."

"It never came up in conversation," he said with a shrug, "besides, it's not something I go around telling everyone I meet. I do it for myself, not for anyone else's benefit."

"Well, I think you're really good. You should display them somewhere."

"I don't know... I like having them here; they're memories from all the places I've visited. It's different than taking a picture of something, you know? Pictures, they capture images, but they can't capture the feeling of a place. To me, these are more about how I felt when I was there. Either the colors, or the crowds, or the landscape—these are my memories, and now that I'm not sailing anymore, they're all I have left."

Lorelei was struck by the depth of his statement. Here was Tyler, uncompromisingly honest, a man who last night said he had no one and nothing to live for, but who created such emotion and feeling using the simple lines of his paintings that it took her breath away. She was enthralled at how he captured details from his memory and put them onto canvas; splotches of paint and brushstrokes created images and details of countries and cities she could only imagine. It wasn't unlike singing; the singer channeling emotion into rhythm and melody so that the feeling of a song is conveyed to the listener. Music after all, was little more than lines and dots on a piece of paper without someone there to transform it into something beautiful.

As Lorelei browsed the gallery that was Tyler's room, he filled a suitcase with clothes from his dresser, neatly folded and arranged. He opened the closet door on the other side of the room where hangers clacked against each other as he sorted through his shirts.

"Hey, Lorelei," he called. "Can you bring me that bag that's next to the bed, just there on the floor?"

She turned around, looked down and picked up the blue backpack that was leaning against the nightstand. Bathed in sunlight from the window, Lorelei stood beside a large easel that was facing Tyler and held the bag outstretched toward him. His gaze caught hers for a moment. He looked at the easel, and then back up at her. Tyler's lips parted slightly and his eyes grew wide.

"It was you," he whispered.

CHAPTER TWENTY-FIVE

Tyler looked at her intently, analyzing her features, trying to confirm his suspicion. Lorelei stood frozen in place. Finally, she spoke, "What? What was me?"

"There," Tyler pointed at the canvas beside her. "It was you all along. I just never put it together."

Lorelei took a step forward and looked at the painting on the easel. Her own eyes stared back up at her from the portrait, those translucent blue-green eyes of the sea. Those were unmistakable. It was the portrait of a woman, her body perched above the surface of the ocean with golden-brown hair rolling in curls over her shoulders and chest, in front of a scorched sky. Her mouth was agape, her chin tilted up to the heavens—she appeared to be singing. Was this what she looked like to him as a siren? This was certainly not the vision she had of herself. The painting clearly depicted a woman, not the girl that Lorelei knew herself to be.

"Who, or um, what is this?" Lorelei stammered.

"That day the vessel exploded, this is who saved me. This is what I remember," he moved toward her and lifted her chin with his fingers, studying her eyes, "your face."

Lorelei blushed and turned away, "I don't know what you're talking about."

"You don't have to deny it. I know you're the one that saved me out there. This is really why you came to see me, isn't it? I knew there was something about you from the moment I laid eyes on you at the bar last night. Why else would a beautiful young girl throw herself at a stranger like me? I thought maybe I was just lucky, but I knew there had to be more to it than that, and you looked so familiar, I just couldn't put my finger on it."

Lorelei panicked. Her heart pounded in her chest. She thought about running, but her feet wouldn't move from the spot. "No, it's not, I mean, I'm not…"

Tyler smiled at her, "I don't know what you are, but I know this. I know this with every ounce of my being. You aren't human, are you, Lorelei Clark? At least you're not like any other human I've known. You're something altogether different, but you did save me, and you've come back to me now."

"I'm human," Lorelei scoffed, offended, "make no doubt about that."

"Yes, maybe you are," he said. "You look human enough now. But out there, you were something else—something otherworldly, like a guardian angel."

"You don't know what you're talking about," she rolled her eyes. "That's not me, it was only your imagination," she replied.

"Last night you said you believed me, and now it makes sense why you would. You were there, so of course you would believe it. Just admit it, Lorelei. Tell me what you are."

"Tyler, please, enough of this. Just stop."

"No, I have to know the truth. You saved me that day, but I need to know why. Why me? What made you pick me? And why are you here now?"

Lorelei grimaced. "It's not what you think."

"Then what is it, huh? Are you a mermaid?"

"Don't be ridiculous. There's no such thing as mermaids."

"You could have fooled me," Tyler was losing his patience.

"You really want to know?" she was starting to get upset. "I don't think you really do. I don't think you could handle it if I told you."

"Try me," he challenged her. "We're in this together now."

"This isn't going to be easy to explain. It's not something I even knew about until last year," Lorelei fidgeted with her hands and looked down at the floor. "Nobody else is supposed to know."

"C'mon, who am I going to tell?" Tyler caught her gaze, his deep brown eyes imploring hers. "Trust me, I won't say a word to anyone."

"Okay," Lorelei took a breath and steeled herself, "I'm a siren. That's what I am."

Tyler cocked his head, furrowed his brow, and made a little grunting noise. She tried to gauge his reaction, but she couldn't tell if he was confused or merely thinking through what she had just said.

"You mean like the Greek myths? Odysseus and all that?" he asked.

"Well, kind of like that."

"They... they *kill* people."

"It's not like that..."

"But you saved me. If you're a siren, shouldn't I be dead?"

"Well, yes, but..."

"Yes?" he cut her off, his voice growing louder. "So did you mean to kill me?"

"It's not like that, we don't just go around murdering people."

"So why didn't you do it, huh?" He gestured wildly. "You killed all of my friends, but not me?"

"Do you want to know or not? I can't explain if you keep interrupting."

Tyler clenched his fists and nodded, "You're right. I'll let you explain."

"It isn't like what you learned about in school. Sirens don't go out to sea to lure men to death. We have to do it. It's not that we want to, it's more like a job."

"Like a contract killer?"

"No," she shot him a look. "Sorry, I'm not explaining it right. Do you believe in fate?"

He thought for a moment and then replied, "Maybe, I mean, I'd like to think I'm in control of my own destiny, but I also think sometimes there are forces outside of our control that influence us, that can change our future. Maybe that's fate."

"Okay. So, let's say there are these forces out there—we'll call them fate. Fate acts on things that are outside of your control, like an explosion on a ship. And in that explosion, people were injured and some of them died. I'm supposed to sing to those dying in the ocean to help ease their pain and fear, to give them an honorable death. Sometimes people are simply in the wrong place at the wrong time. You were one of them. You should have gone down with that ship, and as a siren, I should have made sure of it."

"And how do you know it was my fate to die?" he asked.

"We know ahead of time. When we go to the shipwreck or accident or whatever the case might be, we hear something that sounds like a song, an energy that runs deep through the water. We allow it to sing through us and the Song guides people to their death. Before I came for you, I sang to another man. He was injured so badly he was in total agony. When I was with him, the fear in his face was replaced with complete peace. I did what I could for him, and he died happy. I was supposed to do that for you but I couldn't. I never intended to save you."

"So why did you?"

"It was my first time, you know. I tried to sing to you, but you wouldn't go easily, and I panicked. There was something about the way you looked at me—I couldn't let you go."

"If I hadn't seen it with my own eyes, I wouldn't believe you." Tyler sat down on the window sill and looked up at her, then quietly asked, "What was his name?"

"Who?"

"The one you killed before you found me."

"Tyler, I didn't *kill* anyone... but I do know his name. It was Ronald."

"Ron?" he said, aghast. "My god, he has children, three teenagers all still at home. He was a good guy, a real family man. How could you take a man like that?"

"It isn't my choice. If it were up to me, not a single person on the ship would have perished. I don't make those decisions, but I did choose to save you."

"Honestly, I don't know if I should be angry about this or grateful. If you saved me, I still don't understand why you couldn't have saved the rest."

"It wasn't my place to save them. The others were already taking care of them."

"There are other sirens?"

"Yes, there are others."

"And you know them?"

"I live with them. They're the ones who told me what I am. They've been teaching me how to do this."

"And what do they think about what you've done?"

"They're definitely not happy about it. I've violated their rules. I shouldn't have messed with fate."

"That's why you're here, isn't it?" Tyler didn't look angry anymore. He looked genuinely concerned, but not angry.

"Yes. They wanted me to fix it."

"So you were sent to kill me?" Lorelei was shocked at how well he was taking the news. He hardly questioned the existence of the sirens, or of their abilities, but seemed to accept it all rather with ease.

"They didn't give me much of a choice."

"You could have said no. You don't have to do what they tell you."

"I know, and I tried to get out of it, but if I didn't agree to it, one of the other sirens was going to come and find you. They told me this is what had to be done, but they're wrong. I can't bring myself to hurt you, and I'm not going to let them hurt you, either. That's why we have to leave town."

"I don't know, Lorelei. You pretty much just admitted that you came here to murder me, and now I'm supposed to trust you enough to go away with you?"

"First of all, stop calling it murder. It isn't like that. I told you, we don't kill people, we only help them die. And secondly, if I really wanted you dead, do you think I would have admitted all of this to you? I don't want the others to find you, and the only thing I can think of is for us to leave this city."

"I don't want to run. I think we should stand up to them."

"No, you definitely don't want to do that. The others are much more powerful than I am, and they would see to it that you died quickly. They're good people, really, but this fate thing is their whole life, their reason for being. I don't know that I could stop them."

"I'm certainly capable of being able to stand up to a *woman*..."

"It's not about physical strength. She'd have power over your mind. You wouldn't be able to resist her."

"Yeah, right. I think I'd be able to defend my *mind* against her."

"Like you were able to do last night?" Lorelei asked, raising her eyebrows.

"What are you talking about?"

"Oh, nothing..."

"No, you can't say something like that and then dismiss it without telling me what you mean."

"Well, I might have done the same to you last night at the bar."

"What did you do to me?" he stood up and stared at her fixedly.

"I... kind of used my powers to lure you out of the bar," she confessed.

"What? No... no, I wouldn't have gone with you unless I had *wanted* to go."

"You only wanted to go because I seduced you," Lorelei cowered sheepishly.

Tyler backed away from her, "You really were going to kill me, weren't you? That freak storm at the pier, that was you, wasn't it?"

"No! That wasn't me, I swear. I don't know what that was."

"Don't lie to me. That must have had something to do with you, or... your kind," he looked disgusted. "You lured me out there to drown me by calling up that storm, didn't you?"

"Tyler, no, that's not what happened! You think this is what I want? As it is, I've gone against fate and disobeyed the other sirens, and truthfully, I'm scared shitless about what's going to happen to me. To both of us. All I know is that they told me there would be terrible consequences if I didn't set things right, so I came down here to do what I had to do, even though it made me sick to think about it, okay? It's true, I took you to the pier to let fate finish what I had failed to do, but when you kissed me, everything changed. I felt something for you, and I had to keep you alive, to hell with the consequences. Now, if you still don't believe me, I'll leave; I'll go right now on my own, but I want a chance to try and protect you. I want you to live."

"This is too much for me to process right now. I'm going to need some time to think about it."

"We don't have much time to wait. I have no idea how long it will be before they find out you're still alive. I have a feeling they probably already know."

"Look, I'm really trying here, but this isn't the kind of thing you can just expect me to be able to go along with right away." He walked toward the door, "I've got to get out of here for a while."

"Where are you going?"

"I don't know, but I need to get some air," he slammed the door shut behind him.

Lorelei turned around, alone in the empty room. She looked at the portrait again, Tyler's memory of the creature that had saved him. It must be confusing to learn that it wasn't a rescue mission like he'd assumed, but a botched execution instead. She rubbed her head in her hand and glanced out the window in time to see Tyler emerging from the house into the streets below. He wasn't safe out there alone. She ran down the stairs and opened the front door. He was just turning the corner down the street and Lorelei took off after him.

Keeping her distance, she followed him past the houses, shops, and restaurants on Ferry Street and down Van Buren until they reached the end of the road where a little league team was playing on the baseball field. He walked briskly, and she tried her best to keep up with him without being seen. Past the park, he crossed a busy road that ran perpendicular to the large metal bridge that hung over the Passaic River. The riverfront was empty and Tyler crept through the brush and trees before emerging in the shadow of the bridge beside the river.

Lorelei hid behind a parked car and watched him pick up some stones and throw them into the river, one by one. His proximity to the water made her anxious. She could envision the river rising to a swell like it had the night before and washing him away, but for now, everything was calm. Slowly, she snuck up to the side of the bridge and started down the hill. A bit of gravel under her feet gave way and she slipped. Lorelei grabbed at a nearby tree branch, but the branch broke and she fell sideways on her hip. Tyler turned around to see her sliding toward him.

"Lorelei?" he called up at her.

She didn't respond. Gravel had scratched through the skin on the palm of her hand and part of her shirt had snagged on a bush. Tyler climbed up to where she lay on the ground, rubbing her sore hip.

"Are you okay?" he asked, assessing the damage.

"Yeah, I think so," the side of her leg hurt as she stood up. He brushed off her pant leg and reached for her hand. As he swept the gravel from her palm, Lorelei winced and pulled it back. His eyes met hers and a familiar flush crept across her cheeks. She let him take her other hand and he guided her down to the riverside.

"You were following me?" he asked.

"Sorry," she said, "I just wanted to make sure nothing happened to you."

"Looks like I'm not the one you should be worrying about. You ought to spend more time watching out for semi-steep gravel hills."

"Very funny," she said. "You're not mad?"

"No, I'm not mad at you. I'm not happy about the situation, but I guess in the end, you've never actually done anything to hurt me. And I've been thinking about what you said, about leaving town."

"Did you make a decision?"

"I'm prepared to leave for now, but how long will we have to stay away?"

"I don't know."

"I know this city may not seem like much, but this is my home. I don't want to leave if I may not ever get to come back."

"I wish I could say we'd be able to come back in a few weeks, but I can't. I simply don't know. It isn't easy for me, either."

Tyler gazed over the river. "Show me what you do."

"What do you mean?" Lorelei was taken aback.

"Your powers," he said, "you must be able to do something. I want to see it now that I know what you are."

Lorelei walked up to the edge of the river. She looked around to make sure no one else was nearby and listened for a moment, but she couldn't hear the Song. She took off her shoes and walked a few steps into the water. Holding her hand over the surface of the still river, Lorelei closed her eyes called it toward her like she had done so many times before at the cove in Chatham. When she opened her eyes, a spinning orb of liquid had formed just below her palm.

"Wow," Tyler's jaw hung open. He reached out to touch it, but as soon as he did, the orb broke and crashed back into the river, splashing them both. Tyler stared at the ripples forming on the river, "This is real, isn't it?"

"Yes, this is definitely real," she replied.

"And you are… a siren."

Lorelei nodded.

Tyler's face suddenly registered the gravity of the situation. If Lorelei's power was real, then so was the danger they faced. "I'll go with you, wherever you think we should go. If you think we need to leave, I believe you."

"Thank you," she said.

"I should be the one thanking you," Tyler's voice was low. "I've been so concerned with how this was affecting me, I didn't stop to see the risk you've taken in coming this far. You'll have to be patient with me, though. This is a lot to try to understand, but thank you for telling me the truth."

"I know it is," Lorelei remembered her own terrified reaction the first time she had seen the sirens emerging from the water. In comparison, Tyler had handled it quite well.

They stood at the water's edge in silence for a few more minutes before they walked back through town to the house. He packed his things, left a note for his uncle, and made them each a sandwich for the road. They loaded the Jeep, and Tyler took the driver's seat and backed away from the house. Lorelei glanced up at him; behind his stoic expression, she could sense his sadness as they left the place he called home.

CHAPTER TWENTY-SIX

The industrial harshness of the city faded away to houses and lush trees as they drove through the outer suburbs of Newark. With the radio on, Lorelei and Tyler said few words to one another. There were things she wanted to tell him, but she didn't know how to put into words her feelings of regret and guilt, and even deeper than those feelings, another one buried deep inside that made her nervous to be around him. Instead, she sat in silence, watching the landscape between the small New Jersey towns flying past. A few hours into the trip, she asked Tyler to stop at a mall just outside of Philadelphia. She was still wearing the only clothes she had brought with her, and now they were caked with mud and torn from her fall by the river. Lorelei went to a few of the familiar chain stores and purchased several pairs of jeans and shirts in her size without trying them on before going to one of the department stores where Tyler, obviously bored, waited in the juniors' department while Lorelei picked out an assortment of underwear, socks, and a light coat.

Back on the road, a female indie singer wailed incomprehensible lyrics to an acoustic guitar on the radio while the bright sunlight beat down on the hood of the car. Lorelei found her atlas and traced their route to the town of Waynesville in the mountains of North Carolina. It would be another nine hours before they arrived at their destination and it was already afternoon. She took the sandwiches from the backseat, unwrapped one for Tyler and saved the other for herself for later.

"Thanks," he said, taking a bite of the sandwich. "You know, I feel like I've told you everything about my life, but I hardly know anything about yours."

"Not much to tell," Lorelei started, "I grew up in Colorado, in the suburbs outside of Denver. My parents were pretty normal. My dad is, well, he was an engineer and mom's a consultant for a security company. I'm an only child, and I've got a couple cousins that lived nearby."

"What about friends?" he asked.

"Besides my cousins, I didn't have a lot of close friends back home. I started studying music pretty young, singing in the school choir, and my teacher referred me to a private coach." Lorelei ran her fingers through her hair, "I poured myself into it, but I had to give up a lot of the normal childhood and teenage things so that I could focus on my training. I spent so much time training and traveling and performing that I never had the chance to make very many friends, especially once I was in high school. I'm definitely a perfectionist—I get it from my mom. I would spend entire weekends working on a piece until it was absolutely flawless. By the time I was fourteen years old I was already singing complicated arias and oratorios."

"I'm impressed. I spent most of my weekends in high school drinking with my friends in our parents' basements," Tyler chuckled. "Your parents must have been proud."

"My dad was really supportive, he always went with me whenever I traveled, but my mom thought it was frivolous. If you've ever heard about stage mothers, mine was the exact opposite. Sometimes I think her resistance to my wanting to be a singer is part of what drove me to want to do it even more."

"And what brought you all the way out here from Colorado?"

"The beginning of my senior year, my vocal coach introduced me to a professor at this really top-notch music conservatory in Maine—one of those places I always dreamed of attending, right up there with Julliard. I auditioned for her and earned a scholarship. I moved out in June."

"I thought you said you were living in Cape Cod…"

Lorelei gulped, "I left the conservatory after my dad died."

"When was that?"

"Last year, over fall break."

"I'm sorry to hear that," Tyler took Lorelei's hand in his. She turned and looked out the window, trying to push down the tears that were welling up in her eyes whenever she thought about her father. "So that's why you moved?"

Lorelei was grateful that Tyler had changed the subject, "I was having a hard time readjusting to school after the funeral, but one day I received a letter from my Aunt Helen inviting me to visit. I'd never even met the woman, but I thought if I left Calais it would help me clear my head."

"And did it?"

Lorelei gave a half-hearted laugh, "Well, let's just say once I found out about all the siren stuff, it took my mind off my dad's death, but it was replaced with a whole new set of worries. If I knew then what I know now, I wish I hadn't left Calais."

"Would you have had a choice?"

"I don't know. I doubt it. You can't run away from your fate."

"You never know. Maybe you could have made a different decision, Lori."

"My dad used to call me Lori," she said. "It's strange to hear someone else say it."

"Sorry, I didn't know. I won't call you that if you don't want me to."

"No, it's okay. I kind of like it."

It was strange, having someone to talk to about these things. The Deleauxes had made it clear that they did not discuss what they were with anyone outside of the family. *Just one more rule I've broken*, she thought. And yet, being able to confide these things with another person, and to have him actually believe her, was reassuring. She leaned her head back and shut her eyes, letting her mind drift to the place between waking and dreaming.

Lorelei woke to the sound of the car bell dinging. She sat up. They were at a gas station, and Tyler was outside filling up the tank. She opened her own door and stepped out into the crisp air. Lorelei stretched her arms up over her head and yawned. They were between the interstate and a large harbor with sounds of cars zipping by reverberating around them.

"Where are we?" she called across the roof of the Jeep.

He looked up at her, "Just south of Baltimore. We were getting low on gas."

"How long was I asleep?"

"Just a little over an hour, I think." The pump clicked off and Tyler replaced the nozzle in its holder, "You want anything from inside?"

"A bottle of water would be good," she said.

Tyler left Lorelei alone standing beside the gas pumps and walked into the convenience store. The gas station was separated from a pier by a small strip of weedy grass. Tied up to the pier, an empty cargo barge bobbed gently. Toward the south was an inlet that cut through the city. Across the inlet, a green knoll jutted out into the sea, atop of which was an impressive Revolution-era fort guarding the harbor. Lorelei walked the length of the parking lot, stretching her legs.

"Ready to go?"

Lorelei turned around as he lofted the bottle of water toward her. She caught it in one hand and walked back with him to the car. She buckled herself in and Tyler started the car. He merged onto the highway, following the few other cars that made their way south to a set of tollbooths. Ahead of them, the eight lanes of road intersected with the harbor and slipped below the water. The entire highway was routed underneath the inlet. They were about to travel directly beneath the sea. Lorelei knew in an instant this was a very bad idea.

"Turn around!" she yelled.

"What?"

"Just turn around, Tyler! We can't go under there… ," her voice filled with panic.

"We can't turn back now, it's a one-way highway. What's wrong?" he handed a few dollar bills to the tollbooth attendant.

"Don't you see?" she pointed up at the water. "We're too close to the ocean. It makes me nervous."

"It will be fine. Just relax." Tyler flipped on the headlights, and continued the descent down the highway to the mouth of Fort McHenry tunnel.

"You didn't tell me we were going through a huge tunnel under the water."

"Calm down. It's enclosed in cement and it's perfectly safe. We'll be through it in just a minute."

The four lanes heading southbound were separated into two tunnels of two lanes each. Tyler took the tunnel on the left. Lorelei remembered the moments as a child when her parents would take her to the mountains and she would attempt to hold her breath until they made it all the way through to the other side. There was one tunnel that she could never make it through without gasping for air by the end, and she was breathless like that now. Flashes of light pulsated on the roof of the car as they drove beneath the fluorescent lights that illuminated the tunnel. Solid concrete walls surrounded them on both sides; it was like being buried.

They had been in the tunnel barely a minute when the lights of the tunnel started to flicker. A moment later, they went out altogether. The line of brake lights ahead glowed in a river of red. Without the overhead fluorescents guiding their way, the tunnel seemed endless, their headlights like lanterns in a cavern. The cars slowed and finally came to a stop. Lorelei eyes adjusted to the sudden darkness and she glanced at Tyler, the silhouette of his face barely visible.

"What's going on?" her voice quivered.

"I'm not sure," he paused, "but blackouts happen all the time. I'm sure this is completely normal."

"No, something is wrong. Something is definitely wrong."

"Don't freak out, Lori. We'll be fine."

"It doesn't feel right, Tyler." An overwhelming feeling of anxiety had found its way to her stomach and taken root there.

"It's okay. Look, the traffic is moving now. We'll be out of here in a few minutes."

The car moved forward slightly with the line of traffic. A loud bang reverberated through the tunnel followed by the sound of twisting metal like the groaning of a machine.

"What the hell was *that*?" she sputtered. "And don't try telling me that was normal."

"I... I don't know," he replied. The cars slowed again. Tyler rolled down the window and stuck his head out, trying to look ahead, "If these people would just keep moving..."

The creaking metal sounded again and a drop of water landed on their windshield. The small drop of water beaded up and rolled down the glass. Another drop of water landed on the roof, and then another, until the increasing staccato of water hitting the roof sounded like a light rain. They turned and looked at one another, each barely able to see the other in the dark. Tyler pulled ahead until the bumper of the Jeep was nearly touching that of the car ahead of them. The water leak was now a solid stream of water, pouring on the car and cascading down the rear window.

Another stream of water gushed from a rivet on the ceiling in front of them. It showered down in a dark arc, glinting back at them when it passed the beams of the headlights. Tyler laid on the horn. "Move!" he screamed.

As though on command, the cars began to move again. Another rivet broke free and spilled water down the side of the wall. They drove through the waterfall that had formed inside the tunnel.

"I told you this wasn't a good idea!" Lorelei shouted.

"You can yell at me later," he said, "just let me concentrate right now."

A huge tile fell from the ceiling, landing on the hood of the Jeep. Water poured into the tunnel in torrents as more of the tiles fell. Everything seemed to be collapsing around them. The traffic had picked up speed, people in the cars ahead realizing the danger they were facing. Having slowed to a stop after the lights had gone out, everyone was now rushing to exit the tunnel as quickly as possible. In the lane ahead, an old Honda had stalled in the flood.

It was positioned directly under one of the huge water downpours. The cars slowed as they inched their way around the disabled vehicle. Tyler pushed his way to the left, just beside the stalled car. He scraped the side of the Jeep on the concrete corner of the elevated walkway.

"Is anyone in there? Are they okay?" If the tunnel flooded and innocent people died, Lorelei wouldn't be able to forgive herself for bringing this upon them.

"They're up there," Tyler pointed at a couple who were running along the elevated walkway on their left, sprinting toward the exit.

Once Tyler cleared the stalled car, he sped forward. Bits and pieces of the ceiling fell, pelting them with debris. Each time a bit of the ceiling collapsed, another spillway of water opened behind them. Faint light appeared in the tunnel, signaling that they were almost to the other side. The headlights of the other cars were on their tail. Tyler deftly dodged around a chunk of concrete that had crumbled on the highway. The light from the end of the tunnel was growing brighter, but behind them a wall of black water had formed and was heading toward the vehicles like a tidal wave. If the flood of water overtook the cars, everyone trapped in the tunnel would drown.

"Stop the car!" she screamed.

"Are you crazy?" Tyler yelled. "We're almost out of here!"

"Stop the car. NOW!" Lorelei yanked the wheel, smashing the car into the wall. Tyler's torso thrust forward toward the steering wheel upon impact. The cars behind them screeched to a halt.

Lorelei jumped out of the Jeep and spun around just in time to see an SUV hurtling toward her. She backed up against the door as more vehicles whizzed by, then sidestepped to the rear of the car where she turned to face the oncoming traffic. The sound of the rushing water hurtling through the tunnel was deafening. Lorelei steadied herself on both feet, took a breath, and raised her hands with her palms toward the wave. *Please let this work*, she thought. She closed her eyes and pushed against the water, as she had done so many times in the cove outside of Helen's home, trying to change its course. Lorelei tightened the muscles in her arms, locked her elbows, and willed the torrent to obey her. She opened her eyes. It was working. The water stayed in place, splashing and frothing, but not moving forward. The two people they had passed moments ago ran by and the cars that remained in the tunnel shot past her.

Even from a distance, she could feel the weight of the water pushing back at her. Arms shaking, she leaned into the Jeep for support. It felt like the wave was crushing her. Lorelei dug her feet into the ground and gritted her teeth, perspiration dripping from her brow, then pulled her arms into her chest and heaved them forward with one last powerful motion. With that, the water retreated slightly. Lorelei pushed herself from the rear of the Jeep and took a step forward, leaning into the weight of the flood, forcing it back into the tunnel. Another step followed and the water continued its retreat. Her back ached, but she had the water under her control.

"Lorelei!" a voice called out from behind her.

"Is everyone out?" she didn't turn around, but remained planted firmly in place.

"What are you doing?"

"Go check! Make sure everyone made it out of here!"

Tyler ran toward the light. Lorelei took deep, steady breaths and lifted her arms up higher, the weight becoming more bearable. The wall of water had retreated behind the curve of the tunnel so she could no longer see it from where she stood, but she could still feel the presence of its force digging into the palms of her hands. She leaned forward, shoving her arms straight out from her body. Even with the impending wave under control, more water was pouring in through holes in the ceiling and she was standing in a pool that came midway up her calves. There was something snaking around her ankles, not unlike the tendrils of the Song and mist that enveloped her when she transformed into a siren.

"They all made it out," Tyler was at her side. He was out of breath, panting.

"How far are we from the end?" she asked.

"Not far. Maybe a hundred yards, maybe a little more. We've got to get out of here before this whole thing collapses."

"Go start the car," she instructed. "I'm going to hold it off, but as soon as I'm in the car, let's get the hell out of here."

Tyler nodded in agreement and went back to the Jeep. He had to crawl in through the passenger's side since the left side of the vehicle was pinned up against the wall. Lorelei moved backward, step by cautious step until she was beside the car. She let out a scream and pushed with all her strength one last time before she jumped in the car.

"Go!" she shouted, slamming the car door shut.

Tyler put his foot down on the accelerator and plowed through the water toward the light at the end of the tunnel. The wave of water spilled out from behind the curve in the distance and gained momentum as it got closer. Tyler focused on the road ahead, and finally the exit came into view. The Jeep roared, water splashing up in a huge spray from both sides. The wave touched the bumper of the car, pushing it out toward the light. Tyler and Lorelei emerged from the tunnel and sped up the ramp to higher ground. The water gushed from the exit before dissipating across the many lanes of the road, no longer the threatening force that it was in the contained space. Several parked cars at the top of the hill blocked off the highway, their drivers walking around bewildered. A police officer spotted the Jeep, ran over to the car, and banged on the window. Tyler rolled down the window.

"Are you both okay?" the officer asked, looking over Tyler at Lorelei, whose entire body was trembling from physical exhaustion.

"I think so," Tyler replied.

"Ma'am, are you okay?" the policeman asked.

"I'm fine," her voice was weak.

"She's in shock," Tyler said, "but I don't think she's hurt, at least not physically."

"You'll need to wait here. The ambulance is on its way," the officer left them and ran toward a man who was lying on the road hyperventilating.

"Are you all right?" Tyler's asked. His eyes scanned her body for injury.

"Just lightheaded, but I'm okay," she said.

"Here, lie down," Tyler reached over her body and pulled the handle of the seat to recline her backward. He looked down at her, his face above hers, and shook his head.

"What is it?" Lorelei asked.

"What you did in there was incredible," he said. "That was either the bravest or the stupidest thing I've ever seen anyone do."

"I had to help them. I didn't have a choice. I'm just glad it worked."

The sirens of multiple ambulances filled the air. Tyler put his hands on the wheel and drove to the right side of the road, around the cars that were parked at the top of the hill. He sped away just as the emergency vehicles were descending toward them. The blinking red and blue lights were the last thing Lorelei saw before she fell into the dark solitude of unconsciousness.

CHAPTER TWENTY-SEVEN

A cool breeze blew in from the open window in the bedroom, rustling the dusty blue-checkered curtains. Lorelei was wrapped in a tattered quilt, her head resting on a feather pillow all on a dark-stained log bed in an unfamiliar room. She vaguely remembered Tyler carrying her in from the car and placing her in bed, pulling the covers up around her shoulders. The austerity of the room was evident in the unfinished knotty-pine floors and empty walls, the corners of which were covered with cobwebs. Hazy sunlight filtered through tree leaves along with the sound of chattering songbirds.

Lorelei sat up on the edge of the bed and placed her bare feet on the floor. She remembered the moment right before she had passed out from exhaustion once she and Tyler had escaped from the tunnel in Baltimore, and although she knew where she was now, she was surprised to find that she had slept straight through the night. Several shopping bags containing her new clothes were propped up in the corner of the room. There was a bathroom adjoining the bedroom and lying on the sink was a neatly folded set of towels. She turned on the faucet in the bathtub. It sputtered some rusty colored water for a moment before it cleared up. Lorelei wrinkled her nose, but climbed under the lukewarm shower regardless. It smelled a bit metallic, but it was better than nothing. After washing up, she put on a pair of new clothes and left the bedroom.

Tyler was still asleep on a faded blue sofa just outside the bedroom. Lorelei carefully walked through the main living room past the tiny kitchen to the front door, opened the wooden latch, and stepped outside. The covered porch overlooked rolling green hills and a larger mountain off in the distance. The hillside was scattered with trees and lush grasses, and at the bottom of the slope, a winding creek trickled over smooth gray rocks. A narrow dirt driveway led up to the cabin. Lorelei looked down the hill, but she couldn't spot the main road, and there were no other houses as far as she could see. They were completely alone here in what felt like the middle of nowhere. She filled her lungs with the sweet morning air and sat down on the porch stoop. The cacophony of the forest was buzzing so early in the morning; squirrels ran atop the tree branches and a pair of blue jays hopped among a clearing of wildflowers. It was as though Lorelei had stepped into some rustic, backwoods alternate universe.

The door creaked behind her and Tyler came into the light. A pair of cargo shorts hung down to his knees and as he stretched, the muscles of his tight, muscular torso flexed. His tousled hair stuck up from his head, each tuft pointing in a different direction. He smiled at Lorelei and she felt a little flutter in her stomach.

"So what do you think?" he asked.

"It's nice," Lorelei grinned. "What a beautiful view."

"Glad you like it. Sorry the cabin's such a mess. No one's been out here for a while to clean it."

"It's not that bad," Lorelei lied.

"You feeling better?"

"I guess so."

"You were totally out of it. I woke you up a few miles outside of Baltimore just to make sure you were okay, but you wouldn't stay awake. I figured it would be best if I just let you sleep."

"I don't remember that."

"I think you were pretty wiped out from what happened in the tunnel," Tyler paused. "By the way, what exactly *did* happen in the tunnel?"

"It was going to flood and I tried to hold it back. To be honest, I wasn't sure it would even work, but I had to try."

"This is freaking crazy," he rubbed his head. "You could have died, you know."

"Yeah, I know, but somehow I knew I could stop it. Helen taught me to move bodies of water, so I figured if I could make water move, maybe I could also hold it in place. I'm just glad it worked."

"Me, too," Tyler laughed. "You are an endless mystery, Lorelei."

"How so?" Lorelei shot him a glance, not sure if she should be offended.

"Well, at first you come across so, I don't know, shy almost, but you definitely take control when you need to, even when it scares you. I'm never sure what you're going to do next."

"Is that a good thing?"

"Oh yeah. It's exciting." He hopped off the porch and turned to face her. "So, you have any big plans today?"

"You're joking, right?"

"Well, we probably need to take a trip to town and get some supplies. We need some food and firewood at least. You want to come?"

"I'm a bit tired. Can't we just stay and rest here for a while?"

"Well, you can stay if you'd like. I won't be long."

"Nope," she said, "I'm not letting you go alone. I guess we can go now."

"Great, I'll go get dressed," Tyler leapt from the ground to the porch with one giant stride. He was gone only a minute before he reappeared, wearing a red polo shirt, his hair now in place.

The overgrown driveway meandered down the hillside from the cabin where it met up with a two-lane dirt road. It was ten more miles before they encountered any sort of civilization. The picturesque town of Waynesville looked like it was sleeping amidst the gentle hills, its main street practically a nostalgic postcard. At the general store, they picked up some kerosene, several bundles of firewood, cleaning supplies, and four jugs of purified water. Lorelei bought three books for herself, knowing she would need some form of entertainment back at the cabin. They had an early lunch at a dive restaurant before going to the grocery store and loading up the car with what seemed to be at least three months' worth of necessities.

Once they arrived back at the little cabin, Tyler unloaded the car while Lorelei started cleaning out the kitchen. The refrigerator was coated in a layer of putrid brown slime. She held her breath, sprayed it down with bleach, and wiped away the filth, gagging at the odor. Filling the sink with hot, soapy water, Lorelei washed and rinsed every dish and piece of cutlery that existed in the cupboards. She piled the dishes on the counter to dry and then turned her attention to the dirt-specked floors. Tyler scooped out the ash inside the brick fireplace and dumped it outdoors. He swept the floors in the main living room and helped Lorelei wipe down the cupboards and put the dishes away.

"You want to take a break?" he asked.

Lorelei was on her hands and knees, wiping a sticky spot of heaven-only-knows-what that was next to the sink. She looked up at him, "You read my mind," she said. Sweat was beading on her forehead. Tyler helped her to her feet and they sat in a heap on the sofa. "It's getting there," she sighed.

"A woman's touch," he handed her a glass of water. "Hank and I are pretty good at ignoring the dust."

"Dust? That was more than just dust. I think there was something growing in the fridge."

"Maybe you're right. It was pretty gross. But we have all the time in the world to clean. We can do the rest tomorrow."

"Okay, I won't argue with that. At least we won't be murdered in our sleep by dust bunnies."

Tyler looked at his watch. "It's almost six. Are you getting hungry?"

Lorelei hadn't felt hungry until he mentioned it. "Sure, I guess I could eat."

Tyler stood up, "Good. I'll go start dinner then."

"You want any help?"

"No, you just relax. I'm cooking for you," he tapped her nose with his index finger and then went outside.

Lorelei peered out the window and watched him stack firewood in a pit then stuff crumpled newspaper underneath it. He lit the paper and it started to smoke before little flames erupted, licking the wood until it crackled. Tyler came back to the kitchen, chopped up some ingredients, mixed a few things in a big green bowl, and went back outside, carrying everything on a tray. The smell of the campfire drifted in through the open door.

"You're going to love this," he yelled from outside.

"I'm sure I will," Lorelei called back. She had no idea what he was making, but he was happy, so she didn't care.

Over the next half hour, Tyler was back and forth between the kitchen and the campfire, taking various items out with him. After he was satisfied that dinner was ready, he invited Lorelei to join him outside. He had spread a blanket out on the grass not far from where the fire was burning. Two plates were placed on the blanket, and upon each plate were two foil packets and a slice of cantaloupe. Lorelei took a seat beside him.

"You want some wine?" he asked.

"Just a little bit."

Tyler poured a full glass of red wine and handed it to her.

"Thanks," she said, taking a sip. She carefully peeled open one of the tinfoil packets. Inside was what appeared to be a cooked onion, "Um, what's this?" she asked, feigning enthusiasm.

"Oh, here, let me show you," he took the onion and split it apart, revealing a perfectly cooked meatloaf hidden inside.

"That's pretty impressive!" she took a bite. It wasn't bad, for having been cooked on a campfire. Inside the other foil packet were some chopped potatoes, lightly salted and cooked until they were tender, and just a little smoky. "Where'd you learn to make this?"

"From my dad. We used to come here in the summertime to go fishing when I was a kid. He taught me how to build a fire and make a couple simple things. It was either this or hot dogs."

"This is definitely better than hot dogs," Lorelei took a bite of the savory meatloaf and another drink. She wasn't sure if the wine or the fire was making her hot, but her face was warm and flushed.

"I'm glad you approve," he said, his eyes dancing with the reflection of the flame.

After they finished eating, Tyler poured them each another glass of wine. The sun descended behind the Smoky Mountains, its rays gleaning through soft, white clouds and adorning the hillside with a muted glow, and filling the sky with radiant amber and mauve hues. Crickets began to chirp and somewhere in the forest a mournful owl called out its evening song. Lorelei leaned up against a fallen log to watch the sunset and Tyler went inside, returning with a blanket to cover her legs.

"One last thing," he opened a paper bag and pulled out a box of graham crackers, a package of marshmallows, and a bar of chocolate. "Care for something sweet?"

"Oh, I love these!"

"Here, you open these, I'll go find some sticks," he rummaged around near the trees before he returned with two long branches. He sat on the ground beside Lorelei, took a jackknife from his back pocket, then trimmed the bark from the ends of the branches and sharpened them to a point.

"Thanks again for dinner," Lorelei said, roasting a marshmallow over the dying flames.

"No problem."

"I'm really sorry I dragged you into all this mess."

"Why are you sorry? You saved my life, and not just once, but on at least two occasions now. The fact is, we're here and we're safe. So maybe our lives have taken a slight diversion from what we planned, but that's part of the journey, right?"

"I guess so," Lorelei sighed. She looked up at the sky and could see a few stars beginning to peek through the dark-blue, evening sky.

"And if I'm going to be stuck out here with anyone, I'm glad I'm stuck with you," he gently nudged her with his elbow.

Lorelei was lightheaded. She hoped he was right, that they were safe here, and they were in this together. In fact, she rather liked being alone with him. After all, he was undoubtedly good-looking in a carefree, masculine way, and he was strong and resourceful—

all good qualities in a man that she might have to live with for quite some time. He was the first person who wasn't either another siren or messenger that she'd ever been able to talk to about what she was; he believed because he had seen it, and he wasn't afraid of her. She didn't have to hide what she was from Tyler, and she trusted that he would protect her, as she would protect him. *If it could just be like this always,* she thought, *maybe it wouldn't be so bad to stay here forever.*

"Here, you've got a little… ," he brushed his thumb on her cheek, wiping away a bit of sticky marshmallow that had fixed itself there.

They both stopped, as if frozen in time, their eyes locked on one another. Lorelei's whole body tingled being so close to him. He leaned in, his lips caressing the place where the marshmallow had been, then trailing toward her mouth where he kissed her very gently, his lips only lightly grazing hers before he backed away, searching her eyes for a reply. The first time they kissed he had been so physical, so demanding. Now when he kissed her, the passion in his eyes burned like the fire beside them, but he gave her the choice to decide. Lorelei wanted him, too. She trusted this man, more than anyone else. She put her hand around his neck and pulled him closer to kiss him again. Their mouths touched tenderly. They didn't have to rush into anything. They had all the time in the world here, with each other.

She stopped kissing Tyler for a moment and just looked at him. Her face lit up with a smile. She didn't know if it was infatuation or simply puppy love, but whatever it was, being beside him was perfect. It was Lorelei's act of rebellion that had created this situation, and in her defiance of fate, fate had, in a way, brought them together. It was all so dangerous and beautiful at the same time. The firelight reflected in his dark-brown eyes. *I'm thinking too much*, she thought. *Relax.* And with that Lorelei let herself fall into him, like diving into a deep pool of warm passion.

Her hands reached up and touched his rough cheeks, feeling every contour of his handsome features. His lips pressed more urgently against hers, seeking more and more of her. He tasted like marshmallows and chocolate, a heavenly combination. Tyler's hands tangled roughly in her hair, and then moved down to her neck, her ribs. He pulled her gently against him and Lorelei sat delicately in his lap, his strong arms wrapping around her, encompassing her, worshipping her. Lorelei's mind was both whirling and totally void of thought. There was only Tyler, only here, in front of the smoking campfire and under these bright stars. It was late when they pulled away from each other, exhausted and never having felt so alive. She stared down at him, waiting for the moment he would reveal that this was all a mistake, that he should have never left New Jersey with her, a monster in her own right. But he didn't. His eyes hungrily took in every inch of her, and he reached for her again, kissing every part of her face, burying his face in her thick curls.

"Lorelei," he whispered, his voice loud amongst silent trees, "I think I'm falling in love with you."

Lorelei pressed against him, amazed at how her skin and spine burned in the cold night air. He closed his eyes and climbed off the log they had been sitting on to stretch out on the soft ground. Lorelei lay beside him, her head nuzzled against his sweatshirt.

"Lorelei?" he asked.

"Yes?"

"Sing to me."

And so she did, putting voice to a dreamy and intimate sort of melody; all the while, the many stars above them blazed their approval.

CHAPTER TWENTY-EIGHT

Morning broke and cascaded drops of liquid sunshine over the tiny cabin. Lorelei rose early, still dizzy from the night before and unable to keep a grin off her face. She straggled into the kitchen in her pajamas and set a pot of water on the stove to boil. The pile of blankets on the fold-out couch rustled as its resident came to life, stretching and grunting. Tyler sat up and rubbed the sleep from his eyes. A ray of sunlight perched on his cheek and bathed him with an ethereal glow. He smiled, his eyes twinkling, and Lorelei's knees were suddenly wobbly. She wanted to kiss him again right now, launch herself at him and revel in his embrace, but she restrained herself, settling to give him a nervous little wave of her hand instead.

"Good morning," he said. "Did you sleep all right?"

"Yeah, I slept great."

"You look beautiful."

Lorelei reached up and felt her hair, a mess of curls that had half fallen out of a ponytail and were piled atop her head like a bird's nest. "You're sweet," she said. "Want some coffee?"

"Sure, if you're making some."

Lorelei took two mugs out from the cabinet. She scooped a few spoonfuls of coffee crystals into one and placed a teabag in the other. Tyler rose from the couch and entered the kitchen where he planted a kiss on the nape of Lorelei's neck and rested his chin on her shoulder. She closed her eyes and breathed in the scent of him.

Tyler stepped away and opened the refrigerator door. He took out some eggs, milk, cheese, and bacon, and made two omelets. Lorelei sliced some fruit, placed it on the plates next to the eggs, and then they took everything outside to eat. Like a little old couple who had spent their entire lives together, they sat side by side on the porch with their feet dangling off the edge. Lorelei picked at her food, taking only a few bites, but she drank the mug of tea before it got cold.

"Another day in paradise, huh?" he asked.

"Guess so," Lorelei leaned back on her arms and took in the forest around them.

"It's peaceful here, isn't it?"

"Yeah, it's wonderful, all we could really ask for. Peace… and safety."

"Well, it's not much, but it has its charms," he took a bite of fruit. "I was wondering if maybe you'd like to go for a hike sometime today."

"Sure, I'd love that. After we finish getting this place cleaned, we can get out for a while. Are there a lot of trails around here?"

"Yeah, there's an old one that leads from the main road up to Richland Balsam Mountain Trail. We could try that one. I don't expect we'd actually climb the mountain or anything, but it's a nice trail that Hank and I use to go fishing down at Lake Logan."

"That sounds good. After lunch."

"So, it's a date?"

"Sure, it's a date." A date with Tyler. How strange. So they were *dating*? Lorelei wondered what this made her—was she his girlfriend? It seemed they must be more than that, after all, she had already shared her most intimate secret with him. And now they had been forced to live together, though secretly that situation made her quite happy. It was a strange circumstance, for despite the deep connection she felt with him, they had only known one another for a few days, and had spent a great portion of their time together running away from the threat of a supernatural attack.

"I wish I could paint you," he said, "just like this, no makeup, nothing fancy, just... you. I love this—being here with you, and you so happy."

Lorelei blushed. Tyler gave her a peck on the cheek and stood to take the dishes into the cabin. Daybreak in the mountains was breathtaking. Lorelei noticed that, for the first time in quite a while, the knots in her stomach had almost disappeared. Surrounded by natural beauty, in the company of Tyler, and not worrying about being asked to attend to her duties as a siren—she was filled with a quiet comfort. She didn't know how to capture it, this feeling of true happiness, something that since her father's death had become mysteriously elusive. While she watched the morning break, she sang to herself, a song she had studied from the Compendium.

> *This soft morning haze is the twilight's ascent,*
> *Though equally arrayed in pensive sentiment,*
> *And while it sits, pondering,*
> *The blooming sun, the sphere of life,*
> *Launches over the modest blushing day,*
> *While, like a wounded soldier, the darkness*
> *Has crept out of its grasp;*

An eternal game of cat and mouse they play.
The range extends and adorns the horizon and
The new morning is gilded with birdsong.
These mountains I would watch for hours
In darkness to see this new birth,
Half in stupor and half in awe,
I rise majestic with the sun and
Worship in this great cathedral Earth.

She brushed the dirt from the back of her legs and went inside, piling their plates in a sink full of soapy water. She put together a checklist of chores to be done. Lorelei pulled down the curtains throughout the cabin, washed them in the bath tub and hung them from the porch railing to dry. Tyler climbed up on top of the cabin and pulled clumps of slimy leaves from the gutters. He repaired a few loose shingles and when he had finished, he and Lorelei worked together to scrape away the moss that was growing on the north side of the cabin.

With everything cleaned up, the place was almost nice. It was small, cozy, and suitable enough for the two of them to stay there for quite some time, at least until winter came. Lorelei had never had a place of her own beyond a dorm room, and even though this cabin wasn't really hers, it was the only home she needed. *We could paint it in the spring. Maybe light blue,* she thought, and began scouting about for a plot of land where she might be able to start a little garden. For the time being, she was content to play house, but they couldn't stay here forever. She still had a fair amount of life insurance money left in her checking account, but it wouldn't last forever. Tyler had mentioned a possible settlement with the owners of the destroyed cargo ship, but that probably wouldn't happen for a very long time. At some point they would both have to find work and someplace more permanent to settle, but for now, she was content.

The chores took longer than expected, so they weren't able to leave for the hike until mid-afternoon. The weather was still good and Tyler reasoned they still had plenty of daylight left for a decent hike; he packed a backpack with some necessities—bottled water, granola bars, a telescopic fishing pole and a box of lures, a roll of toilet paper, two of Lorelei's books, a blanket, and a map. They threw everything in the Jeep and drove for several miles along the curvy mountain road before turning down a dirt road. Wild viburnum bushes with their clusters of little white flowers lined the road; regal maples and the fanning green leaves of ash trees blocked out the overhead sun.

Tyler pulled the car into a nondescript parking lot on the edge of the deeper woods. A trailhead marked the path ahead: *Great Balsam Ridge Trail.* Lorelei got out of the car; her nose filled with the sweet smell of Fraser firs while the gentle coo of a mourning dove sounded in the forest beyond where they stood.

"All set?" Tyler asked.

"I think so… don't go too fast though, okay?"

"C'mon, a Colorado girl like you ought to be able to handle these hills."

"Being from Colorado does not make me a hiking aficionado, you know."

Tyler chuckled and swung the backpack around his shoulders. He set off into the woods and Lorelei followed behind him. At first the trail was relatively easy; the path was smooth, meandering up and down the hills, peeking through flower-decked meadows and across fallen logs that traversed glassy streams. As they went along, the trail increased in elevation, and the path itself became more rugged. Tyler helped Lorelei over the rocks that were scattered in piles covering the trail.

"Can we just... stop and sit for a minute?" Lorelei was out of breath.

"Just a little farther," Tyler replied, "we're almost there."

"Almost where?"

"You'll see," Tyler forged ahead, leaving Lorelei straggling behind him. The trail straightened out a bit and circled around a low hillside. Bright sunlight crossed their path, blinding Lorelei, but as soon as she stepped back into the shadow she could see an old house with a tall chimney ahead of them. It was a two-story, brick house with a crumbling facade, the roof pocked with holes, and one of the walls half fallen to the ground. Tyler ran ahead, jumped across a little stream and bounded toward the dilapidated house.

"Come over here," he called.

"Hold on, I'll be right there!" Drenched with sweat, Lorelei approached the creek before her and knelt beside it. She reached into the cold, refreshing water and splashed her face. She rose to her feet again and leapt over the stream to join Tyler beside the old structure, "What is this place?"

"This is the old Hamlin House. It's been here forever, but it's been unoccupied for a long time. Old man Hamlin died when I was a kid."

"You remember the guy that lived here?"

"It's hard to forget somebody like that," Tyler started walking through the bushes toward the back of the house. "The Hamlins were mountain folk, real backwoods kind of people. No running water, see—there's what's left of the outhouse," he pointed at a small outbuilding that was leaning sideways. "They hunted or gathered whatever they needed and otherwise kept to themselves.

The only Hamlin still around when I was growing up was Tobias. He had the nastiest, shaggiest beard and had such a thick accent you could barely understand him, some old Appalachian dialect."

"How'd you know him?"

"Everybody in town knew the old man, and when he came to the point he couldn't take care of himself, the townspeople would help him out a little, even though most folks were a little scared of him. He just pretended not to notice. My dad helped paint the house one year, and if we caught fish down at the lake, we'd always leave a few on his doorstep. The old guy died out here one winter—froze to death in the house. Guess he had run out of firewood and a place like this never had electricity or any sort of heating."

"That's so sad," Lorelei picked up a shard of blue pottery that was wedged between two stones on the ground beside the house and put it in her pocket. "Why don't they tear it down?"

"Lots of reasons. It's pretty inaccessible, so it's not easy to bring a bunch of heavy machinery this far out in the woods. Then there's the historic preservationists who think it should be saved, which is nice in theory, but nobody seems inclined to actually want to pay to restore it. But I think the real reason is because the people in town think it's cursed."

"And why do they think that?"

"Tobias had a daughter named Isabel. Her mother died in childbirth and Isabel was a weak, little baby. She was always sick and as she grew up, he refused to put the child in school or even take her to the doctor. The courts decided that it was in the little girl's best interest to be removed from his care and placed in a home. One day they came to take her away and Tobias stood up to the police—he aimed a shotgun at them. You have to remember, he was just a mountain man; he lived by his gun. I don't think he actually meant to do anything with it, but they didn't give him a chance to back down. One of the policemen fired first. The bullet shot through the wall and hit Isabel. The official story is that the little girl died here, but there are rumors that she lived and was taken away from her father. People think Tobias placed a curse on anyone who would try to take anything away from him ever again."

"That's terrible. But how do they know the place is actually cursed?"

"A couple years ago the county tried to tear this place down," Tyler pointed to the wall that was partially collapsed, "but the workers left spooked after only a few hours on the job. They claimed to have seen strange lights in the woods and heard the sound of a child laughing. Some say the ghost of little Isabel is still haunting this house."

"They're scared of ghosts? Shouldn't they know better than to believe in that sort of thing?"

"You tell me. Up until just recently I wouldn't have believed in sirens, either."

"Yes, but…"

"So it only stands to reason that if creatures like you exist, other things that we would have once considered myth or superstition might exist as well."

"I guess you have a point."

"I'm not necessarily saying that I personally believe in them, because I have no idea if they exist or not, but I wouldn't put it outside of the realm of possibility, knowing what I know now. Haven't you ever been curious?"

"About what?"

"That maybe there are other beings out there with powers like yours, you know, I mean, not your specific powers, but beings that have other superhuman capabilities."

"No, I can't say I've given it much thought."

"You never even asked the question?"

"Nope."

"Man, that would be the *first* thing I would want to know."

"It never came up in conversation, and to be honest, I had enough difficulty accepting what I was that I don't think I would have wanted to know. Even if that were the case, I don't see how it would be any of my concern, anyhow."

"It's no big deal," he said, "I was just curious, that's all."

Tyler jumped through one of the lower-level windows and put out his arms to help her inside. Plaster was crumbling off the interior walls where the elements of nature had been allowed to wear it away. Some of the interior rooms still had wallpaper, though it was greatly faded. In the kitchen, one room that still had all of its walls intact, there were a number of old kitchen items—a dairy churn in the corner, a wash basin with two steel buckets inside, and several very ragged cross-stitched items left hanging on the wall. In the living room beyond the kitchen was an old upright piano missing several keys and at the bottom of the piano was a hole where a family of mice must have chewed through the wood to make their home.

Lorelei tried to imagine the young Isabel, isolated from society and any semblance of normal life, learning to play this piano, but the thought itself seemed odd; if she were out here all alone with an unrefined father, there would have been no one to instruct her. No, this instrument must have belonged to her mother. But why would a woman refined enough to play the piano and spend long hours doing cross-stitch marry a man who was so different from her, out here in a place that would have been so far from her home? Being in the deserted house made Lorelei sad—it was like looking in on another person's life, and a particularly tragic one at that.

Tyler, satisfied with his investigation of the building, led Lorelei back outside. They walked farther along the trail past the remnants of a decaying barn. Just down the hillside from the barn was a quiet grove of trees where Tyler spread out the blanket that he had tucked in his backpack. He lay down on it, facing the sky, and put his hands behind his head. Lorelei rested her head on his chest and started to read one of her books. She felt him breathing beneath her, deep and rhythmically. The book held her interest for a while, but when her eyes grew heavy, she put it away and rested.

Tyler shot upright. Lorelei's head hit the ground and she was unceremoniously jostled from her sleep. It was already twilight. They had been lying there in the forest a very long time, long enough that the sun was retreating from the sky.

"Did you hear that?" he whispered frantically.

"No, hear what?" Lorelei sat up and looked at him. "I can't believe it's already so dark out. We'd better get back…"

He held up his hand, "Shhh… listen."

She tried to hear what it was that Tyler had heard, but there was nothing.

"Did you bring a flashlight?" she asked.

"Hold on, be quiet," he stood up and looked into the woods, "There's something out there. I just heard it."

"It's probably an animal…"

"No, it sounded human."

Lorelei was puzzled, "Like someone talking?"

"Like laughter—" his voice stopped and Lorelei heard it, too. He was right. There was definitely something that sounded like laughter off in the distance. Her ears perked. She knew it could be something else, perhaps some strange birdcall that they were misinterpreting, but it sounded distinctly human.

"Let's get going," she said. "I can't believe I slept for so long."

"Hold on a minute, I want to know who's out there."

"Whoever, or whatever it is, let's just leave it alone and get back to the car, okay?"

"Look!" Tyler pointed into the forest, "See the light out there?"

There was indeed a light in the forest, like a faint bobbing lantern, flashing intermittently, and then disappearing, only to reappear in another position a moment later.

"What is it?" he walked toward the light.

"Tyler, stop!"

"Just wait right here, I'll be back in a minute. I just want to see if it's her."

"Who?"

"The Hamlin girl."

"Isabel? Tyler, it's an urban legend. There are no *ghosts* out here."

"You don't know that. I'm going to check it out. I'll be right back. Don't go anywhere."

Tyler ran into the forest. Lorelei was hot with exasperation and frustration. Stuck in the middle of the woods, abandoned by her guide, and alone in the dusk, Lorelei was furious. He had no right to do this to her. Moonlight beamed down on the little patch of ground where she stood, but the forest was dark.

She called out his name, but there was no reply. The wind began to blow through the trees and create a low sound, something between a whistle and a hum. The breeze on her bare skin made her shiver and row upon row of tiny goosebumps raised up on her arms. Her heart was racing. *What's taking him so long?* Underneath the hum of the wind, Lorelei heard another sound. It wasn't the laugh she had heard before. This noise was quiet and distant at first but it grew louder. Piercing and unmistakable, this was the sound of the Song. *Shit.*

Lorelei's head was spinning. This couldn't be happening—they were hundreds of miles from the ocean. They were supposed to be safe out here. *It's just my imagination,* she thought. But as hard as she tried, the sound grew more and more pressing. And Tyler was alone out there with whatever fate had in store for him. She leapt forward, her feet crunching through fallen leaves and undergrowth. Moonlight poured over the treetops, their dark shadows disorienting her.

Lorelei screamed for Tyler repeatedly until it hurt her throat. She jumped across a little stream and when she landed on the other side, she noticed that the ground beneath her feet was wet. By now she was well off the trail. Even if she doubled back to the place where Tyler had left her, she wasn't sure she'd be able to find the spot again. She stopped running and closed her eyes to listen for the Song. It was still weaving through the trees, but she focused on it until she had pinpointed which direction it was coming from, then adjusted her course, and continued ahead. The ground was no longer merely damp; it was now akin to tromping through puddles. Her shoes were soaked through; splashing water accompanied every footstep. Lorelei's body trembled, both from the cold and the uncertainty of being alone on this Appalachian hillside. She was lost.

CHAPTER TWENTY-NINE

Pale moonlight streamed through the woods ahead, where just beyond a thick nest of bushes, the forest opened to reveal a clearing. Lorelei ran toward it, sloshing through ankle-deep water. Maybe she could get her bearings there, find Tyler, and get the hell out of here. She hurtled over the cumbersome ground cover and sank knee deep into the water, realizing too late that the clearing she had seen from the forest was a lake tucked in among the trees, and she had just run straight into it. The fog was so thick that it completely covered the lake in a swirling, smoky haze. *This can't be happening.* She yelled his name into the night air, but there was no answer. He had to be around here somewhere. They had only been apart a few minutes. Whatever was happening, he wasn't safe and Lorelei needed to find him, fast.

The loud crack of a tree branch breaking turned Lorelei's attention to the right, but the shore was obscured amidst the fog. Her eyes focused as best they could through the hovering mist and she detected movement in the distance. Beside the lake, the figure of a man emerged from the trees, slowly walking toward the water. Lorelei screamed for him, but he didn't respond, steadily moving forward, step by step. She broke into a run, desperate to reach him before he crossed into the lake. Water splashed up around her. Her pace slowed by the mud caking around her feet, straining her every step. Lorelei headed toward the trees, where the water was not as deep and the mud was less consuming. She pulled on tree branches in an effort to brace herself from falling even as her feet slid in the muck.

Tyler stopped walking and stood still, just at the water's edge. Besides the sound of Lorelei's feet splashing through the water, everything was quiet. She ran ahead, separated from him by a mound of rock and earth. She climbed over the rocks and slid down the other side, pulled herself back up on her feet, now sprinting toward Tyler as fast as her legs would allow.

Out of the corner of her eye, several dark figures appeared in the lake almost as though they had simply formed in the mist. Four heads bobbed in the water, at least thirty yards away from where Tyler was standing. The water about them shimmered with an opalescent sheen, like an oil spill. The surface of the water seemed to be boiling and the figures rose up, their shoulders now visible above the lake. As Lorelei drew closer, she could tell they were women, though their faces were unfamiliar to her. They couldn't be sirens; their features were not as fine and fair, and their skin had a gray pallor, not the milky glow of the sirens. Besides that, their eyes were solid black, as dark and empty as a moonless night.

The four women emerged from the lake effortlessly until only their hips and legs were beneath the surface. The fog collected itself around them in thick, black ribbons. Their long hair billowed around their heads wildly, giving the appearance that they were floating underwater. One of the women in the middle of the group reached out for Tyler, and he mindlessly stepped toward her and into the lake.

"Stop!" Lorelei screamed as she closed in on him, grabbing his arm and yanking him around to face her. Tyler's eyes were blank. He pulled against her and took another step closer to the women.

Lorelei shoved him hard and put herself between Tyler and the four figures, blocking him with her arm. "Who *are* you?" she yelled toward the mist.

There was no answer. It was as though they couldn't see her. Lorelei spun around and braced her arms against Tyler's shoulders. "Wake up! They're trying to take you! You've got to snap out of this!" In a moment of frustration, she drew back her arm and smacked him on the side of the face. He shook his head, and for a moment, Lorelei could see a glimpse of Tyler beneath the trance. It didn't last long. Moments later, he was again glassy-eyed, looking ahead as though he could see right through her.

"Leave him alone!" Lorelei screamed through the fog.

Their dark eyes focused on her. The woman on the right, the one who seemed to be the youngest, put her finger to her lips.

Lorelei remembered all the instructions Helen had given her in the cove about controlling her emotions to harness her power, but this wasn't the time for that. Her anger rose to a crescendo and she released her emotions to unleash pure fury. She thrust her hands into the lake and sent up a violent spray of water, then clinched her jaw and swooped her right hand in a semicircle from her left hip, over across her body, and up past her right shoulder. Water sliced through the air, pushing the women several feet backward. The figures charged ahead, anger now evident upon their faces. Lorelei dipped her fingers into the lake, stirred the water, and created a massive wave that rolled across the lake. The crest surged above their bodies and they disappeared into the darkness.

"What's going on?" Tyler asked. He was free from the trance and genuinely confused to be standing here beside her, almost up to his waist in lake water.

"You've got to get out of here!" she yelled. "Run!"

"Why? What's happening?"

"Just go! Now!" she shoved him.

Tyler took a step backward, almost tripping over his own feet, and then ran out of the lake and up the hillside. Lorelei returned her attention to the four women who were slowly rising out of the water once more. There was no longer any anger in their eyes, no emotion at all, just an eerie blank gaze.

"You can't have him!" Lorelei's voice shook, but she stood fast as they approached.

The ground beneath her feet started to tremble, causing the water to ripple. Above the troubled water, the mist circled faster and faster, spinning upwards into a cyclone. Through the veil of mist, another dark figure arose like an apparition; its arms angled out to the side, its long hair a tumultuous, windswept tangle like Medusa. As its body took shape, the wind that encircled the figure died and the thick fog retreated to cover the surface of the water. The body ascended from the lake and moonlight struck its face. Lorelei recognized her as clear as day.

Calliope.

Lorelei's jaw dropped in awe. This was not the Calliope she had seen transformed in the ocean beside their home in Chatham— that beautiful, mystical creature that had accompanied her into the sea. The creature that hovered above the water now was beyond terrifying, a monstrous transfiguration. Her eyes were like black pools resting on sharp cheekbones that were covered in thin gray skin, with clearly visible blue veins running beneath. She fixed her cold stare at Lorelei and her lips curled into a scowl.

"Lorelei," she spoke, her voice like venom, "you pathetic, unworthy *child*."

Lorelei bit her tongue. If Calliope wanted to hurl insults at her, she knew she probably deserved them, but to hear her use the word pathetic made Lorelei's sense of pride bristle.

"What's wrong, little girl?" Calliope moved menacingly toward the place where Lorelei stood, the other women closing in behind her. "Helen's little pet... you are so weak... weak and stupid."

"Why can't you leave us alone?"

Calliope cackled, "You still don't understand, do you? This is your fault. It was your selfish desire to play the hero that led us here. You're a pitiful excuse for a siren, and truth be told, you shouldn't even exist. You've disgraced our family, just like your mother before you, and I intend to set things right."

The words stung Lorelei like a slap to the face. "I'm not letting you have him!"

A calculating smile spread across Calliope's face. "Lorelei, I've been patient with you, but you refuse to listen to reason. I will give you one last chance to step aside before you get hurt."

"No!" Lorelei pressed her palms into the water and lifted them over her head. The water cascaded beneath her hands creating a dense wall that separated her from Calliope. Lorelei took a step forward, pushing the wall of water as she went.

"Lori!" Tyler called. He was standing just a few feet behind her.

"What are you doing? I told you to get out of here!" she yelled, her arms still outstretched in front of her.

"I couldn't leave you."

"I can handle this! They're after you, not me. You've got to—" her voice was cut off as Calliope's hand burst through the barrier, wrapping her long, cold fingers around Lorelei's throat. She pulled Lorelei's head through the veil of water and held it face to face with her own. A black, viscous substance trailed from the corner of Calliope's eyes along the side of her face. Lorelei struggled to pry away from Calliope's grip and the wall of water came crashing down. Calliope squeezed harder, her fingertips grasping around Lorelei's trachea, pushing her down until she was on her knees, waist deep in water. Lorelei gasped for air and arched backward violently, but Calliope held firm.

"Did you think you could hide from me forever?" she asked, her soulless eyes unwavering.

"Let her go!" Tyler rushed forward, but as he did, Calliope flicked her wrist and sent a wave of water toward him, knocking him into the lake.

"Take care of him," Calliope said callously. The four figures approached and summoned Tyler again.

"No," Lorelei sputtered.

"What is it about him?" Calliope asked. "Why do you care so much for this boy? It's tragic really, you've done so much to try to save him, and now you're going to watch him die." She moved her hand from the front of Lorelei's throat and placed it around the back of her neck, then with her other hand, she held Lorelei's jaw and forcibly jerked her head to face the women as they led Tyler deeper into the lake.

"Tyler!" Lorelei screamed. He turned around, panic in his eyes. Without laying so much as a finger on him, they had him completely under their control. The youngest-looking one opened her mouth and let out a shrill cry that rang across the lake. Blood trickled out of his ear and ran down his neck. Violently, he bent forward at the waist, his head submerged below the dark waters. "Please, don't do this… ," she begged.

"I'm not doing anything. This is the natural course of events. It's just his time."

Lorelei struggled to stand and something sharp jabbed her side. She reached in her pocket and found the little shard of pottery that she had picked up back at the Hamlin house. She gripped it firmly and, with one direct and forceful move, thrust the jagged end of the shard deep into Calliope's left thigh. Calliope released Lorelei and let out a ferocious shriek. Lorelei ran away from her and toward Tyler. His body had betrayed him, bent at the waist with his head held in the water by these creatures. They noticed Lorelei approaching and one of them turned to face her. She had a prominent nose, an angular, pointed chin, and blonde hair that undulated above her head.

The figure glided through the water until she was directly before Lorelei. Lorelei balled up her fingers, reached back, and let her fist fly at her face. The woman ducked to the side and caught Lorelei's wrist in her own hand, digging her nails into Lorelei's arm. Lorelei spun and twisted her arm until she freed herself. She pulled her arm forward across her chest, and then shot her elbow backward, striking the woman in the nose. She doubled over, both hands clutching her nose and screaming. The other women stopped their assault on Tyler in reaction to the shrieks of pain that were now sounding over the lake. Tyler stood upright, his eyes connected with hers and he reached out for her.

She took a step forward, but something tugged at her ankle and she fell down face first in the lake, her foot having been pulled out from beneath her. She lifted her head out of the water and gasped for air before being tugged under again. Lorelei's hip hit the bottom of the lake and her body was dragged several feet. She kicked fiercely, but whatever had her wasn't going to let go. Eventually, her free foot found the bottom of the lake. She reoriented herself and pushed her body upright until she was standing. Her other leg was bent at the knee, still held from behind. Calliope's face was beside hers, a gruesome gray visage streaked with black tears.

"You little bitch!" she hissed. Her left hand grabbed Lorelei around the neck and her fingers, like talons, dug into Lorelei's shoulders and pushed her under the water. Lorelei thrashed like a wild animal, her fingernails scratched at Calliope's hands, but she remained fixed beneath the surface. Through the water, Calliope's face was distorted; she looked like a ghoul in the moonlight.

Feet kicking and arms madly swiping at Calliope's face, Lorelei was running out of air. If she drowned tonight, no siren would come to offer her any comfort. There was only this monster hovering above, its thin lips grinning in triumph at her suffering. Lorelei prayed for transformation, the moment that she would connect with the Song and become a siren, but the change didn't come. The noise of this darker song vibrated through her chest, but Lorelei remained in her fragile human state. Her body needed air and her lungs involuntarily contracted, pulling a mouthful of water down Lorelei's throat. Her chest burned. A flash of light filled the sky behind Calliope. With what little consciousness remained, Lorelei gave one final kick, and to her surprise, found that she was no longer pinned below the water.

Lorelei pulled her torso upright until she felt the cold night air sting her cheeks. She coughed hard, sputtering up some of the water she had inhaled. She sucked in the life-giving oxygen and waited for the blood to return to her head. Her senses returned to her and she looked around for Calliope, but the creature that had only moments ago been trying to drown her had seemingly vanished. Something struck Lorelei's side. On the surface of the lake a severed hand was bobbing with a silver spear lanced through the wrist and an emerald ring on the fourth finger. Lorelei screamed, picked up the spear, and threw it as far away from her body as she could launch it.

The sky was filled with light, a bluish glow that illuminated the trees at the edge of the lake. Lorelei held her hand above her eyes and squinted to try to see if she could determine the source of the light. She knew that a brain depleted of oxygen might have visions of things that weren't really there, but what she saw at that moment on the edge of the lake certainly seemed real. There was a woman standing there, facing Lorelei and emanating light. She had on a full vest of armor; a silver breastplate covered her chest and thousands of shiny metal scales surrounded her hips and thighs, stopping just at the knee. Dark leather boots went halfway up her calves and a sword hilt rested at her side. A silver helmet covered her head, but long, black hair hung below the helmet, gently blowing in the breeze. Lorelei rubbed her eyes, unsure if the vision was real, and when she opened them, the armor-clad woman and the light had disappeared.

Lorelei trudged toward the shore, still coughing. Whoever the woman was, her arrival had heralded Calliope's disappearance, though Lorelei hadn't exactly seen what had happened. She remembered the severed hand that had floated past her after she emerged from the water. The emerald ring was unmistakably Calliope's, but who had thrown the spear that had detached her hand from her body? Had it been the lady she'd seen on the shore?

Tyler. She had almost forgotten about him. Lorelei clambered out of the lake and called out his name.

"He's over here!" a male voice answered. Lorelei followed the voice behind some bushes where two men were kneeling next to Tyler who was lying in the brush.

She rushed over and knelt beside him, stooping to cradle his head in her arms. He opened his eyes and looked back up at her.

"Hey," he said weakly, "you okay?"

"I'm fine," Lorelei made a quick assessment of her body. Her neck and wrist were sore, but she was still in one piece, "Are you... hurt?"

"I think I'm okay," he coughed. "Are they gone?"

"I think so," she looked back at the lake, but there was no sign of life out there anymore.

"They tried to kill me," his blue lips quivered.

"I know," she brushed the hair out of his eyes and held him close to her chest, letting her body warm his. "You're okay now. We're going to be okay." She tried to believe it, too.

CHAPTER THIRTY

"He's all right, Lorelei, but you need to give him room to breathe," the man said. Lorelei looked up at the face of the man who had spoken to her.

"Aeson?" her eyes grew large. "What are you doing here?"

"We came to help you," he replied.

"Who's *we*?" Lorelei asked.

"This is Paul," he motioned to the middle-aged man with him who had curly, brown hair graying at the temples. Lorelei eyed the stranger skeptically.

"He's another messenger," said Aeson. "I brought him for backup."

"Calliope… she tried to kill me."

"I know. She's not right in the head anymore. She's gone rogue."

"What do you mean?" Lorelei asked.

"She disobeyed Helen and left Chatham two days ago, hell-bent on finding you. She's left the assembly for good."

"The other women with her, were they sirens, too?"

"They used to be," Aeson said, "but not anymore. They're all banshees now. They tried to drown this one, but we were able to pull him away. We didn't know Calliope had recruited anyone else to her cause. I didn't recognize all of them, but the blonde one was definitely Silviana Musgrove."

"Who is she?"

"She's from the colony in Savannah. I've met her a few times before. Never thought she'd be one to turn banshee."

Tyler groaned and tried to sit up.

"Easy there," Lorelei told him. "Not too fast."

"I'm okay," he replied.

"We're going to need to evacuate this area. Do you think you'll be able to walk out of here?" Paul asked him.

"I think so," Tyler said.

"Let me help you," he reached out and helped Tyler to his feet. Tyler stood up and put his arm around Paul's shoulders. He stumbled a little, but eventually found his footing and Paul helped him up the hill.

"Here, Lorelei," said Aeson, "take a flashlight." She caught it as he tossed it to her, then flicked it on, lighting the forest floor to help guide Tyler and Paul.

The trip back to the car was slow going. It took over ten minutes before they had even reached the path near the Hamlin House, where they stopped to allow Tyler to rest before continuing on their way. The trail seemed so much longer under the cover of night, with the hooting of owls echoing in the trees around them. At least the path was downhill most of the way, and eventually, Tyler had regained enough strength that he didn't need Paul's help to walk. When they had finally made it back to the parking lot, Aeson took the keys to Lorelei's Jeep and helped Tyler get into the backseat. Beside the Jeep was another car, a small sedan that Aeson and Paul had driven here. Paul got in the sedan and followed them along the windy roads.

"Thank you," Lorelei said. "I don't know how you found us, but I'm glad you did."

"I told you to call me if you needed anything," Aeson said sternly. "I meant it."

"I'm sorry," she said. "Things got out of hand."

"I'd almost lost you once before. I didn't intend for it to happen again."

They drove through the dark mountains in silence. She didn't like being chastised, but she was too grateful to contradict him. With Aeson here, she could stop worrying so much. Despite all the effort she had to stay away from the Deleauxes, having him next to her gave her a certain sense of peace.

"We have a lot to talk about," said Aeson.

"I know," Lorelei sighed. "Let's just get back to the cabin first."

She guided him up the mountain roads until they finally reached the small cabin. He pulled up beside it and turned off the Jeep.

"I'm not mad at you, Lorelei. I just want to keep you safe."

"I understand. I won't let it happen again," she said and she meant it. Lorelei was tired of running, tired of fighting. If Aeson could offer her safety, she would gladly take it.

The four of them entered the building and Lorelei led Tyler into the bedroom where he put on a dry pair of sweatpants and a T-shirt and came back out to rest on the couch. Lorelei covered him with a blanket. In the kitchen, she ran a washcloth under hot water and returned to Tyler, gently placing the warm cloth on his head. She sat beside him for a long time, softly stroking his hair until he closed his eyes.

"You probably need to get some rest, too," Aeson said.

SERENADE

"I don't think I can sleep right now," Lorelei held her hand out to show him it was still shaking.

"Here," Aeson pulled a flask out of his back pocket and handed it to her.

"What's this?" she asked.

"Whiskey. Drink some... you need it."

Lorelei took the flask, fumbled with the cap, and took a long gulp. It burned her throat. She coughed and a little of the liquid spilled down her chin. She wiped her lips with the back of her hand and then took another swig.

"Easy now," said Aeson, taking the flask back from her. "Feel better?"

"Yeah, I actually do." The warmth of the liquor glided through her body.

"She's a minor, Aeson," Paul shot them a look of disapproval.

"After what she's been through tonight, if anyone deserves a drink, she does."

"Just be careful," Paul said in a low voice. He stared at Lorelei, as though he were trying to recognize her.

She sat down on one of the kitchen chairs and asked, "How... did you find us?"

"We knew you were south of Baltimore," said Aeson. "That whole thing with tunnel has been all over the news, but we didn't know where you were headed. You weren't easy to find, but it was Deidre who coerced one of the bank clerks into telling her when you used your debit card. He called yesterday and said you'd made several purchases in Waynesville, North Carolina, so we drove out here, but we had no idea where you were staying. Helen's been in the cove for days listening for any sign of you."

"Listening for me?"

"You're all connected to each other. If you made contact with any body of water that runs to the ocean, she'd know where you were. She finally felt your presence and called us, but we weren't the only ones who tracked you here." *The stream on the trail.* Lorelei remembered plunging her hands into the cold water and splashing her face. *That must have been it.* "Ever since Calliope left looking for you, Helen's been beside herself."

"I don't understand... I thought you all agreed with her," she said. "You all said Calliope was right. Even Helen agreed Tyler had to die, so why didn't you let the banshees take him?"

"The day after you left, we were given specific instructions not to follow you, to leave you alone, whatever happened, and if you chose to let him live, that was your decision alone."

"Who told you that?"

"The Elysienne."

"The *what?*" Lorelei asked.

"She's a seer," said Paul. "The Elysienne governs the messengers and sirens alike; she's more powerfully bound to Idis. The messengers have a very specific and limited ability to see the future, but the Elysienne has a greater connection to the Sight."

"The Sight?"

"Sirens have the Song, and messengers have the Sight," he said. "They're both elements of the same source, they just manifest themselves in different ways. It's what lets us know when the sirens are going to be called. But we can't see everything. The Elysienne's vision is broader."

"So why did Calliope follow us if this... Elysienne... told her not to?"

"Calliope refused to accept it," said Aeson. "Her whole life she's been taught to obey fate or suffer the consequences. When she saw you were going to get off without any sort of punishment, she became unhinged. We tried to stop her, but she was too far gone. She took the power unto herself and decided she was going to teach you a lesson. I guess the irony is that in her disobedience to both the matriarch of her family and the Elysienne as well, she was cast away from Idis and turned banshee."

"But if the two of you followed me out here, aren't you also disobeying the Elysienne?"

"When I became a messenger, I swore to protect the sirens under my charge. I vowed to protect you from all harm. That is the oath that binds me. My allegiance is with you… always."

"You need to get some sleep," Paul interrupted. "Aeson and I will stay on guard through the night."

Lorelei looked up at him incredulously, "How do you expect me to sleep after what happened out there? I almost drowned tonight."

"That's why you need to rest," he said. "The only reason you recovered faster than this young man is because you're a siren, but that doesn't make you impervious to the physical effects of nearly drowning if you went through it unchanged. You're only human— you need to let your body recuperate."

Paul's eyes were kind. She wanted to believe him, but her mind played out a thousand different scenarios in which he and Aeson left with Tyler during the night and finished him. How could she believe that they wouldn't harm him, that their motivation was any different from Calliope's?

"I can see you're troubled," Paul said. "Don't be. You're safe now. I give you my word that no harm will come to you, or him, this evening. We'll watch over you."

Lorelei resigned herself to trust him. If they'd wanted to, they could have simply let the banshees kill Tyler at the lake, but instead they had pulled him from the lake and resuscitated him.

Lorelei took one last look at Tyler sleeping soundly before she retreated to the bedroom. Paul and Aeson stayed up through the night taking shifts patrolling the cabin for any signs of trouble.

It was early morning when Paul woke Lorelei from her sleep. She grumbled and rubbed her eyes. It took her a moment to remember the face of the man at her bedside.

"Good morning," he said. "We'll be leaving soon, and I need to speak with you before we go."

"Right now?" Lorelei pulled her covers up around her shoulders.

"Yes. It's important."

"I just woke up. Can I at least get dressed first?"

"Yes, put on some clothes and meet me outside, but be quick about it." He left the room.

Lorelei was annoyed at his abruptness and she didn't like that he had barged into her room uninvited and woken her up, but she wasn't about to argue with him. He was confident, direct, and had taken charge of the situation, and in a way, Lorelei was relieved. She rose from the bed, put on some clean clothes, twisted her hair into a braid, and left the room. Tyler was still sleeping, so Lorelei walked quietly through the cabin and unlatched the front door where Paul was waiting on the front porch.

"You wanted to talk to me?" she asked.

"Yes, we have to make plans. For you, and for… him."

"Tyler," she said, "his name's Tyler."

He nodded, "Yes, for you and Tyler."

"What kind of plans?"

"For your protection, primarily. The banshees that have been hunting you were scared off last night, but they're still a threat. There's a very real possibility that they'll come looking for you again. We have a plan to keep them from finding either of you."

"And what do you suggest?"

"Aeson will drive you back to Chatham. You'll be safer there with Helen. As for Tyler, I'll take him somewhere the banshees won't be able find him."

"No," Lorelei's pulse quickened, "he should stay with me. I've been the one protecting him all along. He can come to Chatham, too."

"No, he can't. Calliope's main interest is in finding him—she only attacked you because you were in her way. If he's at Chatham, he won't be easy to hide, and when Calliope finds out he's there and comes hunting for him, you'll be at risk. We cannot afford to jeopardize an entire assembly of sirens over one man. Your purpose is too great."

"Then I'll go with you."

"Lorelei, none of what you've done changes the fact that you are still a siren, with duties to perform as required by your position," his voice was certain and unapologetic. "Your place is with your family. You are still young and have much to learn. You cannot abandon your post, or else you might as well join up with Calliope."

"This isn't fair!" Lorelei yelled. "After all this, I'm supposed to just go back to Chatham and pretend like nothing ever happened?"

"That's exactly what you're going to do. You will resume your training, Tyler will be safe, and we hope that eventually Calliope will be found and brought back under control."

"And once you find her, Tyler can come back?"

"Maybe," he said, "but I have no idea when or if that will happen. It's highly likely you may never see him again."

Lorelei suddenly resented Paul. He had come into her life and her home, and was dictating the terms by which she would have to live. Who was he to make this decision? In this year alone, she had lost everything—her father had died, her mother had stopped talking to her, Helen and Deidre had taken the side of the woman who would ultimately try to kill her. Tyler was the only one she could talk to, the only person who understood her. She wasn't going to allow this stranger to tear him away from her.

"No. No, this *plan* doesn't work for me. We'll have to think of something else."

"Please don't make this difficult," he rubbed his temples with his fingers. "We've already exhausted the possibilities and this is the best decision for everyone. He'll be out of harm's way and you'll be back where you belong."

"I don't care if that's what *you* think is best, I've done too much to let him go. He needs me to protect him."

He paused for a moment. "Lorelei, I know you care for him. I can see it in your eyes. I understand how much it hurts to lose someone so important to you, but if you love him, you have to let him go."

"How could you possibly understand? You don't have a clue! He's staying with me. That's final."

"Lorelei Clark, I am the Emissary of the Elysienne. My decision, not yours, is what is final," his broad shoulders towered over her and his eyes conveyed that his patience had waned. "You may not like this decision, but you will do as I tell you."

"I'm not some child you can just order about. I deserve to have a say."

"You've had your say, but if you care about Tyler, you will release him into my custody. Calliope will not rest until she's satisfied that he's been eliminated, since you were unwilling to do the job. The fact that he's received a reprieve from the Elysienne and is being provided refuge is practically unheard of, not to mention an extremely gracious offer. You can't run forever. The banshees will catch up with you again, and Calliope will finish the job. The only way you can truly keep him safe is to let him go."

Lorelei's eyes brimmed with tears, "I... I don't know how."

"It's going to be all right," his voice was more sympathetic. "It's never easy, but sometimes you have to make a rational decision even when your heart wants something else, even if it means letting go of the one you care about more than anything else. It's a difficult sacrifice."

She knew he was right. "Where will you take him?"

"I can't tell you that," he said. "The less you know, the better. Just know that he'll be comfortable, maybe even have a chance at happiness and peace rather than a life spent on the run. Isn't that what you want for him?"

Lorelei looked up at Paul and sniffed. She wiped her eyes with the back of her hand and nodded, *Yes.*

"Then you will say goodbye to him." Paul reached out and squeezed Lorelei's shoulder then walked around the side of the cabin.

She sat in silence looking over the rolling mountains and sunny meadows. It was too beautiful to bear. Just yesterday, this sight had enthralled her, but this was the last time she would ever watch the morning from this hill. She took a few minutes to pull herself together and went inside to start packing. Tyler was still sleeping. She didn't have much, so it didn't take her long to load the car. As she was bringing her last bag of clothes out to the Jeep, Aeson approached from the woods.

"Seems like we're alone out here. There aren't any signs of the banshees."

Lorelei didn't look at him. She opened the car door, threw her bag inside, and headed once again toward the cabin.

"Hey," he called after her, "what's wrong?"

"Everything!"

"Paul talked to you already?"

She spun around to face him, "Yep, told me all about his little plan and I have absolutely no control over any of it."

"Listen, I know he isn't the most tactful person, but he's only trying to protect you. We both are."

Lorelei wanted to tell him she didn't need their protection, but it wasn't true. She did need their help, and like it or not, she wasn't in a position to go it alone anymore. But it didn't make her any less angry. She went back into the cabin and left Aeson standing alone outside.

Tyler was awake now and was folding the blankets on the couch. When Lorelei walked in he looked at her and smiled, then reached out his hand. She moved closer and he enfolded her in his arms and kissed the top of her head.

"You're so beautiful," he said, playing with one of the tendrils that had fallen from her braid, "not sure if I've told you that enough."

Lorelei held back her tears. She wanted to stay here forever, embraced in his arms, the outside world nothing more than an afterthought. She traced the scar on his cheek with her finger. Every little detail of his face—his firm jawline, his dark eyes, the wisps of hair that fell over his forehead—she committed them all to memory. "I don't want to forget anything about you."

"What makes you say that?" he asked.

She nestled her head against his chest and didn't say a word. He wouldn't understand.

"What's going on, Lori?" he cupped her face with his hands.

"We have to leave each other for a while," she said. "You have to go away and where you're going, I can't follow."

"Why?"

"Paul thinks it's best that they hide you from Calliope. He's taking you somewhere safe where she won't find you, but he won't tell me where it is."

"I'd rather stay with you."

"She won't stop looking for you, and as long as you're with me, we're both in danger. Believe me, I don't want to do this either, but he says it's the only way, at least until they can find the banshees and put a stop to this."

"So it's not forever," he said with a hint of enthusiasm, as though he were trying to convince her. "We'll be together again soon."

"It's not a guarantee. There's no way of knowing where she is or how long it will be until she's found, and to be honest, I'm not sure who's supposed to be looking for her. It might just be a waiting game."

"Is this what you want?"

"Of course it isn't!" she started to cry again. "I don't want to lose you."

"You'll never lose me, Lori. I'm enraptured by you. I won't leave unless *you* want me to. You have me under your spell."

Oh no, she thought, *the spell.* Was it possible? Deidre had told her that once a siren seduced a man, he would remain under her allure until she released him from it. Was all of this just an effect of some kind of supernatural brainwashing on her part? The thought terrified her. She needed him to love her, just because he loved her, not for any other reason. Otherwise, it all felt like a lie. Lorelei clung to him. She prayed this was real, that the things he had said he felt for her were real, but she wasn't sure anymore. If there was any chance he was only infatuated with her because he was spellbound, she had to release him from it.

"I can't stand the thought of being apart, but you have to go. We can't be together."

"Even if we're separated by the ocean itself, I will love you, Lorelei. There's nothing in this world that will keep me from you. I'll make you this promise: when we're safe again, I will find you. I will find you and I will love you, all the days of my life."

Lorelei kissed his neck, her lips quivering. For several minutes, she just held onto him, not wanting to leave his side, and then she betrayed her own heart and whispered the words she dreaded to speak aloud, "I'm letting you go. I may never see you again. This is goodbye. Forever."

CHAPTER THIRTY-ONE

The Carolina landscape passed Lorelei's eyes in a blur. She stared out the car window, unfocused. Her body was so heavy she sunk into the seat like a rock, lacking the energy to move. Lorelei rested her face up against the glass and shut her eyes. She had run out of tears about a hundred miles ago; the act of crying had drained her of all energy and left in its place a dull, pounding headache. The last image in her mind had been of Tyler standing on the porch of the cabin, his hand lifted up in a cursory goodbye. Even now she regretted leaving him, unsure of where he would be taken. She could still smell him, feel the way he pressed against her and kissed her deeply before they left. It was Lorelei that had been the one to pull away in order to break free from his embrace.

Thankfully, Aeson hadn't tried to talk to her as they drove. She didn't want to be consoled at this moment. Her sadness, at the very least, was evidence of her connection to Tyler, proof that what had happened between them had been real. Now as they drove farther away from him, Lorelei had fallen into a trance, hypnotized by the green forest. Aeson had carefully planned their trek back up through Virginia toward New England, intentionally avoiding any routes that came too close to the ocean.

To avoid the water was to avoid any unnecessary risk, even though they were fairly certain Calliope would focus her efforts on finding Tyler, not Lorelei. She prayed Paul was right, that with Tyler safely hidden away, Calliope would no longer be a threat to him. It was like some mythological witness protection program with the messengers safeguarding him at an undisclosed location, hoping to ferret out the villain. What kind of life was that? A life of secrets, of constant vigilance, and of looking over one's shoulders— that kind of life wasn't easy. Even though she wanted him to be happy, to live without fear, she also envisioned that he would eventually move on, maybe even forget about her and find love again, and that didn't sit well with her either. The thought of Tyler with anyone else made her miserable, so she tried to push those images aside and allowed the fast-moving landscape to numb her senses.

Daylight passed into darkness and Lorelei fell asleep while Aeson drove through the night. When they had eventually reached their destination, he pulled up alongside the Deleaux home at 4 Nehwas Road. The lights in the house turned on when they arrived, and Helen stepped outside to greet them. Aeson gently awakened Lorelei and opened the door for her. She put her feet on the ground, and followed him up the steps and into the house. Helen followed without saying a word and closed the door behind them. As though in a dream, Lorelei trudged up the stairs to the third floor and fell into bed. She faced the wall and started to sob again. The door to the bedroom opened, but whoever had opened it didn't come in any farther, and simply watched from the stairwell. She didn't know who it was, and she didn't care.

When morning finally came, Lorelei arose and opened the windows out to the balcony. Returning to this house was very strange—as familiar as everything was, she didn't feel like she belonged here anymore. She imagined how awkward it would be to make conversation with Helen and Deidre again. Would they ask for an apology? Would they expect her to offer an explanation as to why she disobeyed Helen's orders? All of this aside, she had many unanswered questions about what had happened. She needed to know why Calliope had become so enraged as to try to kill not only Tyler, but her as well.

She walked downstairs where Deidre was waiting in the kitchen, her effervescent beauty illuminating the room. She sprung out of her chair and threw her arms around Lorelei.

"I've missed you so much. We've been so worried about you. We never imagined this could have happened."

Lorelei forced a smile. "I'm glad to see you, too."

"You have no idea how scared I've been. Aeson told us what happened when he found you. I mean, we all knew Calliope was angry when she left here, but I don't think we ever imagined that she would try to hurt you. We're family, it doesn't make sense. I'm so glad you're okay."

Physically, Lorelei was unharmed, but emotionally, she was battered. Though weary from recent events, she longed for Tyler. It tugged at her heart, relentlessly reminding her of what she had lost.

"Helen wants to see you," said Deidre. "She's waiting for you outside."

Lorelei took a deep breath and walked out the kitchen door to the gardens that opened up to the shore. At the edge of the cliff, a solitary woman stood, her head held high facing the sea, silver hair falling down her back, and wearing a long, black dress with a loose skirt that rustled in the wind. She turned as Lorelei approached and walked toward her slowly.

"You've returned to us," she said.

"It wasn't my choice to come back," Lorelei replied.

"Idis brought you here once before and has returned you home to us again. Your place is here with us. This is your calling."

"Why me? I'm not cut out for this. It feels like becoming a siren has taken everything from me, like this has all been some sort of test."

"Maybe it has been," Helen turned back to face the water. "Our ways are not the ways of Idis. All of our journeys are filled with sorrow and we each have our own grief to bear. It is always a part of us, something we must swallow up inside until we learn to make peace with it. If not for our own pain, we would not be able to know true empathy; we could not have mercy on those that we would escort into death."

"It's too much. I don't know if I'll ever be able to be happy again."

"Oh, you will. You'll know happiness and love—all of the wonderful things in your life will come to be. But to know happiness, one must also experience grief, for without darkness, what is the light?"

The sound of the surf hitting the beach echoed up from the cove. Lorelei looked out over the ocean, covered with a blue sky, majestic in its grandeur, beckoning her. Even without hearing it, she could sense the Song playing through the rolling sea, its melody enchanting and mysterious. A rush of wind encircled her, its call undeniable. This was her destiny, her duty to humanity to stand as sentry to the great gates of mortality.

"Can you forgive me, for all the things I kept from you and for putting you in such a dangerous situation?" Helen asked.

Lorelei couldn't be angry with her. The things Helen had done were a result of her intense belief in fate as the foremost power that governed all lives. "Yes. It's in the past now, if you'll forgive me as well."

"Without question. Today is a fresh start, for all of us."

"I have to ask a few things, though."

"Anything, my dear," said Helen.

"Calliope tried to drown me," Lorelei stated as fact. "I don't understand why."

"I know. She was very angry."

"Angry enough to try to kill me?"

"Lorelei, there's a lot of history in our family," said Helen. "Your mother and Calliope were very close once, but they were torn apart, the schism in their relationship brought about by their mutual affection toward the same man. Your mother won, in the long run, and you were the result of their relationship, which Calliope has always resented. I didn't realize she had any animosity toward you until you defied fate, but I believe that moment solidified it for her. She saw your mother in you—headstrong and, in her mind, disrespectful. Looking back, I'm sure she disliked you from the very beginning, but your decision justified her actions, and in taking your life, she would also be causing Cassandra great pain by destroying her only daughter."

"Calliope had feelings for my father?" Lorelei couldn't picture the two of them together.

"Oh yes, very intense. They were even engaged once."

So her mother had stolen Calliope's fiance. It explained why Lorelei had sensed an icy reception from Calliope since the beginning. No wonder her mother hadn't divulged the Deleauxes' existence to Lorelei. She had taken the man that Calliope loved; certainly that was reason enough to avoid her presence.

"Calliope had a righteous indignation at what she saw as a violation of our sacred trust, and sought to correct that which had been breached. The fact that you were Cassandra's daughter made it that much easier to go after you and make you pay for what you had done."

"I guess that makes sense," said Lorelei, "but why didn't someone tell me sooner?"

"It wasn't my place to say anything about it. It happened a long time ago. Your mother was very young, and she hurt her very dearest friend. I'm certain it wasn't her proudest moment."

Lorelei could picture her mother, ambitious and determined, fixated on her father, as focused to win him over as she became so easily focused on any other number of projects. The fact that he belonged to another woman would be little reason to admit defeat. In fact, she may have seen it as a challenge.

"Did you know Calliope was going to become a banshee?" Lorelei asked.

"Calliope has always been faithful to her duties, so no, I couldn't have guessed it, but now that she has fallen from us, I can see that there was always something about her that relished death a little too much, as though she enjoyed the task at hand. While I have grown to accept my role over time, it is always with sadness and trepidation that I lead the fated to their death. With Calliope, that wasn't the case. She took a great amount of pride in her work, and was very skillful, but sometimes she seemed to delight in sending those fated to die to their graves. The act itself gave her pleasure, but I never thought she would abandon her calling. I really thought she was committed to Idis."

"So why did she leave?"

"The Elysienne had given us explicit instructions that we were not to follow you. The night Calliope departed, she left behind a letter accusing me of being overly sentimental toward you, of not seeing you for who you truly were. She wrote that leaving us was necessary and that once she had 'taken care' of you, she would return to the house and replace me. It is her opinion that my ways are outdated, that I am too superstitious."

"She thought she could come back?"

"Not only does she think that my position is unmerited, she also concluded that the Elysienne should be stripped of her title for not pursuing you and Tyler herself."

"Really?" Lorelei was shocked at Calliope's insubordination.

"Yes, and that was the final straw. In separating herself from the rule of the Elysienne and leaving this assembly of her own choice, she became a banshee, using her power without any thought to the consequences. A siren acts on fate's behalf—she does not decide for herself who will live and who will die."

"And that's what a banshee does?"

"Well, a banshee can do any number of things. When we speak of banshees, we are talking about sirens who are simply no longer heeding the call. Most of the time they do little harm, but sometimes they tap into a darker song that can enhance their power, making them monstrous things. I fear this is what has happened with Calliope, and not only that, but she has found others willing to abandon their calling to seek greater power with her."

"There were four of them there that night. They were all terrifying."

"I know. They have deserted their assemblies as well, following Calliope's misguided attempt to change the way things are. Together, they could be very dangerous, for they are following no one but themselves. They may be quite difficult to capture."

Lorelei remembered Paul saying that she wouldn't see Tyler until Calliope was brought back under control. How much more difficult would it be if these five women were banded together?

"I think she's injured," said Lorelei. "Even as I was drowning, something came and speared her arm. I wasn't sure what I saw, maybe I was delusional from the lack of oxygen, but I could have sworn there was someone else there, another woman. When I came out of the water, I could see her standing on the side of the lake. She was clad in armor and radiating light. It may have been an illusion, but I remember it clearly."

"It was no illusion. She was sent to your aid. She was the one who saved you from Calliope."

"She was real? Who was she?"

"That was a valkyrie, Lorelei. That was your mother."

Night came and the Deleauxes retreated to their rooms. Lorelei watched the moon rise over the ocean until it hung in the sky above her. She took out one of the dresses Deidre had bought for her in Boston and changed into it. It was a long, blue dress made of chiffon, and it hung perfectly on her figure. The neckline plunged over her collarbones, leaving her milky white shoulders bare. She swept her hair up into a messy chignon at the nape of her neck. Lorelei's heart was heavy, and the sea sought her companionship, promising to ease her pain. She would heed its call tonight, returning as a long-lost friend.

Lorelei lit a candle, carefully placed it in a glass lantern and gracefully descended the main staircase in bare feet. She crossed the gardens silently under the light of the stars. The candle illuminated her path as she traversed the rocky bluff and came to the very edge of the cliff jutting out over the cove. Below her, the water serenely reflected the moon's light, sparkling like living diamonds. Lorelei set the candle on the ground and walked forward until her toes gripped the very edge of the cliff. She looked down and saw that the drop was great, but she had no fear.

She was consumed by a broken heart. Had it been love? She wasn't sure if it was possible to love someone she'd barely known, not like this. And yet, if she hadn't loved him, why was it so hard to be apart from him? Why did she ache whenever she pictured his face? The sea comforted her; her pain was part of the suffering of all humanity. That which was both the Song and Idis sang for her now; that which both gave life and took life away directed her footsteps. Glistening tears fell from her green eyes, plummeting to the water below. With a broken spirit, she raised her voice once again and sang a song she had learned as a child, but had never fully understood until now.

Come back... Come back... Come back...

My sincere thanks:

To those who have offered encouragement and support of my dreams: My amazing church family at St. Matthew's and the choir members who enrich my life every week. Cynthia, the world's best single-gal neighbor and spinster sister. Sara and Elizabeth, for your friendship and support—may your daughters be as lovely as you are. To all my teachers and mentors along the way, who taught me both the beauty of music and of the written word.

To the people who have held this book in their hands and watched it grow: Erin, my first editor, who was there with me from the inception of this story and saw me through until the end. Karen, for your much needed feedback and encouragement. Wayne Elizabeth Parrish, whose keen eye and attention to detail helped this story improve. Crystal Patriarche and Heidi Hurst at SparkPress, a BookSparks imprint, thank you both for believing in my story and for your wisdom and guidance. And more than anyone, this book would not exist today if not for the inspiration (and sometimes a duly deserved kick in the pants) from Colleen

Oakes. You helped me find my voice and believed in my story, a story that is as much yours as it is mine.

To my family who shaped me into the person I've become: My mother, who always supported my voice and whose hands taught me a love for all things culinary. My father, whose quiet determination taught me to try my best and to have personal integrity. Kaki, whose practicality and wisdom encouraged me to move forward. And lastly, to Lauren, Hanna, and Maddie, each of whom in some little way makes an appearance in this book. I'm so lucky to have you in my life.

About the author:

Emily Kiebel was raised in Colorado and went on to study classical music and English at Concordia University. She found a love for singing early in life and pursued her passion for music while in school. She now sings professionally and directs a local church choir. When she's not writing or singing, she works as a logistics analyst. In her spare time, she can be found exploring the beauty of nature with her beloved dogs, Ginny and Diggory, cooking for friends and family, traveling, and dragging her friends to obscure historical sites. This is her first novel. She is currently working on the sequel to *Serenade*.

About SparkPress

SparkPress is an independent boutique publisher delivering high-quality, entertaining, and engaging content that enhances readers' lives. We are proud of our catalog of both fiction and non-fiction titles, featuring authors who represent a wide array of genres, as well as our established, industry-wide reputation for innovative, creative, results-driven success in working with authors. SparkPress, a BookSparks imprint, is a division of SparkPoint Studio, LLC.

To learn more, visit us at www.sparkpointstudio.com.

CPSIA information can be obtained at www.ICGtesting.com
Printed in the USA
BVOW01s1352180514

353447BV00003B/3/P